THE DEARLY BELOVED

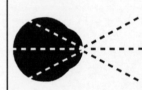

This Large Print Book carries the
Seal of Approval of N.A.V.H.

THE DEARLY BELOVED

CARA WALL

THORNDIKE PRESS
A part of Gale, a Cengage Company

GALE
A Cengage Company

Farmington Hills, Mich • San Francisco • New York • Waterville, Maine
Meriden, Conn • Mason, Ohio • Chicago

LIBRARY OF CONGRESS CIP DATA ON FILE.
CATALOGUING IN PUBLICATION FOR THIS BOOK
IS AVAILABLE FROM THE LIBRARY OF CONGRESS

ISBN-13: 978-1-4328-7125-3 (hardcover alk. paper)

Published in 2019 by arrangement with Simon & Schuster, Inc.

Printed in Mexico
1 2 3 4 5 6 7 23 22 21 20 19

To my parents,
Myrle and Duane,
who somehow taught me everything I
know without ever telling me what to do

PROLOGUE

On the day Charles Barrett died, James MacNally closed the door to his study, sat down in his chair, and laid his head on the thick edge of his desk so he could weep. His wife, Nan, did not knock to be let in, though his rough, heavy sobs hit her like stones. She knew James's own death would wring the same sounds from her, if he went first and left her adrift in the world, unmoored.

Nan knew, full well, that life was a series of bereavements and each stole from her one load-bearing beam, one bone. Nan almost always believed, as her father had, that even deep wounds could be repaired, that God healed all parts of us like skin: no matter how sharp the cut, it would someday knit itself back together and leave only a scar. The hallway in which she stood, for example, had once been blue with a dark wood floor, but there had been a flood. When the old boards warped, Nan replaced them with pretty flowered tiles.

But this was not a wound; it was an amputation. There was no proxy for Charles. There was no replacement to be carted in like a sofa or hung, carefully as a picture, to hide the hole in the wall. James and Charles had ministered together for forty years. They had witnessed each other in pain, in desperation, in crises of faith, even as they struggled to inspire a congregation, to help them make sense of the course of events that engulfed the world. It was a lifetime, as long as the lifetime James had spent with her. And now, he had no one to tell him what he needed to know, which was: How did I come to love someone so much I cannot bear his passing?

Nan felt empty and old. She reached for the black telephone sitting on the hall table and put the palm of her hand on its curved handle. She wanted to call Charles's wife, Lily, but she did not dial. It was the right thing to do, and who else would do it? But she knew Lily would not answer the phone.

Lily would greet widowhood in a tall, straight-backed chair, facing a window; she would sit there without company as long as she could. That was the difference between them, the fundamental architecture Nan had never been able to conquer. She was

8

soft; Lily was straight. She wavered; Lily was plumb. Even now, Nan felt herself casting about for a reprieve; Lily would already know they had reached an end.

The story that was the four of them was over.

■ ■ ■ ■

Part One

1953–1962

■ ■ ■ ■

ONE

On both his mother's and his father's side, Charles Barrett was descended from old Boston families. His father was the head of the Classics Department at Harvard, where he taught seminars on the Romans and Greeks.

"Societies fail," his father told the freshmen year after year, "when men are rewarded for seeking pleasure instead of responsibility." His tweed jackets rasped as he cracked notes on the blackboard; his comments on papers, written in gaunt handwriting in deep blue ink, were direct and critical. At the dinner table, just before pushing back his chair to retire to his study, he often said, "Obligations are the fuel of life, Charles. Reputation is their reward."

Their shingled, sharp-roofed Victorian house was painted grey with brown shutters. Inside it was stern, angular, and choked with books, each chosen deliberately: a col-

13

lection of translation, biography, and historical analysis his father would one day bequeath to the library — a legacy of edification. Charles's mother hid her romance magazines behind a bucket under the kitchen sink, and Charles fell on the comic books other boys brought to faculty parties, gorging himself as quickly and stealthily as his contemporaries emptied the cocktail glasses the grown-ups left behind. He never took a comic home, because his father did not believe in leisure or in letting one's mind run free, without purpose. If he had seen Charles with so much as a paperback, he would have assigned Charles an essay to write or a problem to solve.

Thankfully, each June, Charles and his mother packed the station wagon with canvas totes full of shorts and white sneakers and escaped to her parents' square, damp summer house on Martha's Vineyard, which was full of rag rugs, needlepoint pillows, and dogs. Her tanned parents were waiting when she and Charles stepped out of the car onto the crushed-shell driveway. His grandmother hugged him tightly; his grandfather clapped him on the shoulder, and said, "Stack of funnies on the table," words that caused Charles to race into the dining room, dropping his bags hastily in the front hall.

Charles felt his full self in that house, bigger than himself — free and happy. His mother's sisters laughed often, walked barefoot on the lawn, meandered into town for ice cream with their arms linked together. Her brothers joked with Charles around the barbecue; he and his cousins built model airplanes, flew kites, and captained remote-controlled submarines in the salt-water lake behind the shed. Summers were when Charles learned how to sail, play tennis, fix old shutters, season butter for lobster, and introduce a new person to a crowd. Summers allowed him, though he was an only child, to feel part of a brood, a clan that sailed through the world together, as stately and festive as an ocean liner.

His father visited for a week each August, sat on the beach in khaki pants and blue button-down shirts, never took off his shoes. He was not like his wife's family, and he did not like his wife's family. Despite this, Charles's aunts, uncles, and grandparents respected his father. It was hard not to. He had set forth a paradigm for himself and followed it to the letter. He was well educated, eloquent, gainfully employed, and saved from arrogance by the fact that his accomplishments were verifiable and significant. For all their diversions, Charles's mother's family esteemed intelligence and academic debate. Still, they took turns sitting next to his father at dinner, so that no one had to talk to him two nights in a row.

Charles had always known he would go to college, just as he had always known that to go anywhere but Harvard would cause his father to grumble and sigh. He wasn't unduly bothered by the expectation — he loved Harvard. He loved its tree-filled commons, its stone courtyards, its brick facades, and the snippets of conversations that fell out of its open windows. He could picture himself there, walking to class in a blue blazer, books tucked beneath his arm. He could imagine the smoky smell of autumn slipping into classrooms as his professors entered, hear the gentle *pop* of new texts opening, see clean notebook pages white and blue beneath his pen.

Because, even though he sometimes wished he could spend his whole life playing baseball, standing in the outfield, tossing lazy balls at the deep green end of summer, when the air stayed warm well after dark, he knew he was very much like his father. Though he loved to feel his cleats kick up dirt, smell the chalk of the baselines, catch a ball in his mitt and throw it back, his body lengthening as the seam slid off his fingertips, he also loved books and everything in them: Latin, physics, algebraic equations and algorithms, the end-stop lines of geometric and philosophical proofs. Though he often longed to lean out over the side of a little boat, bracing his feet on the mast while the wind hurled him forward, pulling the line close to his hip, he also wanted to write papers, debate ideas, use his mind to read closely and accurately, formulate answers to every hidden question.

He enrolled at Harvard and majored in medieval history.

It was there, in late May 1954, that Charles sat in the library reading a book about Catherine of Aragon. He loved the library, its mahogany shelves that climbed to the ceiling, its bounty of lush pages majestically restrained. He loved it especially on days like this, when it was empty, steeped in quiet, electric with promise, as if the books were breathing, alive as big dogs sleeping at the foot of his bed. He reveled in that particular stillness, in which he felt as if he could, at any minute, turn a page and recognize everything there was in the world to know.

His junior year was drawing to a close; as

soon as exams were finished, he would set off for another summer on the Vineyard. He was looking forward to vacation. He was ready to be without coat and tie, to sleep late, walk on the beach, and read whatever paperback novels happened to be on hand. It occurred to him that he should take his cousins' children some comic books, carry on his grandfather's tradition, but he realized, with a pang of disappointment, that he did not know where one bought comic books — his had always been hand-me-downs. He marked his page and crossed the long marble room to ask the librarian, Eileen, keeper of the key to the rare manuscripts collection, whether she knew where to buy some.

"Comic books?" she asked, eyebrows raised. "I don't think so." She pushed her chair back and craned her neck to ask the woman in the office behind her. "Marilyn, do you have any idea where to buy comics?" The woman in the office must have shaken her head because Eileen turned to Charles and said, "Apologies."

Charles moved off to the side of the desk, abashed at having bothered a librarian with such a trivial question. But before he went far, he turned back to ask Eileen if she had a phone book. A girl had moved to the front of the tall desk. Eileen was stamping her books, and as she slid the last circulation card into its cardboard holder, she asked the girl, "You don't know where to find comic books in this town, do you?"

The girl looked up, thought for a moment, then said one word: "No."

It was not the flat clap of a mother's angry no; it was not the timid no of someone who wanted to always, and to everybody, say yes. It was a full, round, truthful no — not off-putting, not regretful, just an answer. It perfectly matched the girl who had spoken it. She was tall and straight-standing, wearing a navy blue skirt and a white shirt one might wear to play tennis. Her hair was thick and brown — not a deep, shiny, fashionable brown — just a serviceable, reliable brown, the color of a pony. It was cut in a plain bob. She was slightly tanned and very freckled. She looked exactly like a girl Charles might meet next week at a party on Martha's Vineyard, except that her face was entirely sad.

He didn't think she knew she looked sad. He thought she probably looked in the mirror and saw a well-designed face, with strong cheekbones, a straight nose, and perfectly fine, rounded pink lips. He thought she probably brushed her hair every morn-

19

ing and thought to herself, *Good enough.*
He acknowledged that there were men in
the world who would think she was beautiful and men in the world who would find
her plain. He found her both — ravishingly
beautiful and exquisitely plain. She was slim
and sturdy as a board, lit up with health,
and quietly, eternally sad. She looked
exactly like a medieval queen.

The girl picked up her books and walked
away. Charles leaned over to Eileen without
thinking and asked, "What's that girl's
name?"

Eileen answered, "Lily."

Lily Barrett's parents were killed in an
automobile accident when she was fifteen.
This fact seemed absurd to her. If she had
been told it might happen before it happened, she would have said, "Don't be
ridiculous." When she talked about it afterward she said, "I know it's ridiculous."
Often, the person to whom she was speaking did not think it was ridiculous at all.
But it *was* ridiculous. Whose parents died?
Certainly not anyone's she knew. The parents she knew were dentists and head-
mistresses, men who washed their cars on
Saturday and women who cultivated roses
in their spare time. And really, how could

her parents be dead? Last time she had seen them, they were standing at the door, dressed for an outing. Her mother was closing her purse, her father shrugging himself into a jacket. What was it — a birthday party? A wedding? An appointment at the bank? She hadn't asked.

They had come into the living room to say their goodbyes. Lily was lying on the blue tweed sofa. "We'll be home by six," her mother said, leaning over to kiss Lily on the forehead.

"Love you," her father said, wiping away the red lipstick her mother had left on her skin with his thumb.

Lily had rolled her eyes. *Rolled her eyes.* She was in the middle of *Jane Eyre,* and she wanted to finish it that afternoon. She wanted to eat potato chips, drink ginger ale, and swallow the black-licorice paragraphs whole. Her parents went out the door. Even after the room fell still, Lily could smell the straw of her father's hat and her mother's lemon perfume. Outside, her cousins were playing in the backyards of the houses on either side of her own; she could hear the younger boys shouting, "This is a stickup. No, *this* is a stickup!" She knew the older girl cousins had been sent outside to watch them, sitting on the steps with their striped summer skirts tucked under their knees, talking about boys, folding and refolding their socks so the lace trim fell just so around their ankles.

Lily thought they were frivolous. They thought Lily was dull. That didn't stop them from bothering her, though; they were forever asking her to sit with them while they embroidered, or swing with them on the porch swing, or walk into town. The boys wanted Lily to play checkers with them, or help them find their archery sets, or referee their games of tag. If they had known she was home alone, they would have snuck inside to pull her hair. So she stayed in her living room all day, with her library book and its thick soft pages, its crisp cellophane wrapper that crackled slightly whenever she moved.

Lily was the lone only child in her big family. Her mother was one of four beautiful sisters, all of whom had married upstanding men. For wedding presents, their father had given them a string of sturdy white houses, lined up in a row on a leafy street in Maryville, Missouri, near the university on the west side of town. While their husbands served on the city council and ran the rotary club, Lily's mother and her sisters took turns walking the children to school in the morning and picking them up in the afternoons. Birthday and anniversary celebrations rotated from dining room to dining room, lemonade stands from porch to porch. There was no yours and mine, only ours. Lily's mother was the youngest, the most beautiful, and the most doted upon. Her father was the tallest, the best dressed, and the most fun.

At the hospital, Lily was given two gold wedding rings, two watches with leather straps, and her mother's ruby earrings in a small brown envelope. She did not see the bodies. As she was waiting for her aunt Miriam and uncle Richard to finish talking to the doctors, she took the watches out and put them on; her father's was too big, slipped off her wrist, and had to be held in her palm.

It was still light when they drove home. Miriam, stunned and pale, did not notice the car had stopped until her husband opened the door and touched her shoulder. She got out and helped Lily out behind her, but then stood, as if lost, on the green stretch of lawn that spanned the family homes like an apron.

"Go home, love," Richard said, turning Miriam in the right direction. Then he took Lily's hand, led her up to her own wide, covered porch and sat next to her on the thick, weathered swing. The two of them stayed there for what seemed like hours, without saying a word. There was a slight breeze. The cicadas came out, and then the lightning bugs.

Uncle Richard was a big man, tall, who wore blue-and-white-striped shirts and kept his grey hair in the same buzz cut he had been given in the army. His stillness was as big as his being, and even then, tangled in shock, Lily realized this was why he was sitting with her, rather than anyone else. Not just because he had been first to the hospital, or because he was the oldest man and only lawyer in the family, but because he was solid enough to feel real while everything else in the world dissolved.

"Want to go in?" Richard said, finally.

Lily shook her head.

"All right. It will be here tomorrow." He looked over at her. "It's your house," he said. "It will be until you don't want it to be. We'll leave it unlocked, and we won't go in it much without you."

Lily looked at him.

"So you can come here for privacy," he said. "But you'll live with us."

It was then that Lily started to cry, because the offer to live in someone else's house

24

made her feel completely and utterly alone.

For most of Charles's undergraduate life, the history of the Saxons, Plantagenets, Lancasters, and Yorks had stretched out across reading tables in front of him, full of petty politics and sweeping consequences, courtly love and syphilis, mental incapacity and strength beyond compare. There were wars brothers fought as enemies, and wars they won as allies. There were castles and feasts, the boundaries of Europe changed over and over, and there were the Crusades, which took his mind to the mosques and mullahs of the Middle East. He studied well and got good grades, for which he worked diligently. He wanted to distinguish himself as an academic in his own right, separate from his father. He sought no favoritism, but he sometimes thought he was being graded harder than his classmates in an effort by his professors to prove beyond a shadow of a doubt that they were showing him none.

Those professors were not pleased when Charles decided to take a class given by Tom Adams, a young academic prodigy who ran seminars called If Henry the Fifth Were Alive Today, Could You Have Conquered Islam?, and Was Korea a Crusade?

25

It was Tom's class on Korea that caught Charles's attention, along with the rest of the school's. It was being given just as young men who had fought in the war were enrolling for their long-delayed freshman year. Their presence alone disturbed Charles's classmates, all of whom were the right age to have served, but none of whom had signed up. They had chosen their student deferments, read about the fighting in newspapers, caught glimpses of it on the televisions in their house common rooms: footage of men in shirtsleeves and loose helmets, crawling over dirt, weighed down by their backpacks, their hands and faces bare as bullets exploded next to them in the ground. Now those men were years behind them, and there was a palpable sense of awkward guilt in the air. Tom's course seemed in poor taste to some, but those who signed up for it found the chance to discuss war with actual soldiers the most affecting experience of their college careers.

Charles's father found it ludicrous. "That man," Charles's father told him, "needs to align himself more closely with tradition." He pointed meaningfully at Charles, and Charles nodded deferentially, but spent the night before registration sleeping in the drafty hall of the history building to guarantee himself a spot in Tom's fall tutorial: Martyrs and Their Murderers.

Tom Adams was not much older than his students; he wore the same penny loafers and horn-rimmed glasses they wore and had the same cut of tidy dark hair. But when he walked into the room on the first day of class, he was not like them at all. He was intense, electric, and inspired. They leaned forward in their chairs.

"We study the past to illuminate the present," Tom said loudly, staring at them. "Is the present, then, illuminated?" He paused, shook his head, paced the perimeter of the room.

"Study does not engender wisdom," he continued, his voice stern and challenging. "Analysis does not inspire insight." He raised his eyebrows, exhorting Charles and his classmates to pay attention. "Only empathy allows us to see clearly. Only compassion brings lasting change."

Tom strode to his desk, hoisted himself up to sit on one corner. "I am going to ask you to imagine yourself into the history we read. I am going to ask you to *feel* it. Because only living it will convince you to stop it from happening again."

Charles knew that, in a classroom down the hall, his father was giving his own beginning-of-the-year speech, about discipline and meticulous scholarship. "Do not extrapolate; do not embellish," he was saying. "Never underestimate the gravity of your undertaking: to analyze the ages, to evaluate what has come before."

Tom put his hands in the pockets of his sport coat and smiled. "Everyone imagines himself a king," he said. There were chuckles around the seminar table.

Tom nodded indulgently and shrugged. "That's perfectly fine," he said. "It's what makes history fun." He opened a drawer and took out a thick stack of stapled paper — the semester's reading list. "But I'm not going to encourage you," he said, throwing a syllabus down in front of each of them with a thud. "Kings are champions of the status quo. I want you all to pay attention to the serf. I'm certainly going to work you like some." There were scattered grins; Tom stared them down. "I'm going to force each of you — you of sound, incredible, impressionable minds — to understand at least one thing here that will make you want to change the world."

Charles felt chastened. He *had* been imagining himself a king. While boys his age had set up tents in South Korea, he had studied. While they slept on cots, he had played a game: the study of history for history's sake. Now, for the first time, he was asked to ponder the purpose of his studies.

Charles realized with a start that if his father thought harder about it, he would see that he and Tom held the same goal: to inspire students to strive for excellence, achievement, insight, and understanding. His father believed their training should include intellectual rigor and ruthless critique. Tom believed it should be built on imagination and depth of feeling. But their motives were the same: to pull their students into the world of useful men.

Lily's family's grief was immediate and un-assuageable. They fell apart. Entirely. Her aunts took to their beds and the older girl cousins wept for days; in hysterics, they called their friends and cried on the phone. Even months later, there was almost always an aunt weeping over a mixing bowl or wiping her eyes with a flour-dusted apron.

Lily's mother had loved to bake, had held court in the kitchen as she cut out sugar cookies or spooned biscuits into a skillet. She had talked and baked, and Lily's older girl cousins had hung on her every word, copied her dresses, styled their hair to look like hers. Now they told Lily, "I wanted to be like your mother. I wanted to *be* your mother. Now I don't have any idea who I want to be."

Lily had never wanted to *be* either of her parents. When they were alive, she hadn't fought for space on a kitchen stool next to the girls or hid under the dining room table with the boys while their fathers played endless rounds of hearts in the evenings, hoping to shoot the moon. She had just read all day and wished she lived someplace where she could do that without a boy cousin trying to steal her book, or a girl cousin asking if she had seen her other shoe, or one of her aunts asking her to clean up the dining room table, simply because she was the only child sitting still enough to be found.

Even in grief, Lily wanted to be left alone. She wanted to remember her parents the way they had been with *her.* The way the three of them had walked home together at the end of every family dinner holding hands. The way her mother had brushed her hair before bed and the way her father had stared into the refrigerator, looking for one last cold 7Up to drink before he went to sleep. Her parents had not been like her, but they had been *hers,* and it was unbearable to watch people grieve for parts of them she had never really known.

For the first year, she carried a book with her constantly, like an oxygen tank. When she was forced to venture out without one — to help carry groceries or bike one of the younger children into town — she lurched, limped, looked for things to hang on to. The outline of the world — trees, pavement, hands, the tops of buildings against the sky — was too keen, too ready to fall and slice. The unplanned chaos of people moving about her was too much to bear. She needed flat angles, thin pages, to sit quietly with her hair tucked behind her ear.

The problem was that she could no longer follow a story. Every plot seemed contrived to her: the author's intent too clear, the layers of gears revealed. Characters were strangers. No matter how hard she tried, she could no longer care for them. They were just bland letters on a page.

She could still manage schoolwork. In fact, she liked school even more now, because it hadn't changed; there were still assignments given, with expected page lengths and footnotes to be organized, grades received. Her teachers would have given her a pass, she was sure, but they couldn't stop her from handing in work or discourage her from revising for hours to make certain her As were not given out of pity.

Her parents had never cared much about school. "Don't be so serious," they said. "Get out and have some fun." But there was no fun to be had now, so she spent her afternoons in the library, reading textbooks and filling notecards with citations. The library closed at five. Lily packed up slowly and waited as long as the librarian would let her before heading home. It was easiest to time her arrival with Richard's, so that she could slip in behind him as his children ran downstairs. Every night, as he hugged them and asked about their days, Lily crept away into the living room and continued studying, alone, until dinner.

After a year passed, Richard and Miriam's house settled back into its routine. The children fed the dog under the table and stole pieces of cake off each other's plates. Miriam shook her head in exasperation at their antics, shooed the dog outside fifteen times a day, and constantly exhorted everyone to do their chores. But not Lily. She no longer had chores. She was a guest, a doll from another dollhouse family.

Sometimes Lily went back to her old house, climbed the porch steps, opened the door, and flipped the light switch on the wall. The blue living room couch, the hooked rug, the two wooden chairs, the tall lamp with its tasseled shade were still there. The kitchen table and its chairs, the beds in the bedrooms, the bathroom sinks and the mirrors above them had not moved. But grief was there, and absence, and loss. Lily could not stay too long, never past dark. If she did, emptiness bloomed inside her, as big and cold as a night without stars. Sometimes she worried that the darkness would dissolve her, erase her like chalk until she was nothing. One endless ache and then gone.

After a few months more, there was a discussion about money. Richard sat her down in his office and put her parents' will on the desk in front of her. It was six pages long. He had unstapled it so that he could turn the pages over into a separate stack as he read them to her, two white rectangles on the dark wood, one striped with text, the other blank: two eyes, one opened and one closed.

"It starts with small things," he said. *We, Ava and George, being of sound mind do bequeath* was followed by a long list of items that felt trivial to Lily, but she knew would feel important to those who received them. To Aunt Miriam, they left the family silver, which everyone said should have gone to her in the first place. To nieces, they left pieces of jewelry, to nephews, radios and watches. To a pair of uncles, they left two cars Lily never knew they'd owned.

"Those were hot rods," Richard told her. "They fixed them up together." His voice was apologetic. She wondered if he thought there was any Earth on which she would ever consider sitting in one of her parents' cars.

"Now, Lily, no one wants any of these things soon. In fact, I haven't told anyone but you about the will. But at some point, people will start asking, and I wanted you to have the facts."

She nodded. It was as if her parents had left her a Christmas list, asked her to go to the store, buy the presents, and wrap them.

Richard turned another page. "And finally, to our darling daughter Lily," he read. "We leave everything else we own, anything in our possession not mentioned above, including all the money we have managed not to spend, and the house if it is still standing, and of course, all the love we have for her, forever."

She had begun to cry, silently, at *darling daughter,* the now-familiar heat of grief climbing like a rash up her throat, behind her cheekbones, to her eyes. By *love*, tears dripped off her chin onto her lap. Richard handed her a handkerchief and turned to the last page.

There, Lily saw a list of three bank accounts and the value of the house. The amount was absurd to her, because she had never thought about money beyond nickels for library fines. Everything she needed had simply appeared. She did not know how to take this in: her parents' worth in numbers on the page, the squiggles of a language she had not been taught to read.

"We'll pay for everything you need right now," Richard told her. "We want to. But I also want you to know that you're not dependent on us for your future."

Future was not a concept Lily could understand.

Still, she tried to move on. She presented everyone with their gifts from the will, and then some. She gave away all of her parents' clothing. Her cousins and aunts took her mother's dresses, blue-flowered and pink lace. Her uncles did not fit into her father's suits, but they took his ties and lace-up shoes. She let the smaller cousins have all the toys and books they wanted. She found that the fewer things she owned, the easier it was for her to contain her grief, to pack it away in the closets and sideboards of her bones.

But every day there was an uncle standing on the lawn, wearing one of her father's hats, shaking some small, broken thing and saying, "If only George was here to get this up and running." There were pictures of her parents in silver frames on the mantel of every house she entered, placed at the front and freshly shined.

"Remember when he tried to fix the roof and nailed all those shingles on backward?"

"Remember how breathtaking she was in that ivory strapless gown?"

Lily couldn't get them to stop talking, couldn't make them understand that every memory unfurled her grief again, like a great wind heaving through the shelves of her being — plates broken, silverware scattered, sheets falling, unfolded, to the floor.

Slowly, she realized that the numbers on the page were like the pieces of a model airplane: everything she needed to build her way out, to get herself somewhere, anywhere, she could be something other than an orphan. So when she was seventeen, she asked her aunts about college, saying, "I want to go to Boston."

She didn't particularly want to go east. But she desperately wanted to meet people who did not know the details of her life and with whom she did not have to share her story. She wanted to go somewhere she could choose a day, any day, on which she did not have to think of her parents. She applied to, was accepted by, and left to study literature at Radcliffe.

TWO

James MacNally grew up in Chicago, in a small house embellished with lace curtains and starched doilies that did not effectively hide the shabbiness of the dark furniture beneath them. His mother worked at the telephone company and his father was a drunk. His life was cluttered with siblings: two older brothers who left shoes on the staircase and three sisters who left hairpins on the sink. There were shared bedrooms, not enough bathrooms, and many, many arguments about who had to wash the dishes after dinner and who ate the last piece of bread.

James often escaped the chaos of his house to wander the bristly, pocked streets of his neighborhood, where he learned to smoke, look angry, and kiss girls without their brothers finding out. He was tall enough — by the time he was fourteen he was five foot ten — not to get picked on and wiry enough to run fast when he did. When he came through the door each night, his mother said, "There's my scrappy one."

Each night he complained, "Ma," and each night his father called over the back of the living room couch, "There's worse things than that to be called, Jamie." And then he proceeded to list them until he fell back into what the family persisted in calling sleep.

"Don't judge," James's mother admonished him and his siblings. "He's a good man. He fought the war to give us what we've got, and it killed a lot of him. What's left we are going to leave be."

Most of the men in James's neighborhood had borne some brunt of the Second World War. They were a gruff, quick-tempered group who had seen hard combat, humped their packs, slept on the ground. They had endured the low ceilings and dank odors of boats, the claustrophobic bellies of tanks, and the frantic tilt of airplanes. They had felt the honeycombs of grenades in their hands, the wind of shrapnel in the air. They had pulled the triggers of machine guns and pistols, hanging on — always hanging on — to the weapon that might deliver them from evil. And, despite their efforts, they had been shot, bled through their bandages, carried roughly from the battlefield, sewn up in army hospitals and sent, mercilessly, back to the front. Most of the boys James knew were afraid of their fathers, because they knew their fathers had killed men; could fight to the death with hands and knives and guns.

Most of those fathers had come back from the front and carried on. They had built walls between the war and their lives at home: high, thick, barbed-wire walls that allowed them, every weekday, to shower, shave, put on a hat, and go to work. On weekends, they kept working: they climbed onto roofs to tack stray shingles, pounded nails into loose porch boards, pulled dead branches from trees, raked leaves into piles and set them on fire. On Saturdays, they taught their sons how to throw footballs and ride bikes, keep their heads down, their elbows up, and how to land a blow to the throat.

James's father had not built a wall, and so the war had followed him home like radiation, like mercury: a silver-plate, X-ray poison laying bare the bright white weakness of his bones. On Mondays, his father dragged himself, rumpled and unshaven, to work in the steel mills, where he loaded I-beams onto trucks until the whistle blew.

But then, not bothering to take off his stained uniform jumpsuit, he threw his hard hat and blackened gloves into his locker, fell in with the other men broken by war, trooped to a bar, and drank with them until the liquor made them maudlin and their sons came to take them home.

James and his brothers knew all of those sons. They met one another's eyes as they paid their fathers' tabs and bent to pick their fathers' coats off the floor. They made a point of meeting one another's eyes at school, too, and at parties, where they glimpsed one another standing against walls, catching the beers that were thrown at them and flipping them open. But they all knew that each of them would nurse those single beers all night long and that, on their way home, most of them would leave the cans on windowsills half-full.

James and his brothers and the other boys knew every one of the ways they were different from their fathers. They were taller or stockier or better at baseball; they were quicker at math, had a head for science, didn't hit their girlfriends. They carried those traits like lucky pennies in their pockets, hoping these were the charms that would make them different from their fathers forever.

James wondered what those boys would think if they knew he had tried whiskey once, from a friend's flask, in an alley. He wondered what they would think if they knew how much he had liked the burn in his throat and the warmth in his belly and the way it made him dreamy and confident all at once.

"My arms are heavy but my heart is light," his father liked to slur on his way home from the bars.

Before he'd tried whiskey, James thought this was pathetic. But after he'd had a real drink, he understood. Whiskey made everything fine: his father, his cramped house, the dullness of his classmates, the dead end of their neighborhood that led only to the army, the steel mills, or the bars. He knew he had to escape; the yearning for a way out was a constant, blazing cramp in his side. If he had to stay here, he wouldn't be out of the bars for long.

Nan's real name was Mary, and she was from Mississippi. She was from the slow majesty of the great river, the comfort of her old white house with its mahogany floors and the family furniture kept for a hundred years. She was from humidity, sweet iced tea, football, the smell of gardenias in the spring. She was a Girl Scout, then a cheerleader. She did well in school, had pretty friends, dated handsome boys and never wanted to go too far with them, or too far from home.

Her father was a minister. He had a deep and abiding faith in the Lord, as he called him, and a deep and abiding empathy for Those Less Fortunate. He thought Nan, despite her privilege, should have a true view of the world, so he took her with him on his pastoral rounds to hospital beds and jail cells, to small, musty houses and foster homes filled with crying children. Nan was expected to smile cheerfully and shake the hand of everyone she met.

"And I mean everyone," her father said. Nan adored him. He was serious and calm; he never rushed her or shushed her, never expected her to know things she had not been told. He simply kept a guiding hand on her back as she shook hands with an army colonel and his wife who was dying of cancer, drunken men on narrow sidewalks outside of bars, and garage mechanics who left grease on her palm. He taught her to say *How are you today?* and *What can I do to help?* He might correct her if she had not made eye contact, or if she had stepped back as someone had leaned toward her, but he nodded proudly when she corrected herself, and as they drove home he always said, "Thank you for coming with me today."

Nan's father wore khaki pants and short-sleeve shirts on these visits. Nan's mother would have preferred him to wear his collar, but he said, "That's for the pulpit, Ellen — the only place where I should be seen as separate."

Nan's mother was a gracious woman. This meant, in their congregation, that she was somewhat stern but impeccably mannered. She ran everything in the church that did not take place in the sanctuary: coffee hour, Bible study, youth ministry, Sunday school. She organized them with diligence and efficiency, and her best friends were the women who helped her, who came over for coffee to discuss who should be made an usher or a deacon, whether girls should be required to wear gloves at the teen social, which flowers were best in each season at the altar. They also talked about the school board, the football team, who'd had words with whose husband in the grocery store, whose mother was drinking again, who'd bought a new car they couldn't possibly afford. But at the end of the afternoon, Nan's mother always said, "I think it's time to pray," and they all took hands, begged forgiveness for their gossiping, guidance for their leadership, health for their families, and love for one another. Nan often watched them kiss each other goodbye, waving as they started their cars, secure and happy in their places as confidantes to the minister's wife.

Nan was known as a lovely girl. This meant she was well behaved to the point of boring, which was her only acceptable choice. *Bright* would have meant she was too smart for her own good, *popular* that she flirted with too many boys, *troubled* that she'd done much more than that. Her father was known as remarkable, because he raised eyebrows in the congregation for his populist leanings, and also earned respect with his easy charm and deep commitment to Christian principles.

Nan hoped that, when she was allowed to outgrow *lovely,* she would become both gracious *and* remarkable, a perfect union of her parents. She was often reminded, however, that there was a distance to bridge between them. "It takes a backbone to be a minister's wife," her mother said. "And devotion to be his child."

Sometimes, Nan was not sure to whom that devotion was owed. When she was eight and a half, before a pastoral visit with her father, she tried to dress herself in jeans and a sweater, telling her mother, "If Daddy doesn't want to be separate, I don't want to be either."

"Mary Nan Louise," her mother answered, pulling the sweater away from her and holding out a blue-and-white Swiss dot dress. "Your daddy may want to look like everyone else," she said, "but everyone else wants us to look better. When we look nice, we give them hope that there is a reward for giving up sin."

Nan scowled. She knew her father did not believe that; he believed everyone was equal in God's eyes.

Her mother pointed a finger at her. "You are a minister's daughter. It's a very particular position. My job is to teach you how to handle it well."

So, from her mother Nan learned how to host coffees (serve cookies, not cake), how to write thank-you notes (in blue pen, not black), and how to make everyone feel at home (ask after children and dogs).

And from her father she learned that not everyone went to school, or ate three meals a day, or had a bathroom inside their home. Some people broke the law, some people hurt their families, some people didn't even believe in God. But everyone deserved God's mercy and her respect.

Together, they taught her the vital importance of manners. "Manners exist so that everyone feels comfortable," her father told her.

Her mother continued, "So that in any situation you will know exactly what to do."

Crafted of love and certainty, Nan's life cruised pleasantly in its well-marked lane until the Sunday, when she was ten, that a man took his clothes off in the middle of church. Overcome by the spirit, as her father explained it afterward, a man they had known for years took off everything he was wearing and stood naked in the aisle. Nan was on the dais, part of the children's choir, singing "Just a Closer Walk with Thee." Her father came down from his place behind the altar, put his hand on the man's shoulder, said something low in his ear, and led him out of the church into the vestry, where they sat until someone brought the man's pants and sweater.

Her mother, frantic, rushed from her seat in the front pew to cover as many children's eyes as she could. But in the moments before her mother reached her, Nan stared at the man, stunned by his pale pink skin, the blond hair on his chest, the blond hair down below, and the flaccid pink member, the same color as her little pink jacks ball. He seemed so clean to her, so scrubbed and shiny in the morning light.

Later, her father said, "You must not be embarrassed by what you saw. It was a human body. The human body is a clear and honest thing."

For the first time in her life, Nan did not believe him. If the human body was clear and honest, why had the entire congregation gasped and turned away?

Her mother said, "It never happened. Forget you saw anything at all."

Nan did not think she would ever forget, but she did as she was told. The next time she saw the man, she shook his hand and looked him in the eye. She did not let him see how much he had unnerved her, how hard it was to see him again, even fully dressed. She did not let herself think of him as different, or as troubled, or as dangerous. And she tried not to let the incident change *her;* she continued to sing in the choir, practice her piano, use her manners with her teachers and her friends. She tried not to wonder why it had happened, why she — who had always been the best lovely girl — had seen a naked man, standing there, staring at her. She tried to have faith that there was a purpose to it, that God had a greater understanding of these things, a purpose and a plan, no matter how much of a shock the sight had been.

Toward the end of his senior year of high school, James turned eighteen and went to register for the draft, as the law required him to do. The registry office was a store-front by the L tracks, with an army-green awning and three American flags flying on the sidewalk. James stood at the counter and filled out his card next to another boy who looked remarkably like him — worn coat, old boots, no hat. A thick-necked man in uniform approached them, slid a bro-chure across the plywood counter.

There was a war on again, this one in Korea. The sober fathers clenched their jaws when they read about it, said little, stared into the distance. Their stillness frightened James; it confirmed his fear that there was nothing to be done about the tragedies of the world, no way he could escape his father's disgrace.

"Let me tell you what we'll give you if you sign up," the army man said. His fingers were thick; his wide wedding ring reflected the American flag in the upper right corner of the flyer. James wondered if his wife was proud of him.

"Nope," James told him without looking up. "I'm going to finish my senior year."

This was his coin, his difference. He was smart, and he *liked* school — all of it — the petty bullying, the gossip, the sports, the books, the classes. He didn't understand the kids who sat in the back and passed notes. He knew it was important to look tough, to seem uninterested, but he didn't understand kids who actually *were*. Didn't they see that this was their only opportunity to experience something beyond their small, immediate lives?

The other boy took the brochure, folded it in half, and stuck it in his chest pocket.

"You don't want to take your chances?" James whispered to him.

"I know my chances if I stay here," the boy answered, putting down his pen.

James thought about that all the way home. Maybe the boy had a point. Maybe the army was a viable escape. Maybe a uniform would keep him from drink, instead of pushing him toward it. Maybe he would be sent to Korea. Maybe he would come back strong and capable. Maybe once he left he would never have to come back. He was propping up that hope like a tarp over his fear when he got home. His mother was sitting at the kitchen table, her hair frizzier than usual, cheeks flushed, twisting a letter in her hands.

"Oh, James, sit down with me," she said desperately. "I've got something you need to know."

He sat down. He had never before seen his mother in this state — sitting on the edge of one of their hard chairs, back straight, face tense, eyes so open as to look crazy.

"Right, I've got to tell you before your father wakes up," she said, glancing nervously toward the living room. "So just let me talk." She took a breath. "My brother Phillip, you know about him . . ."

James nodded.

"Don't *say* anything, James," his mother cried, jerking forward toward him, "I've got to get it out."

"I didn't . . ." he began. She closed her eyes and tilted her head back. He fell silent. He looked at the dishes in the sink.

She began again. "My brother Phillip, the one I've told you about . . ."

James did not nod.

"He wanted to become a priest. You know my mother was Catholic . . ."

He had not known her mother but did not shake his head.

"Well, she was, and she went to Mass every single day, left us kids at home so she could sit through it in peace. But my brother Phillip was curious about church, and he snuck off after her one day, followed her right in and sat in the back. When he came home he said to me, 'It was so beautiful, Alice. Right there, I knew everything I ever needed to know.' Well, that made me a little jealous, I don't have to tell you, because I'd like to know everything there is to know, too, but I don't."

James, unused to his mother telling stories, was caught so off-guard by this one that it left him slightly out of breath. But he managed to think that he, too, might like to know everything there was to know, especially about school and war and managing not to have a life that made you drink. He listened carefully.

"He didn't come with us to America when we moved here. He stayed in Ireland, and I understood. He stayed behind, presented himself to a church, and almost became a priest." She took a breath and leaned forward. "He didn't quite make it — you'll have to ask him why. He ended up a banker. But he's always lived a life of faith, and now he says he's managed to save up quite a bit of money and he doesn't know what to do with it, really. He told me, in this letter, that he should give it to the church, but he's at quite a wealthy parish, see, and he thinks they have enough, really, so he'd like to do something nice for you instead."

James almost said something, in his surprise. His mother held up a hand.

"I've written to him about you and told him that you're smart, that you're in your seat at school every day, and that except for that, I think you might be down at the bar. He asked if your brothers are drinking, and I told him they are, not terribly, but still. I told him you're going to start, too, if nothing keeps you from it. If you get stuck here, in a place that feels like a prison, you won't have anywhere else to turn. Don't think I don't see that part of your father in you, because I do."

James stayed still and upright. He noticed that the tree beyond the window was flushed green, about to bud.

"I told your uncle how you have to register for the draft, and that I can't let you go into the army. *Can't let you,* James," she said, striking the table with her finger, her voice urgent as a rifle. The late-afternoon sun was bright behind the branch. His mother sighed.

"He wrote back and asked me if I thought

school kept you from drinking, and I considered it, and I wrote that yes, it did, because it gave you something else to think about. He wrote back again and said we should keep you thinking, and he's sent me money now, quite a bit of money, and you're to use it for school."

James sat silent.

"You can talk now," his mother said.

"School's free," was the only thing he could manage.

"Not college," his mother corrected him.

He was as stunned as he would have been if she had punched him in the kidney.

"He wants me to go to college?"

"Yes."

Unexpectedly, James thought he was going to cry. He felt hot tears race up behind his eyes, his nose swell, and his throat close as if it were on fire. This man, this uncle he had never met, had somehow seen the constant struggle it was not to give up, to keep hoping for an alternative to boredom and despair. He had known that black graduation gowns and dull army uniforms were pushing James to desperation. He had known, had somehow known, that the long, clean halls of school, the hard games of basketball, the fresh, curled hair of the girls who stood in front of him in the lunch line were the only things keeping him from giving in to it. His uncle had understood, and his mother had understood, and they wanted to help him. It had been a secret for so long, and now it was in the light.

"I want to go," James said, and so he did.

When Nan was a senior in high school, her father asked her to meet him in his office after school. It was an oddly formal request, because Nan often spent the afternoon hours in that office, working on her homework as he wrote his sermons. He could have spoken to her informally on almost any day of the week.

Her father's office was attached to the house by a door off the front hall; it was an easy trip from the cushioned and curtained domain of her mother into the dark wood and straight planes of her father. She had gone back and forth a million times without a thought, but that day she paused and knocked on the door.

Her father opened it for her, instead of calling her in, which put Nan on edge. "Come and sit down," he said, which made her worry. This was not the way they did things in their family, not one-on-one. News was given at the dinner table, with the lace tablecloth under their plates and their napkins on their laps. She felt pale and small in the shadow of the book-lined walls and the large antique desk that faced the window. Silently, she took one of the two leather visitor chairs; to her surprise her father did not retreat behind his desk, but sat in the chair next to her, pulled it closer, and took her hand.

"This will be hard for you to hear," he said, "but I don't want you to go to Ole Miss next fall."

Nan went numb and completely still. Everyone she knew went to Ole Miss. All of her friends, their boyfriends, her mother, even her father. It was the only future she had ever contemplated.

"Why?" she asked without moving, as if her stillness could preserve her.

Her father sighed. "I've been thinking about this for a long while," he said. "I can't in good conscience just let it lie. Your life is sheltered, Nan, too sheltered. Shelter stunts the soul. It keeps us small and makes faith easy." He squeezed her hand. "You have a lovely faith, Nan. A sweet and loving faith in God, in me, in your mother, and your friends. But I want more for you than that."

Nan wanted more than that, too. She wanted to be a Kappa, study home economics, go to dances, and get good grades.

"What will I do instead?"

"There is a school in Illinois. Wheaton. A good friend of mine teaches there. It's Christian, and it has a world-class music program."

"Illinois?" Nan asked. The word was oily and slick on her tongue.

"I want you to think of this as your mission, Nan," he said. "I want you to get out of this small town. I want you to see a bigger picture. I want you to decide for yourself what kind of person you want to be."

"Does mother think I should go?"

"No," her father said. "She thinks you're too young."

Nan felt sick; she bent her head to her lap. She realized, with a jolt, that her parents had been fighting about this for months. Just last night, Nan had stopped herself from entering the kitchen when she heard their voices.

"She'll miss the season," her mother said. "She's been waiting her whole life for this, and if she's gone, all the good boys will be taken."

Her father said, "The season is at Christmas, and she'll be home for that. She *hasn't* been waiting her whole life to be a debutante, and if a boy likes her and isn't willing to wait for her, then he isn't much of a man."

"You're filling her head . . ." her mother said.

"With what?" her father interrupted. "With a challenge? With independence?"

"Yes."

Her father sighed. "I have to," he said. "No one else will."

Nan thought they had been talking about a Bible camp or a ministry trip. Nan had thought her mother would win.

In her father's office, Nan covered her ears with her hands so she could hear herself think. Her parents had fought. Her father had won. His prize was to send her away. She felt blank, like the church after a service, filled with the silence of having been full and then emptied.

Her father kept talking. "It's an overnight train ride, and you can come home for all your vacations."

"Can I go for one year?" Nan asked. She sounded like a child; she could feel the petulance in her voice like a thorn. Her father closed his eyes.

"I'd like for you to think of it as your college career."

She understood, then, that this was not a discussion. The decision had been made.

She left Mississippi in late August. Her mother helped her pack, stuffing shoes with old stockings and rolling them in rags before she laid them in the suitcase.

"I can talk your father into one year," her mother told her.

"It's all right," Nan said, folding a dress in half. "I'm ready to go."

"And then you'll come back," her mother continued. "You'll hardly miss anything."

They finished packing in silence, the only sound the tissue paper they laid between each layer of clothing. When they were done, when there was nothing in Nan's drawers, when her closet was empty and her vanity bare, Nan lay awake in her bed and prayed. She knew she should thank God for this opportunity, but instead she prayed for courage in the face of fear. She prayed God would show her the meaning in the crumbling of her world.

THREE

Tom Adams stopped Charles after class one afternoon, called him over to his desk as the rest of the students emptied out of the room. Charles hitched his books up under one arm so he could straighten his tie. He didn't think the summons strange. All of his professors paid him certain special attentions: assigned him extra books, pointed him in the direction of respected journals, offered to fix him up for lunch with venerable editors, authors, scholars they knew. They were ensuring the right recommendations, the best course of study. They were establishing for him an unassailable reputation of merit, so that his father could keep his hands clean, could just nod with satisfaction when the right graduate school envelope arrived.

Tom Adams helped, too, in his own way: he slipped hard-to-find reference books into Charles's campus mailbox, forwarded him invitations to department gatherings. Today, though, he was unusually hesitant. He frowned, looked down, tapped a finger on his desk.

"Well," he said after a moment. "This is a sensitive question, but I'm going to ask it." He straightened, tapped his finger on his desk again. "Are you a churchgoing man?" He looked warily at Charles.

"Not really," Charles said.

His father thought religion was a farce. *The illogical province of primitive man.* In the classroom, he taught it as an instrument of power — a system of rules, with attendant punishments and rewards, wielded by cunning men to keep less cunning men in line. Its persistence in modern life frustrated him, especially because it required him to go to church three times a year: Convocation, Christmas, and Easter. This was the tithe of attention expected of the civilized, academic man, proof of morality and respect for tradition.

On those days, Charles's family attended service in the same spirit they went to the dentist: at a determined time, in a determined place, Charles in his tweed coat and brown lace-ups, his mother wearing a hat and her most expensive gloves, his father stiff with frustration for a social convention

61

he knew advanced his reputation but which was also a complete waste of his intellectual time. During the sermon he scribbled fierce notes on the back of an offering envelope with one of the church's tiny golf pencils. *Sentimental,* he wrote, *repetitive, you've got to be kidding,* and often: *translation,* sharply underlined. During prayers, he closed his eyes, bowed his head a fraction of an inch, as if the soft words might have actually been comforting him. Not until he was in graduate school did Charles understand this meant his father was sleeping.

"I mean, every once in a while."

Tom Adams nodded, started to gather his notes into a leather bag. "Well, in any case, there's a lecture tonight I think you might like," he declared. "Given by a friend of mine. 'The Reality of Faith in the Middle Ages.' "

Charles frowned at him, confused by Tom's reticence. He seemed almost embarrassed, and Charles had only ever seen him fiercely self-assured. Charles hesitated.

"It won't be as disturbing as it sounds," Tom said with a disconcerting smile.

"All right," Charles said. It didn't sound disturbing to him at all and wondered why Tom thought it might.

The lecture was held in a small room,

close to the library, lined with folding chairs and warmed by a fire in the hearth. The chairs were filled with boys he knew: many from his own classes, some from his dorm, others he had seen in the halls. Most turned when Charles walked in, nodded their hellos or raised a hand in greeting, but the atmosphere was curiously hushed.

Tom's friend, surprisingly, was a priest — Father Martin. He was a real priest, in black pants and a black shirt, a white collar, a small silver cross around his neck. He was young, as lively and athletic-looking as Tom, who was speaking with him quietly, happily, who ended the conversation with one hand on the priest's shoulder in the manner of old companions. Charles realized he had never seen someone look glad to see a priest in his whole life.

It wasn't a long lecture. It was about Joan of Arc.

"We know much about Joan," Father Martin said, leaning forward on his chair, elbows on his knees. "Even though history was written by men. For some reason, men found this particular woman worthy of mention."

Charles and his fellow students nodded.

"She was a French peasant. She believed she had visions, claimed the saints told her

63

to drive the English out of France. She dressed as a boy and managed to convince her king to send her into battle at the head of his army."

Father Martin paused for a moment and smiled.

"The Dauphin must have been desperate, yes? To send a woman into battle?" Around the room men smiled. Father Martin nodded and continued. "He was. Every obvious, rational military strategy had been tried and failed."

Charles was enjoying this story. He knew it already, but Father Martin was a compelling speaker, sure-footed as he walked them down the path.

"And what do you think of Joan?" Father Martin asked. "Do you find her strong? Daring? Crazy?" The fire crackled in the hearth. "I expect most of us think of her as tragic. What a pity to die so young, for faith, in such a futile way." Charles and the other students nodded once again. Father Martin took a sip of water.

"Let me pose a question," he said, pausing for a moment, taking a breath. "What if God is real?"

The room was still and mute. This was a house of academia, where intellect and ambition were idolized. Where research, analysis, and insight were required. Where proof was always the goal. To admit that God existed was as shocking as taking off one's shirt in the middle of a meal.

"All right," Father Martin amended, "what if God was real *then*?" A foot scuffed on the carpet. A throat cleared. "What if instead of being naive or foolish or mad, Joan actually did speak the word of the Lord?"

The room was stunned.

"I think many of you find it hard to imagine — really imagine — a time in which God felt immediate. A world in which it made sense for armies to be led by girls who saw saints. But to understand history, you have to find a way to accept the possibility that Joan was sane. That her visions were real. That the king's decision to employ her was sound."

Despite the looks of disapproval the audience was giving him, Father Martin continued. "My friend Tom, here, asks you not to think of yourself as a king. But I ask you to consider this: as king, you would have believed, ardently, that you were the heir of God on earth. *The heir of God.* You study men's wars and their courts, their manners and land usage. And yet, you find their faith quaint and outdated. It diminishes them, somehow. But what if God is real?"

Father Martin smiled. "Rest assured," he said. "I am not here to convert. I simply want to open a small door in your mind. Tom asks you to understand historical figures as real men. And to do that, you must let yourself experience faith. To feel the urgency of their belief in God. For it was a reality in the Middle Ages. Not a question — very, very real."

That was it. Not a lecture, really, more of a curved lens through which to examine the world, an interesting sidebar to Charles's studies. But it took hold. In the days that followed the lecture, Charles felt odder than he had ever felt before. There was a lump inside his chest, solid and damp like wet clay, as if Father Martin had opened a door in his rib cage and slipped an unfinished piece of pottery inside of him, turned Charles into a kiln. He could not shake the feeling of a shape drying to completion, the colors of its glaze becoming vivid. It was hot, so intense sometimes that Charles was afraid it would shatter, so unbearable that it drove him out of bed into the cool night, where he could parse its urgency into footsteps, breath, and forward motion.

It felt like an answer.

He had not known the question was God.

He had not been aware that he had even ever wondered about God, not really, not deeply. But here was this certainty, arising in the same way clarity rose out of Charles's papers after hours of his sitting with scattered ideas, writing and rewriting, twisting words like brass links into a chain until his argument was sound.

The pain he felt, now, he realized, came from forbidding himself to believe it, this answer to a question he did not think he had asked, this confidence growing in him — both secret and certain. God existed; God was real. He could not explain this new conclusion, except to say that when he put it away, it was agony, and when he brought it out, it was the deepest, most beautiful relief he had ever known.

After a month, he went to Tom Adams's office hours. He meant to begin with a question about a paper, to mention the lecture casually, just as he was leaving. Instead he stood in the doorway and said, "Do you believe in God?"

Tom looked up from his desk. "I don't know," he said.

Charles sat down in the old chair tucked in the corner. "But Father Martin does."

"Yes."

"And how does he know?"

67

Tom smiled. "He says it's like knowing that your mother slept with the milkman. You wish you didn't have to know, but there it is."

"And you don't know."

"My mother never slept with the milkman," Tom said. Then seeing that Charles was serious, he said, "I have never been certain about faith. I expect the same enlightenment of it that I expect from study. But, even when I pray, I still see things in the world I don't understand. Martin tells me I should stop assuming God is so like me. He says the challenge is not to understand, but merely to believe that all things are understandable."

Charles felt pale. "I think," he said and cleared his throat. "I think that may be how I feel."

Tom was silent for a moment. "Then you're lucky," he said finally. "And I don't think you know yet just how lucky you are."

Charles did not feel lucky. He felt like he was going to have to tell his father that his mother slept with the milkman.

He chose Sunday dinner, because that was the time allotted in his family for serious things.

"Mom, Dad," he said, when the table was empty — before dessert, but after the chicken and potatoes had been cleared away. "I'd like to discuss graduate school." His voice was careful and slow. He chose words he knew would calm them both: *discuss, graduate, school.* His father held up a hand.

"I'm afraid not," his father said. "I can't know anything about your process. You'll apply, that's fine. But it can't look as if I've encouraged you or biased you in any way. I can't be in front of it or behind it. Discuss it with your mother," he said, rising from the table.

"But you're not behind it," Charles said, without careful thought. His father raised an eyebrow.

"Mind your talk to your father," his mother said. She began to cut the cake.

His father sat back down. "Charles," he said, "you're a brilliant student. I'm not flattering you. My colleagues tell me so, and I am inclined to believe it." Out of the corner of his eye, Charles saw his mother smile.

"I am also inclined to believe that, though there are those who toady up to me, there are also those who would like to see me go. I don't keep tabs on who outnumbers whom at any given moment. My support of your application could help, but it could hurt, depending on who has the final decision. It's better that I remain removed."

Remain removed, Charles repeated to himself, what a cunning encapsulation of his father's life.

"Thank you," Charles said. "But it's something else I need to tell you."

His parents both looked at him. His mother, holding a piece of cake on the flat edge of a spatula, seemed alarmed.

"I think I'd like to go to divinity school," Charles said. To his chagrin, his voice was small and quiet. His parents did not answer. There was a moment of silence during which his mother transferred the piece of cake to a plate and put it in front of his father, and still no one spoke.

Suddenly his father smiled. It was a real smile, a big smile, a smile Charles had never seen before.

"Hah!" his father exclaimed, clapping his hands together. "Hah!" He stood up then sat back down. "You've done it," he said, leaning toward Charles. "You've done it brilliantly." He sat back and took a bite of cake. "It's brilliant," he said, chewing.

"What's he done?" his mother asked, putting a piece of cake in front of Charles.

"He's come up with a way to completely divorce himself from my shadow." His father shook his head, almost in glee. "I didn't

70

think it could be done. I didn't see how it could be done — it's bothered me all these years, ever since he started liking history. How was he going to make it on his own? How was he going to prove to everyone he didn't need me?"

Charles had never seen his father so animated. He wondered if this was what he was like behind the closed door of his study.

"You could have gone to a different school, of course, but that would have been silly. You would have given up greatness for independence, which isn't what I call a fair trade. So you came to Harvard, and I have been trying to stay out of the way. But divinity school, of course. Of course! Especially with medieval studies. You'll continue Latin, and Greek. Greek!" It was as if his father's hair was standing straight up on his head. "You can finally study the Greeks! And the Romans! You can finally study them because you won't have to study them with me!" His father paused to catch his breath. "It's brilliant," he said peacefully. "It's almost the same course of study. You'll publish something excellent, and any department will let you cross over. Divinity school. It will probably even lend you more cachet."

Charles wanted to let the moment live. A doctoral degree was six years. Six years in which he could bask in the glow of his father's pride. He didn't want to see this glorious, effervescent being become again the grey tweed man it used to be. He wanted to make his father happy.

But as his faith had fallen deeper into him, like drops of indigo in a glass of water, Charles had been thinking. His future was academic; it always had been. His talent was research and writing, distilling thoughts into theses and supporting arguments, crafting paragraphs that fit together like ice cubes in their metal trays. Expressing ideas clearly was his life's work. And now his ideas were about God, about life and how to live it better. As much as it surprised him, he no longer wanted to be a professor, and so though it pained him, he was forced to say, "Actually, sir, I think I'd like to preach."

His father wiped his mouth, set down his napkin, rose from the table, and left the house, slamming the door.

Charles had been prepared for that, but still did not like the finality of it, the emptiness in the room. His mother reached across the table to pat his hand. "Your father will come around," she said. "It's just a shock, especially after you'd made him so happy. At some point, he'll find it noble; he'll write some paper about the history of religious callings."

Charles smiled; it was true. His mother cleared her throat. "Do you," she looked down, then back up. "Do you feel you have a call?" she asked.

"Yes," Charles said. "I do. I'm absolutely certain that God exists. I can't tell you it's rational, only that it's immediate, and urgent, and true." It was the most personal thing he had ever told her.

His mother frowned slightly, then looked at him directly. "A minister," she said. "It seems useful, doesn't it? It seems like a pleasant way to spend a day."

"Thank you," Charles said. "That's just the way it feels to me."

And so Charles started his doctorate in theology, reading the Bible for the first time, studying Hebrew, Greek, papyrology, and biblical archaeology. It was not that different from his study of history, except that it was entirely personal: each assignment, each text, each lecture pertained to the way he would use his faith. Or rather, how he would explain it, how he would bring its peace into other people's lives. Before his first semester was over, he knew he had made the right choice. He was happy — as happy as he had been during his childhood summers, but in a deeper way, because this interlude would not come to an end. When he graduated, he would take a post as an associate pastor, and when that term was done, he would find his own church: a place to minister and serve. It was remarkable to look out on his future and see no impending disassembly of his contentment.

Lily had chosen Fridays. On Fridays, she did not think about her parents at all. It was a relief.

All of Radcliffe was a relief. Though the dormitory was crowded and loud, and girls congregated in the hallways at all hours, smoking cigarettes and singing bits of popular songs, Lily quickly learned that a DEAD END sign hung on her door discouraged people from knocking and that she could skip the weeknight coffees in the living room. This anti-social attitude branded her a grinder who cared about grades more than anything else; it was not a flattering reputation, but she did not mind it. There were plenty of other grinders to sit with in the dining room at meals, textbooks open on the tablecloths, girls who accepted her as a colleague and did not expect her to be their friend.

At the end of her freshman year, she enrolled in summer school. She had gone back to Maryville for Christmas and discovered that, in her absence, her family's grief had scabbed over. Their sadness had thinned and lightened, new skin had grown, fresh and pink. While she was away, they had been able to forget the accident. When she returned, they had been forced to pick up their rakes of grief and drag them along the ground.

So she formulated a plan. She would not go back again. She would finish her undergraduate degree in three years, take her master's degree courses in what would have been her senior year, and continue on to a PhD. If she went to summer school every year, she could be finished with all her classroom studies in eight years, and her dissertation in two after that. Then she would find a teaching position — not at Radcliffe, which still did not hire female professors, but perhaps at Mount Holyoke or Smith. She could live a life full of colleagues and students, assignments and grades given, research and footnotes to organize. Her schedule would be set, and there would be enough faculty meetings and parties for her to not be totally isolated. The prospect of it was the first taste of comfort she had found.

In the middle of what would have been

Lily's senior year, she was well into her master's degree. She was decidedly tired of communal living, especially now that most of her classmates were engaged and conversations in the hallways were about how to plan a day-after-graduation wedding while taking enough courses to get a diploma. She was glad her accelerated schedule meant she spent all of her time in the library, and it was there, in January 1956, that Lily met Charles.

In the two years since Charles had last seen Lily, he had never really stopped thinking about her. During Father Martin's talk, Charles had pictured Joan of Arc as looking like Lily, plain and indomitable. When he first read the story of Ruth, he had thought of Lily; something about the famine and the precision of the gleaning made him remember her. So, when she walked in front of his desk, wearing a grey skirt and red shirt, she had been so constantly at the back of his mind that he wasn't actually surprised to see her.

"Hi," he said without thinking. Lily stopped and turned to him, as slim and straight as the spines of the books on the walls behind her.

"Hello," she said suspiciously. "Do I know

76

you?" Her voice was as low as he remembered, and her hair was as straight and brown. She had, obviously, not noticed Charles sitting there.

"I was looking for a comic book store once, a long time ago," he said.

"Oh," she answered. Charles could tell that she did not remember him at all. He watched her shift her weight to accommodate the stack of books she was holding. The soles of her shoes scuffed against the marble floor, the sound of a teacher demanding silence.

"I've been thinking about you," he said.

"What?" Lily took a step back, pulled her books up to her throat.

"Oh, I'm sorry," Charles said, standing up as if to wipe the terror off her. His chair scraped and yelped as he pushed it back. "I didn't mean . . . I can't think why I told you . . . it's just. Look," he said, grabbing his camel jacket off the desk, struggling to put it on. "I'm not crazy. Really. I study at the Divinity School."

Lily turned her head, looked at him from the corner of her eye. "Divinity?" She raised an eyebrow and gave him a dismissive smile. "I don't believe in God at all."

Charles was so stunned that he let her walk away.

FOUR

James went to the University of Chicago. It was near his house on the South Side, but his uncle had given him enough money to live in the dorms, so he did. He knew it was best to get out of his neighborhood. He wanted to start anonymous and new.

His dorm room was shabby and historic, as big as the entire downstairs level of his childhood home. He had a roommate, Bill, from New York, who told him the building they lived in was one of the oldest on campus, that the funny little windows they couldn't open were called casement windows, that he should take three hard classes and two easy ones, so that his homework wouldn't take up all of the time he would need to date girls.

James liked Bill because Bill was at ease in his own skin, could talk to anyone, and took it for granted that he and James would be best friends. Walking across the cleanly trimmed campus lawns, Bill ran monologues. "That's Jeffries, he lives one floor below us. He's brilliant at math and has a gin still in his closet, I hear. And that, over there, is Emmeline Waters. Her father is the dean of the English Department, but she only dates seniors. That's your first period classroom over there; mine's the other way. Meet back here after third and we'll have lunch. But not at the dorm — in the pub." James didn't understand why Bill had adopted him, and he did not care. Without Bill, he would have been lost.

His classes were uncompromisingly difficult, even the easy ones. He was assigned hundreds of pages of reading a week and papers one after the other, a gristmill of words and ideas he could not quite understand. His classes were small, and his professors expected discussion; they called him out if he did not participate. He was exhausted. Bill managed to finish his assignments in time to take girls to dinner, leaving James hunched over his small dorm desk, rubbing his forehead in frustration, textbooks and pencil shavings littering the floor.

"I have every faith in your powers of intellect," Bill said as he exited. "But could you please figure out a way to speed them up so that we can have some fun?"

James knew that Bill's free time was a result of careless studying and haphazard essay writing. At the end of his first semester, Bill got a raft of Cs and laughed about them. James got a raft of Cs and wrote his uncle an apology.

I study constantly, James wrote, *but I can't figure out what they want from me.*

What do you want? his uncle wrote back. *Surely not to spend every waking moment chained to your desk. There is more to college than academics.*

James exhaled for the first time in months. Then he turned off his desk lamp, lay down on his narrow bed, and slept for twenty-four hours. He awoke stiff, dry-mouthed, and disoriented. It was early afternoon; outside his window, dry February snow blew in circles on the ground. The stack of textbooks on his desk was as strict as ever, but he did not want to study. He smiled; it was the first time he had admitted that. He did not want to study. But then, what did he want to do? He thought for a moment and realized he wanted to be himself. For months he had been nobody: a reader, a listener, blank and amorphous, painstakingly translating the instructions that would help him take on form. He felt deaf and dumb. The silence in his room unnerved him. How could he have spent so many months motionless and alone? He wanted to be in a room full of people, to be part of a pack, to roughhouse as he had with his brothers, to joke and laugh and be loud.

Bill was dating a tall girl named Millie, who studied music. Every weekend, Bill got together with a group of guys to hang out with Millie's friends, all of whom also studied music. James started to tag along. It was too cold to walk anywhere, but Bill had a car, into which could squeeze four guys and four girls, if they were willing to sit on laps. The boys wore button-down shirts; the girls wore plaid circle skirts and bright sweaters. Their breath fogged the windows; their perfume crept into James's hair. The group never went too far from campus, just four or five blocks. It was far enough to feel like an adventure, but close enough that the pizza was cheap and the bars were filled with people they knew.

His classes were not any easier, but his uncle had been right; there was more to college than the library and the classroom. On his nights out, James learned much about his new world. For instance, he discovered that no one in Bill's crowd was going to shoulder him up against the bar and dare

81

him to do something about it. There was no need for James to hang back, size people up, figure out whom he could take easily or who might knock him down.

At first, it was disconcerting. James felt uncomfortable. He stood at the edge of groups, laughing at other guys' jokes, deciphering what they considered funny and what they considered coarse. He discovered that he should sit back in a booth and relax, that he could cross his legs without it meaning anything, that drinks were bought in rounds, beer in pitchers instead of pints. He got used to guys shaking his hand in greeting, clapping him on the shoulder. He began to trust that if one of them borrowed five dollars, it would always be repaid.

Still, James felt uneasy. He had thought that once he learned to fit in, there would be more. That once they had all gotten to know each other, conversations would move past sports and cars, perhaps expand to include politics or careers. James wanted to learn how these men's minds worked: What did they worry about, if they did not have to worry about money or fighting or food? They did not tell him, and James could not figure out if it was because they were not that interested in him or they were not that interested in the world.

■ ■ ■ ■

Nan spent her first semester at Wheaton writing letters to her mother. She told her mother about her roommate, Carol, who was from New York City and so would have her coming out at the Plaza. *It sounds very grand,* Nan wrote, *but intimidating.* She wrote that her room was cozy, the food fine, and the girls friendly; someone was always on hand to zip up a dress, lend a bobby pin, hold a door. She wrote that she enjoyed literature and French and that daddy had been right: the music department was terrific. She did not write any more about it, because she did not think her mother would understand. Her mother had grown up in a church that had discouraged listening to music, beyond hymns, of course, and so her mother thought of music simply as one of the sounds of worship. Nothing more.

Nan had joined her church choir when she was seven, partly to have something to do besides sit by her mother in the front pew, partly so that she could stop wearing itchy stockings, since her legs would be covered by robes. But from her first rehearsal, she was overwhelmed by the harmonies and the descants, dissonance and resolution, how so many different notes sat together in one chord and how each one was necessary for that chord to sound whole. She, herself, sang second soprano, but she was fascinated by the depth and intensity of the basses. In the sanctuary, their voices blended with the low notes of the organ, steady as a metronome; in the practice room, the power of their sound was startling, even more so as she matched voices to faces and discovered that the most luxurious tones were sung by the plainest, smallest of men. There were, it seemed, many secrets in music, and she wanted to know all of them.

At eleven, she asked for a piano and had taken lessons twice a week, learned to read time signatures and clefs, rests and fermatas, sharps and flats. She had been given solos at church and in the musicals at school. She was known as the girl who could sing. But, at Wheaton, she was discovering that her experience was the equivalent of a mechanic knowing how to change a tire. Now, she was in classes where they were assigned symphonies to read like books. They picked them apart like taking out stitches, laying the sleeves and collars and skirts out flat, then learning to put them back together. They compared different composers who worked in concurrent years and compositions in the same style that had been written hundreds of years apart. One of her professors held class in an auditorium that housed three pianos, so that students could play different pieces of music simultaneously and then talk about how they fit together, where they fell apart.

Nan did not have the words to explain how this affected her. She could say that it felt like she was a piece of muslin and the lessons were embroidered onto her. Or she could say that her assignments felt like a thousand-piece puzzle, and every time she put one together, it became a part of her. But she was afraid those words would sound crazy to her mother, and that the intensity with which Nan would write them would sound crazier. So she wrote about the weather, how the trees were encased in ice and there was hot chocolate in thermoses on the dining room sideboards all day long. She did not want her mother to worry, because Nan wanted to stay.

She was making friends in her music classes, and she liked the church on campus. The congregation was almost exclusively students, which was new for Nan, and somewhat strange, but it meant that there were parties every weekend. Not Kappa parties, but parties just the same.

Most weekends, one of the girls in James's group performed in some sort of recital. These were given in various small concert halls on campus, all of which were hushed and carpeted, with a blue curtain that opened to reveal a piano spotlit on the stage. To his surprise, James enjoyed these. It was easy to sit in the darkness and listen to girls sing. There was no mystery to it, nothing to decipher, he could close his eyes and simply feel the fullness of the chords, notice the way the melody wound its web-like way around the room.

He had never been exposed to serious music before, never heard Italian arias or cheerful German folk tunes. It was a relief to encounter something new and not be expected to remember it, to take notes on it, to answer questions about it, or analyze its salient points. After a while, James stopped accepting the mimeographed programs the ushers handed out as the audience walked in. He didn't care what the music was called or who wrote it; he just wanted to listen.

It was at one of these recitals that James first saw Nan. She was the accompanist. She sat in the spotlight on the shiny black piano bench, her back straight, fingers poised over the keys. She had wavy blond hair held back from her eyes by a rhinestone pin. She wore a plain navy blue dress, a simple gold necklace, and no nail polish. She was almost plump and as pale as milk.

James was used to paying attention to the singer, the girl who clasped her hands beneath her breasts and pushed her voice up and out, flinging it to the back of the room. The singers always wore nail polish, bright pink or red. Nan looked at the singer while she played, nodding her head as the other girl did, waiting for her to catch a breath before she continued playing. Nan held her mouth slightly open, leaned forward, almost, but not quite, mouthing the words of the song. James could not take his eyes off her. She was not singing. She was accompanying. *Accompanying,* he said to himself, what a wonderful word.

After Nan's recital James's group went to the pub on campus, as usual. James knew, now, that the way to approach a girl was to buy her a Coke. If he asked if she wanted a drink, she might say no. If she said yes, he had to leave her and spend ten minutes at the bar while she talked to everyone who wasn't him. Some girls said no to a beer, but no one said no to a Coke, so he bought

87

two and searched the topography of heads until he saw a blond one wearing a rhinestone pin.

James had never noticed just how many girls there were. They circled around Nan like geese, a maze of pale cardigans and pearl earrings. Bill had managed to infiltrate the circle, to sit on a barstool with Millie on his lap. James watched him whisper something in Millie's ear that made her peal and blush. James hung back; he was afraid that once he got close to Nan he might crowd her, break something, lean too close and spill ice on her skirt. His head felt loose, too large for his body. But he forced himself to push forward, edging between couples, smelling the mix of perfumes.

As soon as he got to her, Nan looked up. Her eyes were blue.

"Great recital," he said, handing her the tall glass, which was sweating.

"Oh," she answered brightly, "I missed four chords, but I was happy with the timing. Thank you."

"You're welcome," James said. "Having fun?" He felt wooden.

"I am!" Nan said. "We don't do this kind of thing at Wheaton."

"You go to Wheaton?" It was an hour-and-forty-five-minute train ride away.

Nan nodded. "I just filled in tonight, for a friend of a friend." She was smiling at him, small, neat, and clean. The top of her head came to his shoulder. She smelled like vanilla.

James was already working out a plan to borrow Bill's car.

On Tuesdays, the day on which he had no afternoon classes, James drove forty-five minutes to Wheaton, paid for visitor parking, and met Nan outside her French class to walk her to her dorm. He sat on a bench outside while she went upstairs to change for dinner, and they ate at one of the places in Wheaton's small campus town. He drove up again on Saturday mornings and they spent nice days in the park, rainy days in the library.

Nan seemed to think this behavior was perfectly normal. Girls from James's old neighborhood would have teased him, accused him of pestering them, mocked him for the persistent gleam in his eye. Bill raised his eyebrows every time he handed James the car keys and said, "She better be worth it." Bill was the only other person who knew that James was now cramming all of his schoolwork into four nights a week because, in order to afford all this courtship, James had taken a job bussing tables at a pizza parlor Friday and Saturday nights.

It *was* worth it; Nan was the gentlest and most considerate person James had ever known. She listened to him as he talked about his academic struggles and lingering sense of alienation. She did not speak until she had thought for a moment or two; then she said things like *Some people don't think about how their actions make people feel* and *Obviously, you're going to do well in school, it may just be harder than you want it to be.* James could have taken them as platitudes, but when she spoke, she looked him in the eye with an expression that was neither pitying nor patronizing. She meant what she said; she wanted to help him look at his life in a different way.

James wasn't stupid; he knew Nan was too good for him. From first glance, he could tell she had money and a lineage, grace, kindness, and generosity. He knew what it meant to date girls whose fathers had money. He needed more than a job — he needed a career.

He wrote to his uncle for advice, as he often did. *I must find something to do, and no one here wants to help me. The professors are caught up in ideas and theories; their students run in circles around them, barking to be heard.*

I wondered when you'd outgrow them, his uncle wrote back. *More quickly than I thought. What are you studying?*

Philosophy, James told him. *Anthropology, Rhetoric, Latin II.*

His uncle answered, *Philosophy, anthropology, Latin — the underpinnings of religion, the very subjects that drew me to God.*

Over the next few weeks, they exchanged a dozen letters, from which James learned that his uncle worked in finance because he liked numbers, specifically their round weight, like that of marbles, sensible and clear. At the same time, James learned that his uncle experienced God as a tangible entity in his life, unseen but present, most often at dusk, and that he prayed to Jesus, the Virgin Mary, and all the saints, according to their particular auspices.

James ignored his uncle's theology and wrote, finally, *They're all so busy being clever they've forgotten that once I graduate, I've got to get a job.*

And what job would you like to find? his uncle asked.

I don't know, James answered. *I want to be useful. I want to see results. I don't ever want to have to go back home.*

His uncle took longer than usual to reply.

I think you should know, he wrote, eventually, *that I tried to help your mother. A hundred times I tried to help her, and she wouldn't let me.*

Because she was afraid?

Because she wouldn't subject your father to the shame of being supported by another man. That's the choice she made.

James had never realized his mother had been given choices. He took some time to write his answer. When he finally did he said, *I don't ever want to have to stand by and watch people suffer. I want to confront the things that need confronting. How do I do that?*

Politics, his uncle answered, *medicine, religion, education, law.*

James nodded as he read the letter. *Law,* he thought, *I'll be a lawyer, and Nan will be proud.*

On Tuesdays, Nan arrived early for her afternoon French class so that she could get a seat by the window and watch for James to come loping up the pathway in his khakis and grey tweed coat. At first sight of him, she closed her notebook and put her pencil in her bag, so that she could pack up as quickly as possible and be the first person

92

out the door.

Nan had always expected to meet her husband in college. She had assumed some boy would find her pretty and charming, like her more than he liked other girls, trust her enough to let her choose a house and raise his children. She had assumed she would find a boy she thought was handsome, who was on his way to making money, whom she trusted to buy her jewelry and pick out their cars.

She had not expected James, with his wry smile and messy hair. She had not expected to wake up in the morning and wish he were with her, to hurry through breakfast, leave class directly at the ring of the bell so she could be with him more quickly. She had not expected to feel panicked when he was late or relieved when she saw him, to relax when he put his arm around her. She had not expected her heart to race furiously when he kissed her, or to want to be with him more than anyone else. She had not expected to need him as surely as she needed shoes. She had not expected him to become so quickly, so irreversibly, essential.

She wanted James to love her. She knew he was wary. He often walked awkwardly, one shoulder hunched, tense, ready to run away. She recognized his vigilance; she had seen the same look of distrust in so many eyes on her visits to parishioners with her father. It was the look people had when they needed to be treated with dignity after so much of life had been unfair. She wanted to wrap her arms around him, hold him as she would a frightened bird, thumb on its back, fingers on its shaking, feathered chest.

She thought he might be worried that she was as silly as her friends, only interested in clothes and cars and television. So she told him about music: about learning how to tune a piano, to transpose a score, her first experiments in conducting. She told him about her mother and father, and how they had fought about her leaving home. She told him how homesick she was, sometimes — how much she missed the smell of mown grass and the ironed sheets on her childhood bed. As she spoke about them, she realized she was letting them slip away.

She invited James to church. The prospect terrified her. James had told her he was not religious; he had meant it, and the determination in his voice had given her great pause. Of all the things she thought she could give up for him, she could not give up her faith in God. She had pondered this as deeply as her father would have wanted her to, and she had come to the conclusion that her faith was an essential part of the person she wanted to be. Who would she be without God? What purpose would her childhood have served? Whom would she thank for her blessings? How would she understand the workings of the world? How would she accept its mysteries?

On the appointed Sunday, James arrived in a coat and tie that he had obviously borrowed from Bill. Nan was instantly less nervous; it was a gesture that meant he was willing to try. They arrived for the eleven o'clock service ten minutes early and sat in the third pew. Nan was usually in the choir stalls, as she had been since childhood, but she didn't want this to be a performance. She didn't want James to be her audience. She wanted him to be her date, her partner. She wanted to listen to the word of God with him, to have a shared experience of faith. She wanted it so badly she felt made of glass.

It had been years since she had sat in a church pew, facing the altar instead of standing with her back to it, looking out over the congregation as she sang. She felt ordinary and plain. But she didn't mind, because she was sitting next to someone whose hand she could reach out and hold, marveling at how astonishing it felt to love

God and man so fully at the same time.

James, however, was obviously distracted. It seemed he could not be still. He opened and closed the hymnal and the prayer book, read ahead in the bulletin, took his offering cash out of his pocket much too early, folded and unfolded it until the offering plate finally came around. He rubbed his temples during the sermon and sat on his hands during the prayers. Nan had never seen him so uncomfortable, and she sat through the service wondering if he would ever want to try it again, anxious that this Sunday would be his last.

FIVE

For three weeks, Charles tried to forget Lily. He attended class, ate in the dining hall, wrote papers, and went to church on Sundays. He read the newspaper, shined his shoes, took his blazers in to be pressed, all while trying to forget Lily's brown hair and slight frame.

It did not work. He wanted to know her. He wanted to put depth and shadow and texture to her outline. He wanted to discover the timbre of her voice, to watch her hands move as she talked, to know her stride, her pace, to hear her snap at him in annoyance, to feel her hand on his arm as she made him pause to look at something that had caught her eye. He wanted to know how she sat, how she held her cup, how she brushed her hair. He was surprised by how much he wanted to see her room, to know what color it was painted, what light it got, whether her desk was wide or narrow. He wanted to know how she moved in the world, so that he could recognize her in a crowd just from the way she tucked her hair behind her ear.

But she did not believe in God, and he did. In any intelligent analysis, it was an insurmountable divide. Wars had been started for less, civilizations razed to dust. He supposed he should try to find a girl who understood the deep comfort and broad joy God gave him, who smiled when he talked about becoming a minister, who told her family their plans with pride. He made a point of looking at other girls in the library. Some of them were there to study, lugging stacks of books, wearing tweed skirts, cardigans, and lace-up shoes. Some were there to meet men; he could tell by their tightly curled hair, bright blouses, and open-toed sandals. Any one of them could be the right girl for him; but not one of them was Lily.

It was strange to him that so soon after finding his faith — after believing every need could be fulfilled — a new longing had been awakened in him. A longing for a girl who did not believe in God. But then, his mother did not believe in God, or his father, or Tom Adams — who was, perhaps, the person he most admired in the world — yet he loved them, and they loved him. And also, there was a chance that any girl he dated would reject something inherent about him, wouldn't like history or Martha's Vineyard or comic books or baseball. He, in turn, might dislike her brother or her cat or how she spent her money. So why should he give up on Lily before he'd even tried?

He appealed once again to the librarian, Eileen.

"Look," he said to her. "I'm not crazy. You know me. I study divinity. I think I might be totally in love with that girl, Lily, and I've got to know where she lives or her phone number, or something." He felt like a scrambling puppy.

"She studies English literature," Eileen said.

So Charles stationed himself in the lobby of Radcliffe's English building. He did not know Lily's schedule, so he started his campaign first period on Monday morning, arriving ten minutes before dismissal, hoping to catch her as she came out of a class. He sat on a slatted wooden bench outside the administrative office, his eyes trained on the wide expanse of the marble staircase to the second floor. There were other men there with him, suitors waiting for their own unforgettable girls. Eavesdropping, he realized that most of these boys were English majors, like Lily, and that they could vigorously debate the merits of English literature versus American literature versus literature in translation. These boys seemed to him pale and floppy, and he wondered whether this was the sort of boy Lily admired.

As he waited, Charles worried that Lily would equate him with other divinity students, men who disdained atheists, who worked to debunk disbelief, whose faith called them to save unenlightened souls. He puzzled over how he would explain his own faith to her, how to make her understand that he knew God, but he did not need others to. How to explain that God was like a mentor, a person whom Charles admired, whose company he enjoyed and whom he asked for advice. That analogy left out the *feeling* of Charles's faith completely, but Charles thought it would help Lily see him as sensible and levelheaded. He wanted to describe his faith as one part of him, like being tall or needing glasses — intrinsic and essential, but not something others needed to possess as well.

The bell rang. Lily did not emerge from a classroom, so Charles walked back through Cambridge to his own second period class, the class he skipped the next day so that he could pace the long halls of Lily's school building, still wondering what she would think of him.

His father thought he was crazy. "God," his father said, rolling his eyes, "the greatest myth ever adopted by humanity."

Tom Adams agreed. "God," he said, shaking his head. "Not what I saw coming. I thought you were going to be my competition. I thought you were going to write the books I wanted to write. I thought you were going to write them better."

Charles had thought that, too. But now he knew his studies had been his preparation for ministering. There was suffering, and he could help. There was loneliness, and he could keep company. There was despair, and he could hope. Charles did not question this calling. It was as certain as the facts of his life that had come before. But now he knew his call was not everything. Now, there was Lily.

Charles returned to look for her again the next day. His in-class essay had taken longer than he'd thought it would, even with his rushing it, and he arrived later than he'd wanted to, dropping onto the bench hot and slightly out of breath. Carrying his books had made his palms sticky; he wiped them on his pants then raked them through his hair. He looked up. The bell rang across the marble floors, a door opened at the top of the staircase, and Lily emerged. She was wearing a grey dress with a full skirt, no stockings, flat shoes. She was pushing a notebook into her green Radcliffe book bag, and she did not see Charles at first. He was glad, because if she had looked at him, she would have seen his face awash in incredulity as he realized that it was not their difference of faith that was absurd — it was the depth and certainty of feeling that he had for a girl he did not know.

His attraction was as unavoidable as a baseball spinning toward him, as his raising his arm to catch it, feeling it land hard in his mitt, the force of it reverberating through his shoulder, simple and solid and obvious. He was relieved when Lily looked back into the classroom to say goodbye to her professor. He needed a moment to take her in, a moment to compose himself, to realize that he felt in that moment exactly as he'd felt in front of Father Martin: that when given the possibility that God — and now love — might be real, he couldn't possibly turn away.

When Lily came down the stairs of the

English building to find Charles waiting on a bench in the hallway, she thought, *How ridiculous,* and averted her eyes. She recognized him by his height; even sitting, he was a full head taller than the other boys on the bench. He wore a perfectly normal tweed blazer, white shirt, and khakis. It did not occur to her that Charles might be waiting for another girl; she turned away from him because she had absolutely no idea what to do with a boy with such a look of determination in his eyes.

She had just left a discussion about *Leaves of Grass,* during which she had been reminded how different she was from other people. Her classmates needed to discuss what Whitman was *trying to do* with his fragmented language, to ask *what does it mean?* Their sincerity made Lily feel as if she was watching them from the distance of the moon. How could she be the only one who knew that some experiences could not be translated into language, could only be measured or explained by the gaps left between the words? She left class with a silence inside of her, a memorial to what was missing.

And now there was a boy who wanted to talk to her. A boy in a striped tie and penny loafers who jumped up to follow her as she strode quickly past him down the hall. He caught up to her before she reached the door, the rough sleeve of his jacket just grazing her bare arm; he smelled like cedar.

She stopped with an audible sigh and looked up at him, wary. He really was absurdly tall; she had to step back to see him properly. His eyes were grey, which surprised her. She had expected them to be as brown as his shoes, and for them to be insistent. Instead, he was looking down at her with an expression that Lily, even in her annoyance, could only describe as nervously kind.

"I'm Charles Barrett," he said. "I'd like to take you to dinner." His voice was round; he spoke loudly, and two boys in bow ties standing by the bulletin board turned to stare. Another jostled past him so forcefully that he had to take a step closer to her to avoid being shoved aside. Lily took a step back. She wanted him to go away. She wanted to ignore him, to push past him without saying a word. But she did not want to make a scene.

"How did you find me?" she asked.

"I asked the librarian," Charles said. "Don't be angry. She knows me. I'd like to take you to dinner."

Lily scowled. "Why?"

Charles looked startled. "To get to know you," he said.

"Absolutely not," she answered.

Charles took a step back. "Pardon?"

"I don't think you *would* like to get to know me. I've told you what you need to know. You're studying to be a minister and I don't believe in God."

To her surprise, Charles smiled and looked up at the ceiling. "That's true," he said, looking back down at her. His skin was pale; his hair fell over the left side of his forehead. "I'd like to take you to dinner, anyway. Please?"

Lily glared at him, stiffly aware of the passing crowd and the raised-eyebrow looks her classmates were giving her. She could see them lifting their notebooks to cover their mouths as they whispered to one another. Rumors would sprout and twine around the two of them as long as they stood there, as long as they gave everyone something to see. She could not stand it.

"One dinner," Lily said. "And then you have to leave me alone."

Charles left the English building draped in a golden relief so heavy it made him want to lie down. He had expected Lily to reject him, had prepared to make his case. Still, in the moment after she had said *absolutely not,* when her eyes were hard and dismissive, he had felt utterly undone, as if someone had opened a window and taken away the whole living room.

But he had won a dinner. One dinner in which to persuade her to have another. How would he do that without discussing God? It was all he had, really, all that he was: a man who wanted to become a minister. He spent his days in church-adjacent rooms parsing men's callings and their hopes of sharing them with others. He spent his evenings absorbed in Hebrew translations, authenticating primary sources, reading testaments — reading everything — with an eye to how he might use them in a sermon, or in counseling, to illustrate or shore up his own words of wisdom and advice.

Lily wanted to hear none of this. He would only be able to tell her that school was easy for him and dancing was not, that his mother made him anxious and his father made him sad, that he loved the Vineyard and sailing and eating lobster on the deck before the sunset, in the clear, bright days of summer. As he showered and shaved and put on a clean shirt, he wondered: Would it be enough?

Lily dressed for dinner with as little effort as possible in a straight navy skirt and navy blouse, red lipstick, and four quick brushes of her hair. She locked the door to her room, put her keys in her purse, and went downstairs to wait for Charles on the bench outside the dorm, so that the other girls would not see him pick her up.

He was exactly on time. He smiled at her as he walked up the path, studiously casual in a grey wool blazer over a navy sweater and white shirt. His hair was neatly combed and still damp from the shower. He smelled like shaving cream.

"Hello," he said.

Lily raised her eyebrows as she picked up her scarf from the arm of the bench where she had laid it and put on her gloves.

They walked to a tavern nearby, where they sat across from each other in a dark wooden booth. The table between them was sloped and scarred with initials. Instead of looking at Charles, Lily let her eyes fall on the tables around them. Other booths were full of people, their tables crowded with glasses and pitchers of beer. She was surprised, as she often was, that her classmates

107

lived noisy, companionable lives. When she finally looked at Charles, who had not taken his eyes off of her, she saw that he was approachable and earnest; there was no grief in his eyes, no sign of a fare hard-paid.

"Let's not talk about divinity," she said.

"Okay," he said.

She said, "It's just that I think God is wishful thinking."

"What's wrong with wishful thinking?" he asked.

"It's wishful," Lily said.

"You must have wished for something that didn't come true."

"Yes," she told him.

"What?" he asked.

She shifted in her seat, tried to lean back, but the wall of the booth was too far away.

"Let's not talk about divinity," she said again.

So they talked about school, and Lily found herself admiring the way Charles's eyes lit up when he talked about history. They talked about the library, and she had to appreciate his reverence for it, the gratitude with which he described its solemn rooms. After they'd finished their first drinks, he told her about Martha's Vineyard, and she could easily recognize the pictures he painted of his cousins — they were as lively and attached to one another as her own. While they were eating, he told her about his stern father, his accommodating mother, the thin, silent house in which he'd been raised, and she was glad to see some sadness in him, a close familiarity with solitude.

She told him about the paper she was writing on *Leaves of Grass* and how much her professor hated the thesis, but would have to give her an A anyway, because it was so well researched. She told him that she had her senior suite all to herself because her roommate, Rosemary, had gone back to homecoming at her old high school and never returned.

Her overwhelming sense, as she spoke, was that Charles was listening. When her eyes landed on him, he was considering her words, every one of them. His attention was alarming. She could not meet his eyes directly. She looked down or over or away and her hands moved across the surface of the table, adjusting the silverware, fiddling with her straw.

Dessert came — two ice cream sundaes in tall cups with long silver spoons. She had not suggested they share, and he had not seemed to mind. They ate in silence. The waitress took their plates away. The seat beneath Lily was hard. The only way to sit comfortably was to lean forward, legs crossed, elbows on the table. Charles was looking at her, waiting for her to say something. His silence pulled at her like a tide.

"Fine," she said abruptly. "Why on earth do you believe in God?"

Her face was flushed and her expression reconciled. It was the first time Charles had seen her look anything but pale, and he thought she looked beautiful. He wanted to tell her they could talk about God another time, but he wasn't sure there would be another time.

He took a deep breath. "I don't exactly know," he began. "From the moment I was presented with the idea, I believed it. I can't imagine not believing."

Lily narrowed her eyes, seemingly unmoved. "Do you think you have some sort of call?" she asked.

Charles looked at the straight angle of her shoulders and the long line of her neck. She was weighing him now; he could not lighten the scale.

"Yes," he said.

"To what religion?"

"Presbyterian." It was the church he had gone to with his parents, and the most democratic and practical religion he could find.

"What do you have to do?"

"Preach. Counsel. I talk with people about their deeper beliefs. Not what they do for a living, but why they do it. I get to know people. I see what's underneath — what gives them comfort, what brings them joy."

He knew this sounded hackneyed, but it was true.

"Do you pray?"

"Yes." Before prayer, his life had unfolded in a place of hard study and debate, where men believed in the power of their minds. Prayer gave him a respite from that skepticism, a way to ask for comfort.

"About what?"

"Mostly, I sit quietly. I ask for help in thought, clarity of understanding. I try to see beyond whatever obstacle I'm experiencing. I ask to see the possibility of its resolution. I know I can't find all the answers, but I think they're out there." Through prayer he had seen, immediately, how much easier life was when he had faith.

"Don't be ridiculous," Lily said.

Charles frowned at her, taken aback. She was angry now, her eyes fierce. She looked like his father, outraged at the absurdity of an unproven thesis.

111

"It's not ridiculous," he said, keeping his voice serious. "It's what I believe." He leaned forward, ready to say more.

"Shush." Lily glared at him. "I'm thinking."

Charles sat back and watched her still, delicate face as she thought.

At one time, Lily had believed in God. She had gone to church and Sunday school, which was taught by her grandmother or her great-aunt, depending on the year. Mostly, they played with the faded animals that made up Noah's ark and cooked pretend chocolate cakes in the yellow plastic oven. If they managed not to act like hooligans, they were given a root beer Dum Dum before they went home.

"Jesus likes well-dressed children," her great-aunt reminded them, "and little boys who don't pick their nose."

Her parents' funeral was in a church. Their caskets were grey, with white roses on top; her aunt Cassandra had asked the florist not to use lilies. Richard sat in the front row with her and held her hand. It was very bright inside, so she closed her eyes for most of the service. She didn't cry. Everyone else did; Miriam kept passing tissues down the rows. Lily just waited for it to be over.

The minister had preached that God had a reason for her parents' deaths, a purpose only God knew. So, for weeks, Lily racked her mind to discover that purpose. Was it to spare her parents from aging, to let them exist for their loved ones as ever young, ever handsome, ever charming and at ease? Or, Lily wondered, was their death meant, in fact, for her — did she need to wake up, to grow up, to suffer, to learn? And if so, why? Was she so judgmental, so impatient, so spoiled? Were her parents so casually ex-pendable? She began to panic because she could not discern the logic of it, which meant she was stupid, which meant she was losing her mind.

Then a thought came to her, a simple thought, clear and unbidden. *There is no God.* The idea was followed by a velvet abyss of silence so deep that it stopped time for a moment, as one stops for a fear-frozen deer in the middle of a road. She stared at it, unblinking.

Could it be? Was God not real? Had God not punished her or her parents? Had they not been watched and found lacking? Was it possible that there was no magical being, no loving benevolence, no outraged tyrant, not even a mirror reflecting her back to herself? Was it possible there was just nothing? Did life run out as commonly as a ball of yarn, knitting needles waving in suddenly empty air?

The idea was so electric that Lily held it at bay for a few days. When it had stopped hissing and cracking at her, when its sparks fell impotently to the ground, she allowed it to be real. And then she understood.

There was no God.

There was no master plan, no prewritten destiny, no plot, no judge, no sentencing. There was no God. There was only circumstance and coincidence. Life was random, neutral, full of accidents. There was no redeeming value in her parents' deaths, just debris to be cleared, trees in the driveway after a storm. Her relief was as liberating as a lemon ice on the hottest day of the year.

And now, here, was a boy who was telling her, with his whole being, that he believed in the loving benevolence, the hidden meaning, the plot and purpose. He had described his faith clearly; she could not mistake its outline. It sat between them as fresh and essential as the pale frame of a new house. Her heart was racing. She was afraid. And yet, she did not stand and walk out. Charles had given her a plain truth, and somehow it calmed Lily, opened a still space inside of her, smooth as a lake at dawn.

114

Without warning, Lily looked Charles in the eye. "My parents died," she said.

Charles held her gaze without answering. There it was, he realized, the barest bone of her, bright as the moon on an autumn night that was full of the smell of woodsmoke.

Lily did not want to be dating. One of the girls on her hall was dating, and it involved flowers, phone calls, hair curlers, and laughing in ways the girl had never laughed before. Lily did not ever want to act that way.

And yet she found herself thinking about Charles all weekend. She was acutely aware that he had not said *I'm sorry.* He had not said, *How terrible for you.* He had not said, *God works in mysterious ways.* He had sat across from her, sturdy and kind, and absorbed her grief without comment or pity.

She did not remember the route they had taken home. The waitress had put the check on the table and Lily had excused herself to the ladies' room. When she came back, Charles had held her coat for her to slip into and followed her out the door. It was cold, but they had decided to walk; she had watched her shoes fall into step next to his. They did not say a word to each other until they reached her dormitory, when she had turned to him, nodded her head, and gone inside.

So, when she found Charles waiting outside her class on Monday, she wondered how he could have possibly thought their date went well. She walked quickly down the stairs and stood squarely in front of him, confrontational.

"You were supposed to leave me alone," she said.

"I didn't want to," he answered. Lily glared at him.

"You didn't call me," she said.

Charles nodded. "I didn't know what to say." He spoke with easy honesty.

"About my parents?"

"Yes."

Lily was tempted to tell him there was no way he could be a minister without having a pretty good plan in place when he was called on to comfort and console. But then she realized he meant that he didn't know what to say to *her,* because his pretty good plan involved talking about God.

"Do you have a class near here?" she asked finally.

"No," he said. "I came to walk you to your next one. What is it?"

"American Lit," she said, turning on her

heel to leave. Charles fell into step beside her.

"Is it good?" he asked.

Lily shrugged without looking at him. "Passable. But I don't like Thoreau."

"What do you like?"

They had reached the glass door that led out of the building. Lily stopped and looked at him, annoyed. She did not want to tell him what she liked. She did not want to find out what he liked. She did not want to talk at all. She resisted the urge to roll her eyes, sighed heavily, and handed Charles her books.

"Come on, then. Even though we're only going right next door." She pulled on her coat as he slid her books on top of his own, tucked the whole pile to his chest, opened the door, and waited for her to walk out in front of him. They walked down one set of icy steps and up the set directly next to them, where Lily took her books, said thank you, and went inside.

On Tuesday, Lily found Charles waiting once again. "Do you not have a class of your own?" she asked.

"Yes, but I don't mind being late." Charles shrugged, the tweed of his blazer rasping against the collar of his blue shirt.

"Every day?" Lily raised her eyebrows,

handing him her books. They walked outside, down stairs, then up stairs. Bells rang
inside the buildings, and Lily said thank
you.

"For the carrying or the company?"
Charles asked before she had gotten inside.

"The carrying," she said, without looking
back.

On Wednesday it was raining, and Charles
arrived with a large black umbrella.

"Do you want to carry this or my book?"
he asked. It was a pointless question; there
was no way Lily could hold the umbrella as
high as the top of his head.

"Do you just have the one?"

"Yes," he said, handing it to her. "Don't
worry, it's not a Bible." He was grinning.
He was *teasing* her. It had been years since
anyone had told her even the smallest joke.
But here was Charles, straightforward and
charming and preposterously pleased.

On Thursday, Charles was waiting for her
again, looking thoughtful. He took her
books, as usual, and held the door open for
her without saying a word. Then, at the bottom of the steps, he stopped, faced her
directly, and said, "Look, Lily. You must
know I come all this way just to see you."

She turned to face him and met his
thoughtful tone. "Of course," she answered.

"If you want me to stop, you should say so."

Lily said nothing. On the one hand, she still did not want to be dating. On the other hand, Charles was not totally objectionable. From what she could tell, his mind was clear and his ideas were organized. Plus, he *was* handsome. That, she could not avoid. Mostly because the girls on her hall had whispered it to one another all week. "Lily's got a boyfriend," they said. "And he's a looker."

"He's not my boyfriend," Lily shouted into the hall.

But they persisted. "Well, he should be," they said. "His father's a dean and he has family money." "He's a shoo-in for faculty, if he decides to teach." "My brother says he's brilliant." They wouldn't leave Lily alone about it, and slowly she began to see that it was not terrible to be a little bit more like the other girls, to not be so different, to be defined by something she had rather than something she'd lost.

Charles had their books pressed between his arm and his rib cage, both hands in his pockets. "All right," he said. "If you don't want me to stop, I'd like to take you to dinner again."

"Tonight?"

"No," Charles answered. "On Saturday."

Lily's heart sank. She knew what Saturday night meant. Friday was for girls who were fun but nothing serious. Saturday was for courtship.

"I'll tell you tomorrow." She scowled.

That night, Lily talked to her uncle Richard on the telephone. "He wants to take me to dinner," she complained.

"I'm sure lots of boys want to take you to dinner," Richard said. "They just don't have the nerve to ask."

"I wouldn't call this nerve."

"What would you call it?"

"Stubbornness."

Richard sighed. "Lily, that boy likes you. And you're being mean."

"I know he likes me," she said. "I don't know if I like him."

"Of course you like him," Richard said. "If you didn't, you would have told him to mind his own business."

Lily thought for a moment about how much she should tell Richard, how much of what she said would get back to the whole family, how much she could bear others knowing about her life. "He believes in God," she said finally. "And I don't."

"I believe in God," Richard said.

"True, but so does Miriam. Wouldn't it

bother you if she didn't?" There was a pause in which she could almost hear Richard thinking.

"Maybe. But Miriam doesn't like to read."

He had her there. Miriam didn't read, and Richard did, constantly. Lily wondered what it would be like to marry someone who didn't have the same need for plot and character and story, for words and words and words. Unbearably lonely.

"Does this boy read?" Richard asked her.

"I have to assume yes," Lily conceded.

"Then try not to make him work so hard."

Charles was, indeed, late for his third period every day. That was how every one of his classmates in Intermediate Greek knew he had found the woman he wanted to marry. True, Lily was not encouraging in the slightest. But he had spent nearly a week watching her face as she talked, and her expressions revealed what an effort it was for her to keep up her indifferent facade. She had ten thoughts before she said a word, and ten more after she'd said it; he could see them in her eyebrows and the way she bit her lip. She seemed aggressively Spartan, but she cared about her appearance: her skirts and blouses and cardigans were finely made. He guessed she would never admit to being sentimental, but she wore her Radcliffe ring on her pinky and a leather-banded Cartier watch that was too big and not new.

She reminded him of the rosary beads he had once seen at the Cloisters. No larger than walnuts, each one had opened like a locket to reveal entire scenes from the gospels in miniature: crosses the size of peppercorns and saints as slender as toothpicks, with eyelashes and fingernails almost too small to be seen. They must have taken years to carve, the monks hunched carefully over every movement, still and precise and attentive. Lily seemed to Charles like both the beads and the carvers: intricate and patient, closed and waiting to be seen.

He spent Thursday night in the library, wondering what he would do if Lily turned him down. If she said no, he would have to give up completely; having asked her to make up her mind, there would be no point in trying to make her change it. He wondered if he should just not show up the next morning, surrender before she could reject him. But he couldn't stand the thought of whom she might walk with if he weren't there, and he could not stand the idea of her walking to third period alone.

So, on Friday, before he even took Lily's

books, he said, "Well?"

"Tomorrow?" she asked, as if she had forgotten to check her calendar.

"Yes, tomorrow," he said, holding his breath. It took her so long to answer that he knew she was calculating something in her mind.

She was, in fact, calculating whether she could love him. Not that he expected her to, after just one dinner and four walks to class, but she could tell he was hoping, and the truth was that she did not think she could love anyone. She could love things, like linen sheets, peonies, and strong tea. She could love Richard and Miriam, because she was grateful to them for all they had done for her. She could remember loving her parents and could still recognize that feeling in the characters and plots of the books she read. But the prerequisite for love was trust; and Lily did not trust anything.

Her silence became uncomfortably long, but she didn't rush herself. She stared at Charles's shoes, then his white shirt, then the bare trees and redbrick buildings behind him, blocking out the opinions of the other girls, trying to decide if she, herself, liked seeing Charles at the foot of the English Department staircase more than she liked not seeing him, if she liked walking to class

123

with him more than she liked walking alone.
The answer was yes. Unfortunately.

Six

Of all the things James had imagined about college, it had never crossed his mind that he might meet a girl he wanted to marry. James had longed for girls before, admired their beauty, stared at them for hours, but only because they were vibrant and happy. He had wanted them because he wanted something in his life that he did not want to make go away. He had never thought of marriage, because his parents' marriage was the circumstance that most frightened him, the prison where he and his family lived in poverty under a gin-sodden roof that leaked rage.

But Nan did not see life this way. Her life was constructed of three things she loved: her family, music, and God. It was to these three things she would compare James, the measure by which she would decide if she loved him. It was these three things James would have to accept in order to truly love her. Family, he knew, was inescapable. Music, he understood. He accepted the fact that during their walks, dinners, and lunches in the park, Nan was always half distracted by melodies in her head, notes stacking themselves up and down the treble clef. He found it charming that when she talked, she used her hands as if she were conducting. He knew she'd had a bad day if she did not have a little song or part of a symphony to sing for him.

Her love for God, however, gave James pause. He did not believe in God; he had to be honest with himself about that. He did not believe there was an eternal, ethereal intelligence guiding the daily lives of all the people on Earth. He didn't believe there was meaning to be found in suffering or that any intelligent being would have created war. And he could never put his trust in any entity called *Father*. Every time he heard that word his whole body clenched into a punch he wanted to throw.

No one had ever challenged him to think differently about this. Men in his neighborhood did not believe in God, or if they did, they knew that God was not with them. Their wives went to church, but men — depending on their character — slept late, read the newspaper, or worked on their houses. God was women's work, the province of softer minds that had not seen the second between breath and nothing, how long it could take to die, how absent God was on the battlefield. James believed that God was left to those whose faith had not been tried.

But Nan's father was a minister, and her faith was in every word she spoke, every touch she gave. To love and be loved by her in any meaningful way, James would have to at least go to church.

Services at the Wheaton chapel were ecumenical. James was glad for that; it was easier to listen to an expression of values rather than the tenets of a particular faith. The eleven o'clock service was crowded every week, and the congregation was full of students. The men wore blazers and the women wore dresses, sometimes with small round hats and white gloves. How on earth, James asked himself, did so many people of his own age decide to believe in God? Where did they come from? What were their parents like? Why did they take time out of their week to worship?

At first the services themselves had been so new to James that he could not quite follow the standing and sitting, the prayers the congregation joined and those it did not, the offering and doxology sung from a memory that James did not possess. He merely hung on, trying to find the pattern, as Nan handed him well-worn red hymnals and Bibles turned to the right page. The sermons were the one respite in which he could relax, listen, and try to understand what the people sitting next to him found so appealing.

This minister, a small, balding, quick-spoken man, said often that faith, at its simplest, was the acceptance of the possibility that things one had never seen could be real. James could accept that; he knew there was more to the world than he had ever experienced, and his time at college had showed him just how limited his experience was. The prayers recited each week were expressions of gratitude, and that was easy for him, now: He was grateful for his uncle, for his mother, for his friends, for Nan. The scriptures read in this church most often described a God of love, and James finally knew what love was: the amazement of encountering someone astounding, like an ocean full of snow.

Because Nan knew everyone in the room, it always took longer than James liked for them to leave coffee hour, but he met at least ten new people a week: English majors, math students, future lawyers and engineers. They all shook his hand warmly and looked him in the eye; James had never experienced a community so free of arrogance or disdain. At first, it made him uncomfortable. But as the weeks passed, he began to look forward to the hour spent in the fellowship room, with its blue carpet and bay window view of the walled garden that set the church apart from the rest of the campus. He began to recognize faces and see them as individuals — sunny, serious, smart, fun — understanding that they were distinct individuals, even in their faith in God.

Why did you want to be a priest? James wrote his uncle.

I had a call, his uncle wrote back.

What stopped you? James asked.

I didn't want to live in poverty, his uncle answered. *I'd already lived that way; I wanted to escape it. So I took a break. I wanted to wait until my call returned. But it never did; God never asked me to serve again. And now I give almost all my money away, anyway. Funny. But I do like the choice. I like knowing I don't* have *to give it away. I like that I still do.*

James's prelaw classes were proving to be long and complicated; every case seemed constrained by those preceding them. Lawyers, he came to understand, served the law;

129

they hardly ever changed it. Politics was corrupt, medicine beyond him. Education intrigued him not at all. A thought began to grow in him, lurking in the lining of his sport coats, sliding out of every notebook he opened: the people in the world to whom he was most indebted — his mother, his uncle, and Nan — believed in God. With growing clarity, James understood that his goal had always been to get out, away from a circumstance he found intolerable. But now he *was* out, and he needed to make that mean something.

James's mother invited Nan to dinner. On the appointed Saturday, his mother nagged him and his brothers to move the furniture, handed his sisters brooms. Together, they cleaned the entire house, top to bottom. James tried to tell her Nan wouldn't go in the bedrooms, wouldn't look behind the cupboard doors.

"Yeah, Ma," his brother Alfie said, "She's already met Jamie — she's not expecting a palace."

James's mother flicked him on the shoulder with her dishtowel. "I want this house to look respectable," she said.

James wanted her to get up off her knees and stop scrubbing the floors with a wooden

130

brush, to get out of her housecoat and slippers, because he didn't want to see how much work had to be done to make him respectable enough for Nan. He didn't want to see that all he had to offer were his studies and his determination. It was not much, and he was afraid.

When the house was clean, James's mother shooed James's siblings upstairs to take baths and iron their collars. James had taken the night off from the pizza parlor and borrowed Bill's car. As he shrugged himself into his blazer, his mother put her hand on his shoulder and held out a ten-dollar bill.

"No, Ma," James said.

"Yes, James," she said. "For gas. We all want to meet her, so we're all chipping in to get her here." James was surprised at the relief that swelled inside him. For so long, he had been alone in his hope that Nan might love him. And now he had company.

Nan smiled when she came out of her dorm. When they pulled up outside his house, she smiled again.

"It's just like you told me," she said. It wasn't. The house sparkled. All the lights were on, there were crisp white doilies on the back of the sofa, and his dad was awake, clutching a cup of coffee between shaking hands.

"Oh!" his mother cried and hugged Nan tightly. "Oh," she said again, and wiped her eyes. Nan had brought her flowers, and his mother put them in a cut glass vase. James wondered from which neighbor she'd borrowed it.

His brothers had combed their hair and his sisters were wearing lipstick. James was a bit overwhelmed that they understood how much this mattered to him. Nan sat among them as if she had always known them, asking them questions about their work and remembering all of their names. They ate roast beef, potatoes, and coconut cake, and after dinner, his father asked Nan to sing.

She blushed. "Oh, I don't really sing," she said, "I play the piano."

But his family pressed her, and she agreed, standing in the dining room, her hands clasped at her waist. She sang a little song, one she'd sung for James a hundred times, and when she was done, his father whistled and his mother cried.

"I think they're wonderful," Nan said on the way home.

"They think you're a celebrity," James said tiredly. He felt stunned, literally, the same way he had felt after each of the three times in his life he had been punched in the jaw.

He did not know how else to feel. His fears had been for naught. And still, as James had watched everyone being their best selves, pulling themselves together and getting along, he had been aware, so painfully aware, of how different Nan was from all of them. For her, the evening was one more lovely night added to all the others she had known, set close beside each other like a string of pearls. How could he ever re-create it, again and again, across a lifetime? The chasm between their upbringings seemed dark and large. He had spent the night wondering how it could be mapped, navigated, bridged. He was worn out by the failure of his imagination, which seemed only able to ask him: *What is the point of climbing down into something from which you can never climb back out?*

Nan turned to him. "Listen to me," she said as sharply as he'd ever heard her speak. He looked at her. She was sitting straight up, twisted toward him. Her cheeks were pink, her mouth tight, her eyes glistening. She pointed at him. "You're afraid I'm someone I'm not. You're afraid that because I have a tennis bracelet and more than one pair of dress shoes that I'm too wealthy to love you."

James kept his eyes on the road in front of

133

him and did not answer.

"Well, I am wealthy," Nan continued. "I've always had more than enough, and that's nothing to be ashamed of. It doesn't mean I'm going to act like Millie. Millie would have thought your house was crooked, your mother's dress was cheap, and your sisters were going to be spinsters. Millie would never have come here, would never have even thought about dating you once you told her where you came from. I thought your family was wonderful. I think your sisters are pretty, your brothers tell good jokes, and your father is so proud of you he managed to stay sober for one whole evening. I think that whole house made you just what you are, and that's why you love me."

James realized she was crying. She bowed her head and began to rummage through her pocketbook. He handed her a handkerchief from his breast pocket. She took it without looking at him, pressed it to her eyes. He wanted to reach out and take her hand, wipe the tears away himself, but he was a tin man, stiff with shame.

"You hardly said one word to me tonight," she said, her voice muffled. "I know it's because you thought I was going to see where you came from and never be able to look at you again."

She was right, of course. Nan saw everything clearly; she knew what people were feeling and she acknowledged it. She never made a joke or looked away. James loved that about her.

Nan put the handkerchief on her lap, straightened, and stared at him, fierce. "I was taught to speak to everyone," she said. "And I was taught to love everyone."

James nodded without looking at her. This was her religion: to see and help. But he did not want to be one of the people her father made her visit. He didn't want to be a person in need. Nan shook her head sternly, as if James had spoken out loud.

"Don't do that," she said. "You know what I mean. You know I mean I love you most of all."

He did. And as soon as he heard Nan say it, James took her hand. For as much as he did not want to need her, did not want her to see him as he really was, and did not want to spend his whole life trying to live up to her, he loved her, too.

James understood, with a dread that felt like a fishhook, that he was going to have to meet Nan's family before he proposed.

They undertook this at Thanksgiving. Nan

135

boarded the train with two little leather suitcases; James borrowed a canvas duffel from his brother so as not to pack his things in a paper bag. She kept her ticket neatly between the pages of her book; he stashed his in a back pocket and gave it to the conductor rumpled and crushed. She had ridden this route often enough to sleep and read; he had never been out of Chicago and kept his eyes glued to the window the entire way.

Mississippi was hot. The city around the train station was dry and dusty, but as soon as their taxi reached the outskirts, the landscape burst into being around them, humid, green, heavy with the smell of honeysuckle. Lush trees shaded white picket fences and houses that rambled across cleanly shorn lawns. James looked at her and raised his eyebrows.

"I am not too good for you," she said.

Nan's parents lived in a white house with two thick columns holding up the porch roof. They were waiting on the smooth front steps to hug Nan and shake James's hand. "So glad to meet you," they said. "So happy you're here." The four of them spent three days driving big cars around the country-side, visiting various family members. They sat at a long table filled with silver bowls and platters for Thanksgiving dinner. The high polish of Nan's life made James even more acutely aware of how coarse his own upbringing had been and how undeserving of her he might seem. But still, after they had eaten and the guests had left, James screwed up his courage and asked Nan's father if he might have a moment of his time.

"Come into my office," Nan's father said.

James followed him out of the dining room, into the front entryway, and through the door to his office. The heels of his shoes were loud on the wood floors.

Nan's father used his chin to gesture to a chair in front of the window that overlooked the grey stone church. James sat down.

"I like to sit here when I know someone's about to come see me," Nan's father said, lowering himself into the chair across from James. He loosened his tie, undid the top button of his shirt. He nodded at the sanctuary across the street. "If it's a simple problem, they come right over here. If it's bigger trouble, they stop over there and pray first." He looked out the window and tapped the arm of his chair with a finger. "I like to know how much trouble they're in before they sit down with me," he said, turning his gaze to James.

The chair James sat in was sturdy and well built; the wall behind him was heavy with books. Nan's father's desk was oiled and gleaming. Nan's father's shoes were new. It was worse than James had imagined it would be, this feeling of wearing a thin sweater and having nothing in reserve.

"You're going to ask if you can marry my daughter," Nan's father said.

"Yes," James answered.

"Why?"

James thought: *Because she is jolly and pretty and bright, like a firefly, blinking in and out of hedges and trees. Because I imagine her in the kitchen, washing dishes, looking out the window and humming to herself, her brow knit in concentration. I imagine myself coming up behind her, putting my arms around her, resting my chin on her shoulder. I imagine her face turning up to me, bright and pale and astonishing, and I imagine her lips just before I kiss her, full and parted, almost singing the words of a song. Because I think beyond kissing her, because I think about her naked and warm under clean sheets and damp from the bath. I imagine her bare ankle rubbing against my own. I imagine her hair disheveled; I imagine myself smoothing it out of her eyes. I imagine making toast with her and eating it at a round table. When I do, I am just as crazed with passion for her as I would be in bed. There is no difference between imagining her naked and imagining her with a kerchief over her hair.*

"Because I love her," he said.

Her father said nothing, staring in James's direction but past him, as if he were trying to solve a math problem written on a chalkboard behind James's head.

"How will you support her?" Nan's father asked.

James had anticipated this question. He knew from Nan that her father respected anyone who worked hard, no matter what they earned. But he had not asked if James was a hard worker, and after spending a day in this house, James had a better idea of what Nan's father meant by support. He did not mean food on the table and a new dress once a year. He meant cars in driveways and trees on the street. He meant friends and parties and pretty things when Nan wanted them. James had thought his answer would please Nan's father; now he was not so sure.

"Actually, sir, I'm thinking about becoming a minister."

Nan's father lowered his chin and raised his eyebrows over his glasses. "Do you believe in God?" he asked.

It was an honest question; Nan's father wanted an honest answer. That was fine. James had already decided he would tell Nan's father the truth, and if Nan's father accepted it, then James could live his life clearly and cleanly. James just wished his honest answer was one he knew would hit the target instead of an arrow disassembled, its parts strewn across the floor.

"To be perfectly honest, I don't know."

Nan's father gave a sharp laugh. "Then I wouldn't recommend it."

James knew he sounded childish, foolish. He scrambled to explain.

"My father went to war, sir," he said. "It ruined him, and it would have ruined all of us — my whole family — if my mother had let it." James had not realized that before and was glad to understand it now; he relaxed slightly as he continued. "My father hated God. He blamed God for the war, for not keeping him out of it, for his drinking, for all the evils in the world. He couldn't stand anyone worshipping. Once, he woke up early and caught my mother dressed for church. 'Goddammit, Alice,' he said. 'There's no great protector. No one is listening. Not to you or anyone you know — great spoiled women who got to stay home from it all, who got to stay here and

140

pray for us. Well, it didn't work, did it? All of your praying didn't do one bit of good.' "

James found himself out of breath, his heart pounding. Nan's father turned toward the window and gazed intently at the sky. He was giving James some privacy, and James was thankful for it; he pressed the heels of his hands into his eyes, breathed in and out.

"Your mother was religious?" Nan's father asked. His voice was deeper than before, less confrontational, and James was relieved by an easy question.

"After a fashion, as much as she could be," James answered.

"Did she pray at home, talk to you about God?"

"No."

Nan's father sat back. He took off his glasses and rubbed his eyes, looked up at the ceiling for what seemed like a very long time. When he finally spoke, he said, "You are aware that most ministers feel they have a calling?"

James had to force himself to look Nan's father in the eyes. His stomach tingled; his legs were jumpy. "Yes," he said.

"It's quite visceral," Nan's father said. "Bone-deep. Without that kind of certainty in God and God's purpose for me, I'm not sure I could do what I do. Do you feel that you have any kind of a call?"

"I'm restless," James answered. "I'm impatient. I want to do something useful."

Nan's father said nothing. James shifted in his seat and scratched his head with both hands. "I have found comfort in going to church with Nan. But at the same time, it creates this urgency in me. It's hard to sit still, sometimes, through all the music, and the announcements, and readings they don't edit down. I like it; I'm grateful to Nan for bringing it into my life. But sometimes I want them to just get to the things that matter, to talk about the things that are wrong with the world and how to fix them."

"What's wrong with the world?" Nan's father asked.

"People don't have enough money," James said, pushing his hair back from his forehead. "People are sick, or in jail, people feel alone. They have given up, surrendered, stopped living in any real way. People are angry."

Nan's father sat calmly. "Does that matter?" he asked.

"Yes."

"Why?"

"Because when they suffer, we suffer with them. Whether we know it or not, we suffer with them." James was startled by the anger in his own voice.

Nan's father assessed him, staring at him and through him simultaneously, his eyes curious. To James's surprise, Nan's father suddenly nodded and seemed to come to a decision.

"I'll tell you what I'm hearing," he said. "You feel you have a duty to work for the world, in the world. And some part of you wants to believe in God."

"Yes," James affirmed. "I do. Every time I go to church, I wish I could believe wholeheartedly, without reservation, without any nagging doubt."

"And you feel you can pray, study Scripture, say the blessings with sincerity?"

"I do," James said. "I may not believe in God, but I believe in ministry. I want to do for others what my mother and uncle did for me. I want to give them chances. I feel I have a debt to repay."

"Fine," Nan's father declared forcefully. "God doesn't always come in visions or dreams, and God rarely comes in certainty," he went on. "God has come to you in restlessness and yearning. God has come to you in questioning. God has come to you as a challenge. It won't be easy, but it's a

143

perfectly acceptable calling. Where will you study?"

James had only begun to think about this, but he knew enough to proffer an answer. "I know Nan would like to come home," he said. "And I'm sure that would make you happy."

Nan's father shook his head ruefully and smiled. "Oh, no," he said. "You can't study in Mississippi. The Baptists will eat you alive."

"In that case," James said, "my uncle has offered to help me find a place at a university in England."

"Very good," Nan's father said. "Intellectual, used to skeptics: a perfect fit. I give you my blessing."

The next summer, James and Nan were married twice. Once with her family in her father's church, where Nan wore a long white gown and veil, and once with his family, by a justice of the peace, for which Nan wore a white suit and hat. They went to Maine for two weeks, stayed by a lake, and when they came back, Nan packed to leave her world again, this time happily, this time for London.

SEVEN

For the rest of the school year, and the whole of the next, Charles and Lily had dinner every Friday and Saturday night. They sat in various booths in various restaurants, and Lily asked Charles questions like, "If God exists, why are men killed in battle? If God exists, how can we be afraid?"

To all of these, Charles answered, "I don't know."

He could have given her his working hypotheses. He could have said, "Men are killed because other men kill them, and I'm pretty sure God doesn't actually want us to be afraid." But those answers would have given her something to argue with, a logic to pick apart. Charles did not want to bicker with Lily. He was willing to discuss the failures and successes of organized religion, but that wasn't what Lily wanted to explore. She wanted to determine whether his faith was permanent. She wanted his final answers, his certainty, and under her particular brand of scrutiny, *I don't know* was the only statement he could make that hewed closely to his truth.

Sometimes, this infuriated Lily. How could Charles not know? After all his study and thought and church and prayer, how could he accept that there was no answer? What would it take to make him scoff at superstition, to make him accept the flimsiness of his worldview? She wanted to poke at his conviction with a stick until it collapsed, until she persuaded him it was fantasy. But he did not give her the chance. He indulged her in debates about history, politics, war, peace, wealth, and poverty. But he would not let her present her arguments against God; neither would he submit arguments in God's defense. It was a fair bargain, Lily had to admit. Still, she continued to test him, to gauge the nimbleness of his mind and his willingness to accept her defiance. The tenor of their courtship was set, and it was contrary: Lily disagreed with everything Charles said.

Over months of debate, Charles's mind sharpened. He understood that, with Lily, he had to be clear and quick. He could not speculate or equivocate; he had to take a stand and support it with facts. He could tell he had become a worthy adversary when Lily took a little longer to formulate her rebuttals. In the pauses, Charles loved to watch the expressions move across her face as she searched for her defense, found it, and wrangled it to run her way.

He did wish he could share more of his uncertainties with her, wished he could tell her the things he *wanted* to believe even though he did not, yet. For instance, he did not quite believe the Bible was the word of God. He wanted to; his career would be so much easier if he could, but the Bible was full of a God that bore no resemblance to his feeling of faith, to his sense that, in the midst of any agony, there was a part of every being in which all was well.

He also did not quite believe, yet, that he could be a good minister. He was worried he had spent too many years steeped in academia, too much time studying the past, not enough time in the real world. He wanted to believe that he was right about his call, that he understood his mission correctly, that it was, indeed, to put into words the alchemical comfort he felt when he prayed. But sometimes he worried he would do the worst job of his life in the pursuit of the life he most wanted.

He knew Lily would not understand his

wanting to believe something that he did not already. She would not accept that, in lives of faith, wanting to believe was everything, when in lives of academia, wanting to believe was a failure of scholarship. So he kept his doubts from her. To share them would cloud the issue, which was that he had no question about his faith in God. He simply let her measure him, discern how much room he would take up in her life.

Lily accepted his patience. She understood that he would not give up God for her, that their future was hers to decide. In many moments, she felt crazy for dating him. What did his faith have to offer her? God had not eased her grief. God had not renewed or healed her, even in Charles's presence. In fact, in trying to decide if she could love him, she had thought of her parents every day, wondered what they would have thought of him, decided they would have found him steady, calm, and intellectual, just like her. And so, in the months they had been dating, she had felt more bereft than ever.

Still, she did not send Charles away. Dating him was lectures and dinners and long evenings in the library. It was insight and breadth of knowledge and desire to learn. It was exactly what she had wanted out of

Radcliffe, only it was with a boy. A boy whose height and voice and scent had become familiar, whose hand she held, for whom she honed her best ideas so that she could earn his respect. She had never felt this way, even with her family. With them, she had felt different; with him, she felt entwined.

It was preposterous. He had an entire part of his life that he could not share with her, that she could never understand. But then, so did she. She had told him, of course, how her parents had died, what her life had been like beforehand, and then after. She had given him the history of it. But just as he did not tell her about God, church, ministry, and colleagues, she did not tell him that she often woke at night with a tar-dark dread inside her, as blistering as her first moments of orphanhood when she realized that no one was alive who truly loved her, that she could be forgotten, that she was lost and no one would claim her as their own.

Thus, their scale was equal. He had his faith and she had her grief, the parts of them that were unspeakable, in the face of which words were flimsy and inept. They both understood what it felt like to change in an instant, to become an entirely different person, to be shown a landscape they had not asked to be revealed. Without his faith, he could not understand the depth of her grief. Without her grief, she could not fathom the lightness of his relief. In this way, they were each other's mirrors, each reflecting back to the other a pilgrim on an unsought road.

One spring night they went to a lecture on contemporary art, which Charles had chosen because it was one topic about which they had not yet argued. They sat in the first row, listening to the strangely rasping voice of the lecturer as the slides shone for a moment then disappeared. Lily smelled, as she always did, of gardenia. When the lights came up, they were the last to leave the auditorium; as they waited in the line up the aisle, Charles scratched his cheek and said, "I didn't like that very much."

"I didn't either," Lily answered.

Charles looked at her, clearly surprised. She laughed. Sound came out of her in a burst, and she clapped her hand over her mouth to muffle it. Her eyes were bright; she looked ten years old.

"What?" Charles asked.

"I just never thought we'd agree on anything," she said. "It's a shock."

This Charles knew, as he stood in the

sloped, carpeted aisle, was a miracle. Lily did not laugh often; now her face was bright. There was a pocket of quiet around him; the moment was completely still. Lily had laughed, and it reignited his sense of purpose. He would serve God and he would serve her. He would do anything to make her laugh again.

They found themselves outside as the crowd dispersed, standing together on a campus path as the loudly chattering groups faded away. It was cool, and Lily had brought a cardigan. Charles held it so she could slip her arms inside, and as she did, there was a moment when his arms formed a circle around her, when he felt her warmth in the cool night air, when he wanted, desperately, never to have to let her go.

And yet, he asked her this question: "Do you *truly* not believe in God?"

It was the wrong time to ask it, but he was beginning to doubt that the right time would ever come. They had been dating for months, skirting around the fact that their entire courtship hung on this one question. He knew the answer, but he wanted to hear her say it; he wanted to gauge the way it hit him, hoping it would not feel heavy or hard.

Lily frowned harder than usual, made to turn away. Charles kept his hands on the lapels of her sweater, lightly, just enough so she could not retreat.

"I don't," she said, and, to his relief, it did not gut him, not in the way it might have done, before he knew her.

"Do you truly not *want* to?" he asked.

She nodded. He felt oddly calm, somehow glad that the parameters of their relationship were clear and strong; that he had not been mistaken or misled.

Lily's face was grave, all trace of laughter gone. "Let me ask *you* a question," she said. Charles braced himself.

"Do you believe that someday you'll convince me to find faith in God?"

He was startled. It was one of the easiest questions she could have asked him.

"No," he said.

"Do you secretly *hope* that someday I will find it on my own?"

This was not an easy question. "No," he said. "I don't think that's possible. But I do hope that someday you will find relief, deep peace, and joy."

Lily took two steps back and put both hands on top of her head. "That's ridiculous," she said.

"Why?" he asked. She shook her head so forcefully he was certain she would leave, almost put his arm out to stop her. But he had to ask her one more question, the question that mattered, the question that had slunk behind him as he walked through his days, lingered, persistent as a black cat at the door.

"Do you think you can ever love me?"

She let her hands drop to her sides.

There it was, she thought, the crux of the matter, the X on the map. How could she bear to love him when love brought loss? How could she love him, when she lived in the dark and he lived in the light, when the fact she believed most certainly in life was that love led to agony?

She was exhausted. "I don't know," she said.

Charles was acutely aware that, after almost two years, he had still not kissed her. He had not yet seen any look in her eye to convince him she longed for him. She had never once accidentally grazed his leg while reaching for the salt or leaned close to him at the movies. But still, how could she not know? She, who had plotted the course of her life in excruciating detail, her trajectory predicted in a series of indelible, straight lines?

"Why not?" he asked, suddenly angry with her, hurt by her primness and her intellect and her seemingly complete disregard for

153

his feelings.

"Because you want too badly to make me happy," she said. Even now, witnessing his anger, she could feel his desperate hope. He had accepted that she would never believe in God but could not bear the fact that she would always be sad. It was a pity, because she did love him. That truth had lurked in her for months. But what did it matter?

"You'll never be able to make me whole."

They did not speak for weeks. The end of the school year was approaching. Lily received her admission to the PhD program, and found a room in a boarding house on Irving Street where she could live when her four years of allotted on-campus housing ran out. She met the women living there already and liked them. One was studying Eastern art, the other theoretical physics. They were as serious about their academics as she was. While the bent-on-marriage girls steamed their white dresses and chose names for their future babies, Lily asked her new roommates if they thought it was actually possible for her to finish her coursework and dissertation in five years.

She had not abandoned that plan. Charles had three more years at Harvard after this one, and then he would be called to a church as an associate pastor for two years. If they were still together when he got the call, she would have to decide whether or not to go with him. She had done her research: If she continued her tradition of summer school, she could finish her coursework and teaching the same June that he would graduate, and then she would have only her dissertation to complete, which she could do anywhere. It would have been possible to finish her studies and support his career.

Now, it was impossible. Charles had let go of her sweater and left her standing on the sidewalk alone. He had not been waiting for her outside her class the next day or the day after. She did not see him in the library. He did not call. And she missed him. He loved her, and she had told him the one thing she knew would drive him away.

Graduation approached. Lily ordered her robes and booked a room for Miriam and Richard, who were coming up for the ceremony. As she had not told them about recent events, they were looking forward to meeting Charles. Lily found herself wishing she could introduce the three of them, that they could eat lunch together and drink champagne while she felt proud.

Exam week came and went; Lily passed

155

every subject with straight As. She did not celebrate. She packed her suitcases, sat on the edge of her stripped bed, and stared at her bare walls. The dorm was hot and stuffy. Parents had begun to arrive, and girls were laughing merrily in the halls. In her room, though, all was quiet, except for Lily's billowing acres of loneliness.

She did not want to love Charles. Love was packed up tightly in brown boxes in Miriam and Richard's attic, boxes she had no desire to open. She didn't want to be like every girl in her family, all of whom had grown up, found a husband, stayed in the same town, never spent one moment alone. For her, alone was no longer a state of being cured by company; it was her definition, it lived in her very flesh.

She turned on her light and sat very still on the edge of her bed. She thought about Charles, about his familiar face with its plain chin and its nose flattened where it had once been broken by a baseball. She thought about his carefully ironed collars and the straight line of his new haircut. She thought about his patience, his quick wit, his willingness to listen to what she had to say.

Twenty minutes passed. She went downstairs to the dorm living room and dialed the telephone.

Charles answered.

"Hello," she said.

On the other end of the line, Charles closed his eyes. He had not walked away because he was angry. He *had* been angry — angrier than he ever thought he could be — but he had left because he hadn't wanted Lily to see his face. He hadn't wanted her to see how sad he was for her, how hopelessly and utterly sad. And he hadn't seen her or called her because he didn't want to admit that she was right: He *had* wanted to make her whole. He had hoped he would be enough to make her happy. If he could not make her happy, what was the point?

"There are no classes tomorrow," Lily said.

"I know."

"So you won't be waiting for me."

"No," he said, but inside him something broke and spilled out a thimbleful of hope.

"I'm sorry," Lily said. "I was unkind."

"Yes, you were." He did not want to say more.

"My parents were in love," Lily said, "so I know it's possible. I know people *can* love each other wholeheartedly. I don't know if I can love you that way. But I can try."

And so, their first kiss was on the walkway

157

leading to her dormitory, at two in the afternoon on the day before her graduation, when Charles arrived to find Lily waiting on her front steps. She stood up and walked toward him; when she reached him, Charles realized something had shifted, that her eyes were saying *I don't want you to go.*

He leaned into her, but she stopped him with a hand on his chest. There was one more question.

"Do you *really* not need me to believe?" she asked.

He had already thought about this, thought about it hard.

"Not in God," he told her. "I just need you to believe in me."

Charles was, actually, the one thing in the world in which Lily believed the most. And so she nodded and, finally — finally — his lips met hers, warm and strong. When she put her arms around his neck and he put his around her waist, he knew they had turned the page. He felt he had been given the answer to every question there was to know.

"Please don't ask me to get married," she said, when the kiss had finished.

"Are you kidding me?" Charles asked, incredulously, but he waited two more years, so Lily could feel certain their engagement would not derail her PhD.

Then Charles bought her a sapphire ring, and they turned the wedding planning over to their aunts in order to spend their last unmarried year in uncomplicated academia. The day after Charles's divinity school graduation, they were married on Martha's Vineyard, in the living room of his grandparents' house, with all their collective cousins and aunts and uncles gathered around. Lily wore a simple white satin dress and carried a bouquet of climbing roses that Charles had cut down off the trellis that morning. In a gesture that both gave him hope and broke his heart, Lily had said, "Let's wear my parents' rings."

They did, and as he slid her mother's on her finger, Charles saw a small smile he had never seen on Lily before, as if she were, at last, a little bit less sad.

EIGHT

In London, James and Nan found a flat in Kensington, on the top floor of a white row house among identical row houses, all of them prim behind black gates, a long, green garden spread out behind them like the sweep of a skirt. The flat had two coal fireplaces and lead-paned windows. From the living room, Nan could see the current of people walking to work each morning, huddled under their umbrellas.

James began his divinity studies at King's College London. He left early each morning, placing his rinsed coffee cup by the side of the sink. What coffee they could find was awful, instant. Nan easily switched to tea, but James hung on, stubbornly, swallowing with closed eyes. She marveled at his persistence. She had never known anyone so unwilling to compromise.

Nan constructed their household thoughtfully. She found food stores she liked — a butcher who smiled at her, a green grocer who didn't mind if she touched each apple before she chose. She learned to bring her own shopping bag, to always ask if there was something nicer in the back. She tried to cook something new for dinner every night and had figured out how to make enough so James could take leftovers to school and she could have a lazy little lunch without cooking more than once a day. She learned how to keep the pantry stocked without buying so much that bread went stale or peaches brown. She discovered what the two of them were like, together — what time they preferred to eat dinner, what they enjoyed for snacks in the afternoon. She liked marriage. It was a puzzle, and it was not hard for her.

She rented an upright piano and a sewing machine. She was relieved that neither bothered the neighbors. In fact, the landlord and his wife — Henry and Lucinda — professed to like the piano. If they were in the garden while she played, they clapped after every piece, their applause clattering through the window.

"Brava!" Henry, a tall, barrel-chested doctor, shouted.

"Come down for tea when you're done," Lucinda yelled.

Nan liked both of them. Henry was stately and dramatic, given to gesturing while he talked, even when holding the butter knife or jam spoon.

"Tell me, Nan," he said. "How is married life? Babies soon?"

"Careful, darling," his wife said, taking the saltshaker from his hand.

"Babies soon," Nan said, and blushed. She and James were trying, often. It was only a matter of time.

"Oh, wait as long as you can, love," Lucinda said, setting down a plate of sandwiches. "Babies take over. They absolutely take center stage."

"Rubbish. Muck," Henry said genially. "They're absolutely wonderful." He took a bite of scone. "You come to me when you're enceinte, my dear. I'll send you to someone I know."

"Henry," Lucinda warned him, tapping the back of his palm with her finger. She turned to Nan. "What are you doing up there? How is it looking?"

The flat had been drab when Nan and James moved in: brown sofa, dark wooden chairs, dour carved headboard. Nan had made long, double-lined curtains from a yellow cotton embroidered with green leaves and bluebirds. She sewed matching throw pillows for the couch, with silky blue-and-green fringe. She made pale orange, floor-length covers for the pocked wooden side tables. She put wedding pictures on the mantel, in silver and tortoiseshell frames. She arranged the furniture to hide the thin spots in the rug. She bought new pillows for the bed, and better light bulbs for the reading lamps. She made dishtowels from leftover fabric.

"Would you like to come and see?" she offered.

"Oh, yes!" Lucinda jumped up from the table, pulling her bright red shawl off the back of her chair. "You stay here, dear." She put a hand on Henry's shoulder when he started to rise. "Give us girls a moment. I'll be back."

They went up the carpeted staircase together, Lucinda wrapping herself in her shawl. Nan turned the brass doorknob, stepped inside, and gestured for Lucinda to join her, pleased to see the delight on Lucinda's face.

"It's just lovely in here," Lucinda said, running her hand over the polished telephone table in the entryway. She continued into the living room and took the fringe of one of the throw pillows between her fingers. "You've positively made it a home."

"I like to make the best of things," Nan beamed.

"I remember first being married," Lucinda said. She walked to the mantel and picked up the photo of Nan resting her head on James's shoulder. "It was hell."

Nan was still standing in the doorway.

Lucinda put the picture down and rubbed her eyes. "We had no money. Henry was a student, so we paid for everything with loans. Everything we did incurred debt. Not what I thought it would be. I expected to putter around, read magazines, get dressed for drinks at the end of the day." She smiled at Nan somewhat sadly and sat down on the sofa.

"We used to have the most awful arguments," Lucinda continued, leaning back against the cushion. "I used to throw things, and Henry used to growl." She smiled at this memory.

"Growl," she said again, beginning to giggle. Her hair and her chest shook, and the red shawl came unsettled.

"Growl!" She was laughing outright now, hooting like an owl, her eyes closed, wiping tears from her eyes.

"Oh, God, it's funny," she said, taking a deep breath. "I mean it isn't, but we were so stupid. It all mattered so much, and we were so caught up in it. Oh," she said, calming down. "When I think of those days." She shook her head. "I was so angry, which was ridiculous, because I was young and beautiful and in love."

She wiped her eyes one last time with the back of her hand. "Well," she said, "that wasn't what I wanted to say at all."

She patted the seat next to her and motioned for Nan to sit down. Nan did, nervously. Lucinda put her arm around her. "What I wanted to say is that I remember how awful it was when we first got married; how none of my friends would talk about their husbands, how everyone closed their doors out of loyalty. What I wanted to say is that if you need someone to talk to about your marriage, I can be counted on. If you're feeling blue."

Nan had a strong and sudden surge of compassion for this woman. How awful those times must have been if Lucinda still remembered them so clearly, still needed to talk and share. Nan took her hand and leaned toward her, full of gratitude for Lucinda's secrets and her trust.

"Thank you so much," Nan said. "But I really, really love being married."

"Well, splendid, then." Lucinda took her arm away and looked around the room.

It *was* splendid, Nan thought. It was an adventure.

After their wedding, Charles and Lily moved to Nantucket, so Charles could be the associate pastor to Harold Evans, a white-bearded, old-fashioned, shirtsleeved man ministering at a small, windswept church. Charles was happy on the island; he walked around the hedge-rowed streets in elated relief. He was amazed that he had found a job, that Lily had married him, that he was living year-round in a place so close to the one he had loved as a child.

He and Lily rented an old saltbox house, grey with white trim. It was left to them almost empty, with scuffed walls, bare windows, and unpolished floors. Lily made it fit for habitation by visiting the antique shops and yard sales on the island. Charles watched with curiosity as she approached each cluttered tabletop display. He took note of which cups she touched and which napkins she did not, which vases she carried to the person sitting behind the cashbox and which she discarded before she got there. She liked white, silver, leather, and navy. She did not like paisley. She did not buy things of poor quality. She was not tempted by low prices. She took careful measurements with a blue measuring tape she carried, neatly rolled, in the top pocket of her shirt. He marveled at how deftly she found what they needed, how every piece she brought home fit perfectly in the place for which it had been purchased.

For her efforts, they had a bedroom painted a deep, rich shade of cream, a spare, inlaid mahogany bed frame, and linen sheets embroidered after the design from an old convent. Their entryway was painted sky blue; the kitchen was yellow and green. There were lamps everywhere. They were all different — some delicate and spindly, some solid and hard to move. The one by the arm of the couch was perfect for reading. The one in the bedroom gave just enough light to help him choose a tie. Charles found himself forming attachments to all of them. He had lived, for almost all his life, with overhead fixtures — lights were either on, revealing everything, or off, hiding it all. Now he could have different moods in the same room; he could turn on all the lamps to celebrate, or he could hide what needed to be hidden. He liked the shadow and the brilliance of this place Lily had created.

They settled into a routine. Lily was deciding on a topic for her dissertation. She had annexed most of the table space in the house for textbooks and scrap paper. She researched and took notes sitting cross-legged on the braided rag rug, her back against the old green sofa, entirely distracted by the project. But every Friday evening she said, "Let me see what you've done," and Charles gave her the sermon he was drafting. This she edited late into the night, leaving it red-penciled on the kitchen table for him to see when he came down to make coffee in the morning. Her edits cut easily through his wordy prose, created rhythm and clarity that he could not achieve on his own. Nothing made him feel closer to her. His love was a steady longing that climbed around him, as if silkworms were using him as a loom.

Still, it was strange to be married. He and Lily had spent such a long time deciding if they could live with one another, and now they did. Now he woke with her curled up next to him, warm in her white pajamas, her hair dark on the pillow. He came home to find her taking casseroles out of the oven. But he still did not feel certain he had access to all of her, could not often guess with any accuracy what was going on in her heart or mind. He wanted to feel as if they had been married twenty years, to know each other's mood by the cast of a head or an angle of the eye. But he did not, and it bothered him.

Charles was also puzzled by Harold Evans. On the one hand, Harold was an educated, cultured man who spoke French and German, published book reviews, and had traveled to Asia and Africa during the course of his missionary work. He played chess, scratched marginalia in his books, wrote at least one letter to the editor of a major newspaper a week. On the other hand, he seemed to regard life as one expansive opportunity for fun. He wore silly hats to the office, invented ice cream flavors, was always the first up to bat at church softball games and the first to strike out, spinning crazily before falling in the dirt. His desk was covered with cartoons clipped from the same papers to which he wrote about world hunger, political prisoners, censorship. Charles had never heard him end a telephone conversation without a hearty, jovial laugh.

It was all so confusing. Charles was not sure what he was meant to be, what role there was left to play, how to complement this man who seemed to be so much to so many people at once.

"Lighten up, Charles," Harold said, clapping him on the back. "You're here to learn. Just watch and absorb, don't worry."

So Charles watched Harold Evans shepherd his congregation, moving from member to member throughout the day, now sitting on a front porch, now helping to load groceries, now dancing a jig at a celebration, now rubbing his forehead while witnessing grief. What Charles learned was that humor eased all situations, and humor was one of two things he didn't have.

He also did not have a wife who believed in God.

He had a congregation who stopped by their house with bundt cakes, wanting to sit at their kitchen table and talk to Lily about their new dog, their new garden, their mother's health problems. And they assumed Lily wanted to talk to them, too. She did not. She wanted to take endless notes on yellow legal pads without interruption. She made a little sign for their door that said: SORRY WE MISSED YOU, PLEASE CALL AGAIN. Charles often came home to find two or three apple pies on the front steps.

Charles, himself, enjoyed the endless tiny conversations; they made him feel at home.

"How are you?" people asked and seemed to genuinely want to know.

"The house is coming along very nicely,"

he answered. "We've put up the storm windows and Lily made some curtains."

"Ah. Blackout?"

"Not yet," Charles said. "We don't mind getting up early."

"Well, come winter, you'll want an extra layer," they said.

Charles nodded.

"How's that chimney?" they asked.

"Holding up."

"Anything we can fix for you?"

"Not yet, but I'll let you know." Charles was grateful for their interest and their care.

Lily did not mind the house she and Charles had rented; she liked its wide plank floor, its simple doors, the sparse geometry of the windows and the rooms. She liked their bedroom under the sharp peak of the roof, where she could lie on cold mornings, warm under four quilts, listening to the rain. She liked the smell of coffee mixed with the smell of salt mist; she liked the big, sloping kitchen table — the one thing the owner had left for them to use.

She liked the austerity of the island in winter. She liked putting on rain boots, Charles's fisherman sweater, and a mackintosh, then heading out into the wind to walk the beach. She had never spent much time

171

by the ocean; she was astonished by its end-less, thick expanse, by the space it created around her and within her. She found she could not let a day go by without standing on the shore, her eyes drawn to the far horizon, the sea always flat as an answer.

Charles was like this landscape, straight-forward and earnest, and she still could not quite believe she had married him. In their wedding picture he was tall, so much taller than Lily that it looked as if her choice had been deliberate, as if one could only marry a man so tall if she knew what she was get-ting into, if she loved him above all else. She *did* love him; she *had* chosen him care-fully. But she had not entirely understood what that entailed.

For a while she had gone to church. She had dressed carefully, always in stockings and a skirt, and she had tried to arrive early, because she knew it would be remarked upon if she slid in after the first hymn. She paid attention, followed the readings in her pew Bible, one finger on the black-inked words. Charles did not expect her to attend; he stayed true to his word that she did not need to be part of his ministerial life. But she wanted to try. She wanted to accept the service as ritual, a lecture, like a slideshow in a classroom. But she could not.

The earnestness in the damp faces of the people around her scratched at her like wool. The need in their hands holding the brims of their hats humiliated her. Their shuffling voices reciting the Lord's Prayer rang shame in her like a tuning fork, a metallic chime that made her bones ache, made her want to twist to get away. It was the same way she felt when Charles asked if she wanted to visit her family: trapped, panicked, short of breath, the wretchedness of fellowship, hope, and faith in anything too painful to bear.

She understood the urge to immortalize the feelings of enchantment, of relief, of the vast comprehension she found by the sea. She respected the desire to encapsulate these feelings in a book, into a paradigm of guidance. But she did not believe it could be done. She still did not believe love was eternal or that she would someday live comforted and consoled. She believed that Charles was Charles, and he could not protect her from the world outside the circle of his arms.

She watched him take phone calls from people in his church about the loss of a job, a business slowing, lack of money. He sat at the kitchen table taking down numbers on one of her yellow pads, making notes, nodding with sincerity.

"Oh, that must be difficult," Charles said. "I see. How hard for you. Is there anything I can do? How can I help?"

It made Lily ache to see him reassure these people, to see them in the grocery store the next day, reassured. Charles's greatest attribute was his ability to remind others of the presence of God. It was the greatest solace he had to give, yet it could not help her.

She studied Mrs. Evans, the minister's wife — plump and brisk in her wool skirts and felt hats — for clues about how to handle her new life. Mrs. Evans was at the hospital every day with flowers for sick parishioners. She called on each of the elderly ladies once a week. She baked cookies for coffee hour.

"Not just cookies," Lily whispered to Charles once, "*meringues*. Do you know how hard those are to do in all this wet?"

"Lily," Charles said. "She does all that because she has nothing else to do. It's an island."

The words struck her sharply: *She has nothing else to do.* They burrowed into her like ringworm.

Nan attended Sunday service at the small

174

church two blocks away from her London flat. James was expected to attend services in the college chapel, or to visit churches all over London, in order to learn how to preach. Nan had gone with him for a few weeks, but James quickly made friends with the rowdiest group of men in his year, most of whom were not married. They traveled in a tweedy, boisterous pack, and she saw what a boon it was for James to worship with men of his same age and temperament.

Her church was small and friendly, cottage-like, its outside walls covered with ivy. It was filled easily by the dozen or so pensioners who worshipped there and whose children and grandchildren often visited. Nan was quickly convinced to sing in the choir, which was made up of the few members who had voices strong enough to lead the hymns. There were no robes or stalls; they simply sat at the end of every other pew, singing whichever vocal part they knew best, ready to hold the elbow of anyone who needed support to stand.

It was not a place to make friends, but it was a relief, a quiet hour in which to attend to her own faith, separate from James's. It gave her the chance to pray in the way she always had, starting with *Dear Lord,* ending with *Amen,* filling the middle with hopes for her life — a happy home, a constant marriage, a healthy child. It was comforting to do things the way she had always done them.

This allowed her, for the rest of the week, to be swept along by James's enthusiasm, by his insatiable curiosity and ceaseless movement. His newfound faith was anything but calm. He arrived home from school with his tie askew, dog-eared pages falling out of his notebooks. He was forever making marks in the margins of books, pacing and talking to himself as he wrote his papers.

In the evenings he trekked Nan all over London to wood-paneled, smoke-hazed pubs.

"Here comes America!" James's friend Dean cheered whenever they arrived, raising his glass, pulling up chairs to the crowded booth. James put his arm around Nan as they sat down. The music was always loud.

"Tell me more about the South," Dean said to Nan, leaning across the table so he wouldn't have to shout. He was fascinated by segregation. "Tell me how there are separate swimming pools."

"There are separate everythings," Nan answered, delighted by the attention.

"But we're working on it," James interjected.

"I know you are, mate." Dean pointed at Nan. "Your husband," he said, "won't shut up about social equality, the inertia of the elite." He took a drink. "Makes all of us feel quite guilty."

Nan nodded. She was witness to James's new fierceness of being. He no longer hung back in a room; he stalked forward, hand outstretched to introduce himself to anyone he didn't know. He asked questions, demanded answers, prodded people to continue.

She was pleased and proud. In Mississippi, James would have been angry; he would have glowered at her friends and family, wanting them to be less cheery, less placid. London made him sturdy. She clung to him a little more as they walked, a little more than she would have at home, and he supported her. It had been a good decision to come here, to this place where there were no traditions to follow, no legacies to overthrow, no echoes of the stiff creature James could have been.

Sometimes Nan's parents sent them a little extra money, which they used to go to the theater. They saw comedies and dramas and musicals. They went to the symphony.

They went to Covent Garden, its streets full of buskers playing accordions and bedraggled violins. To Nan, this was a magic London: music everywhere, the entire district lit up and open late. She loved to sit in a dark theater, in a red velvet chair next to James, listening to him rustle and breathe. She loved having him to herself for two hours, without a book in his hand, without an essay to write, just the two of them, sitting still. She loved that when the lights came up at intermission, the whole audience started to talk at once, convivial and boisterous. In those theaters, with their black-tied orchestras, their backdrops painted with scenes of Venice and stages set with false trees, their actors in ruffled bloomers and pink-rouged cheeks, life was a celebration.

She wrote letters to her parents about all of these things. She took her letters to the central post office, because she liked its soaring, vaulted ceilings, its brass teller windows. She liked to stand at the high wooden counters to affix the pink-and-green pictures of the Queen. It felt like an accomplishment to slide the letters into the slot marked International. The sound the letters made as they landed in the bin behind the wall was like a camera clicking, a flashbulb rejoicing that life was even more of an adventure than she could have dreamed.

They had finally met James's uncle, Phillip. He lived in a tall white town house on Egerton Crescent, which was so nicely appointed with silk curtains and gleaming mahogany side tables that Nan felt like a movie star the first time they went over for dinner.

"Didn't want to feel poor, eh?" James joked after Phillip had hugged them and exclaimed over them and asked them to come inside.

"James!" Nan said, looking over at Phillip alarmed.

Phillip only laughed. "No, I did not," he said. "You already know that. Now come in and have a lovely meal."

They sat in the red-walled dining room, drinking wine, while Phillip told them stories about James's mother's childhood. "She was the pretty one, and she could always make me laugh," he said, looking at James. "Absolutely nothing like you," he said with a wink and a smile. Nan asked about his time training for the priesthood, and he said, "Well, they fed me, which was more than I got at home. And they educated me, for which I will always be grateful. But in the end, it just felt like poorly sized shoes. I was happy in God, but wouldn't be in the job." Nan watched James soak up every word.

"Come into the library," Phillip said when dinner had been cleared. I have some things to show you."

The library was wood-paneled and navy blue. Phillip led them over to a large desk, on which old letters and ledgers had been spread. "These are letters from your great-grandfather to various people, and these are the record books from his farms. And this is a family tree I've compiled." He pulled an unwieldy leather tome from the bookshelf. "Sit down and read for a while. I think you'll find you're not from a line of desperate men. Most of our forefathers were well-off, easy of heart and mind."

James sat at the desk, opened the book, and began to read. Nan saw him visibly relax; his collar, which always seemed bunched up at his ears, lay flat as if he, too, was settling into the warm happiness she herself had found living in this city. She took up one of the stiff letters and tried to make out the angled handwriting.

"I'm going to find even more letters for you," Phillip said after a few moments. "I know a few people at church who share my passion for collecting these kinds of things. I want you to read everything you can that's been written by men who share your . . ." Phillip looked at the bookcase while searching for the word. ". . . uncertainty." He nodded his head. "Men who joined the church because it was the only way they knew to make a living. Men who found that, despite that, it fit them perfectly." Nan saw the worry that had weighed James down dissolving in this new, damp air. It was as if the ocean had absorbed the man he used to be.

To James's great astonishment, he found himself excelling academically. The reading at King's College was as hard as it had been in Chicago — he would never get any quicker at it. But the subject matter — religious theory, Aramaic, Greek, even his first attempts at sermon writing — came easily. This had much to do with the company he was keeping. He admired his cohort of classmates more than he thought he could admire anyone his own age. They had deep minds, dry wit, skeptical natures, and they had all been irrevocably marked by war. James felt somewhat ashamed by how much of a relief it was to live in a city where the scars of war were obvious, where the damage done was external, where there were still empty lots and unexploded bombs. It was exhilarating to have it all out in the open.

Most of his professors had fought in World War II and they talked about war's legacy almost every day: what it meant for faith, and men, when it could be justified, how to honor those who fought while still working to ensure it did not ever touch their shores again. Their lives had dignity, a depth he had not experienced before. He had believed fear was felt only by the dishonorable, that anger cursed only those who deserved it. He thought himself both: dishonorable and deserving. He had felt, forever, the hard, black anchor that was something to hide.

But in London he saw a new response to tragedy: It was not skinned or stuffed; no one kept it in a box, preserving it like an injured bird. People unfastened it, let it fall in the gutter, and walked away, determined not to look back. Instead of adorning themselves with it, letting it define them, people let the wounds heal over and, touching their scars like talismans, set out to rebuild their world.

James was determined to join them. He was determined to find jobs for those who had been maimed, find meals for those who were hungry, petition for those who were victimized. He was determined to fashion a world in which people like his father did not need to disappear, in which people like his mother — and himself — did not need to surrender to distress. He thought he would be able to do that in England.

And then Nan had a miscarriage. James had been taking an exam. He had just finished it, thinking he might get one of the top grades in the class, when a secretary knocked on the door to tell him he'd been called to the hospital. James ran all the way there.

He had not known Nan was pregnant. He had not even really considered the fact that they were trying to have a baby — it was something Nan wanted, and James knew she would take care of everything. He knew it would make her happy, and he wanted to make Nan happy.

He found her in a bed behind a curtain, crying wretchedly, pale and fragile in a striped cotton medical gown. The dress she'd put on that morning was folded on the chair beside her, stained with blood. He realized he might have returned home that afternoon to find her dead, white and lifeless on the floor.

"I want to get up," she said. "I've got to

get out of here." She sat up, pulled the sheet off her legs, but the IV tethered her down.

James knew he had to compose himself. He had to talk to the doctors, nod when they told him Nan would be fine. But it was a horror. That was the only word that sounded the way he felt, as if all the air had left him in one great gust of wind.

"Be patient, love," he said. "There's nothing we can do."

Nan knew he was wrong. There was one thing she *had* to do: She had to keep herself from wondering why she had lost her baby. She had to believe God had a purpose and a plan. She had to find the strength to be grateful for the other gifts God had given her: this city, its theaters, her love for James. But she could not do any of those things in the hospital, in her paper-thin gown, with James looking shell-shocked beside her. She did not know how she was going to be able to do any of them at all.

NINE

Each Sunday, as part of the service, Charles gave what was officially called an "Invitation to the Life of the Congregation." This was a welcome to all who were in attendance and a listing of the events on deck for the week: gardening club, beach cleanup, Bible study, bake sale. Charles thought of it as *the reminder that we are not alone.* A public declaration of places to gather in and interests to share.

Charles wished Lily could hear the invitation. He was worried that she was lonely. These days she did nothing but study, brow furrowed, breathing deep, as serious as she had been when he'd first met her. He wished she would try again to join his congregation, to participate in fellowship in some small way. He had not understood well enough, before, that ministry was not just a job but a lifestyle, and how lonely he, himself, would feel because Lily did not

185

want to share it.

"I believe in all the other things you believe in," she told him. "Ethics and tolerance and some sort of moral code. I believe you help people. But I also believe in just letting people alone. Besides, you would do all of this even if you didn't believe in God. It's just the kind of person you are."

Charles disagreed, "God made me this kind of person. Without faith, I would be a smaller man."

"Don't be ridiculous," she said. "I'm faithless, and I'm not a smaller woman."

He was not sure this was true. Except for her books, Lily had only needed four boxes to pack for the Cape: one for clothes, one for towels and bedding, one for dishes, and one for pots and pans. Charles had sat with her in front of her cabinets and drawers, handing her belongings to her, each of which she had inspected carefully, turning it up and down, before she decided whether it was worthy of the trip. For every possession she wrapped in newsprint and put in a box, one was set aside to throw away or send to Richard and Miriam, whom she had not seen since the wedding.

"Don't you want to keep this?" he had asked, holding up a linen napkin, a cardigan sweater, a flowered teacup. He couldn't bear the thought of her things being thrown away, mixed with other people's garbage.

"No," she said. "It's chipped. It's stained. It has a hole." He held his tongue, watched her discard anything that showed the slightest evidence of decay. He knew she never wanted to live at home again, but it made him sad to see how very little of her history she wanted to preserve.

They had lain in bed in her empty apartment the night before they moved, all the boxes neatly taped, labeled, and waiting in the hall. He thought about how curated her life was, how bereft of nostalgia. She permitted herself nothing unless it was practical, no old letters, postcards, faded quilts, worn sweaters. She owned not one rabbit's foot of comfort.

Charles had wanted, then, and wanted now, to bring Lily out of the cold, to build her a fire: a wild, shaggy, crackling fire — the kind of fire one might build on a field of ice and snow. He wanted to take her north, to Alaska, and warm her hands between his own while she discovered herself in the frozen landscape, both of them looking up, grateful and awed by the northern lights.

He went to Harold Evans for advice. He asked late on a Friday afternoon, after the prayers had been chosen, the sermon written. He asked when their backs ached with fatigue, but they were relieved, content with their work. He hoped he had chosen a time when Harold Evans wouldn't make a joke.

Harold Evans did not. He leaned back in his chair, folded his hands across his chest, and stared at the ceiling. "Why do you love Lily?" he asked. "What do you enjoy about her?"

Charles looked down, straightened some papers on his desk. "She is plainspoken. She is practical. She keeps only the essential. Our life is meaningful and pared down. There are no distractions. She sees plainly and has no time for nonsense."

"But other things are beginning to creep in."

"Yes."

"Dismay. Puzzlement. Worry. Frustration." Harold Evans paused. "Anger?"

"Maybe," Charles answered, looking at his hands. "I hope not."

"Anger about?" Harold prompted.

"Anger that I have to question my faith. Since I love her, I have to ask myself if I believe in my own faith above her lack of faith. It sometimes feels almost as if I am disrespecting her by continuing to believe."

Harold Evans sighed. "A faith, Charles, is one's own," he said, letting his gaze fall from the ceiling. "No married couple has the same faith. And one faith is not better than the other."

Charles did not respond. This answer seemed insufficient. Of course faiths were different. But not as different as some faith and none.

"You are in a difficult and precarious position, Charles, one I have not encountered in my own life or in any other parishioner's." He shook his head. "The only thought I have to offer you is an experimental one."

Charles looked up. Harold Evans took a breath. "Love and faith are very different things. Very different things. We work to have limitless faith — faith that encompasses grief, faith that expands beyond doubt. When we see suffering, and it shakes our faith, we pray for those limits to be removed. As ministers, we help people dissolve the borders of their faith, to become more tenacious in it.

"Love is the enjoyment of something. The feeling of wanting something deeply, of wanting nothing more. Our love of God is not as important as our faith in God. Love wanes. Faith cannot. One can have faith and anger, faith and hate. One can believe deeply and still rail against God, still blame God. In fact, if one can hate God it is a sign of deep faith, because you cannot hate and at the same time doubt God's existence."

"Hm," Charles said.

"Not what you want to hear." Harold Evans clapped his hands together. "Right, then. Here's how it applies to you. You love Lily, but you do not yet have faith in her, or in your marriage. You must find it. Faith will allow you the room for anger, for disappointment, for hate. Love will not. You must believe your marriage will succeed, even through hardship, sorrow, loss. Do you believe that?"

Charles was silent. Then he said, "Not if we stay here."

"Ah, well," Harold said, "that's why this post turns over."

Charles looked up at him. Harold smiled. "It's fine, Charles. I'm used to it. This is my life. I live it out in the community with people, and that is what I preach. How to live. We don't live a big life here, but it's a cycle. Sickness then healing, sadness then joy. And to do it well, I have to get out there and see people. I have to be at the hardware store and the baseball games; I have to go to people's houses and to the hospital. And if I tried to do it alone, I'd be lonely. So, I have rotating associates and I have Evelyn.

190

It's a two-person job. If I want to have any time to preach — to really think about what I'm going to preach, it's definitely a two-person job."

"Is it like that everywhere?" Charles asked.

Harold said, "I don't know."

Lily decided to write her dissertation on the careers of Thoreau's critics. "It's easier to commit to a point of view with which I agree," she told Charles.

"Indeed," he said, raising an eyebrow.

She began taking the long ferry trip to Boston once a month to search for new books and return the ones she had finished reading.

"How is it out there?" Eileen, the librarian, asked, keeping tabs on the couple she had introduced.

"Bleak," Lily answered. She thought of the seagulls crying into the blurred fog of cold mornings on the beach, their pleas echoing into her empty days.

Back on the island, she researched and wrote. When someone shouted and waved to her on the beach, she waved back but did not stop. She went home, spread her books out on the kitchen table, and wrote. She would finish this paper, defend it, and earn her degree. *This is something to do,* she told herself.

She knew she was worrying Charles. When he passed her at the kitchen table he often patted her hair, as one would with a child, and kissed her on the top of her head. She wished he wouldn't; it didn't help. His kind of comfort could not cancel her kind of distress. Why had she married him? She had known that someday he would want her to be happier and she would want him to be more sad. She had known that, despite what they told each other, he would want her to believe in God and she would want him not to. She had known they were different, as direly different as stone and water.

Now she was his wife and, no matter how hard she worked, she was no longer free to choose her future. She lay awake at night thinking about Charles's next call, terrified it would take them to Nebraska, Alaska, Idaho. She had nightmares of small white churches surrounded by shorn winter fields. She tried desperately to keep the anxious look off her face. She fought the hope that he might not like being a minister after all, that he might wake up one day and change his mind.

One quiet night, after dinner, Lily and

Charles sat reading in their living room. Charles had moved a stack of journals to make himself a spot on the couch, his feet up on the table in front of him. He was comfortable; he was often comfortable at night when the two of them sat together without talking, when Lily seemed content, when he did not have to worry about her. He was used to her silence, to the academic crowdedness in which they lived.

He put his book in his lap, rested his head on the back of the couch, to pray or sleep — whichever came easier. Suddenly, Lily stood up. The stack of paper beside her collapsed to the floor. She paced to the wall and back, her pen still in her hand.

"I'm going sort of crazy," she said.

Charles stared at her, registering her panic.

"I'm in the middle of realizing that you're going to be a minister forever," she said. "You're going to be a minister for life. And we might always live in a place like this, a place where I don't have a life of my own, where I only have your circumstances." She sat back down on the sofa across from him. The enormity of her dilemma hung like a cobweb in the room.

They sat together, silently.

"What did you think would happen when

we moved here?" Charles asked Lily, finally.

"I thought I could accept it. Or adapt. I know that this is the job you have chosen. But part of me is hoping you would realize it is . . . untenable."

"Untenable." Charles's voice was very quiet. He was picking at a thread on his trousers.

Lily felt herself grow still. "Let me tell you what I wish," she said.

"All right," Charles answered.

Lily cleared her throat. "I wish I could accept the ministry as a noble profession and be proud of the help you give people."

"But."

"The truth is, I hate this place. And I hate that we are here because of a religion you believe in . . . are able to believe in because nothing bad has ever happened to you."

Charles nodded. "You're right. Nothing bad ever happened to me. *Nothing* ever happened to me. Until I found God."

"That's not true."

"It *is* true," Charles said. "My father never asked me a personal question. My mother started each day at the kitchen table writing a list and spent the rest methodically working her way through it. Every Sunday they went for a long walk and had lunch at the club. I assume they loved each other, but how would I know? All they ever taught me was to respect intellect, good manners, and privacy. And that's what I would have done if I hadn't found God." He let his breath out heavily, held up his palms.

"I have a call, Lily. I suppose it would help if I could tell you about a moment of proof — a dream, a light where it should have been dark, a vision, a voice heard in silence. Maybe I could convince you if I had prayed for something and it had come true." He shrugged. "There were lots of guys at seminary who believed they had visions, heard voices, who experienced their call physically, through one sense or another. But I never had that. My call isn't one of proof. It's one of possibility."

He stood up, walked away a little, then returned. "It's possible there's something more to life than moving from room to room, placing myself in front of people, but still finding myself empty at the end of the day. It's possible I can find out *why* people accouter their lives with houses and dogs and needlepoint pillows, and it's possible this will help me understand why my own life once felt so bare. It's possible that other people want the same connection I long for and that I can give it to them. It's possible that if I treat people kindly, patiently, and with compassion, they will do the same for me. And it's possible that what I can't find in others, I can find in God."

Lily stood very still, waiting for the blaze of his anger and humiliation to wear off.

"That's what keeps me going. That's what makes this possible." He waved his hand between them. "I can love you because I can love God. I can love you because, despite all evidence to the contrary, it's possible this might work."

"I don't hate *you*," she said. She didn't. They were like two planks of wood, cut from the same tree, now pressed back together.

"We won't always live in a place like this," Charles told her.

"We might have to."

He shook his head. "No."

"You might get a call . . ."

"No," he said firmly. "If it will make you unhappy, it is not my call."

Lily drew out the chair next to him, sat down, and laid her head on the table.

"I'm sorry," she said. He put his hand on the back of her hair.

Once back from the hospital, Nan felt a little better. She could sleep without the racket of nurses in the hall, drink very sweet tea, and eat cookies. Her mother sent fudge that melted in transit, but which Nan scooped out of the tin with a spoon.

The doctors prescribed fresh air, and she obeyed them. While James went back to school, she took the train out to the old manor houses — Ham House, Chiswick, Sissinghurst — to explore their gardens. There she found acres of silence surrounded by hedgerows and crushed gravel paths. On cold days the dampness seeped up under her skirt; on hot days, leaves hung heavily on their branches. She bought a map and guidebook at each one, followed the walking path, knelt down to examine the flowers closely: gentian, purple aster, clover. She touched each leaf, each petal, felt them fuzzy or spiny or sticky in her hand. Her coats absorbed the dark scent of soil.

"You smell green," James told her.

Nan kept a small brown notebook and sketched the paths as she walked them, feeling her way through their angles, searching for their centers. Each garden had one, a point from which all else grew, the stitch where symmetry began. She knew when she found it, recognized the moment when the heft and breadth of the quadrants equalized around her, when she became the fulcrum. For long moments, she reveled in the order, breathing deeply in the straight equation of the tending and the reward.

She started to grow herbs on her windowsill, calling farms and nurseries to find certain cuttings; she ordered a raft of seed catalogs in advance so she could read them through the winter. It was what she would have done if they had stayed in Mississippi. She would have planted her garden and watered it: tomatoes, sweet peas, radishes, and beans. She pushed tiny seeds into dark potting soil, found some comfort in the idea that each small plastic pot held a grafting of her old life and her new.

In the spring, Phillip found the letters he had promised James at the country home of two book-collecting members of his church, who invited them all to lunch and a viewing of their shelves full of diaries. Nan and James and Phillip took the train up together; Phillip brought the paper and shared a section with each of them. Nan put hers in her lap and looked out the window, wanting to watch the iron outskirts of London turn into the damp grey roads of the countryside, full of dull white houses, soft green trees.

Phillip rustled his paper, clicked his tongue. "Tell me," Nan heard him say to James. "I'm interested in Dr. King."

Nan was tired of this topic now. She was

tired of being a novelty; her home considered an outrage. She did not turn to join the conversation.

"I expect you find him quite inspiring," Phillip said to James.

"Indeed," James said. "I'm in awe of his determination."

"Do you think he will succeed?"

"I do."

James was right, Nan knew. Dr. King would succeed; he had to. Her father wrote her letters about it every week, calling the movement *a commitment to human dignity.* Nan was worried about him, preaching those things from his particular pulpit, standing determined and measured in front of his congregation, asking them to admit that they were wrong. Painfully aware that *wrong* was one of the worst possible things to ask a person to be.

Phillip put his head to one side and said, "Change can be violently difficult."

The two men sat silently for a moment. Then James said, "I disagree." His voice was tense and restless. He had turned sideways, his tweed jacket stuck on the rough mohair of the train seat. "It can happen so easily. Faster than you even want it to. Once you ask for it, everything can turn on a dime.

The whole world could be different tomorrow."

He was right, Nan thought. Change did come fast and easy, as fast and easy as the flow of blood.

She turned back to the window. *I'm glad you're not here,* her father had written. *People we know are saying such terrible things, Nan, doing such inconceivable wrongs. You wouldn't recognize them.* She didn't read these letters to James, because James would rejoice in them, full of the wonder of justice and courage. He wouldn't understand that her world was slipping away, like the fields outside this train window. Soon there would be nothing to go back to. Mississippi would be a different place. Better, fairer, healthier for all, but not one she would recognize.

"We've arrived," Phillip said, as they pulled into a station. They all stood up. James put his hand on the small of Nan's back.

The book collectors lived a little way off the road in a cottage with climbing ivy framing the door. The wife, Leonora, met them on the walk, wearing an old skirt and rubber boots.

"Come inside!" she said heartily. "Arthur is just trying to decide what you might like to see first."

"I hear you have some letters," James said, shaking her hand eagerly. "From men studying to be pastors."

Leonora winked at Nan. "A man after his own heart, is he?" She spread her arms out to herd them inside, a border collie nudging sheep. "You two go in there." She pointed James and his uncle toward the library, where Nan could see Arthur bent over a manuscript set on a music stand.

"You," she said to Nan, "come with me. We'll leave the boys to those crispy letters. I have something just for you." She went over to a bookcase in the hall, far away from the dangerous light of the window. She pulled down a blue box tied up with a matching ribbon.

"Collector's box," she said. "I don't much go in for them — bloody expensive to have made, but this was an exception." She carried it to a table. "Close those curtains, will you?" she asked. "The English countryside is a wonderful place for books — hardly any sun at all — but you can't be too careful." Gingerly, she undid the ribbon and opened the box, revealing what looked like a school notebook with a grey-green cardboard cover.

"Phillip mentioned you've taken to English gardens," Leonora said. "So I thought you might like this." She opened the cover. "Vita Sackville-West. She wrote gardening articles, you know, and she wrote them all by hand, all out in books like these. There are four of them. Museums have three, but we found this one. Lucky." Nan pulled up a chair. The book looked so fragile, so pale, and yet so inviting.

"Come on then," Leonora said. "I've got to get lunch on, but you have a read."

"Oh no, I couldn't," Nan said.

"Why not? Books should be read. That's why we collect them. Don't want them all to go into museums, under glass. Go ahead; learn something. It's what keeps writers alive."

Nan sat down and read. The pages were soft as satin in her hand. There, in delicate, green-inked handwriting were fourteen articles, with spelling corrections penciled in, whole sections crossed out and rewritten in the margins. The words were ordinary. They spoke of soil temperatures and angles of the sun. They explained methods of composting, the effect of eggshells buried close to roots. There were odes to oak trees and Queen Anne's lace, advice on which gloves to wear when pruning holly and ivy, all the plants with bushy, sharp edges and the fruit trees with the stickiest of sap. There were pages about the greenhouse, where roses and hollyhocks, orchids and iris were carefully seeded, their beds thoughtfully planned. Vita Sackville-West believed she could grow anything anywhere, that hostile climates could be tended and made to bloom. A whole life could be created and made meaningful around doing so. It was almost comforting. But Nan was not a seedling in Vita's calloused hands.

Most of Nan's life had been lovely, as lovely and easy as a walking tour. She had grown up in a climate where gardens were obvious. Where every neighbor's backyard was fertile; where any corner of land could yield daylilies, lemon trees, magnolias, plums. She reached out to touch an ink spot on the page. There were no secret tricks, no miracles revealed, but as she read Nan felt, for a moment, as if she herself had been put under glass. As if she were as sheltered as the flowers growing in the moist heat of greenhouses. She felt as if she were on a stage, slowly rotating, knowing the curtain would open onto a completely different place in time.

My life is no longer easy, she thought. She had been trying to make her days as tidy as patches of land in the countryside, as windproof as their farmhouses' tight thatched roofs. But James was trying to make himself as powerful as the train they had ridden in on — as loud, as fast, as scene-changing. He had a vision; he believed he was right, and he would spend his life trying to make it come true.

"Do you know what I'd like to have?" she said to James when they got back to the flat. "Ice cream. Real American ice cream on a fresh-baked sugar cone." English ice cream was watery and bland.

She was really saying: *I want to go home.*

■ ■ ■ ■

PART TWO

1963–1965

■ ■ ■ ■

Part Two

1963-1965

TEN

Third Presbyterian sat on the corner of Twelfth Street and Fifth Avenue: a dull, brown, brick building with a tall, square steeple. To its right was the church office building, a four-story rectangle of newer brown brick, with double glass doors and a balcony off the second floor. To its left sat the manse, built at the same time as the church and in the same style, with a gable roof and gothic windows. The three church buildings were set apart from the city streets by a black wrought iron fence, which would have rendered them overbearingly formal and somber except that the church gardens were full of dogwood and hydrangea, which in spring bloomed uncontrollably, white and pink. Charles and James and Nan and Lily had first seen the church at the messy end of winter, 1963, when the buildings and branches stood out starkly against the grey city snow.

Third Presbyterian was well respected and traditional; a place where women wore hats to Sunday service and men wore suits and ties. It resembled its uptown, society-church cousins in the quality of its organ music, its choir, and the success of its fund-raising. But since church attendance was not a social requirement downtown, Third Presbyterian members believed their faith was more authentically chosen, a little deeper, more closely held.

Third Presbyterian was in trouble. Five years earlier, the church's search committee had hired Sebastian Taft, a minister from Connecticut. Their previous minister had retired after twenty years, and Third Presbyterian wanted a fresh point of view. Their city was changing: It was the age of sky-scrapers, cars, and highways, which required whole city blocks to be razed and colonized by diggers, cranes, and jackhammers. Third Presbyterian had lost many members to the suburbs, and many more had also begun to dream of quiet lawns, tall trees, places for dogs and children to run.

Even the members committed to staying in the city found they wanted their church to become a haven, an escape from the disruption. They looked, specifically, for a pastor from outside the city, someone who could tell them what life was like in a prettier, cleaner place. They had wanted a village feel, someone who could preach the wisdom of a small town.

Sebastian had interviewed with five glowing letters of recommendation on distinguished, heavy paper. One elder from his previous church actually wept on the phone, moaning, "He's such a stalwart; I just can't believe we're going to lose him." He arrived with thirteen black robes and fifty-two bright, colorful stoles hand-embroidered by his old parishioners, one for each Sunday of the year. He shook everyone's hand enthusiastically, with quick, sharp pumps. He cocked his head to one side when spoken to, nodded with affected interest, and ended every conversation with a loud *Thanks* and a jovial slap on the back.

He enjoyed pageants and enlisted children to march through the sanctuary in costumes, with their pets — goldfish and hamsters and guinea pigs. He festooned the church with purple wall hangings and white satin bunting. He shined the crosses; he oiled the pews. He wrote poems in the shape of the cross and manger, candle and flame; he printed these on the fronts of the worship programs. He wrote his own loose, casual prayers to replace the ones that had been said for fifty years.

As promised, he increased attendance, but the new additions were members from his old church, groupies who drove in on Sunday to hear him preach. He did not bring in students or young families; he did not stem the tide of defection to towns nestled safely above the Triborough Bridge. As promised, he preached a message of hope, which the congregation found too hopeful. At Easter he declared, "Even in death there is a happy ending." The few city-dwelling members these meditations did bring in were as brightly optimistic as Sebastian. They complimented his sermons about lambs and harvest, the ark as a symbol of everlasting hope. They appreciated his gaudy decorations and jovial hellos.

Long-time Third Presbyterian members came to recognize that Sebastian hailed from a church where suffering was cushioned by green lawns and plushly upholstered cars. He wasn't equipped to help Third Presbyterian think through the upheaval it was experiencing. He did not understand the friction of the city, its grey stone stress and the agony of its disrepair. They came to understand that he had no desire to wade into rough waters. He simply wanted, like Noah, to ride out the storm.

As a full year passed, they began to suspect that Sebastian was not writing new material: his sermons were general and somewhat glib. They made no mention of events they read about in the newspaper, good or bad. They asked him politely to reinstate the traditional prayers. He refused, as placidly as a mule. They asked him to curtail the pageants. He refused, with a stubborn smile. And then, at Christmas, he made his boldest move.

For a hundred years, the Third Presbyterian congregation had sung Joy to the World as the last Christmas Eve hymn, then emptied triumphantly into the silent streets of New York full of life and hope and the clear brass notes of the organ. It was their most treasured tradition, a night when they felt emboldened in their faith, empowered to scatter it in front of them onto the streets of the city like gold. Instead, Sebastian decreed, the last hymn would be Silent Night, and as they sang they would light candles, filling the church with a soft, shimmering glow. It was beautiful; it was sophisticated; it was reverent. But where was the celebration? They tiptoed out into the New York night, lonely and perturbed.

The magnitude of their mistake in hiring Sebastian was shocking. He had no respect for Third Presbyterian's cherished identity, no desire to further its long-standing mission. He wanted to create a church in his own image, pleased and facile and smug. Third Presbyterian's congregation discovered that they did not want a shiny, Christmas-ornament version of faith. They wanted to talk about *belief,* how to find it and what it meant for their lives in a changing world. When, four years later, Sebastian contracted gout, they knew they should feel sorry for him. Still, there were various quiet celebrations when, for medical reasons, he retired early.

"We want," the new search committee wrote, "a minister with the highest academic credentials, who struggles with the incongruity of faith in the modern world. We want a minister who looks for answers in a dignified way. We are not interested in the trappings of religion, only in the deep, incisive examination of Christian principles and the ways we may apply them to our lives. We want to restore our self-esteem."

To this call, both Charles and James had answered.

Scheduled for their Third Presbyterian interviews on the same day, Charles and James sat in a wide, second-floor hallway, outside a heavy wooden door, waiting to be invited in. They had not been introduced and took that to mean they should not speak. But they saw each other.

Charles saw a wiry man, a wound-up clock ticking with purpose. He could see it was an effort for James not to pace, thought he could hear him humming with energy, like a light bulb. He saw the kind of man who made him most nervous, who formulated his thoughts quickly and voiced them with force. If this was the kind of man the church wanted, then he, Charles, with his love of obscure texts and academic analysis, did not stand a chance.

James saw a tall, hale man whose good navy blue blazer, monogrammed shirt, and khaki pants evoked a wealthy, literary upbringing. Charles's slight stoop and the glasses in his breast pocket spoke of intellectual ability; his steady gaze suggested a deep respect for the thread of history. If Third Presbyterian wanted an academic, James thought, then why was he here?

Alan Oxman, the chair of the search committee, came out to greet them. "Sirs," he said, "please come in."

James and Charles stepped into the church's library. After the bare hallway, the room was a surprise: warm and welcoming.

To their left was a large fireplace with a marble mantel; to their right was a wall of leather-bound books. In front of them was a long, polished table flanked by the church members who would decide if Charles and James deserved a job. The two men stepped onto the thick carpet and, making their way around the table, shook hands with their interviewers. They were each given a chair, in which they sat without taking off their jackets. Though the windows on the far wall were open, the room smelled distinctly of wood and wax.

"Let's get started," Alan Oxman said. The interviewers opened their file folders, positioned their pens in their hands. The room stilled. A woman with short brown hair and a plaid dress turned to Charles. "How do you picture God?" she asked.

Charles answered, "I don't picture God; I just believe."

A man in a pin-striped suit and red tie turned to James. "What are your thoughts on dying?"

James answered, "Scares the hell out of me."

The interviewers chuckled, nodded, wrote notes on their yellow legal pads.

Alan Oxman flipped through some pages in his folder, then looked up and leaned

214

forward, put his elbows on the table, and steepled his hands under his chin. "Tell me," he asked, "What do you consider to be your most personal mission?"

Both Charles and James paused to think before they answered.

Charles answered first. "To help people think clearly," he said. "To help them see past fear and disappointment to possibility."

"Thinking's not enough," James exclaimed. He exhaled impatiently, sat forward in his chair. "We can't just think about a man living on the street corner. We can't just *think* about war and race and cruelty," James continued. "I'm going to preach about social justice."

Alan Oxman sat back, looked at the ceiling, cleaned his glasses on his tie, gave no impression that he felt the tension in the room. Finally, he said, "I'd like to know what each of you considers to be your greatest personal flaw."

Charles thought, suddenly, of a story his father told to all his classes, about a professor who kept a rabbit. The rabbit had been the professor's childhood pet. It ate from the professor's hand, went into its cage quietly at night, and twitched its ears when called, as if it recognized its name. But the rabbit never accomplished anything the professor could really brag about. It had gotten old and fat, but the professor allowed it to roam the house freely, and would as long as he earned enough money for a maid to pick up the pellets.

One night, as the professor sat reading in front of the fire, the rabbit shuffled into the room and stopped directly in front of the grate, one hind paw on the hearthstone. The firelight cast its shadow on the floor. As the professor watched, the rabbit leaped farther than the man had ever seen any rabbit leap, and spun in the air before landing heavily on the ground. Then the rabbit leaped again, straight up, in front of the red and gold flames, and turned another pirouette, the fire casting shadows on the turn, as if there were three dancers twirling before the professor.

When the professor invited a friend over for dinner the next night, he invited his friend to sit in a chair by the fire to finish his wine, anticipating the rabbit's next appearance. The rabbit made its way to the hearth and sat down, looking at the two men.

"Just wait," the professor said. "Last night, he did the most incredible thing."

The men waited for hours, but the rabbit did not move and finally the friend went home to bed.

"In this story lie all the foibles of history," Charles's father told his students, assigning each of them a paper positing what they were. There were various correct answers, but Charles's father's favorite was: Never assume success, especially when its circumstances are not under your control.

Charles brought his attention back to the search committee and said, "I tend to assume that things will work out the way I hope they will."

Before anyone could respond, James said, "I'm impatient. I can't let anything be."

They left the room together and shook hands at the door.

After some weeks, during which the search committee considered references, reread mission statements, and combed through CVs, Charles and James were called in again. They sat in the same warm library, surrounded by books and windows and people who might give them a job. Alan Oxman stood at the head of the table.

"We want, as you know," he proclaimed, "a certain dignity and intellect." He nodded at Charles. "Which we believe we have found."

He turned to James. "We also find we need a call to action, a certain spark to pull

217

us from our reveries," he said, "which we believe we have also found." He cleared his throat and looked at the others around the table. One or two nodded at him and he nodded back. He turned to James and Charles, some of the ceremony gone from his face.

"We have, as you may or may not know, been through a trying time, and entered this process with a large degree of trepidation."

"The last guy was an idiot," the woman in the plaid dress — Betsy Bailey, they now knew — exclaimed quietly. The search committee laughed; James and Charles shifted uncomfortably.

Alan Oxman continued. "We find you each have qualities we admire, and we are not willing to choose one over the other. We find we would like to protect ourselves by building in a choice. So, gentlemen, we are offering you a joint pastorship, the job split fifty-fifty. We think it's going to take more than one minister to restore us to our former glory."

In this way, James and Charles found themselves standing in the doorway of a small office into which two desks had been squeezed, facing each other.

"You could move the desks," Alan Oxman said.

Charles shook his head. "No need."

James continued, "If we're going to preach together, I suppose we should be able to look each other in the eye."

They were given a secretary.

"I am Jane Atlas," she declared when they met her. "I am seventy-two years old. I have been at this church since 1920. I wore a short skirt and bobbed hair to my interview," she told them. "They thought I was scandalous. But I typed better than anyone else who'd accept the pay." She handed each of them a blue ceramic mug of coffee. "Still do."

She was a tiny woman, with a neat silver bob and the deepest, fullest voice either of them had ever heard; it commanded from them the same awestruck silence as a large chieftain beating slowly on a round, ceremonial drum.

"Elocution lessons," she told them. "My mother made me take them. She wanted me to be an actress. She wanted me to be in silent films. I told her I didn't need elocution lessons for those and she said, 'But of course you will — everyone will be watching your lips move.' She took me around to every shady man she knew, and a few she didn't, and every single one of them pinched

219

my rump. That was it for me. I came to work at a church. She squawked like a chicken, but here I am. I don't think she ever understood that all I wanted was a little bit of peace."

From this information, James understood that Jane didn't feel the need to earn their respect; she simply expected it. Charles understood that she had left a chaotic life for some serenity, which they were not to disturb.

"The first thing we've got to do," she told them as they set their coffees on their desks, "is take down that dreadful man's flibbertigibbets. You carry those," she said, pointing to six empty boxes sitting in the corner of their office. They each took three and followed her as she led them through the door that connected the church building to the church itself. The sanctuary was cool and quiet, a long rectangle with a marble floor and high, vaulted ceilings. The dark wood pews were set with faded blue velvet cushions and red hymnals with frayed spines. James and Charles were to sit apart from the congregation, up three marble steps, behind a large mahogany altar. To the right of this altar was the small pulpit, carved of freestanding marble. This was for the lay reader and announcements. To the left of the altar was the preaching pulpit, up twelve rickety stairs, from which James and Charles would impart wisdom every other Sunday in turn.

Charles was relieved to be starting the day in the sanctuary. He always felt comforted by places of worship, reassured by their thick walls and calm air. He enjoyed the privilege of spending time in them on days when there were no services, when he had no responsibility to inspire others and could let himself relax. James was glad the building was not too grand. Large and impressive, yes, but seemingly designed by practical men to be sturdy rather than ornate, a simple building built of wood and stone. He could see why Jane wanted so badly to remove the white satin bunting Sebastian had hung from the balconies and the tasseled gold banners he had pinned to the doors.

"Take all of it down," she ordered, so Charles and James each climbed up to a balcony and untied the bunting, letting it fall to the floor as Jane stood on a stepstool to wrest the gaudy banners down. When they were finished, they gathered the material up and dropped it into the boxes, closed the lids, and taped them shut.

"Good riddance," Jane said, as they

stacked the boxes in a neat row. "Now sit."

She gestured to the high-backed wooden chairs behind the altar. Charles and James did as they were told. From that vantage point, they could see the whole of the church more clearly: the very back corners of the balconies, the small stained glass circle above the closed front door, the way the pews lined up like the strings of an abacus, with Jane Atlas staring intently at them, the lone counting bead.

She walked over to the first pew, opened its little wooden door, and took a seat inside. Charles had rolled his shirtsleeves up to dismantle Sebastian's sets. His pants were wrinkled and had a smudge of dirt on the knee. He began to tuck his shirt in, ran a hand through his hair. James glanced over at his movements and hurried to do the same.

"It doesn't matter what you look like," Jane said, her deep voice echoing in the empty hall. "I'm not going to take your picture. I just want you to get the lay of the land."

Charles was used to preaching from behind a music stand set in front of the altar, close enough to touch the parishioners in the front pew. Here, the congregation would have to turn their faces up to him, as if to the sun. The anticipation of it was disconcerting; people who looked up expected more.

James could not take his eyes off the center aisle, down the middle of which ran a long fracture, caused by the unsupportable weight of the crowd in the balconies on a day when Third Presbyterian's most famous minister, Harry Emerson Fosdick, had caused the church to be especially full.

"Intimidating, isn't it?" Jane asked, following his gaze.

It was, indeed, James thought. An unavoidable reminder that there was once a man who so filled the church he nearly broke it down.

"Now, stand up there," Jane told them, pointing to the steps of the high pulpit. James and Charles glanced at each other. Jane pointed to the high perch again. "You first," she said to Charles.

Again, Charles did as he was told, rolling his shirtsleeves down as he climbed the rather fragile spiral staircase to the octagonal wooden box. He took his place behind the brass podium and placed his hands on either side of it, looking down. The sanctuary seemed even more formal and vast from this height but Charles, to his surprise, found the vantage point a relief. The pulpit was cramped and hot, but it encircled him almost completely and in it he felt protected. He thought he might be able to speak well from here, able to give sermons that leapt up into pirouettes, inspiring in his congregation moments of fire-lit, incredulous awe.

"Fine," Jane Atlas said. "You're quite imposing. There's no need to stoop to read; you can raise that podium. I'll make sure it's done." She turned to James. "Now you," she said.

James waited at the bottom of the stairs until Charles came down, then climbed them carefully, one hand on the rail. The steps were worn smooth; the wood had a particular smell of antiquity. He took his place behind the podium and was, for a moment, overcome with panic. The box confined him.

"Does everyone preach from up here?" he asked. The church erased his words as soon as he uttered them. Jane Atlas looked at him with a hard stare that cut through him instantly. She was slight as a child in the pew.

"Yes," she said. "And I'm glad you won't need a box to stand on. You're a normal height when you're not next to him." She motioned at Charles, who had not returned to the altar, but slipped into a pew across the aisle from her.

"Come down now," Jane Atlas said, so James did, coming to lean against the pew in front of Charles.

"I assume you'll alternate weeks to preach?" she asked. Charles and James nodded. She nodded back. "What about the other stuff?"

James looked over at Charles. In the weeks since they had been given their positions, they had written to each other regularly, happy to discover that though they had their differences, they both dealt with new situations by being prepared. Still, it was one thing to make plans on paper, another to say the words aloud.

"We thought we'd split the other responsibilities by natural affinity," Charles said. "So I'll take counseling and home and hospital visits."

"And I'll take fund-raising," James said. "And community outreach." They both spoke quickly, like schoolboys hoping they had said the right thing.

To their relief, Jane nodded. "Good," she said. "That way everyone will know which one of you to ask about what. And Sunday school?"

Charles and James looked at each other

blankly. They had forgotten that one.

"That's all right," Jane said. "There's a committee." She cleared her throat and stood up.

"Now, I've got something to say to both of you." She smoothed her skirt, stepped out of her pew, and walked over to look directly at them. In the stillness, Charles noticed how thin she was and that she was wearing stockings with sturdy black lace-up shoes. He was aware that, despite the resonance of her spirit, she was old. He felt the urge to reach out and help her, but stopped himself. He knew she was going to say something critical, something grave enough to cut through her good manners and her reserve. Jane raised an eyebrow, as if she had read his thoughts.

"I've seen a lot of young preachers," she said, "and none of them are very good. They're inexperienced, insecure, and they underestimate their audience." She gestured to the empty pews around her. Then, abruptly, she raised her hand and pointed at Charles and James. "You've got a congregation in trouble," she said. "Your members are desperate for dignity. They used to have it — the minister before this last, silly one — was here for twenty years. They respected him. He had a steady hand on the rudder

226

and he had seen God. Not over the washing line in a white robe — but in his wrestling with why we live and what is waiting for us in the end. He had conviction; he believed that God is watching, God is interested, God is kind." Jane took a deep breath and let it out with a sigh. "But then he left, and they hired what's-his-name. And now they're angry and embarrassed and ashamed."

She crossed her arms in front of her and looked at them, assessing. "You two need to be the right choice. Do you think you are?"

It was not a question she expected them to answer, that was clear. It was a doubt she wanted to plant in them so that it could bother and burrow and itch.

"I can help you with the paperwork and the committees and the personalities," Jane said briskly, back to the business at hand. "And if you can't preach, I can fix that. But I can't make them respect you. And you can't earn their respect in a day. I suggest you start by getting them to like you. Go to coffee hour, shake their hands, tell good jokes, and listen to what they have to say. You're young and good-looking, which will get you through the first month. Then we can see where you are."

By the time she had finished talking, she

was already turning away. Charles and James stared after her as she shuffled out the side door.

Charles leaned forward, his elbows on his knees. James cleared his throat. "I think I should tell you," he said, "that I'm not entirely sure God is watching, or is interested, or is kind."

There was a moment of silence, then Charles said, "Surely there's more."

"I believe in the urge to be good, to stay good, to do good in the world," James continued. "But I don't think God exists in the way people would like to believe; I don't think God saves the day. I think it's up to us. We know the rules, and we're the ones who have to play the game."

"My wife is going to like you," Charles said.

"Really?" James asked. "That's something of a relief."

Charles smiled and then said, "I believe in God. I think God gives us wisdom, infinite numbers of entirely different ways to understand the world. It's an absolutely clear feeling for me, like walking into a room full of books all opened to exactly the page I want to read."

They were silent for a moment. With only two people in it, the church felt cavernous.

They both looked at the crack in the floor and wondered how to become the kind of men other people respect.

"Well, thank Saint Pat for that," James said. "One of us certainly should."

They heard Jane Atlas's shuffling stride as she returned. Instead of coming all the way back to them, she leaned in the side door and spoke loudly. "I forgot to ask," she said. "Which one of you is taking the manse?"

The spell of camaraderie was broken; the two men looked down and away. This was the most awkward circumstance of their shared position: that the church had a house for only one minister, and one of them had to live there. In all the letters they had written, in all the phone calls they had made, they had not broached this matter, because it seemed so fraught. Because it was of so much importance to each of their wives.

ELEVEN

Third Presbyterian's manse was a small rabbit's warren of rooms, each with a tight coal fireplace. There were casement windows on both floors; the one in the living room had a window seat. Upstairs, there were three bedrooms, one large, two small, and one bathroom with a window that looked out on the garden. Nan fell in love with it right away.

She was beside herself that James and Charles hadn't agreed on who would live there, that the church hadn't pressed them to do so. Didn't they understand that it was urgent? She could not stay much longer in the apartment that she and James had sublet, the one that belonged to a professor friend of Nan's father who was on sabbatical in Italy. It was sunny and genteel, lined with books and carpet, but Nan could not appreciate it. Like everything else in her life, it reminded her that she did not have a child.

There were two bedrooms, but one was empty. The hallway was long and wide enough to accommodate a tricycle, but there was no toddler to ride one. The kitchen had a window seat next to which she could have pulled up a high chair; the table at which she ate with James was sterile and bare. For the most part, she kept her desperation to herself. She went to museums and the movies; she made dinner. But in the evenings, James liked to rifle through the bookcases, piecing together the personalities of their absent hosts by the titles they had chosen, the inscriptions on the first pages, their handwriting in the notes taken in the margins. It made Nan want to scream.

Outside, cars honked in the street; people shouted beneath windows. Bottle tops and cigarette butts clogged the gutters; the city smelled of sewage in the heat. James told her to think of the city like a piece of music, the traffic as its tempo, the shouts and slamming doors its percussion. She could have done that, once. Now she saw everything off-kilter, the treble clef on its side.

She wished James had been called to a small town. She had known they would not go home to Mississippi — her mother said it had changed too much, and her father protested that it had not changed enough. She had known they could not choose where James would work, but she had prayed for a bright church in a welcoming village that had hymn sings and potlucks and prayer circles. If she could not have that, she needed her own house, one for which she could make curtains and choose pillows. One that felt like a beginning, instead of the lobby of a station in which she was waiting for a train. She needed coffee hours, committees, and a position in her community. She needed the manse.

"Please don't be magnanimous," she begged James. "Please don't just give it away."

New York had come to Lily like a miracle. She could not stop marveling at her good fortune. She loved the long, wide avenues that pointed like arrows, up and down. *Go here,* they prompted her. *Try this.* And so she walked all over, stopping in green grocers, art galleries, antique book dealers, rare-print shops. She walked along the promenade by the East River, watching its strong currents swirl and billow. She walked up and down the Hudson River, past the block-long meatpacking buildings that stank of rancid blood and leaked sawdust onto the old city streets. She walked through Central Park, rode the merry-go-round, tried to throw the brass ring into the hole in the wall. She wanted to see all of New York — all of it — old Trinity Church, the new skyscrapers, Grand Central Terminal, the tall, straight row houses in Harlem. She walked across the Brooklyn Bridge and through the old cobblestone streets of that borough. She walked everywhere, imagining herself a nomad, a Bedouin.

She and Charles were renting a small, one-bedroom apartment that looked out onto Sixth Avenue and was loud with the blaring of car horns, bright with the red neon signs of tattoo parlors and pizza joints. Lily, despite her penchant for neatness, loved it. She reveled in the stained bathtub, the sticking windows, the tiny kitchen. She rejoiced at being awakened by deliverymen shouting outside. She liked buying her coffee instead of making it, drinking it out of a blue-and-white paper cup. It felt temporary, anonymous, as if she could fold her life up like a tent, tuck it in her pocket, and move on.

She had found a job teaching composition to undergraduates at the New School. Her students were eager and engaged. Her teaching colleagues were academics exiled by oppressive European regimes. They wore decades-old tweed jackets, pants that hung below their bellies. They drank after class and faculty meetings.

"Dr. Barrett, you must come with us," they said in intriguingly accented English, and she did, following them to bars set below the sidewalks, full of smoke, where they drank vodka and she drank Kir or Lillet from stubby, spotted glasses. They paid in change fished out of pockets full of keys and ticket stubs while she took clean dollar bills from her leather wallet. But they got along very well.

Lily listened, mostly, for they talked without pause, interrupting one another, never asking questions, only interjecting. Lily loved the *rat-a-tat-tat* of it, the efficiency, the lack of indecision. One week they would be sure of one thing, the next week another, changing their minds without a single *Sorry* or *I was wrong.* They talked like speeding trains, veering to the left or right whenever confronted with a switch. They were arrogant and cynical. They were the opposite of church, of God.

"Tell me about the evils of religion," she asked them, after they had drunk enough to lean back in their chairs, close their eyes, let their cigarettes burn out in the ashtray.

"It weakens the mind," one said. "All that

belief in delayed gratification. We should work quickly and reap our reward. Religion makes us complacent about suffering."

These ideas were familiar to her; they fit into the jigsaw puzzle of her own principles.

"And it's naive," another began, "to believe you have a supernatural parent who takes care of you and teaches you right from wrong. I imagine all of these people on the operating table or lying on the side of the highway, thinking, *Soon I will be with God.* Then, just as everything goes black, they think, *How could I have been so wrong?* Well, I am not going to die a dupe. I'm going bravely. I will not be humiliated."

Under the practiced impassiveness she wore as her second skin, Lily was ardently in love with these men. They were the opposite of Charles. They had escaped, erased old histories, constructed new ones. They had filled the ragged space around them with cigarettes, drinking companions, lectures, and fountain pens. But inside, they were angry and bitter and superior; they knew they would never be fully healed. For the first time, Lily had found a place where she belonged.

"I can't live in a house next door to the church," she told Charles. "I'll be fair game. People will want me to *make tea.*"

■ ■ ■ ■

The problem of the manse was still not solved when Charles and James decided they should all go to dinner together, so Lily and Nan could meet for the first time. Lily suggested Chinese, so they met in Chinatown at a neon-signed restaurant with a bright green door. Nan and James arrived first and waited in the vestibule, a fluorescent light flickering overhead. Despite the plainness of the decor, the diners at tables were wearing suits and silk dresses. Nan's white cotton skirt, blue cardigan, and pearls branded her an outsider, hopelessly out of place.

She had felt this way for months, long before they had come to New York, though New York had made it worse. It was an odd, silent loneliness, as if she had been locked in an isolation booth on a game show stage. She took James's hand. She had to rejoin the world, and tonight was the place to start. She might be inappropriately dressed, but she knew how to make a good impression.

James waved, suddenly, and Nan saw Charles and Lily opening the door. Charles was every inch as tall as James had described him, and Lily was poised and stylish in slim black pants and a matching sleeveless top. She looked like Audrey Hepburn.

Nan marshaled her manners and put out her hand. She wanted this to be the first of many dinners, for it to lead to lunches and barbecues and weekend getaways. They would be working together for years, hope-fully, and Nan wanted them to be a team. She wanted it for James, who already had so much respect for Charles, and she wanted it for herself, because she needed friends.

"Hello!" she said, stepping forward.

Lily took a step back. She disliked Nan's hair and her shoes and her bag. She disliked how hesitantly Nan stood next to James, as if she might fall and needed him to catch her. She disliked Nan's pleasant, open face and the eagerness in her eyes. Nan was the spitting image of the girls at Radcliffe who had married early and had babies instead of careers, and she exuded the gentle consider-ation Lily's aunts pressed upon her in seem-ingly endless supply.

She forced herself to shake Nan's hand. It was one dinner. A dinner that embodied everything Charles held dear: a job he loved, a colleague he respected, a cheerful social circle. Surely she could give him one din-ner, after he had given her the glittering possibilities of New York. But she knew she could not give Nan one inch, not one conversation. Even one gesture of friendship would lead to the expectation of more, to Nan hoping Lily could give her what she needed. Lily couldn't stand other people's need. It made her angry. It rose around her like floodwater.

"Look," James said, abruptly, pointing to a group of people at a table in the far corner.

"We shall return," Charles said, putting his hand on James's shoulder. "We've got to tend the flock."

They walked off, leaving the two women alone. The restaurant's foyer smelled of fish and oolong tea.

"I'm so glad to meet you," Nan said.

Lily nodded. A waitress in a blue satin dress waved them over to a round table in the center of the crowded room, pulled out their chairs, set crispy noodles and a bowl of sweet and sour sauce in front of them. Nan smoothed her napkin on her lap. Lily poured water from a plastic pitcher into glasses on the table without speaking.

"James tells me you have a job," Nan tried again, looking at the slim gold bracelet on Lily's wrist.

"Yes," Lily answered.

"Teaching English?"

"Yes." Lily set the pitcher down and picked up her red-wrapped chopsticks.

Across the room, James and Charles were standing by their parishioners. James was shorter than Charles by half a foot, but more animated. Nan could tell by the rhythm of his hands that he was telling a joke. When he finished, the table laughed. Charles put his hand out to quiet them, then told one of his own. The table laughed again; James and Charles nodded and rocked casually on their heels. Nan could see they were already a pair.

"Congratulations," Nan said.

She knew she was being snubbed. She could see it in every inch of Lily's body. But it would not deter her. She settled her gaze on Lily and kept her eyes steady. It took a moment, then two, but finally Lily raised her head and Nan could look at her straight on. Lily's eyes were brown, and for one split second they were startled. Then they froze.

"Thank you," Lily answered. What she wanted to say was *Don't like me. Don't ask me to like you. Don't make me feel guilty.*

The men came back smiling.

"That went well," Charles said, hanging his jacket on the back of his chair.

"Absolutely," James exclaimed. He slid in next to Nan and put his arm around her.

239

Nan returned to herself, jostled out of range of Lily's frost, held close to the warmth of her husband.

Lily put her hand on Charles's knee. It was just one dinner. "Let's talk about something important," she said, as she popped a crispy noodle in her mouth.

"All right," James said, loosening his collar and pushing up his sleeves. Nan recognized the look in his eyes that said *I'm game.* "What do you have in mind?"

Lily slid the sleeve off her chopsticks and laid them on her plate. "Will you tell me about your call?"

Nan understood, instinctively, that Lily was trying to make them uncomfortable. That she was going out of her way to make this conversation hard.

"No." James said, good-humoredly. "Let's talk about something really important: what we're going to eat, and how we're going to fix this godforsaken city." He picked up his menu and grinned.

Charles smiled kindly at Nan. "You married a live wire, too?" he asked. Nan relaxed instantly, nodded at him with gratitude.

They ate their dishes sociably, talked about the Yankees, the Mets, the arrival of Hare Krishnas in the city. When they could eat no more, their plates were cleared and fortune cookies came. Lily opened hers with a crack and pulled out the little slip of paper. She leaned toward James.

"Mine says: Good things will come if you tell me about your call."

James rolled his eyes and leaned back in his chair. "All right," he said. "I appreciate persistence." He put a hand on the top of his head, looked up, thought for a moment.

"Will you accept an incomplete answer?" he asked.

"Certainly," Lily said.

"I'm not sure I really have a call," he said, pulling his cup of tea toward him.

Charles looked at him quizzically. "Of course you do," he exclaimed.

"Of course you do," Nan said at the same time, putting her hand on James's arm, shocked that he still felt this way, enough to say it out loud.

"It's all right if he doesn't," Lily said to both of them. "I'll like him better for it. I like people who refuse to be what they're expected to be."

"Next question?" James asked in his straightforward, impatient way.

Lily tucked her hair behind her ear, assessing. "What's the worst thing that ever happened to you?" she asked.

James raised an eyebrow, but did not look

away. Nan could tell he would take this game as far as Lily wanted to go.

"Once my father came home so drunk he could not get his key in the door," he told her, "so he fell asleep on the front steps in his own urine. What's the worst thing that ever happened to you?"

Both Nan and Charles swung their heads to hear Lily's answer, but Lily shook her head. She turned to Nan. "You first," she said.

Nan hesitated. She knew Lily's question was a test and that any answer she had to give would fail. To demur would seem cowardly, to reveal her truth felt like surrender. Lily did not want to hear about her suffering.

"I've been very lucky," Nan said. "But, really, it's your turn."

Lily almost didn't answer. She felt Charles pause and grow still next to her. She didn't have to tell them. It had turned out to be a fine dinner. A dinner she knew meant the world to Charles. But she found herself compelled to prove to Nan that she was incapable of friendship, not at all the kind of person Nan wanted her to be.

"My parents died in a car accident," Lily said. She had meant for it to sound brash, but it came out flat as tin.

Nan gasped and put her hands over her mouth, her blue eyes wide as a doll's.

"Don't be ridiculous," Lily admonished.

Nan looked at her, confused. "That's awful," she said.

Lily sat very still, pale, her eyes fixed to the plate in front of her. Nan's warmhearted empathy was a tangible presence; it smelled of her vanilla perfume. It made Lily want to gag.

"Were they religious?" Nan asked, gingerly.

"Yes."

"Oh." Nan blinked. "Well, that must have helped."

"No, it didn't," Lily declared. "Not one bit." She wished she could put a line through the whole conversation, crumple the paper, put it in the bin.

"Why not?" Nan asked.

"Because I don't believe in God," Lily said. She felt Charles bow his head next to her, in awkwardness and shame.

"But you go to church," Nan said, almost pleading with her, her face pink and worried.

"No, I don't," Lily said. Her words fell to the table, flaccid and bare.

What a privilege, Nan thought, to believe oneself completely independent, to feel

243

unshackled by social conventions and the worry of what other people might think. What a blessing, to be lonely in that particular way.

Charles took a loud breath, leaned across the table, and took Nan's hand. "She didn't mean to offend you," he said.

"Maybe I did," Lily corrected him. She saw Charles's jaw clench. But she had to be clear: She was not going back — not to Nantucket or Boston or Maryville. Not to church or courtship or grief. She was going to move forward, as fast as New York would let her.

Charles was furious. He did not help Lily with her coat after dinner. He let her pull the glass door of the restaurant open and step out onto the sidewalk without him to block the wind.

"You got what you wanted," he said tautly as they crossed Sixth Avenue, the oncoming traffic restrained, momentarily, behind the straight white line. "We won't have to be their friends."

"You can be his friend," Lily said, one pace ahead of him. "I can't be hers." She stopped once she reached the safety of the other curb, standing under the grey metal streetlight. He stepped up to face her. The traffic rushed by. She shone like smooth and polished marble in the evening light.

"She needs someone to have tea with, Charles. She needs a friend to be glad when she enters a room. She needs someone who will smile and invite her in if she drops by." Her voice, which had been strident, softened at the end. "Am I that person, Charles?"

She was not, he knew. Lily did not want friends. She barely wanted him. She was turning to New York, finding her excitement in the hum of the city. She said things like, "I walked over to the river today. It felt so great I almost kept on going." She said them carelessly, as she came in, unbuttoning her coat, dropping her bag on the floor. Empty space was creeping in between them, as if the ligaments holding them together might dissolve.

It was a dangerous weakness, he realized, this desire he had for Lily to find happiness in the ways that he found happiness. If he did not want to lose her, he would have to learn to let her be.

The office that Charles and James shared was an ascetic one: two metal desks, metal bookshelves, light grey walls, dark grey floors. Only their books saved it from grim desolation. When they moved in, Charles had been almost embarrassed by his endless collection of theology and philosophy, until James had unpacked his huge arsenal of sociology and economics. Their books had seemed to intertwine instantly, weaving them a leather-bound tent, offering them provisions, leaves and leaves of stores.

The next morning, Charles approached its door slowly, embarrassment hot and close to his skin. He liked James, liked him easily and straightforwardly. He believed they would work well together, or he had believed it, before the disaster that dinner had been.

He opened the door. James was sitting at his desk, jotting something down in the dull green notebook he kept for random thoughts.

"So, your wife does not believe in God," he said.

"No," Charles answered, standing in the doorway, uncertain, reluctant to discover how much damage Lily had really caused.

"You might have told me that before, when I was laying out my own confessions."

"It's not the same kind of disbelief."

"I suppose." James put his pencil down.

James liked Lily. She was stubborn, like he was, and for the same reason, too: She already knew the worst that could happen.

She had seen the impact of death, the surrender it demanded: blank eyes, stale clothes, heads laid on tables in exhaustion. She had seen the practicality it left in its wake: a world cleared of procrastination and excuses. Her outlook would not shift, had already shifted, was resting on bedrock. Her eyes were unclouded by the expectation of favors or deliverance.

"She's like the girls from my old neighborhood, and I was glad to meet her."

Charles took a deep breath and relaxed. "I suspect Nan may not feel the same way."

"Nan's been through worse," James said. Then he asked, "Is Lily's lack of faith hard for you?"

"Yes," Charles told him.

"I've been thinking about it. I hope that doesn't offend you." He looked up, and Charles was relieved to see his face held only concentration and concern. Charles shook his head.

James continued, "I've been thinking about doing this job with just my own flawed faith to carry me through. Sometimes I think it would be easier."

"Really?" Charles crossed the room quietly, sat down in his chair.

James ran his hand through his hair. "Nan's faith is nurturing," he said. "It's kind and comforting, accepting and giving. My own is challenging. My urge is to confront, to push, to shake people until they wake up. If I could be that way wholeheartedly, it would be easier. Instead, I think of her faith — every time I meet with someone, every time I write a sermon — I think of her faith and remember that there are people like her in our congregation who need nurturing, who need comfort, who need faith to be quiet and still. The nature of her faith makes me doubt my ability to do my job."

Charles felt heavy with relief. "Thank you," he said.

"You're welcome," James replied, his face genuine, intent.

In Nan's world, people made visits. Her mother made them constantly. To visit, one put on a dress and baked something and put it in Tupperware, which would be returned by means of a short visit to prove the original offering had been consumed. Nan's mother had an entire closet devoted to Tupperware.

To smooth things over with Lily, Nan baked a coffee cake, cocooned it in Tupperware, and walked over to Charles and Lily's apartment. When she buzzed up, Lily did not answer, so Nan left it in the lobby. The Tupperware was returned the next week through James with a thank-you note from Charles. A thank-you in a man's handwriting seemed odd to Nan. Lily had not even signed her name. Nan flipped the card over; the back was blank. Lily had not written anything at all, had not even taken a few seconds to appreciate a cake she had eaten and the time it had taken to bake.

Nan realized, suddenly, why her father had forced her to shake all those people's hands — all those sick people, all those stiff-dressed days — why her mother had taught her to begin a conversation with a compliment, accept the gifts she was given, always use a coaster, smile when others were speaking to her. They had understood what she had not: That people needed permission to exist. Every welcome enlarged their world, widened the hallway around their suffering, saved them from suffocation. Lily made Nan feel invisible.

The two women did not meet again until two weeks later, on the first Sunday after Labor Day, when their husbands were going to preach together for the first time.

Nan put on a yellow shift dress, a matching coat, and a little orange pillbox hat. Her parents had called earlier to wish James luck, to say they wished they could be there. Nan was, in a way, glad they weren't, for the same reason she had accepted that she and Lily would not be friends. This was her church now. She would not have to ask for Lily's opinions or permission; she could organize things the way she liked them, choose the groups she wanted to lead and the meetings she wanted to join. She would have to go to more of them, of course, since she would have no help, but perhaps this was why she did not yet have a child — so she could be present here, fully present for a while. She made the choice to believe that, and it comforted her.

She walked over to church early, hoping to meet a parishioner or two before the service began. But when she arrived, there was only one person sitting in the church lobby: Lily.

"I didn't think you were coming," Nan said. In the plainness of the room, her clothes were very bright.

"Charles asked me to," Lily said. She did not want to be at church. It was sunny and warm outside; the trees were vibrantly green and the streets not yet crowded. Lily wished she could bolt down the garden path, past the black fence, out into the city. But she had never seen Charles so angry, and she had to do something to make amends. She had to give him one gift, after she had taken so many others away. She could give him one Sunday — a tithe of gratitude.

"I hope it won't feel like too much trouble." Nan held her yellow purse at her waist with both hands. Lily wasn't carrying one. Nan wondered where she put her money. They stared at each other.

In the sanctuary, the organ burst into sound. Nan turned toward the music.

"They're starting," Nan said. "I'm going to sit in the front," she said. "Will you sit with me?"

Lily sighed and set her shoulders. "Just this once," she said.

They sat politely next to each other throughout the service. Nan smiled and leaned forward during each piece of music, tapping her foot as the organ played, hands clasped under her chin as the choir sang. Lily remained impassive, standing and sitting as the bulletin directed, holding her hymnal open to the right page, but not opening her mouth to sing.

James and Charles processed in in their plain black robes, tall and impressively stately despite their youth. The sermons were good: brief, introductory, with little jokes that made the congregation smile and nod at one another. They both chose to speak without microphones, filling the church with their deep, unadorned voices, their words carrying without the hiss and crack of artificial authority.

At the end of the service, they pronounced the benediction together: "The Lord bless you and keep you; The Lord make his face to shine upon you, and be gracious unto you; The Lord lift up his countenance upon you and give you peace."

As the choir was recessing, Nan turned to Lily and said, "Do you know my father is a minister?"

"Is he?" Lily asked.

"Yes. And I'd like to live in the manse. I suppose I should ask you nicely, but I'm not a politician. Say no, of course, if you want to. We can always let the men work it out."

To Nan's surprise, Lily smiled. "Good grief," she said, "isn't it obvious? I wouldn't live in the manse to save all our lives."

TWELVE

True to her word, Jane Atlas put together the most productive and seamless ministerial schedule James and Charles had ever seen. After a month, it became second nature. From nine to noon, the two men attended to paperwork, letter writing, and staff meetings. From noon to one, they had lunch and, since Jane believed no one should sit around after eating, they made site visits from one to three — to the hospital, other churches, and people's homes. Jane had taken Sebastian's taxi fund out of the budget. "You're young," she said. "It's a neighborhood church. Walk."

From three to five, the men had office hours. The one who was preaching that Sunday retired to the library to work on his sermon while the other straightened up his desk and cleared his mind for the onslaught of other people's problems. Jane ran those two hours as crisply and efficiently as typeset. The sofas and chairs of the church lobby accommodated eight people. Those parishioners who arrived early enough to sit could stay. Latecomers were told to return tomorrow and to be on time. Once vacated, seats were not refilled. "Eight is all you can handle," Jane told Charles and James. "You're young. Nine would make your heads explode."

On a normal day, there were eight people waiting by two forty-five. They ranged from young to old, and their purposes were as varied as their ages. Adam Clayton, a young man just out of school, wanted guidance on a career that *won't make me feel I've gone into the dark.* Don Fergus had lost his paycheck at the track and needed the help of church funds. Jane sent him into the office with a folded note admonishing: *Do not give him more than thirty dollars. You may take it from petty cash.*

Charles liked walk-ins. He listened quietly while people poured out their stories: mothers whose children were sick, men with drinking problems, old women and men who came because they had nowhere else to go during the day. He made them coffee and watched carefully as they spoke, tried to honor their anguish, the need for help that had overcome their need for privacy. It was not that different from being in class; he was listening to histories, striving to interpret what was said, percieve what was not, and offer compassion and empathy for it all.

James hated walk-ins. The people who came to see him needed things, or thought they needed them: cars, clothes, school tuition. They wanted to find love so that they could feel less lonely. They wanted new jobs so they could feel less adrift. They wanted more money in the bank so they could be generous without it feeling like a sacrifice. They wanted to rail and complain. And they wanted a witness.

"How do you listen to all of it, over and over and over?" James asked Charles.

"I'm good at it," Charles said.

He was. Though he had entered ministry thinking his call was to guide others toward the peace of the faith he had been given, he thought now that his daily calling might be even more simple: pay attention and offer hope.

Ironically, he was deep into a cycle of sermons about doubt. He had begun to address the lingering bitterness of Sebastian's tenure, to meet the congregation's distrust head-on. "Many of you doubt James's and my ability to do this job," he said. "We are too young to understand futility, too healthy to understand illness, too successful to understand failure. In short, we lack the instruction manual of personal experience." The congregation chuckled at that one, which made Charles happy.

"Your last minister left a rift, and you do not yet have faith that we can fix it. Neither do we, but we shall try. Perhaps you could put your trust in that, for the time being."

As the months passed, he spoke about the consequences of doubt: uncertainty, anxiety, emptiness. "It is important to search for the antidote," he said, "and choose to administer it." Had Lily been there, she would have rolled her eyes. But his ideas were well received by the congregation, many of whom congratulated him after services, asked him to lunch, sought him out when they had a joke to share.

In addition, to Charles's great relief, no one seemed to mind that Lily was not there. On the receiving line after services, one or two parishioners asked after her when they shook his hand, but their curiosity was pro forma, and they were perfectly happy with his *Very well, thank you.* Because of this, all of this — the congregational goodwill, James's collegiality, Jane's artful steering of their boat — Charles could enjoy his work fully. And because of that, he was once again beginning to enjoy his wife.

They had spoken little after their meal with James and Nan; Charles had made a point to wake before Lily, dress quietly, and head to work before the alarm clock rang. He had stayed at work later than necessary, coming home just in time for dinner, which they ate while reading their separate books.

But she loved her job and had not been able to stop herself from telling him about it, even when his disppointment had been at its freshest.

"One of my students has long hair," she said. "With flowers in it, and he's a boy."

She grinned at him, lit up with interest and excitement. He could not help but let his anger thaw. He loved seeing her busy and fulfilled, loved watching her grade papers with alacrity and passion, curled up on the floor by the sofa with a pencil behind her ear: a professor, but the exact opposite of his father.

So they cobbled together a stable routine. Lily did not have drinks with her colleagues as often; Charles left coffee for her every morning. She saved the paper until he got home and, after dinner, they spread it out on the floor around them, read passages to each other and snipped articles that might be useful for sermons or lectures. Lily had bought them each a brown accordion file and a pair of scissors.

"Now this," she said, "is a pleasant way to spend an evening."

It was not perfect, but it was better than Nantucket, so much better than the way she had faded and dissolved before his eyes.

Nan and James moved into the manse in October. It was small and dark, but after Nan washed the windows and hung peach curtains in all the rooms, it looked cheery. She made sure to get a flat of tubers and bulbs into the ground before the first frost: purple crocus, yellow tulips, white iris, lily of the valley. She also planted two lilac bushes and a bed of peonies, because the man who owned the nursery said they flowered better their first spring if they were planted in the fall. The thought of all those flowers lying dormant, gathering the sleep they needed to bloom, cheered her as the ground hardened and the snow fell.

Life was beginning to feel easy again. She woke at eight, had toast and coffee with James, then walked him to work, which was twenty steps along the stone path that connected their house to the church. Jane Atlas was always ensconced behind her desk before they arrived. It was clear she did not welcome Nan's presence in the office space. Her *Good morning*s to James were hearty and efficient; to Nan she nodded coolly. If Nan brought James's lunch and stayed to talk while he ate it, Jane knocked on the door to remind him how busy his afternoon was going to be.

"I think you're supposed to stay at home," James said, shrugging helplessly in the face of Jane's disapproval.

"That is not something I'm going to do," Nan said.

Winning the manse had energized her: She had a vision for her role at the church and a plan to make it happen. Jane Atlas might not want another woman around, but Nan had been well trained in ways to convince her.

"I recognize that this is your domain," Nan said, gesturing to the elevator, the waiting room, and the offices beyond. "But I would like to have a role in the life of this church."

"Choir?" Jane Atlas asked.

Nan shook her head. She had decided, early on, that she should not sing in Third Presbyterian's choir. If she processed in in robes, as James did, and sat on the dais behind him, parishioners would be reminded that he was an ordinary man, instead of a man of God. Her mother had agreed. *I think you'll find that you'll be too busy for it, anyway,* she'd written.

But Nan was not busy, and she wanted to be. "Could you at least consider giving me the tasks you cannot stand?"

Jane Atlas stared at Nan for a long moment. Then she opened her desk drawer, pulled out a note card, and wrote down a phone number.

"Let's see how this goes," she said dubiously. "Good luck."

In this way, Nan became very familiar with those parishioners who cared deeply and specifically about which type of polish was used to shine the cross, which brand of cracker should be served on Communion Sundays, whether and how much the sanctuary lights should be dimmed during the sermon, and if the babies being baptized should be required to wear gowns. Nan was aware that Jane Atlas had set these people upon her as a penance for being presumptuous and too full of cheer, but Nan liked these conversations. She believed that these small issues mattered. Each complaint meant a member of the community cared about the church, and her response signified that the church cared for them in return. This was how Nan had been taught to build community; it was the same as gardening, planting one seed at a time.

Part of Nan's job was to comfort the members who had joined the church under Sebastian's leadership. They were unnerved by their two young ministers, confused by the bookishness of Charles's sermons and James's brusque, impatient handshakes on the receiving line. They missed Sebastian's decorations and his merry outlook. When Christmas arrived, Nan made it clear to Jane Atlas that, though the Christmas Eve service should, undoubtedly, conclude with the fanfare of Joy to the World, they also needed to include Silent Night if they did not want a mutiny.

"With candles?" Jane Atlas scoffed.

"And in the dark," Nan insisted.

The service was a success, and in mid-January, while she was manning the urn at coffee hour one Sunday, Nan was approached by Dr. Rose, the church's round, elfin organist who wore bow ties and tweed suits and a pencil tucked behind his ear. He blinked quickly and often. Nan did not know him well, but it seemed he was there specifically to see her.

"I hear you are the tamer of the Sebastian folk," he whispered conspiratorially, as he

261

took his cup and saucer. "And I've just discovered that you play the piano."

"I do," Nan said, somewhat wary.

"And sing. Your husband says you sing very well. That, in fact, you have a degree."

Nan wondered what else James was telling people about her.

"Yes," she said.

The music director put down his coffee and clapped his hands. "You can help me," he said with delight. "Those people are constantly after me to plan sing-alongs and shows, both of which I abhor. But I have to give them something, and I'm thinking it could be a junior choir. At least then they can perform in robes, like civilized human beings."

It was not a role Nan had envisioned for herself. Her mother had never been involved in the music of Nan's childhood church. But then, the organist had never asked her. And Nan still had more free time than she knew what to do with. The idea of playing music for a purpose, of arranging and conducting was irresistible.

"Did you ask Jane Atlas?" Nan pressed him.

"Of course," he said.

Nan looked around the room, at the blue carpet, the people in suits and ties and hats.

She realized this was a call, simple and straightforward — God wanted something from her and Jane Atlas approved.

"All right," she said, "I'll do it."

Before she could even catch her breath, she was choosing music and ordering robes. There were fifteen singers from six families. The girls behaved better than the boys, who swung their feet as she talked, elbowed one another, and forgot to spit out their gum. But it was the boys who were the best performers, who sang with the most gusto when Nan said *Louder,* who she knew would grin when they stood on the steps in front of the altar, faces scrubbed and hair combed. Nan was teaching them two hymns and "Sheep May Safely Graze" in parts for Easter; they practiced on Sunday and Wednesday afternoons.

At first, they sounded worse than an orchestra tuning up. Anne Hammet sounded like a violin bow shredding itself across the strings, Tommy Ahlers couldn't keep time to save his life, no matter how often Nan made him march around the room while he sang. But slowly, slowly, with Nan's endless exhortations to *Listen, listen. Just close your eyes and listen,* they learned to follow Nan's cues: to start only when she pointed at them, sing louder when she

263

raised her hand, and stop when she closed her fist — *Even if you weren't in the right place and thought you had one more line to go. I'm talking to you, Tommy.* Slowly, Nan learned that Brenda Eades, who was in eighth grade, could carry the sopranos, her sister Hillary could ferry the altos along behind, and if she put Tommy Ahler's brother, Peter, in the front row, he would wave adorably at his mother and make the whole congregation smile.

Nan threw herself as best she could into her work. She wrote nonsense lyrics to make warm-ups fun. She gave out stickers after rehearsals, brought lemonade and lollipops on birthdays, and gave each child a chance to play the organ, even the ones who had to stand on the foot pedals because they were too short to reach them from the bench. She complimented them to their parents at coffee hour. Mothers beamed when they saw her. Children ran up to her in the church building to give her pictures they had drawn. She began to get thank-you notes and cookies left outside her door. On her own birthday in March, she got hand-made cards from every one of her students and a huge basket of flowers from their parents.

They love you, the card said.

It was bittersweet to be loved by other people's children, but Nan chose to see it as a sign that her own were on their way. She wrote to her mother about her gains, and her mother replied: *Good girl.*

While Nan made a life for herself at church, James prowled the streets. He strode down Fifth Avenue, loped through Washington Square, followed Christopher Street all the way to the Hudson River, stopped for a moment to consider the abandoned shipping piers. He followed the river downtown for a few blocks, picking his way through broken bottles and scruffy weeds: the city's outskirts, its shredded hem.

Everywhere he saw men in stained pants standing by pay phones, waiting to sell drugs. He saw the men who bought these drugs sleeping, mouths open, in the park. He saw cramped buildings with broken windows, fire escapes hanging off walls, women too scared of knives and fists to take the subway alone. He saw graffiti everywhere, its wild, scrawling colors echoing, reflecting, perpetuating all of the uncertainty — a broken geometry of danger. They were details he recognized, the shrapnel of his childhood. After six years of clean classrooms and intricate assignments, he was back in the clutter and clang of littered streets, filled again with impatience and anger.

In contrast to what he saw on his ramblings, Third Presbyterian seemed privileged and staid. The sturdiness of the brick sanctuary and its fellowship building seemed incongruous in the face of the disrepair around them. The more office hours James endured, the more he realized how insular the congregation was, how alike they were to one another. If plotted on a graph, their needs fell in one high quadrant.

He asked Jane to make sure that, one day a week, his schedule was cleared. He used these days to work the telephone, comb the city. "What can we do?" he asked everyone he came into contact with. "How can we help?"

First, he created a list of groups that needed donations and volunteers: the Foundling Hospital needed clothes and diapers, the Henry Street Settlement needed tutors, the YMCA needed swim instructors. He organized food, clothing, and toy drives. This was a success. Parishioners arrived on Sunday morning with grocery bags full of canned goods, socks, and paperback books, smiled and chatted with one another as they placed their offerings in the crates set out to

266

receive them.

"Thank you," they said to James on the greeting line. "We didn't know how much there was to do."

And how much more there is after this, he thought. At home, he complained to Nan. "How can they be so completely unaware?"

Though Nan loved James for his fierce integrity, there was an outrage in his tone that worried her. Something had changed in him. In London he had been jubilant and determined; now he was brooding and critical, unfulfilled, even by his parishioners' enthusiasm. He was missing her father's deep well of patience and unflagging belief in God's grace.

"Be patient, love," she said, as he had once counseled her.

But James itched to confront the darker issues in the neighborhood: children out of school, parents out of money, muggings, shootings, burglaries, the boys getting high in Washington Square Park and the girls turning tricks on the Bowery. He knew these were hard issues to tackle, ones that involved social services, federal funding, and getting the police to do their jobs. But he couldn't ignore them; he needed to do something more than preach about them, something beyond the monthly allotment of offering funds the church sent to organizations in need.

As far as he could tell, other than money and volunteers, the major resource Third Presbyterian had to offer was space. He, Charles, Jane, and their office hours took up the first floor; coffee hour, the musical director, and the choir room inhabited the second. Above that, there were two more floors of closets full of files, Christmas decorations, and meeting rooms that lingered empty most of the day and every evening.

"What's going on with those?" James asked Jane. "Can we use them for things other than church business?"

"Yes."

"At whose discretion?"

"Yours."

James smiled and commandeered them quickly. Within a month, Third Presbyterian was hosting ten meetings a week. First, James invited the ministers of nearby churches to coordinate social outreach efforts, or at least not step on one another's toes. Then he gave space to community advocacy groups combating juvenile delinquency, street crime, and the spread of disease in the single room occupancy hotels. He organized an AA meeting and a gambling addicts group. Finally, he agreed to let a feminist group meet every Thursday evening on the top floor.

Nan knew this would be a mistake. James's first groups had made sense; they increased the church's outreach and its reputation. But the feminist group was secular, provocative, revolutionary. The first seminar they gave was on women in the workplace, which, to Nan's surprise, many in the congregation attended and enjoyed. They followed up with women in the clergy, which, as Nan could have predicted, stirred up tart criticism at coffee hour.

"You do know that church members attend those meetings?" Nan asked James.

"Of course," he said. "I hope so!" And Nan realized that he did not understand how harshly church members whispered to one another, and what a wind those whispers could stir up.

When the group screened a documentary about prostitution, which was both graphic and salacious, Nan forced herself to attend, so that she could support James and prepare herself for the consequences he refused to see were coming.

To her shock, Lily was also there. Nan had felt secure in the fact that Lily would never be at church, ever. But now Lily was there, and Nan felt so panicked that she slid quickly into a chair in the back corner of the room. Lily sat third row center, chatting with the women on either side of her.

Nan regarded Lily carefully: her hair was still cut in a straight bob; her slim pants and white sweater were neatly pressed. She carried herself with the same precision Nan had seen in her before, but there was more confidence in Lily now, less stiff arrogance. She moved easily, laughing often; she had even kissed one of the women next to her hello. When had Lily made friends, Nan wondered, and how, and why was she gracious to these women but not to her? Why was she here at all? Just by being in the building, in the room, Lily had put Nan on edge, siphoned off her ease, left her brittle and resentful. This was Nan's sanctuary, and Lily's presence made it itch and burn. Nan made sure to leave before the film ended, before Lily could even get out of her chair.

THIRTEEN

To Charles's great surprise, Lily had become a protester. She stayed up late at night making giant placards demanding school integration and denouncing the Vietnam War.

Charles was proud of her but bewildered. A Lily full of purpose was like a sail caught by a stiff wind. She woke up before him each day, was dressed before he went to work. The phone rang incessantly, and she *answered* it. She *talked* to people, called them by name. Last week, when he had arrived home from Wednesday Prayers, there was a group of women in the kitchen, drinking tea and stuffing envelopes. Lily had looked up at him and smiled.

"We're flooding the congressional mailboxes," she said. And when the woman sitting next to her said, "For forty days and forty nights, like the Great Flood. They're going to drown if they don't give us peace," Lily had actually laughed.

Charles knew she had been attending the feminist group, so he made a point of being out of the church building before the meetings began. He did not want to crowd her. Though he longed to put his arm around her in the lobby, to show her off to everyone they might see, he knew that would push her away. And so he went home.

But he heard about the meetings. Partly because James was mentioning them in his sermons and partly because Charles had taken over office hours, which Jane Atlas had renamed the Committee of Complaints.

"He's not speaking for all of us," the new members cried.

"No, he's not," Charles answered. "He's speaking about what he thinks is right."

"He's asking us to change views we've held all our lives," some of the older members told him.

"Yes, he is," Charles said. "That's what you hired him to do." His optimistic manner never flagged, but inside he was worried. Attendance on the Sundays James preached was falling off. Charles was used to the vicissitudes of the pulpit. He knew that sometimes his sermons would succeed, that there would be a moment of reflective silence as he gathered up his notes. He knew he would sometimes fail, would be chastised

272

by the rustle of programs and the blowing of noses before the hymn began. James had moved beyond failure into affront, with parishioners standing a little way off during coffee hour, not quite meeting his eye.

And then the feminist group held a council on abortion. They had not announced the topic beforehand, but they had lined up a group of speakers, two of whom talked about candidates for Congress who supported legislation, and one who recounted her experience in a back room of a doctor's office: rushed, silent, in the dark except for one light between her legs.

Nan was there. She made herself listen to the whole story, which ended with: *They let me lie on the table for five minutes while they crushed the paper and the instruments and their gloves into a black garbage bag. Then they handed me my underwear, and I bled all the way home.* Nan, nauseous and overwhelmed, lurched out of her seat before the last word had finished ringing. She pulled herself up the aisle, grasping the back of each chair she passed, burst out of the grey door and willed herself to James's office, translucent. "What the hell is going on?" she whispered.

James jumped up and put a hand on each of her shoulders. "What happened?"

Nan shook her head. He ran out of the office, pulled open the door of the meeting, and thrust his head inside. When he turned around, Nan was behind him like a ghost, and he pulled her into his arms.

"I'm so sorry," he said.

She knew he was, that he was sorry *now,* because he had hurt *her.* But she knew he was not sorry that he had brought anger and uprising into the church.

The door opened and women came out, puffed up with energy and determination, their murmurs a seismic tremor. Lily was among them, a yellow scarf tied around her hair. James took Nan's face between his hands and pressed his forehead to hers. She knew he was trying to protect her, but how could he, when he was determined to drag this church into the real world, a sack behind him on the road?

Lily stopped beside them. James stiffened; Nan closed her eyes. She wanted Lily to pass her by. She wanted to take a deep breath and compose herself, to be able to pretend that no one but James had seen her overwhelmed and trembling. But Lily had. That was another consequence of James's meetings — Lily had come to his ancillary, makeshift church that had nothing to do with God.

"Progressive," Lily said, her flat voice rounder with respect for James, with interest in him, piqued by his daring rebellion. She approved of his plan to force the church to look at the ills of the world — to really see them — and then march them all on, relentless, without counsel or compassion. If asked, Lily would say she respected James for rushing forward, never thinking about consequences beforehand, never fully accepting them after. If James had let go of Nan, even for a second, Nan would have slapped her.

The phones rang so incessantly the next morning that, at lunchtime, Jane marched into James's office and said, "If you're going to use those rooms for things like that, you're going to get in trouble."

"With whom?"

"Me."

"Why?"

"First of all, because I'm the one who has to write down all the complaints. Most of all, because this church has a history and a reputation, and you don't get to change it on your own."

In her khaki skirt, red cardigan, and lace-up shoes, her grey hair held up in a bun with plain brown pins, Jane was the embodiment of common sense.

"I'm not big on history and reputation," he said.

"And you're not the only one who has opinions," Jane told him.

Jane was right. The panel had undone Nan like a placket of snaps, torn her open so jaggedly that James could not refasten her. She had sat on the floor in front of their couch, tears dripping from her chin, and said, "I would have raised that baby."

James had not known she was still grieving. He had left their miscarriage in London, along with the memory of Nan's blanched face and the acidic fear that he might have lost her.

Jane and Nan were both right; he did not think things through as he should. He had no patience for the calculations. Life was a rigged game, and there was no time for hesitation. Nan thought he did not see the consequences, but the truth was that he did not care what the consequences were — he was willing to summon them and fight them and break every limb in his body, if it would wake his congregation up.

He held Nan, made her tea, tucked her into bed, and lay next to her until she fell asleep. But it was not easy. As he lay there, in nights full of her grief, he saw his faith clearly for the first time. It emerged out of the fog like Charybdis, a stygian cliff into which he could not help but crash. How would they bear it? How would she survive? How could he protect her as he tried to pull the lighthouse down?

On Saturday, he opened the door to his and Charles's office, exhausted, shoulders bowed. The room seemed small and crowded to him. If he'd had the energy he would have escaped the building, roamed the city until dark. Instead, he sank into his chair and sighed.

Charles was at his desk across from him, sober and concerned. "Ever think about backing off?" he asked. His tone was as casual as possible, but he was sitting stiff and upright in his chair.

James shook his head. "I don't want to run one of those churches," he declared, "where everyone comes to feel right, where they sit in services and hear their own beliefs preached back to them."

Charles looked away from James, re-arranged some of the papers lying on his desk. "Sometimes people need to feel right," he said.

James rubbed his palms over his eyes. "I know," he said. "I hear them at coffee hour. *It's not for us to understand. God knows more than we do.* They hope their only job is to live quietly, gratefully, that they can avert their attention for a couple of decades and when they emerge, the world will be a place they can once again enjoy."

"That's not true," Charles said carefully. "They're smart people. They're paying attention. They know what's going on, and they want to help. But they don't want it to be such an issue." He looked at James. "They don't want it to be their sole identity."

James turned to Charles sharply, shoulders forward, eyes tense. "Do you not see the city I see?" he asked Charles, loudly. "Do you not see the injury, the deprivation?" He stood up, walked to the window, knocked on the glass.

"When I look out into the congregation on Sunday, I have to grit my teeth. Everyone out there is so comfortable, so able to afford earrings, ties, the green dollars they slip into our silver bowls. I know some of them grew up hungry and panicked. I know it's hard for them to give anything away, because they never want to feel that way again. But most of them have never even brushed up against injustice. Most of them assume the world is as content as they are."

Charles shook his head, determined.

"You're wrong," he told James. "They want to fix the same broken pieces you do. But they want to feel good about it. They want to feel like it's helping. They want to feel like it's enough."

"It's not enough," James said.

Charles wondered what would ever be enough. James's need for change was insistent, voracious. He wanted the world to be fixed — to be fair, to be reasonable, to be abundant and honorable — and he wanted it to be fixed immediately. He wanted Third Presbyterian's members to do what he said without question, to willingly accept that he was right — no matter how afraid it made them, no matter how confused, how frantic.

And he was right. Charles understood that. Charles saw the same world James did — the poor, the injured, the addicted — but Charles also saw more. When James had given up office hours, he had also abandoned hospital and home visits, the chance to see the futile cases: the terminally ill and those who mourned them.

"You're good at those," he'd told Charles. "I'm good at something else."

It was true, but it meant that James no longer witnessed the paralysis of grief, the exhaustion of illness, the fundamental barriers to action many in their congregation faced every day. James did not seem to understand the need for comfort, for forgiveness and absolution. Charles surveyed James's side of the office, his well-ordered desk, his uncushioned chair, the notes for his next sermon. He wondered what James was working on, what exhortation he would make this week and what complaints it would bring, how many bewildered phone calls.

James never preached about God, or the joy his faith gave him, the solace and direction. James preached about service and suffering. Charles was beginning to think that James's God was a taskmaster, shouting at him to do more, shouting so loudly that James had stopped listening to his own church, stopped noticing it, had lost almost all sensitivity to its needs. He began to think that James's God was conscience, guilt, and desperation.

Charles wished he could introduce James to the God he knew, a God of quiet calm, who gave him strength to preach a message of hope, who helped him contemplate the meaning of eternity and equanimity. He wished he could help James see the worries of this world as small waves in the ocean, tiny snags on a vast piece of wool.

■ ■ ■ ■

But then, that Sunday, a man walked out of the service. This was not unusual, many people came and went on Sundays, leaving to attend to children, find the bathroom, contain a cough. This was different. It was James's turn to preach, and he had decided he would apologize. He recounted the events of the panel, assured the congregation he would supervise the groups more thoughtfully, that there would be less controversy in the future. Charles knew how hard this was for him, and he was impressed by James's composure and sincerity. He knew James was doing it for Nan, that Nan spoke for many in the church.

And yet, in the middle of it, a man cleared his throat, rose, and strode down the aisle deliberately. People turned to watch him. James pretended not to notice. He finished the service: took the offering, sang the hymns, pronounced the benediction. But Charles could feel his anger; James almost shouted the last prayer.

Stalking into the dressing room, James said, "I don't know what they want from me." He shoved his robe onto a hanger, slammed the closet door. "Actually, I do."

He stared out the window as if trying to break the glass. "Mrs. Abbott wants me to preach about Ruth. 'Whither thou goest,' she says. 'I like that one. It's my favorite story.' " He put both hands on his head. "Her favorite story. As if we're in kindergarten."

Charles unbuttoned his robe slowly, slid it neatly onto the hanger. Throughout the second half of the service, he had not been able to stop thinking about the way that Tom Adams had urged him to be brilliant, about Tom's worry that ministry would dull Charles's mind. Now, Charles saw how that might come to pass if he, too, pressed James to stifle his intellect and fervor.

"I don't like David Elliott," he said, placing the hanger carefully on the wooden bar.

"What?" James asked, turning around to stare at him.

"I don't like David Elliott," Charles said more loudly, shutting the closet door with a snap.

James opened his mouth wide. "You like everyone," he whispered.

"I don't," Charles said, shrugging into his blazer. "I don't, and I'm tired of pretending like I do. David Elliott finds fault to find fault. He doesn't listen; he has no interest in understanding. He simply wants to pick apart the arguments, wants me to say nothing that could possibly be interpreted more than one way. He calls me up every Monday morning to tell me where I went wrong, as if he has a right to, as if it's his job."

"It is his job, you know," James said, reluctantly cracking a small smile. "At the *Times.* He's a fact-checker."

"Oh," Charles said, putting his hands in his pockets. Then he stood up straight. "I don't care," he said, lifting his chin. "This isn't the *New York Times.* This is church. I'm not reporting the news. I'm assimilating it. I'm *interpreting* it. I don't know everything."

James sighed. "Thank you," he said.

"For what?" Charles asked, frowning.

"For not being a pious ass."

Charles looked at him, eyes wide.

Jane Atlas knocked on the door. James rubbed his eyebrows. "Jane," he said. "You're smarter than Alan Oxman. What should we be doing?"

"Do you know what Sebastian's first sermon was about?" she asked.

They shook their heads.

"The color of fall trees," Jane continued. "The idea that the color of fall trees means God loves us, that he gives us something to look forward to, some way to enjoy the coming of winter, something to celebrate on our way to a harsh season." She shook her head. "He didn't mention current events, TV coverage, or anything in the newspaper. He spoke about nature. The perfect choice; guaranteed not to offend." She narrowed her eyes at them. "That's what you've inherited," she said. "A rudderless congregation. The old members want to be told that tragedy can be understood. The new members want to be told that tragedy will pass. They can't agree. They want you to hold the middle."

"Hold the middle?" James exclaimed, looking at her unflinchingly. "Is that really what you think is going to change the world?"

"No," Jane said, her voice booming in the small room. "I did. I thought it was what the church needed. But I have changed my mind. Neither of you should have to compromise yourself; I'm quite ashamed that I asked you to tone yourself down." She stared at James as intensely as he was glaring at her and raised an eyebrow. "So, I've decided you two should take a lesson from the choir. Sing your own parts and sing them well. Tune yourselves to each other, speed up and slow down at the same time, balance each other out. When one of you sounds too loud, the other has to sing out just as powerfully. Otherwise you both sound off-key."

The next Sunday, Charles climbed the stairs to the pulpit slowly, arranged his note cards in front of him. On them he had written every complaint brought before him in the last month, every plea for restraint, for encouragement, for tradition, for permission to look the other way. He looked out at his congregation where they sat expectantly in their pews.

"What you've been telling me lately," he began, "is that change is difficult." He paused. "I have no useful answer for that, except to say that it is not as difficult as you seem to think it is. There is right and there is wrong. Other churches are preaching that everyone, regardless of race or gender or income, deserves to live with dignity, is worthy of salvation. We think that's right, and we can't help but reflect that belief to you. You won't all agree with us.

"Other churches are preaching that only some can know God intimately, only some deserve the right to vote and work and marry. We think that's wrong, but we respect your right to join them. You don't have to worship here; you have your choice of

285

churches."

He paused again, looked up, almost expecting someone to leave. He was struck speechless, for a moment, by the silence in the room. He looked at his notes.

"James and I don't have that luxury," he said, more quietly. "We were called. *This* is our call, and we have to fulfill it to the best of our beliefs. Our beliefs, not yours."

There was more, a paragraph that softened the message quite a bit, but James did not hear it. When Charles descended from the pulpit, James sat beside him through the rest of the service, stunned.

"You don't have to worship here?" he asked as soon as they were out the doors.

Jane was waiting for them in the lobby. "Our beliefs, not yours?" She raised her eyebrows.

"Too much?" Charles asked. They both shrugged.

"We'll see," Jane told him.

Alan Oxman paid them a visit first thing the next morning. "I'm here to inquire," he said.

Charles stood up. "I overstepped," he said.

"Don't fall on your sword," James interrupted. "He was defending me."

"Pipe down," Jane shouted from her desk. "Let Charles handle the diplomacy."

Alan Oxman smiled at that and said, "Quite honestly, it's somewhat comforting to hear you both preaching from the same page. But it was too personal, and I've had some complaints about the tone."

"I'm sorry," Charles said.

Alan Oxman looked at him curiously. "Do you believe the things you said?"

"I do," Charles said, in his steadiest voice. "But that doesn't make them appropriate for the pulpit."

The next week, James was in the unfamiliar position of being the minister who needed to return the church to stability. He knew everyone would be reassured if he told them he had a plan — that the meetings and speakers and calls to action were in preparation for something profound, that he had drafted his design on a poster board, set it up on an easel, and would now pull back the curtain to reveal his grand, measured strategy for a better world.

He did not have one. His faith seemed, now, to be one of destruction: his job to expose, provoke, alarm. But Charles was right: his intensity had no focus, his hurricane no eye. He compelled himself to sit quietly for a moment. If this was his last Sunday in the pulpit — as indeed he worried it might be — what did he want to tell his congregation?

The answer was awkwardly simple: He wanted to tell them about war. It was war that had brought him to the ministry. War had caused his hardship, created his most pressing fears. It was the one issue from which he would never be free, the one issue about which he could preach with his full conviction and expertise. And that was a problem, because Third Presbyterian was apolitical. Its founders had believed, unequivocally, in the separation of church and state. Third Presbyterian did not want to stand for movements, or parties, or campaigns; they wanted to keep their church free of the rampant corruption and political violence of their day. As the years progressed, the rules relaxed a bit. Politics could be mentioned, issues explained, but still, no one point of view could be favored. No pastor was allowed to express his particular political beliefs. War, James knew, was undeniably politics, and he had a particular belief about it.

James had been skirting Third Presbyterian's convention for months. His sermons, though sharp, had stayed within the borders of Christian values: food for the hungry, a voice for the oppressed, aid for the poor.

But the new war in Vietnam was chewing through boys and eviscerating families. It was in every newspaper and on every television screen. It woke James up at night, sent him dreams that he had been drafted, bidding him to wonder, once again, if he should just sign up to serve. Instead, he set out to stop it.

He heard about a meeting being held on a Tuesday afternoon at the Greenwich Village Peace Center and walked over to it, arriving just as it was starting. He slid into a seat in the back of the auditorium, expecting to hear speeches about the ideals of nonviolence, the organization of protests, letter-writing campaigns. Instead, the moderator proposed that a boat be rented to sail up and down the Hudson River, simulating an invasion of New York by the North Vietnamese. James was astounded by the intensity of the fantasy — the idea that war could be stopped by a college prank.

He wandered back to the church, into the office, and sat down across from Charles, dismayed. "There's no leadership," he said. "No clear message. No vision. No shared certainty of mind."

Charles nodded. "You want to preach about it," he said uneasily.

"You don't want me to," James replied.

"I think it's dangerous. Especially now."

James stood up, opened his mouth, closed it, paced to the window.

"You can't talk about the war, James," Charles said without looking up. "I've made that impossible. You can talk about anything else. But the war is incendiary. Some people here believe in it. Others don't. You're going to pit them against each other. You're going to start a fight."

"I think it's time," James said.

"If you preach about war this week, after the meeting we just had, I think you're going to get fired."

"Well, then, it's *really* time," James shrugged. From his point of view, Charles had opened a door, and James wanted to walk through it.

He wrote a stirring sermon about the escalating conflict and the propaganda surrounding it. He did not give any warning to Nan or Jane. He simply walked up the stairs to the pulpit, took out his notes, and proclaimed, "Anything that speaks of violence, hatred, warfare, torture, or murder, that robs children of their youth or any other living being of their dignity or of their life, even when done in the name of God, is not about God. That kind of thing is about frail humanity — our impatience and selfishness,

290

our thirst for power, our greed, our fear, and our defiance of God's purpose. It represents not our faith, but our lack of it. None of it is worthy of God's name or blessing."

Nan clutched her handkerchief as she listened to him. He was blistering, rippling like the heat rising off a scorched summer road. He was preaching with conviction, with clarity and a wisdom she had not heard before. But he was doing the one thing her father said no minister could ever do: He was trying to make his congregation feel ashamed. She sat in the pew until the church emptied, until he had finished greeting everyone who still wanted to shake his hand at the door. She was sitting there when James walked back up the aisle from the street door of the sanctuary and Jane Atlas entered from the church side.

"You are a very special kind of fool," Jane said, voicing what Nan so longed to say. "Hang on to your hat, because change is coming, and you're not going to like it."

The next morning, he and Charles were called to meet with members of the session. The invitation was written on thick church letterhead, a copy on each of their desks.

"A meeting to discuss your future," James read from the sheet in his hand. He looked at Charles, the first twinge of dread dark in his stomach. "This can't be good."

"They wanted me to type them up," Jane shouted from her desk. "I told them to do it themselves."

"I thought it would just be me," James apologized to Charles. "I didn't think they'd drag you into it." Charles, full of his own prickling misgivings, wondered how James could be so naive.

As at their interviews, they sat in chairs at the long table in the library. Coffee was set out on the sideboard; the session members helped themselves to it as they made their way in, laid their coats on the backs of chairs. James and Charles stared at them, took note of who would and would not meet their eyes.

Alan Oxman called the meeting to order. "We need to decide how to proceed," he began. Charles felt James stiffen in his chair. He almost put a hand on James's shoulder, but stopped himself. The session members were wearing expensive wool sweaters, silk ties, gold earrings, watches with leather bands. Alan Oxman opened the manila folder in front of him. "I want you to know," he continued, "that there are just as many letters of support as there are letters of outrage. But the rules of this congregation are clear."

James stood and paced to the fireplace. No one spoke. A couple of women bowed their heads.

"And you would like me to uphold those rules," James said. He came back to the table and put both hands on it.

"Yes."

"You hired me," James said. "You read my dissertation. You knew what I believed."

Alan looked down at the table. "We did," he said. "But now you've crossed the line."

He looked to Betsy Bailey. She straightened up and pointed at James, her finger blunt and calloused.

"You keep reminding us how flawed the world is," she said. "About all the problems you expect us to solve." Then, unexpectedly, she pointed to Charles. "And he keeps talking about doubt, and how it's okay."

"Please don't bring him into this," James said. "He's your biggest ally."

"Nevertheless," Betsy Bailey continued, "doubt and disaster are a frightening combination. Especially in this day and age."

James returned to the fireplace, tapped the mantel with his fingertip. Charles bowed his head.

"We recommend," Betsy Bailey started, but James stepped forward, raised his arm.

He didn't want to hear them say it.

"We understand," Charles said.

The committee wanted them to restrain themselves. No wonder James was furious all the time. It felt terrible to be told your church did not support you, that your congregation wanted you to be different, to be theirs instead of your own. For the next week they did not speak to each other about the meeting, because they did not know what to do.

FOURTEEN

Nan did. She called Charles, James, and Jane Atlas to a meeting at the manse. Jane was the first to arrive.

"The boys are freshening up," she said as Nan walked her into the living room. "I told them they couldn't leave the church before they rolled their sleeves down and combed their hair." She sat down on the red sofa by the coffee table. Nan had laid out a pot of hot tea, a pitcher of iced tea, shortbread — which was James's favorite — and cheese crackers, which were her own.

"Are we eating?" Jane asked. Not long ago, Nan would have taken this as a criticism, but now she knew that Jane's deep voice made her comments seem more critical than they were.

"Yes," Nan said. "It's the end of the day, and we'll all need something."

Jane took a cracker and a cup of hot tea, settling into the cushions as she looked around the room.

"You know, it's almost impossible to fire a minister," she said. "That's why so many churches are so awful."

Nan had been on edge all day; nervous about convincing others she knew just what to do. Jane's invocation of possible dismissal did not help.

"I don't think James is going to get fired," Nan answered. "But I want him to succeed. Otherwise . . ."

"Otherwise they'll both quit," Jane interrupted. "James won't stay where he's not wanted, and Charles won't stay without James."

They heard the two men come in the front door, talking loudly as they finished their conversation.

"Don't keep us waiting!" Jane shouted at them. "Come in and listen to what this woman has to say."

Nan had purposefully taken the armchair at the head of the coffee table, so James and Charles had to sit side by side on the sofa facing Jane. They were in a fine mood, given the circumstances, which made Nan angry and flustered. To get them to agree to her plan, she needed them to be more chastened. James looked at Nan impatiently. Nan looked at Jane. Jane cleared her throat.

"I believe Nan has called us together to propose a solution to the mess you've gotten yourselves into. Which is a good thing, because if you two go, I go. And I'd like to stay." Her voice was stern and sharp.

"Is this an ambush?" James asked.

Jane cut him off. "I believe it is a much-needed intervention." She nodded at Nan and motioned for her to begin.

Nan took a deep breath.

"James is going to take some time off," she said, holding up a hand as James leaned forward. "He and I are going to visit my father, who is unwell." She shook her head at Charles's look of concern. "Charles is going to decide that he wants to preach a series — six Sundays — on the historical context of the scriptures. He wants to follow the liturgical calendar to the letter, illuminating what each week's scripture would have meant to the people of the time."

Charles and James sat back, reluctantly catching on.

"James and I will return sooner than we thought we would, and James will be in his office and do his outreach. But he won't cut Charles's series short. He will lead the prayers and blessings. And on his first week back in the pulpit, the children's choir will sing."

James frowned. "You want me to run away?" he asked. "And lie?"

"I want you to take a break," Nan said.

"And I'll do the lying," Jane Atlas assured him.

Charles looked at both women, concerned. "I think this is going to exacerbate the situation," he said.

"I agree," Nan told him. "And that's why we need Lily."

Charles looked stricken, but Jane Atlas hooted in delight. "A distraction!" she exclaimed. "A magician's sleight of hand!"

"Yes," Nan responded. If she had been at all sure this would work, she would have smiled.

Charles nodded. "So I have to ask her?"

"No, I'll do it," Nan said. "She already doesn't like me."

Charles telephoned Lily to tell her that Nan was coming over, and Lily had to let her in. Lily had been working on a lecture; stacks of library books and papers were piled neatly on the rug around the couch. She had just made herself a cup of tea. She held it between her hands as she looked out the window to watch Nan walk up the street.

Nan was brightly dressed, as always, in a light green sweater and darker green skirt. From her high perch, Lily could see the top of Nan's head, where her blond hair was darker along the part. It was pulled back from her face with an emerald bobby pin, and Lily wondered for a moment if the stone was real. Then she watched Nan pull open the lobby door and listened for her steps on the staircase.

She had decided not to clean up her work; she wanted Nan to see the evidence of her job, to perceive that she was busy and productive. And she was not going to offer Nan a cup of tea, though she was going to open the door with her own porcelain mug in hand. She wanted Nan to know this was an interruption and Nan was not welcome to stay.

Nan knocked. The hair on Lily's neck and arms stood up. She opened the door.

"Hello," Nan said. Her face was intent. Lily stepped back so she could enter. Nan looked around the room for a moment; Lily saw her take in the uncurtained windows, the dark blue kilim, the navy sofa, the white walls crosshatched by framed lithographs. She imagined Nan's living room was soft and floral.

"I need you to come to church." Nan

turned to Lily, still standing. "We all need you to come to church. For six weeks. Starting as soon as possible."

Lily laughed. It was not a cold or mean laugh — simply startled and incredulous. "That's what you came to say?"

Nan's expression did not change. "Yes," she said, clutching her beige purse in her hand. "Will you do it?"

Lily knew little about what went on at church, but she did know that Charles was worried about James, that the talks she had attended were offending people, and that Nan had to be desperate to ask her for a favor in her own home. She sat down on the couch, still holding her tea. After a moment of hesitation, Nan sat in the leather armchair across from her.

"Why?" Lily asked. Nan leaned forward.

"Because our husbands are in trouble."

Lily leaned back. "*Your* husband is in trouble," she said.

"They're a set," Nan corrected her.

No, Lily thought, *Charles and I are a set.* They had found their places: both working, both reading, writing, and thinking deeply. Both lecturing; neither dependent on the other for support or company. Bookends; an equal pair.

"I don't think so," Lily said.

Nan put her purse on the floor, clasped her hands together, and leaned forward even more, her elbows on her knees.

"Do you have any idea what goes on — what really goes on — at church?" she asked Lily, her voice challenging. Lily realized she had expected Nan to beg, perhaps cry. But Nan was looking at her as if she were a child threatening not to do as she was told.

"No," Lily said.

"Your husband is an excellent minister," Nan told her. "He really is. He has a way of seeing the world that expands it for people, so they have more room to breathe. James admires him more than almost anyone in the world."

"Of course I know that," Lily said. "I edit his sermons."

Nan nodded without comment. "And my husband is working to counter injustice. A pursuit of which I know you approve."

Nan had her there. Lily *was* impressed by James, by his dogged fearlessness in the face of expectations. She felt they understood each other. They both knew the effort it took to pull up every root they had, to gather them into their arms, to tug them free whenever they tried to burrow their way into the ground.

"They're close to being fired," Nan said.

"They are close to being asked to reconsider their calls. That can't happen."

But it could, and for one shining moment, Lily imagined the possibility. If Charles left this church, he might not want to look for another one. He might decide to become a professor. He and Lily might not have to work in entirely different places, devote themselves to entirely different philosophies. Lily might know his colleagues and their wives, and she might feel comfortable with them — might not feel, as Nan was making her feel now, contrary and unkind. She could be herself, her whole self, and she and Charles could go to dinner parties together, instead of Lily drinking with her colleagues alone.

But Charles did not want to leave Third Presbyterian. Lily knew that. He was confident now, full of purpose and goodwill. He was happy. She had almost forgotten that she wanted him to be happy, that she had chosen him carefully, that he had not been a terrible choice.

"What do I have to do, exactly?"

Nan exhaled, and Lily caught one quick glimpse of how scared Nan had been of her, how terrified that Lily might say no.

"You have to come to church," Nan said, speaking quickly in her relief. "And to coffee hour. You don't have to talk to anyone — in fact, it's probably better if you don't. You need to stay long enough for people to see you and Charles together."

"Because?" Lily asked, skeptically.

Nan sat up, straight and certain. "Because it will remind the congregation that if one of them stumbles, the others will catch him. That we are stable and reliable. That four of us are better than one."

Lily hated the idea of the congregation's attention. She felt vaguely nauseous at the chance that it might lead to handshakes and small talk and invitations. But Charles needed her help and she had not known it, and that made her angry and ashamed.

For a long moment, Nan thought Lily would say no. Her heart began to race and her throat tightened in fear. Where would they go if Lily turned her back on them? Nan wanted to jump up and shake her, make her see how important this was, how precarious and urgent. But she knew Lily would despise an open show of feelings, might even refuse to help out of spite, simply to extricate herself from any tendril of obligation or despair. So Nan sat motionless, almost invisible, as Lily chose a course of action.

Lily stood. "All right," she said. "I'll show

up and look mysterious and keep my mouth shut."

Nan relaxed so fully she did not know if she would be able to get up from her chair. "Thank you," she replied.

From the first Sunday of Nan's campaign, Charles recognized its brilliance. It had been a joy to write his sermon; he was thrilled to return to the familiar trails of history, to ponder questions he knew he could answer, to lay down the cobblestones of a story rather than submerge himself in the existential depths of saving people's souls.

And it was a pleasure to see Lily in the congregation, to know she had chosen to sit in the pew on his behalf, and James's, and Nan's. It grounded him, more securely than he could have imagined, to have the two sides of his life stitched together in the same room.

James was not so certain about it. For the first time, he resented Nan. She was denying him the chance to defend himself to his antagonists, and he abhorred the oily residue of defeat. He fell silent on the train to Mississippi, read his newspaper and looked out the window, trying not to catch her eye. It did not seem to bother her. She was delighted to be going home, content to read her book, to knit, to smile at the other passengers as they passed down the aisle. He was annoyed by the lightness of her being and burdened by the heaviness of his own.

But, once at her parents' house, it was difficult to remain indignant in the face of her happiness. As she washed dishes with her mother, weeded the church path with her father, laughed with her childhood friends in the living room, James saw the Nan he had first met: full of hope and charm and cheer. He had taken her away from this life; he had changed her, and though he could not have charted their life differently, he lamented what it had cost her to follow him.

They went to service at her church, and James was spellbound by her father's presence. He was not only in the pulpit but was, somehow, also of it — an alloy of man and minister, fearsome and approachable, exacting but kind. James felt the tension of the current, upheaving times in the church, but also the long rudder Nan's father had put in the water, his strong hand on the wheel. He wondered how he would ever attain that wherewithal, that command.

When he asked Nan's father about it later, in the same office in which they had sat once before, her father said, "In my opinion, the most important job a minister has is to become a man who can lead his congregation through difficult times."

James nodded.

"This," her father continued, "requires you to become someone they can trust." James flinched; it was a quick and sudden cut. He saw, instantly, that he was not that man for his congregation.

"Nan tells me *you* are the one causing trouble at your church." James nodded. Nan's father shook his head and sighed. "That's one option — standing for what you want to stand for. If you stick with it, you'll earn people's respect. But if you want to earn people's trust, you can't chastise those who disagree with you. You have to include everyone — no matter how misguided they seem to you. You have to give them time to say their piece, look them in the eye, and give them credit for it."

James said, "That is the very last thing I want to do."

"Then you're an activist, James, and you should quit the ministry."

James flinched again. He had seen, in this trip, what Nan had lost in marrying him. In marrying her, he had lost the freedom of choosing any other profession. And he did not regret it. "That's the other very last thing I want to do."

"A divided congregation will always turn on itself, James, and then what use will they be to the outside world?"

It was exactly what Nan had been trying to tell him. As he watched her brush her hair before bed that night, leaning against the edge of the dresser, he said, "Your father is a wise man."

Nan turned to him and smiled. "I know."

"I haven't been so wise."

Nan put down the brush, tucked her hair behind her ears, stood up, and took his hands. "It's all right," she said. "You've been on a mission."

The moment widened around them as if stretched by a fermata. She felt suspended in midair, the lacuna wrapping her like a splint, her scattered parts assembling in an order that made sense. She let the silence linger, a whole bar of rest. She was a minister's wife, and she had done her job.

On the last Sunday of the project, Lily breathed a sigh of relief. She had done as Nan had asked: sat in church, borne the attention, watched the congregation whisper about her. It had been hard for her to stomach; it had been even harder to witness Charles preach about history, to see him revel in his expertise, to be thrilled by his meticulous intellect, imagining the life they could have had, if God had not found him first.

But she had seen the way the gossip had drawn the church together, the way the congregation relaxed into the predictability of Charles's series of sermons, how much fuller coffee hour was on the fifth week rather than the first. When Nan led the junior choir down the aisle, arranged them on the steps in front of the altar, untangled one small boy's blue robe, and lifted her hand to conduct the anthem, Lily had to admit she had underestimated her. Though Nan operated in a small and particular world, she had known what she was doing. And she had been right.

Two weeks later, Nan had another miscarriage. She had not realized she was pregnant. In the planning and packing and rehearsing of the previous eight weeks, she had not thought to keep track, but she recognized the very particular pain. She was glad she had not known, had not told James, because if he had whooped with joy she would have known he was as desperate for a child as she was, she would have known he had been hoping, too. She thought she could not bear to see James as stoically grim as he'd been the time before. When the cramps hit her, she said to herself, *I'm not going to the hospital. I'm staying here, and I'm bearing it alone.* Which was exactly what she did, sitting over the toilet, bleeding, but it was impossible not to tell James when he came home.

Nan had always known, even as a child, that God did not answer prayers for worldly things like candy or new shoes. God answered prayers that helped her help others. God did not change the circumstances of your life; God changed *you.* She had seen it happen too many times to doubt it. She had seen so many people walk nervously down the aisle of her father's church to accept God at the altar, then had seen them find friends, drink less, hug their children more. She had seen the transformative power of the church, and she knew there was a God, even if no one could be sure in what form God came. If you were good, God liked you.

But God had turned away from her. This was how she felt, lying in her bed each night, praying. God was not listening. Or God was listening and not answering, because she had once again prayed for the wrong thing. She had prayed for children. So she began to pray to *not* want children, to be happy with what she had, to be content with her husband, her home, herself. "Help it be enough," she prayed. "I want it to be enough." But it was not enough. She was not changed. She wanted a child.

Instead, that honor was given to Lily. Nan found out about it, a few weeks later, when Lily crashed into Jane's organized waiting room, dazed.

"I'd like to see my husband," she said. Nan had pulled up a chair to Jane's desk, where she was addressing envelopes.

"I *need* to see my husband," Lily amended. Nan felt Jane sigh. Despite Lily's assistance in restoring the church's equilibrium, Jane Atlas was not impressed. *Anyone can be useful every once in a while,* she'd said.

Now she told Lily, "He's busy." Lily looked around the empty waiting room, unsteadily, her movements jerky.

"Are you all right?" Nan asked.

"No," Lily said. "I'm pregnant."

She had come straight from the doctor's office to tell Charles, without thinking about what she was doing, which was a marker of how stunned she was by the news. At the doctor's she had managed to not say, *Don't be ridiculous;* instead she had said, "Oh."

310

"A surprise, then?" the doctor said, washing his hands at the metal sink.

"Yes, quite," Lily said without getting off the examining table.

"Well," the doctor smiled at her. "Babies give us nine months to get used to the idea, thank goodness."

Lily managed to get dressed, pay the bill, and leave the office building. Outside, she took a deep breath; the air was full of the smell of concrete. She would have a child. She had been actively trying to prevent it. She wanted to keep teaching, to have summers off to read, to start a new school year, and then another, a string of years spun into a cocoon out of which she could emerge unmarked by tragedy, a person whose life was not defined by death but by work. Books, students, pencils, lined paper, classrooms: all of these occurring in succession, meant to be enjoyed then finished with. A life built on blocks for which substitutes and replacements could easily be found.

Now she was going to have a baby. Her scalp prickled and her ears rang. She leaned against a fire hydrant and put her head between her knees.

Nan did exactly the same thing when she heard Lily's news; she put her hot, stinging

head between her knees so that neither Jane
nor Lily would see her cry.

FIFTEEN

Charles woke each morning more awake than he had ever been, alight with expectation. He could not stop smiling. He would have a child. A child to sail with, to read with, to talk to while holding hands and walking down the street. He realized how little he had been smiling lately, at least without ruefulness or concern. Now, he was unabashed. He would have a house full of puzzles, card games, and high chairs at the dinner table. For the first time, the cool and bright expanse of faith he always felt around him was inside of him, like a pencil lead, silver and strong, ready for him to put to paper and draw lovely, lucky scenes.

He had not even had to convince Lily. That was a moment of luck Charles could not explain. He had been formulating his argument for months, wondering how to convince Lily she, too, wanted a baby. His determination had dulled in the face of

James and Nan's misfortune; it seemed disloyal to actively campaign for a child when his friends could not have one. But now, it had happened. Just happened, without conversation, without Lily's skepticism or resistance. They were having a child. His prayers were full of gratitude and incredulity.

As it turned out, they were expecting twins. And Charles was even more delighted. The house would be full at once, no waiting for another. He began to wonder more ardently if this was ordained from on high somewhere, as if the universe knew Lily might stop at one child, might go back to work and be content, and had given her two, so that he could have the family he wanted.

"Twins," James said. "Cain and Abel. Jacob and Esau. How very biblical of her."

Charles was besieged by well-wishers, women of the parish who marched to the church to take up a walk-in time.

"When the baby cries, rub him with Epsom salt," some said.

"Oh no, give her just a little bit of whiskey," others countered.

"Bright lights — you wouldn't think it would get babies to fall asleep, but it does."

"Tell Lily," some commanded, "not to go

to them every time they cry."

"Best thing I ever did," others admonished, "was pick my children up every time they whimpered."

On and on their advice continued, punctuated by stories of their own children or childhoods. When their appointment times were finished, the well-wishing women waited in the lobby for their friends to be done. Charles often encountered them there, clucking together, having thought of something else they hadn't told him.

He had never known it could be so exhausting to smile and nod.

"It's like Lilliput," James said. "I see you sitting here every day, and all I can do is step carefully over all these little ropes."

"I enjoy it," Charles said with careful humility. "But I do sometimes wonder if it's a waste of time."

James looked surprised. "You're helping them feel important," he said. "They're getting to tell you something they know."

"Yes," Charles told James, "but Lily's not going to use a single shred of this advice. Even if it kills her. She'll do something completely unorthodox, and there will have been no reason for any of us to have sat through it all."

■ ■ ■ ■

James was more grateful than ever for the manse, had come to respect its basic vocation, which was to nurture, inspire introspection, sequester him and Nan from the distractions of the outside world. It was not meant for guests or entertainment, but for quiet conversation and cups of soup by the fire. He liked its smooth corners and flowered sofas, the curtains and the thick, warm rugs and the polished tables. He did not take it for granted. He was relieved to have this refuge that made it possible for him to go out into the jagged world. But the manse was not a house that inspired change, and it had enveloped Nan, enshrouded her, allowed her to hoard her suffering, to dwell on her pain.

She was letting Jane handle the busybodies and, most worrying of all, had taken a break from the junior choir — left the children in Dr. Rose's less capable hands. It had been weeks since she had joined James at coffee hour. He wanted to move on. He wanted her to do something. He assumed their next baby would stick; he needed Nan to believe that, too. So he told her about the ladies who dropped in on Charles. He knew this would distress her, but he hoped that recommendations for buggies and diapers might get her thinking about the future.

Nan had no energy to think about the future. It was all she could do to go to church, and she did that only because she had fought so hard for James to stay there. She was so angry at God. She could not understand why God had given Lily two babies and her none. Why Charles and Lily were embraced by goodwill but desperate to escape it.

"Those women are doing their best," Nan said. "They want to help." She wanted to fling herself on their bosoms, never to emerge. She wanted to take every shred of their advice, listen to every word about dinner and baths and school. How dare Lily look down on them and their domestic wisdom? It was not something to be pitied. It was Nan's fondest dream.

James was so worried about her that he sent Jane Atlas to the manse. He gave her the key, in case Nan was too tired to open the door. Jane did not even knock. She opened the door, closed it loudly behind her, and shouted, "It's Jane Atlas. I'm coming in."

She heard Nan stand up in the living room, found her — thankfully — fully dressed in a light blue skirt and sweater, bleary-eyed and rumpled.

"Your husband gave me the key," she said. "He wanted me to startle you. Let's have some whiskey."

"I don't need whiskey," Nan said.

"Of course you do." Jane pulled a silver flask out of her purse. She went into the kitchen and opened cabinet doors until she found the glasses. She came back into the living room with two of Nan's fanciest tumblers, etched with flowers and vines. She sat down on one of the red sofas, put the glasses on the coffee table, and poured a finger of whiskey into each one.

"Sit there," she told Nan, pointing to the couch across from her, pushing a glass across the wood. "And drink."

Nan did as she was told. The whiskey numbed her throat. She realized it had been days since she had seen anyone but her husband. She felt stiff and stale. Her days were an ocean of sameness: the same food, the same rooms, every day a house unchanged. Even her favorite arias, played over and over again, gave her no comfort. She had thought she could put down roots in New York. Instead, she felt as rudderless as a broken boat. No, she realized; James was in the boat. She was in the water, holding

318

on to his hand. She needed other company. She needed people who drank iced tea, who had time to linger over conversation, who wanted to talk about music and marriage. She knew she needed help.

"What am I going to do?" she whispered.

Jane surveyed her carefully. "You're going to take a bath, put on clean clothes, eat an omelet and make new friends." Nan stared at her.

"Go on," Jane waved at her. "I'll find the eggs, and then we are going to the knitting circle."

Nan knew that every Wednesday a group of women met in the coffee hour room to knit booties and caps for the Foundling Hospital. She also knew they were all at least sixty years old. She had never joined them, just as she had never joined her mother's friends at their card games. In her house, the young needed an invitation to join their elders.

After Nan had eaten, Jane marched her across the path, into the church building, up the stairs, and into the fellowship room, where she said, "Here's that fresh face you're always telling me we need." Nan recognized them all; they were the ladies who sat in the third row at church, who stood together in a corner during coffee hour. She had said *Hello, how are you?* to them a hundred times and had been met with somewhat curt *Fine, thank you*s that told her she should not intrude. She was surprised to see them out of their church clothes, stylishly dressed and obviously gossiping.

"These are *my* friends," Jane leaned up to whisper in Nan's ear. "You can share them. But you cannot tell the boys. It would ruin my reputation."

Nan found a seat on a blue upholstered chair, next to a woman her mother's age who was knitting so fast Nan could hardly see her fingers.

"I don't really know how to do this," Nan said, as Jane Atlas handed her a pair of silver needles.

"We'll teach you," a woman in a black pantsuit across from her said, tugging a ball of yellow yarn from a chic basket handbag at her feet.

The knitter on Nan's other side, a woman wearing horn-rimmed glasses and a huge diamond ring said, "It's nice to see a young girl who has time for this sort of thing."

Nan realized they had been watching her, judging her as she went about her business of being a minister's wife. She could not tell what conclusion they had come to; they were looking at her as if deciding how to proceed.

The collective pause went on too long, until Jane said, with equal parts gravity and compassion, "Nan does not want to talk about Lily."

And Nan understood: They had been judging all four of them. And Jane had just told them that Nan and Lily did not get along. Nan knew it should have embarrassed her, but she wanted to hug Jane, to kiss her on the cheek for making her life one small bit more true.

The room erupted into lively conversation, and Nan concentrated on looping her yarn around the sharp point of the needle. For the next six months, she spent Wednesdays with that group of women, talking about church and the manse and being married to a minister. She heard stories about dachshunds and dinner parties and Paris. She learned about wills and nursing homes and widowhood. She knitted a scarf, a blanket, and a pair of mittens. She resumed her parish work and returned to the junior choir. Not once did anyone mention Lily.

Six months in, Lily was still stunned. She woke each morning frozen — not cold, but desperately still, as she had held herself as a child when she was reading in the hammock and wanted her cousins to pass her by. She spent her days like this, her feelings in a glass jar on a high shelf, the rest of her blank and numb. She registered Charles's happiness, and was not opposed to it; children should be happy occurrences, and his cheer was so bright that it seemed to hide her dullness from him. It was easy to let him make plans, choose blankets, bottles, cups, and spoons.

But she could not ignore that there were two people growing inside of her. They had begun to move, rolling and kicking so strongly that she sometimes had to sit down. She did not understand their enthusiasm. Did they not know that she lived in a tiny apartment and had nowhere to put them? Did they not know that she wanted to work, not stay home and make oatmeal? Did they not know they were forcing her hand, that now she would have to stay married, stay in New York, be part of a life she was still not sure she had chosen correctly?

These thoughts spread themselves out in her mind like pieces of a jigsaw puzzle. She turned them over, night after night, so that they were right-side up, corners and edges identified. But she did not put them together. If she put them together she would be fused, her life would be fixed and determined, ready to be sprayed with glue and mounted as a trophy on a wall. She wanted to keep the pieces separate; she wanted to live in the spaces between them for a little longer.

But in the spaces were her parents. That was the truth, and as she grew bigger and bigger, slept less and less, she could not remain frozen against it. In the spaces her mother baked cookies and her father fixed cars. In the spaces they stood close to each other at the kitchen sink, washing and drying with a kiss or two in between. In the spaces, her mother smoothed Lily's blankets, kissed her forehead, turned out the light, and her father said, "That book will still be there in the morning."

There was no way to avoid these memories now. The babies were stirring them up as they twisted and turned. There would never again be a day when she would not remember that she was an orphan. The babies had brought suitcases of grief, and they were unpacking them inside of her, leaving the work of so many years in disarray.

At the end of the term, she went out with her colleagues for one last drink. She was tired of Charles's solicitous attention, the way he slid out of bed in the morning as quietly as possible, so she could sleep in, stirred his coffee without clanking the spoon. She was tired of him looking at her incredulously, tired of his happiness, his confidence that their relationship had been restored. She wanted to be with people who didn't believe in miracles.

"Dr. Barrett!" Her colleagues smiled as she stepped down the dark steps into the bar. "Come, come," they said, making space for her at the tables they had pulled together. "We were just discussing economics, but now that you've arrived, we'll turn ourselves to literature."

There was a silence. Lily felt it pulling at her like an undertow. These men had lost their families and jobs and freedom, just as she had. They had picked themselves up and learned to live with it. Just as she had. In the past, that had inspired her, made her glad to be part of their revolution. But tonight, she saw that behind their conviviality their eyes were flat and dull, their pockets empty, all hope stolen long ago. Would she look at her children with the same indifference? She didn't want to. It struck her that she had been wrong about these men. She had admired the ways they were different from Charles without seeing how similar they were to her.

Lily took a deep breath. She would have children. She would have to care for them. She would have to love them. She would have to risk the chance that they might die. The horror of it turned her stomach inside out.

She went home. Charles was sitting on the sofa, nodding into the telephone.

"That must be difficult," he said steadily. "I see. How hard for you. What can I do?" She knew he was talking to a parishioner; she wanted him to talk to her in the same way.

She stood in the middle of the living room without taking off her coat. She watched him nodding in the yellow light of the lamp.

Charles said, "Call again if you need to," and hung up the phone. Then he said, "Hello," and held out his hand.

Lily pulled her hat off and said, "Does it really help these people when you listen and then try to say something profound?" Her hair was full of static, stuck to her head. "I need to know if it helps them."

"I hope so," Charles said.

Lily's demeanor alarmed him. Pregnancy did not agree with her. She was restless and sick, spent nights alternately pacing the halls or leaning, pale-faced, over the bathroom sink. She gained the appropriate amount of weight, but her face had thinned, throwing her cheekbones into high relief and leaving her almost gaunt. She could not sit anywhere for more than five minutes. She was cranky, demanding, and tossed so violently in the night that he often woke up cold, found all their blankets on the floor. As her belly grew bigger and she began to waddle, she was so changed to him that he could not imagine how different she felt to herself.

And when the babies started to kick, he noticed her recoil. He wanted to follow her around, keep his hand to her belly, know what the babies were doing every minute of the day. But she wanted them to stop. She sat down, took deep breaths, closed her eyes until they were once again still.

Now, to his relief, some wisdom within him revealed to him that Lily was afraid. Charles could not believe he had been so stupid or blind.

He put his hand out again. "You know," he said, "I think these babies are going to be fine."

"You can't know that," she said. "How can you possibly know that?" And to Charles's complete surprise, she began to cry. She sat down — still and composed, as usual, but the tears fell from her eyes as if she were so

full of them, they could not help but over-
flow.

"Will you tell me how to love them?"

He was so full of compassion and grief for
her he could not answer. She smiled ruefully.

"I'm like a church member, aren't I?" she
said. "Calling you up for your advice."

"Do you want my advice?" he asked.

"Can you leave out the part about God?"

"Probably not," Charles said.

The next day, Charles went before the session to ask for money to buy a house. He
was expecting two children; he could not
raise them in a tenement. He had a wife
who craved freedom; if he could not give
her that, he could give her a real home.

"I know it's not the best time," he told
the session. "I know we're not working out
like you thought we would." He raised his
hands in front of him. "But James got the
manse," he reminded them. "We'll move
into anything, but it's got to be soon."

Within a month, the session found them a
town house on Twelfth Street. It stood in
the middle of the block, sturdy between its
neighbors, redbrick, tall windows, a plain,
practical black gate guarding the stairs. He
took Lily to see it on a Tuesday. It was late

October, the first truly brisk day of the year. He had not put a coat on over his blazer. He paced up and down through the fallen leaves on the sidewalk as he waited for her to arrive.

"It's too close to the church," Lily said.

It was just across the street from the church's side door. People would see her coming and going. They would know her schedule, which bags she brought home, whether or not she had brushed her hair. But she took a good look at the building anyway, at its straight lines and the panes of glass in its windows. It was almost like looking in a mirror.

"We'll buy a quarter of it; the church will buy the rest," Charles said. "That way we'll own *something*."

"You've been inside?" Lily asked.

He nodded. "Five bedrooms. Can you imagine? And a garden . . ."

In spite of herself, Lily was intrigued. "Let me in," she said.

Charles reached into his coat pocket for the keys. "It's a little beat up," he said, "but I think we can get it ready before the twins are born."

He turned the key in the lock and pushed open the door. He was right: The house was beat up. The staircase had no banister;

plaster peeled off the walls. The moldings had been painted over so many times that they could hardly see the patterns carved into them. But it was a beautiful house. The front hallway floor, under the fallen plaster flakes, was tiled black and white. The staircase leaned drunkenly against the wall to the right of them, but past it Lily could see the kitchen — big — and past that, a glass-paned door that led to a garden. She opened the door to her left.

"A study," Charles said. "It looks out on the church, so if they need me, they can knock and you won't even have to see them."

"Let's go upstairs," Lily said. They picked their way up carefully and found, on the second floor, two big bedrooms and a bathroom with a claw-foot tub. On the third floor there were three small bedrooms and a bath with a sloped ceiling. There was a skylight in the hall.

"What do you think?" Charles asked hesitantly.

Until that moment, Lily had not known why she wandered through the city, why she followed men she barely knew to various and sundry bars. She had not known why she listened to their stories, why she created some of her own, in her head, as she walked;

where she would go, someday, how she would get there, whom she would befriend when she arrived. She did not know; she had not analyzed. She had simply let herself live in her fantasies, imagining herself glamorous and far away. She had wandered because it meant she could be alone, because it meant the landscape was always different, because it meant she did not have to care for anything longer than the moments she held it in front of her eye.

"I don't know," she said, heading back down the stairs. There were no fixtures in the kitchen, but it was big and square, with room enough for a table. The garden was paved with flagstone. There were cedar planters around the borders and a linden tree at the far end.

"Can you live here?" Charles asked. His eyes searched hers.

She stood in front of him and looked up. She had been wandering because she had lost her way. She had not thought of it that clearly before. She had wandered because it seemed her only choice, because Charles would not give up his faith, because she could not find one of her own. She had been desperate, rootless. She had been wandering because she had forsaken her first home, traded grief for freedom, had not known she needed a new one. Now, Charles had found it for her.

He was looking at her eagerly. She would never be free again.

But she would also never be alone. Charles would sit on a hundred benches in a hundred schools, waiting for her to come down a thousand steps, because he loved her. They would have babies and raise them in this house, a house full of noise and laughter. She could not shake the feeling that she had come full circle, that she had lost two people and was being given two more. It was like the clasp of a bracelet once clicked open, now snapped closed.

And Charles had done this. Charles had seen her fear and, against all odds, had helped her. She could give up her doubts now. They seemed as slight as handkerchiefs, and his certainty was as solid as the world.

"Thank you," she said.

Charles saw the look of relief on Lily's face, realized that he had succeeded — he had reached her. He had brought her back to the land of the living.

James called doctors. Every day he chose a name out of the yellow pages and introduced himself as a reverend, which almost always got him put through. All of them said some version of: *Miscarriage can be caused by many things. I suggest you keep trying, and pray. There are procedures we can try — if necessary — but you're young, and it's early days yet. Two miscarriages — early, early days.* He did not tell Nan about these calls. He knew she would hate him for talking about her with other men, and she would hate the idea of involving a doctor in this part of their lives. To her, babies were miracles, not medical procedures. But he had to do something. He always had to do something.

The church was stable. Their ministers had turned into family men. There were children singing hymns and even more children to look forward to. These were straightforward talismans, traditional hopes. The church was once again classic and comprehensible. Attendance was soaring.

James had pulled back from his revolutionary sermons; he knew what a peaceful church meant to Nan. He did not want to interfere with her healing — not that Jane Atlas would let him. She had reassigned him to congregational meetings and monitored his wanderings. He could not let her catch him more than ten blocks from home. But Nan was getting better, and he was getting restless. He needed a new cause to champion.

Nan, too, needed a new project. In September, from her window she had watched children going back to school in new shoes, book bags too big for their small backs. To her relief, this had made her glad. She loved the first weeks of school, when blackboards were clean, binders empty, blue-lined pages blank. It was a new beginning, a chance to reinvent oneself.

Now Nan knew she needed to make a correction. She needed to let go of her bitterness and make amends.

"Let's throw Lily a baby shower," Nan said to the knitting circle.

The usual swift clicking came to a stop. The women looked up from their needles, stared at her incredulously. Nan shrugged without looking at them. "It seems like the right thing to do."

Lily had helped her. When Nan had asked, Lily had saved James's job, forsaken her anonymity, and never demanded anything in return. Now, James told her, Lily was suffering. It was her job to help, and she felt strong enough to do it.

The knitting circle bought soft yarn, mother-of-pearl buttons, and panels of lace from France. They drew cards to see who would make blankets, booties, sweaters, and caps. They knitted in secret, at home, so that when Lily opened her gifts, they could all be surprised. They smiled at one another conspiratorially during coffee hour, and Nan finally felt connected to a circle of confidantes. She knew her mother would be proud.

Nan drew one of the two cards that said baptism gown. For a moment, she wanted to put it back. She knew Lily would hate a lacy costume, no matter how well she knitted it. Lily would hate the whole idea of a church christening, and she would hate Nan for suggesting it. But, Nan thought, the gown wasn't for Lily; it was for one of the twins. And it was for Charles. Surely he would want the children baptized. His family would want to come to the ceremony, and his mother would want her grandchildren well-turned-out. It was tradition. It was for Charles. That's how Nan decided to think about it.

Nan swore James to secrecy — he was absolutely not to tell Charles, but he was worried. It seemed obvious to James that Lily would not want a baby shower — she hated small talk, she hated church, she hated people she didn't know. She was afraid for the babies and afraid for herself. To surprise her seemed cruel. He knew Nan had not considered that, because she was creating for Lily the very thing she most wanted for herself. It was a heartbreakingly meaningful gift, but she and Lily were very different people. He imagined the appalled look on Lily's face as Nan yelled *Surprise!* He imagined Nan's embarrassment when she realized the party was a burden for Lily, the strained civility that would follow, the awkward gaiety of the guests in the room. So he told Charles, who said "Huh" and then "what a nice idea," and then stared at James, nonplussed.

It was painful to watch Nan wrap the gown and tie the white ribbon with care. James was not at all sure he had made the right decision, and as the date approached with no word from Charles, he began to hope Lily might attend after all, that his ruining of the surprise might make the whole party possible.

The night of the shower Nan crossed the path from the manse to the church full of excitement. It had been a hard surprise to engineer. There was no obvious way to get Lily to the church, so Nan had told Charles she was organizing a parenting class that he and Lily should attend. She knew his own excitement, and his worry for Lily, would get him there. She was excited to see them pull open the door, expecting a lecture, and instead find the knitting circle, lemonade poured, gifts in hand.

Nan had knitted the most beautiful dress she could — long and white with tiny crosses embroidered on the hem. She knew Lily would hate the crosses, but the woman knitting the second gown had put them in, and Nan wanted the twins to match. She was proud of it, and couldn't wait for Lily to open the yellow paper and see the effort she had made, in gratitude.

When Nan reached the fellowship room, most of the knitting group was already there, standing in a clump and giggling, clutching bright packages in their hands.

Jane Atlas caught sight of Nan, waved her over. "What's in the box?" she asked.

"Cookies," Nan said, coming back to herself, smiling brightly. "Let's set them out." She had baked sugar cookies in the shape of bassinets, iced pink and blue and green. The knitting circle let out a collective sigh. They spaced them out carefully on a plate lined with paper doilies. Then they sat on chairs in a circle, as they always did, waiting.

The door opened; they put their hands on the arms of their chairs, ready to jump up, but it was only Charles. He stuck his head inside the door and said, "I'm sorry. Lily's sick." Nan knew from the pained set of his shoulders that James had told Charles about the shower, that Charles had told Lily, and that Lily had refused to come.

He smiled apologetically. "Should I stay?"

The women of the knitting circle looked at Nan. "Oh," she said. "No, that's all right. I'll just bring the presents by tomorrow." Charles was visibly relieved.

"Thank you," he said.

For a moment, no one spoke. In the silence, Nan realized that soon all of these women would be gone. All of the women like her mother, who believed in baking and visiting, raising children, and long afternoons spent at home. Soon, all the women who understood her would be gone, and she would be left with women like Lily, who would expect her to make her own, solitary, way in the world.

"Well," Jane Atlas said loudly, clapping her hands. "The party wasn't really for her, was it? It was an excuse to outdo one another. So let's open everything and be impressed." She put a hand on Nan's shoulder, and Nan was comforted.

■ ■ ■ ■

PART THREE

1966–1970

■ ■ ■ ■

SIXTEEN

When Jane Atlas checked herself into the hospital for chest pains, James and Charles visited her the same afternoon.

"You've got your schedules for the week," she said, "and I'll be back Monday. Don't know what you'd do if I wasn't!" Those were the last booming words she said to them. That evening, as Nan was packing a bag of sandwiches for her own visit to the hospital, a nurse called to tell her that Jane had died. Nan stood in her hallway so long without hanging up her phone that Charles got a continuous busy signal and had to run to the manse to make sure James and Nan had heard the news. When James opened the door, the three of them stared blankly at one another, none of them having any idea what to do now that Jane was gone.

Almost every member of the congregation wanted to speak at the funeral, but it was decided that only Charles and James would give eulogies. They set a wide wicker basket on Jane's desk, into which parishioners slid postcards, lined sheets torn from notebooks, and monogrammed envelopes strewn with ink and pencil memories. They soon needed a second basket, which they placed next to the first, so that the congregation could see how united they were in their loss. The baskets made Jane's absence even more conspicuous.

At the service, James spoke of Jane's bracing irreverence and her perennial exasperation with people's confusion and delay.

Charles spoke of her deep compassion, the wisdom she had gathered over decades. "Jane believed so much time and suffering could be saved by listening to one's elders and doing what they said," he began, and the crowd in the pews chuckled. "And she left no one to the agony of going it alone."

He and James went back to their utterly empty office and looked at the schedules she had left them.

"Well," Charles said soberly. "I guess she left *us* alone."

It was 1965. Malcolm X had been assassinated. Martin Luther King Jr. had crossed the bridge into Selma. There had been riots in Los Angeles and a blackout in New York. Gemini 3 had sent two men into orbit around Earth. The two of them had watched these events on the little black-and-white television that sat on their windowsill. Without Jane Atlas to buffer them from the world, they were afraid the history still to come would seem even more unnerving.

"People are going to expect us to figure out what to do," Charles said.

"They hope we know already," James answered.

They knew, at least, to put an ad in the paper. It was small and neatly set: *Presbyterian church seeks assistant. Answering phones, keeping schedules, typing and filing.*

"Let's put 'Bossy okay,' " James said. "Jane would have wanted it."

Instead they put: *Equal Opportunity.*

That afternoon, they got a call.

"Your ad says equal opportunity." The man's voice was like a swinging pendulum.

"Yes," James replied.

"But your church is predominantly white." The enunciation was perfect, the tones round, deep, and controlled.

"Yes," James said.

"White in color or in spirit?" The voice was judging, but not demeaningly so.

James paused. "I'm going to have to say both," he said. "But we're working on it."

The man laughed. "All right, then. This is

Dr. Dennis Price, from the City College of New York. I have a student here who needs a job. He's not experienced, but he is smart. I don't think he wants to be a minister, but he is being raised in a churchgoing family. If he doesn't get a job, he's going to have to quit school. If he quits school, he will get drafted. I have many boys here in the same situation, and I've run out of jobs to give them. May I ask you how you feel about the draft?"

James cast a glance at Charles and raised his eyebrows.

"We are against it," he said.

"Good," Dr. Dennis Price said.

There was a pause.

"I would like you to meet this boy. I would like you to hire him, but I will be satisfied if you meet him. Do you have time today?"

"Yes," James said. It was as if the voice of Jane Atlas had been transplanted into the handset of his phone.

That was how they met Marcus. He could not make coffee, but he arrived every morning with two blue paper cups from the Greek market on the corner. He spoke briskly and intelligently on the phone. He kept excellent schedules. He was always reading the newspaper, but somehow found time to color-code their files.

"It wasn't easy," he said. "Jane Atlas had them organized in some way only old ladies could figure out. Can you read this?" he asked, thrusting a tattered file folder at them. The label, written in black felt-tip pen, looked like symbols on a mah-jongg tile.

"She liked to be indispensable," James told him.

"That's great until you die." Marcus sat down at his desk. "Maybe that's what's wrong with this world. The record-keepers are old ladies who don't leave legible files when they pass on. Maybe that's why we're still in this war. Somebody's old secretary filed the Get Out Quick papers under *snake pumpkin child.*"

Jane Atlas would have laughed.

Third Presbyterian did not question Charles and James's choice. Still, the congregation could not help but notice that their ministers had hired a young black man. They did not say anything openly, of course, so Charles and James could not figure out if it was Marcus's blackness that surprised them or his youth or his maleness.

"Do you think we should have asked someone?" Charles said one day, after they had taken a multitude of phone calls from people just checking in to see how Jane's replacement was doing.

"No," James said.

"Do you think we should *say* something?"

"What, before one of our grande dames gets whiplash from craning her neck?"

"I'd like to stop the gossip."

James nodded. "I think we should ignore the gossip. They know we're right, they just have to get used to knowing it." He wondered why it was that the right thing often took so long to get accustomed to.

He and Charles took Marcus to lunch at the Cedar Tavern. It was where the two of them ate together once a month to check in, to catch up on concerns, to spend time together as men instead of ministers. It was dark and clubby and served good beer and hamburgers. They let Marcus slide into their favorite booth before them.

"What are you studying?" James asked. Marcus was eating everything on his plate as fast as he could.

"Philosophy, history, a little bit of everything."

"What about when they make you decide?"

"Money, probably. Can you study money?"

"If you're white." James put his elbows on

346

the table, which Charles recognized as him getting ready for a fight.

Marcus smiled and kept chewing. "I understand what you're saying." He shook his head. "But you're not going to rile me up today. Right now, I'm taking care of myself. I'm keeping my head down, I'm going to college, and I'm staying out of Asia. When this war is over and I have a degree, I'll figure out how to change the world."

Charles and James were silent. They had not thought of Marcus as much younger than they were, but in that moment they felt how considerably they had aged. They were not old, by any stretch of the imagination, but they were substantially more worn and weathered than Marcus, had loved and hoped and worked and lost and failed and made amends.

James saw himself in Marcus, at least he saw the part of himself that was scared and desperate, that chose a point and threw himself toward it with single-minded energy, so that nothing and no one could knock him off course. And he saw the dread of war, the panic that his whole life could be stolen from him with one tumble of a lottery ticket in the looming brass wheel. How could another generation of young men live in fear? After all James had done, why had nothing changed? Why did the injustices of the world circle like roller-coasters at a carnival — passengers off, passengers on, the track designed to frighten and delight in equal measure, but never to give the riders the controls?

Marcus made Charles feel wistful. He missed being a student, immersed in his own mind, opportunities stacked up in front of him like catalogs. But he was content. He was a minister, a husband, and soon to be a father. These three strong ropes tied him to pier and post, kept him safe at harbor. He glanced at James and saw a fierce protectiveness on his face. He knew their hopes for Marcus were different, but their role in his life would be the same: They needed to shepherd this boy as Jane had shepherded them.

Lily understood that Jane Atlas had not approved of her, but she attended the funeral anyway. As always, she was surprised by Charles's visible joy in speaking to people, in comforting them, in being strong and patient. She was impressed by how completely his voice filled the church when he spoke, how careful he was with his words and tone. She realized those church qualities were no longer just for his congregation

— they had a purpose in her life as well: they would make him an excellent father.

She would not be an excellent mother. She would be short-tempered, quick to criticize, uninterested in toys and nursery rhymes. She had not even been a good cousin. But she recognized that Jane's advice was true: It made no sense to avoid the inevitable.

Construction was finished on the brownstone, and she began to decorate the rooms, taking trips to the Garment District for soft white linens, taupe flannels, thick cotton lining for drapes. Every weekend, she went to the Twenty-Sixth Street Flea Market for furniture, maneuvering herself among stalls crowded with mismatched sets of silver, brass sconces, and hulking cabinets full of chipped china figurines. There, she found two red leather club chairs for Charles's office and a long, smooth, unvarnished wood table for their kitchen. It was pale pine, assembled long ago for a farmhouse somewhere, she assumed, because it was worn to the texture of velvet. She painted eight spindled wooden chairs a glossy white; they circled the table like candles.

She did not decorate a nursery. She knew it would be the room closest to hers and Charles's on the second floor, because it had two windows and was wide enough to accommodate two cribs, two dressers, and a good-sized rocking chair. But she could not bear looking at paint chips, carpet samples, lampshades printed with hot-air balloons and stars. She allowed Charles to believe it was because she did not know if they were having boys or girls but, really, she could not stand the cheerfulness of the show-rooms, the pantomime of excitement the saleswomen required of her, and her own disdain for their assumption that life could be full of joy.

James watched Nan carefully. She hardly left the manse. He came home from work to find her asleep on the couch, the music for the junior choir on her lap. She started books but did not finish them; they lay around the house, spread open to the pages on which they had been abandoned. These days, when he came near her, she looked away. When she did meet his eyes, hers were full of longing.

He watched her working with the choir, despite her sadness, tending to other people's children. He saw the strain it put on her. For so long, all he had wanted was to be useful. But now, it seemed, he could not help his own wife.

"Do you think," James asked Charles one Monday, trying to be nonchalant, "that God has a plan?"

"I don't know," Charles said.

"But if you had to guess."

"Yes. Do you?"

James shook his head. "No. I see suffering that is not caused by anything — not caused by anger or ignorance, not caused by greed. Just suffering. And it is hard to think of that as some sort of strategy. It is hard to think that the church wants me to tell people it is part of a plan."

Charles nodded, but did not say anything.

"I thought," James continued, "that if I chose this life I would always feel . . . full. Connected to something, directed."

"And you don't."

"Nan suffers, and I cannot comfort her. It overwhelms me. It overwhelms this," he said, gesturing around the room. "I thought this work would fix everything."

"But it doesn't," Charles said, certainly.

"No."

"I understand," Charles said, and he did. "Why don't you take a week off? Why don't you and Nan go away?" *Get away from us,* he thought to himself. "That's why there are two of us."

But Nan had no desire to get away. "I

351

can't bear to pack," she said.

Instead, she planted a tree. It was November, and the ground was cold, but she bought a shovel at the hardware store, put on canvas gloves and rubber boots, and dug a hole, stepping on the blade of the shovel, pushing with her heel. It took an hour. Halfway through, she took off her thick sweater and laid it on the ground.

She wanted to give up. Her life was no longer lovely; it was a drought. She woke each morning, scrambled eggs, served them on a plate, set out a fork and napkin, watched James eat them, then washed the pan. She changed sheets, then vacuumed. She ironed; she washed her face, brushed her teeth, pulled back covers, lay down in bed. As she completed each action she thought, *This used to matter.*

She tamped the clodded earth down with the back of her shovel. *This used to matter,* she thought. Hard work, faith, and perseverance had, at one time, been significant. Jane Atlas's whole life had once made a difference, had interlocked with other lives, helped them turn easily, shifted them into gear. Now it was over.

James had told her about the doctors. He said there were small surgeries they could each have. The doctors could clear away some tissue, try to increase blood flow, ease circulation. Nan hated speaking of it, hated the charts and illustrations in the pamphlets the doctors sent. James read them carefully; Nan turned out her light, pretended to be asleep so he could not pass them to her. She was not a line-drawn system on a glossy piece of paper. She was not a collection of veins and vessels, cells and bones. Except they all *were.* They would live fewer years than this tree, and the earth would disassemble them. Jane was already just a cup full of ash.

SEVENTEEN

Lily's twins were born just after New Year's. Boys. The hospital was stark and smelled of bleach. The fluorescent lights and linoleum floor tiles were identical to those Lily had stood under and upon on the day of her parents' deaths. She closed her eyes against them, tried to put the memory out of her mind. She struggled on the bed, nauseous, pushing for so long — too long. The doctor approached her with a black mask and said, "This will be easier if you are asleep."

Before she breathed in whatever gas the mask held for her, she gripped the nurse's hand and begged, "Please don't let my babies die." It was the second most terrifying day of her life.

When she woke up and they handed her sons to her — one for each arm, all wrapped up in striped blankets — she was amazed. They were real; they had come. She had children. People had told her she would recognize them instantly, but she did not. They were complete strangers, red and wrinkled, skeptical, with fingers as long as elves'. She did not know them, and they did not know her, could not recognize her before and after, her brokenness, her tragedy. They were two beings from whom she did not have to hide. If she chose, she could return the book called *Orphan* to the library. She could fold that blanket and put it away.

She looked at Charles, sitting in a chair by the side of her bed and realized that this was how he always felt: grounded and purposeful. She was now a mother, in the same way he was a minister; neither of them would ever be separate from their role. She did not know how she felt about that, yet. But she was, in that moment, so grateful for him, for the house he had found, for the things he had forgiven.

They named the boys Benjamin, called Bip, and William, called Will. They arrived home to baskets of gifts from the women of the parish. Lily took her boys instantly into bed with her, and there they stayed for the first few weeks of life, cuddled together, sung to by Lily, read to by Charles. Lily fed them, changed them, dressed and redressed them, did laundry, cooked meals, wiped the table, put them down for naps, had naps herself, tried to read the newspaper, but settled for watching the news as she fed one and then the other at her breast. In everything she did now, she thought to herself: *My boys will know I did this. Will they be proud?* It was the way she imagined some people felt about their parents.

James and Nan went to visit them. It was a cold day, and Nan was glad for the coats, the scarves, the mittens. They protected her on the way over and gave her something to do in the awkward moments after they arrived. Nan had not been invited to visit the brownstone before. She had not seen Lily since the day she had found out Lily was pregnant. She had hoped the baby shower would build a bridge, but instead the space between them had grown wider, and now Nan was here only because it was something her father would have wanted her to do.

"Come in, come in!" Charles said. He opened the door, then his arms, wide. He hugged them both. "Lily's in the kitchen."

Nan paused in the entryway. It was strange to be inside Lily's new home; it was completely different from the apartment she had seen before. The ceilings were high. The walls were white and there was clean, stark space between them, not quite filled with furniture. There was not a single rug on the floor. The only touches of color were the lush, celebratory vases of flowers. It made the manse seem trivial.

A baby cried. Charles hurried to the kitchen and Nan and James followed him. Lily's counter was marble; her table was a blank plane of honey wood. Lily was holding both babies, sitting on a hard, straight chair.

"I'm sorry," Lily said. Nan thought, for a moment, that Lily was apologizing for her appearance, which was disheveled and stained.

"It's all right," Nan said, unable to take her eyes off the babies, who were both swaddled in white crocheted blankets. She could smell their soap and powder from across the room. One had wiggled a hand free, his tiny fingers grazing the air.

"No, it's not," Lily told her. "I've been rude to you. I didn't understand; I thought you were being desperate. I didn't know what it meant to have a child, and I thought you were foolish for missing something you never had. But I understand now."

Nan knew Lily still didn't understand at all. How could anyone comprehend another's longing when their own had been fulfilled? She felt James's hand on her back, the familiar rub that told her they could go if she needed to.

"I hope you have one," Lily continued. "I will hope for you as hard as I can."

Nan felt like the surface of Lily's table, sanded bare. She did not want Lily's pity.

"Can I hold one?"

Lily held out the little bundles she was cradling. "As long as you want to," she said. Nan put the baby on her shoulder and placed her cheek next to his head. He was warm and breathing.

James took the other baby, awkwardly, aware of the length of his adult arms, the clumsiness of his hands. He held him to his chest. The child seemed to weigh less than a newspaper. James found himself overcome. His throat closed and he had to stand very still to hold back the tang of tears.

He had known Nan was lonely. He had known this life of faith, of study, of friends and conversation was not enough for her, that she needed something more. He had known she wanted, so deeply, so simply, to love — to love as many people as she could, to raise them and take care of them. He had not known he felt that way as well.

That night, as Nan read the paper in front of the fire, James sat down next to her and said, "I think we should try harder."

"What do you mean?" Nan asked, frowning at him.

"I think we should try harder," James repeated, taking her hands in his. "I think we should go to the doctors."

Nan went pale. Her shoulders hunched forward, her chest sank back as if he had kicked her. "No," she said, standing up, going to sit in a chair across the room.

"Why not?"

"Because that's not the way this happens," Nan said. "Life is a miracle. Something you are given or not given. To force it to happen is like stealing."

"Why?" James asked, sliding to the end of the couch, as close as he could get to her without standing up. "Why is it like that, how is it like that?"

He looked intently at her, almost desperately, hoping she could provide him an answer. He felt the same way, that to seek beyond what one was offered caused only trouble, only heartache. Given the state of the world, one should ask only to help others have enough. But that was exactly what he wanted to do; he wanted to help Nan have enough.

"Why should you have to be so miserable?" he asked her.

Nan looked at her lap. "I want it to feel

like a gift," she said, "like Christmas morning. I want it to be full of joy."

James stared at her bent head, wondering how to approach this sympathetically. He understood that, for most of her life, Nan had been given everything she needed without delay: the perfect home, the perfect upbringing, the perfect talent, the perfect education. Before she longed for them, they had appeared, and she had floated along on this current of ease.

"So much of your life has been simple, Nan," he said. "Maybe this is the one thing for which God wants you to work hard." He said it gently.

Nan stood up, pulled the chair in front of herself, leaned on its sturdy frame. She shook her head. James knew he was perilously close to making her cry. He wanted her to hold on, to keep the tears at bay. If she cried, he would relent. He would cross the room, hold her, never speak of it again. Then they would never have a baby. He would never see her happy.

"Do you want a baby, Nan?" he asked, still gentle. "Or do you want to feel chosen?"

She looked at him plaintively. "I want to feel like what we have is enough. I want to be thankful for what God has given me — this house, my students, you. They should be enough, James, they should be enough."

James looked at the fire, the logs growing thinner, crumbling.

"Your father once told me, Nan, that restlessness was my calling. I was ashamed of that for a long time, because it felt like a lie, like something he had made up so he could accept my marrying you. But I understand it now. I understand the feeling that something is not quite right — the feeling that something should be done, changed, fixed — that feeling, Nan, is never wrong. It isn't something to bury or ignore.

"Those feelings that hound you, Nan — they are God. They are God telling you to do something, to be different in some way. Sometimes it isn't right to pray for acceptance of the status quo. If God calls you to upend it, then you should upend it.

"You think God rewards, Nan, I think God pursues."

The twins were not identical. Bip was shorter, stockier, blonder. He moved in a gentle, dreamy sort of way. He was cranky when he got hungry and rubbed his eyes when he needed sleep. Lily thought of him as Charles's child: easygoing, adaptable, curious about the world. Will was dark, wiry, and malcontent. He never cried, not in the way Bip did, but he whimpered constantly and could not be consoled. He did not want a bottle, a nap, or to be held. He was happiest flat on his back in the wide carriage her aunts had sent her, with the hood pulled up to block the rest of the room.

So that was where Lily left him much of the day, even as she carried Bip with her from room to room, laying him on a quilt close to her as she chopped carrots, washed dishes, rinsed diapers. She did wonder if a different mother would have been more attentive to Will, might have tried harder to coax him into contentment. Would she be treating him differently if he were her only child? She checked on him every twenty minutes, peeking into the carriage, hoping he would be asleep. He never was, and when he caught sight of her, he whined. When she drew back, he settled down.

She was exhausted. Her body felt soft and alien, yet she was required to lift and carry and nurse. Her skin felt raw, and yet there was always someone touching her. There was no silence and no uninterrupted length of time in which to read a book. It was a state of being fraught with anxiety and self-doubt.

On top of that, Charles seemed to revel in

fatherhood. He came home for lunch every day, hale and full of cheer, lifting Bip as high as possible, putting his whole face into Will's buggy and kissing him on the cheek, impervious to the way Will closed his eyes, curled into a ball. While he was home, Lily showered, standing under the hot water as long as possible, leaning her head against the tile. When she came down, dressed and dry, Charles kissed her and went back to work, abandoning her for the church.

Months passed. The brownstone became cluttered with silver rattles, plastic animals, wooden blocks, and rubber balls. Lily's days were marathons of watching babies sleep and eat and having no one to talk to. The boys clawed at her, and she was filled with the desire to lie in bed alone, or to leave the boys and walk into the garden, stand there for an hour.

"I didn't think it would be this hard," Lily said to Charles in bed one night after the boys were asleep. "I knew I wouldn't like it, but I never imagined I wouldn't be able to do it."

Charles took her hand. "Of course you can do it."

She had not eaten dinner; she had not washed her hair. Her eyes and throat felt like kindling. She was utterly impaired. "But

I don't want to," she said, quietly. "I want to read books." Tears slipped from the corners of her eyes and slid to the lobes of her ears.

Charles sat up concerned. "What can I do?"

Lily shook her head. "You can't be here all day," she said. He had to work, and she needed to be able to leave the house, drink coffee on a bench in the park, take the bus uptown and walk back home. Miriam would come, if she asked, but Lily had not spoken to her since the boys were born and didn't want to be a burden to her, yet again. Beyond that, there was no one. Lily had succeeded so spectacularly in her quest to be unattached that everyone who might have helped had circled away.

"I can ask someone at church to come by," Charles said. "I can find somebody to help."

"No," Lily said. "I can't meet a new person. I can't make chitchat. I can't be expected to pretend. I just need someone to sit with me and hold a twin." She hesitated. It was an insane idea, what she was about to propose, but she already felt like a lunatic.

"Do you think you could ask Nan?"

Astonished by the depth of her need, Charles did.

364

"Lily wants me to help?" Nan asked him, startled.

"Yes," Charles said, looking at Nan carefully. "She doesn't have anyone else." His voice was full of compassion. "Would that be okay?"

Nan stared at him wide-eyed, stuck in a prolonged shrug. Every fiber of her being wanted to say no. Every fiber of her being wanted to give Lily her comeuppance.

"You don't have to go," James said, when he heard about the request.

"Yes I do," Nan said. It was an impossible question with only one answer. Nan wanted babies, and here were two. Nan wanted to be a mother, and Lily was a mother in need. So, in the morning, Nan took a breath, put on her stockings, dress, coat, and hat and went to Lily's brownstone.

Lily opened the door. There were shadows under her eyes. She was holding Bip, who was clutching the hair behind her ear, pulling it hard toward him. Nan could hear Will crying in the living room. She saw instantly that Lily's need was genuine, and was relieved to know that she could still recognize the depths of someone's suffering.

She took Bip from Lily's arms. He had grown so quickly, could now hold his head up, touch Nan's nose. Without him, Lily looked small and weak. Nan felt sturdy in comparison.

"Thank you," Lily said. "I know we haven't been friends."

"No," Nan said, taking off her coat by shifting Bip from arm to arm. "We haven't. But it's all right. We know each other well enough. You won't expect too much of me and I won't expect too much of you. If I need to leave, you will understand. If you seem distant — well, I know why."

"I'm not used to people being around," Lily said. "And you've been around. I didn't know what to do with it earlier. Now I need it. I'm too tired to not need it."

Nan walked past her to the living room, where Will was sitting in his buggy, red-eyed from crying. Nan sat Bip down next to him.

"Go to sleep, Lily," she said. "Everything will be fine." For one strange moment, she thought Lily was going to hug her, instead she turned up the stairs to her bedroom and closed the door.

Nan rolled the buggy into the kitchen, sat on one of Lily's white chairs, and pushed the boys back and forth until they fell asleep with their arms crossed loosely over each other. While they slept, Nan washed the dishes that had been piled in the sink, dried them, and put them away. She rinsed out the dishrags, hung them on the cabinet knobs to air out, checked the dates on the newspapers, and threw out the oldest. When Bip stirred first, she carried him upstairs to Lily's room and knocked on the door. Lily answered, sleep-heavy and dazed, and Nan said, "Take him to bed with you; he'll nurse while you sleep."

And so began a rhythm of days. Nan arrived at ten in the morning and stayed until three, holding a twin, cleaning the kitchen, wiping the counters, pushing in chairs. Lily often napped while she was there, and Nan took the twins for walks, let them sleep in their stroller. She was not foolish enough to pretend they were her own, and she felt lonely when she walked with them, knowing they belonged to someone else. But she had to admit, it was easier to be included. It would have been so much harder to watch from afar.

After a few weeks, when the boys were on a schedule and Lily was rested, Nan made lunch, chicken salad and pickles, and they ate together at the long table, now stacked with the boys' clean, folded shirts and bundled socks.

After some moments of silence, Lily said, "Thank you."

"You're welcome," Nan answered, wiping

her mouth with a napkin.

Lily took a drink of water. "I don't think I would have done the same for you."

Nan thought for a moment and then said, "No, you wouldn't have."

Lily smiled. "I would now," she said.

Nan felt the lesson like a sudden rain. Lily would, now; of course she would. Every right action begets another; every extension of a hand forms a rope and then a ladder. How many times had her father told her that? How willfully had she forgotten?

"I'm sorry about the baby shower," Lily said. "It was kind, and I was selfish."

Nan shook her head, but Lily continued. "Please don't say it's all right. I know it wasn't."

It was a strange feeling, Nan thought, to sit with someone in total honesty. "It really wasn't," she said, the relief of it making her light-headed enough to smile. Lily smiled back.

"This is what it was like in my family," Lily said. "Women in the kitchen, sharing chores and children. I used to think it was frivolous, but now I know it was necessity."

Nan was suddenly embarrassed; a piece of her was pulled like an iron filing to the magnet of shame. How had she never understood what grief had done to Lily? Why had she never even tried? She leaned forward. Lily rolled her eyes.

"Please don't ask about my parents," Lily said. "Not when I'm actually succeeding at being nice."

Nan sat back. *This,* she thought, *is trying harder.* This was the way in which God was pursuing her. She was charged, yet again, to put her own needs aside and serve others. She had fought against it, but now she was doing the difficult work. *This is my contribution,* she thought to herself. *This is my doing more.*

At one year, Bip began to talk with gusto, shouting his first words — *da, mo* — with great hand gestures to go along with them. Charles fawned over him after each word, so that he talked more and more, waited expectantly for accolades after every syllable.

Will, though, didn't begin to talk. It was clear he understood. He did as they told him to and followed his brother's progress with watchful eyes. Lily assumed he was waiting to see what happened next — how this new phenomenon affected Bip before he tried it on for size.

But the months went by. The comparison was bare and bright. Bip played. He pushed trucks around the floor and carried teddy bears. He held out his arms to be picked up and squealed with laughter when Charles held him upside down. Will held on to things — bears, trucks, dishtowels, socks — and would not give them up. When Lily tried to take them, he howled and turned away, hunched over. He squirmed when she tried to hold him, and held his breath, whimpering, until she let him go. He screamed when Charles tried to pick him up, and did not stop screaming after he put him down.

"Please calm down," Lily said to him calmly. "Please calm down," she said to him urgently. "Please, please, please calm down," she said, holding her hair back to keep it from touching him, sunk on her knees like a pilgrim.

Will sat in his high chair and looked at the tray, moved his finger along the grain of the wood. He did not notice the food she put in front of him, could go for hours without eating. When hunger overcame him, he would fuss and cry, drop to his belly on the ground and whine angrily. Lily would bring him something with a straw. He liked straws, as long as they were not striped and the paper had been taken off. He would eat almost anything through them, and so his diet consisted mainly of yogurt thinned with milk, blended juice, vegetable purees. The pediatrician did not discourage this.

"He'll grow out of it," he said, "and he's getting enough vitamins. Just keep it up." So she did, blending everything she made for Bip into a soup for Will. She felt he needed something more — bread, spaghetti, potatoes — and she put them on his tray each meal, but he did not notice them except to push them out of the way.

He liked to play with dominoes, holding them close to his face and touching each dot on each tile over and over again. Sometimes he would pick up a tile and press it to his cheek with his palm, resting it there for a long, long time. When he learned to crawl, he made his way to the front hallway and tapped each black tile on the floor.

This behavior was the easiest for Lily to bear. It was calm; it was silent. She couldn't bear Will at bath time. As soon as she began to run the water, he began to moan, twisting his hands and whimpering. When she turned the water off and sought him out to pick him up, he began to howl. As she lifted him off the floor, he went stiff as a board, kicked his legs violently.

"Shhh," she said. "Shhh."

She tried the water hot, cold, tepid — it

didn't matter. As soon as his feet touched the slick bottom of the tub, the struggle began in earnest, her kneeling, one arm wrapped like a vise around his upper body, locking his arms to his chest, forcing him to remain sitting, as he bucked and rocked and howled. One night he hit his head. One night he bit her. She gave up the bath and, instead, washed his neck, bottom, hands, face, feet with a soft, warm washcloth. Twice a week, she and Charles wrestled to hold him bent over the sink so they could wash his hair. They cut it short, short, short, so shampooing only took a minute. Still, he howled and fought. After these episodes, they let him rock himself back and forth for an hour, until he quieted enough so they could lead him to bed, where he slept with his head underneath the covers.

He began to lose coordination. Things he could do the month before — pick up a ball, shake his head, run without falling down — now seemed hard for him. He started to hold his left arm at an odd angle, and then they noticed he did not stop twisting his left hand.

"What's that, Will?" Charles asked one night at dinner. "Is it a new dance?" He twisted his hand in the same way.

"Don't," Lily said. She put her hand on

Will's, holding it to the table. "He's been doing it all day. He won't stop," she said. She took a deep, labored breath. "Will," she rasped. "Stop."

Charles often came home from church on Sunday to find Bip napping upstairs and Lily sitting on the kitchen floor, staring at Will while Will stared at the wall. One Sunday, though, Charles came home and Will was standing at the kitchen door, unscrewing the doorknob.

"I thought he might like to play with something real," Lily whispered. "I thought maybe he just doesn't like toys." She took a shaky breath. "He's taken them all off. Every one in the house. They're all lying on the floor." She looked up at Charles. "Please help me," she said. "I don't want to find him so disturbing."

"Something's wrong with Will," Nan told James over breakfast.

James looked up from the newspaper. "What do you mean?"

"I don't see him anymore. Lily keeps him upstairs when I'm there. I take Bip for walks; she and I eat lunch while the boys sleep, but she doesn't talk to me, and as soon as Will starts moving upstairs, she's gone."

Nan enjoyed spending more time with Bip, who was as sunny as a child could be. He loved fire trucks and big dogs, ice cream and fountains. They whiled away long afternoons in Washington Square Park together, listening to musicians playing their instruments, playing hide-and-seek behind the trees. But it felt false to Nan. She knew Lily was suffering; she had lost weight and stopped dressing well. She was distant and grey, like a piano with slack, damp chords. And still, she did not tell Nan anything. She simply gave Bip a kiss, transferred his hand from hers to Nan's, and said thank you. Soon, there were no more lunches, no afternoons folding laundry. Nan was a babysitter, nothing more.

"Has Charles said anything?"

"No," James said. But Nan knew he was shouldering the burden at church. He had preached four Sundays in a row, came home late every night, and had taken to pinching the bridge of his nose to ward off headaches.

"I've asked him if there's anything I can help with," James said, "but he just smiles this empty smile and says *Not at all.*" He was softening the story so Nan would not panic. The truth was that Charles was silent. His clothes seemed too big and his eyes were always red. He had begun to stoop even more. When he was in the office, he simply sat at his desk and worked in silence, came in late or left early. He had asked Betsy Bailey to head the Bible study group. He had shortened his office hours. He had stopped answering his home phone.

The congregation asked after him, constantly calling the office, leaving messages that were never returned.

"I'm not sure what to tell them," Marcus said.

"I'm not either," James replied. He was hurt that Charles was not confiding in him, bewildered that Charles was pushing him away, and angry that Charles was forsaking his responsibilities so blatantly. There was work to be done. The church had supported the election of the first black moderator to the General Assembly. Every bus James sent uptown — to the Central Park Be-In, to Martin Luther King at Riverside Church — had been full. He wanted to build on the momentum; instead he was doing Charles's job: hospital visits, sympathy calls, counseling, twice the number of sermons.

"Why don't you stick to the easy stuff for a while?" Marcus asked. "Oppose a Moses highway? Save a historic building?"

"Not religious issues," James said. He had taken to speaking in half sentences that offered no foothold for debate. "Things people would do on their own."

"It must be intimidating to take on the big stuff all the time. You're a brave man."

"I'm not brave," James told him. "I'm frantic."

Marcus nodded. "So what should I tell people?"

"Tell them Charles is working on a sermon series and he'll be back soon." It was the only excuse James could think of that would keep people from calling even more.

"Is he?" Marcus asked.

James shrugged. "I don't know that he isn't."

Charles and Lily took Will to a specialist.

"I hate waiting rooms," Lily said to Charles as they sat in one, cold and surrounded by beige.

"Reverend and Mrs. Barrett," the doctor boomed. An hour ago, he had taken Will away, asked them to stay put. He was sixty, grey-haired, red-faced, thick-handed.

"The good news," the doctor said, "is that it isn't physical." Charles nodded, but Lily tensed. Good news was never followed by no news.

"The bad news is, there's something going on."

"Something what?" Lily asked.

"There's more good news there," the doctor continued. "Ten years ago, I would have told you he had juvenile schizophrenia. Probably would have blamed you, Mom, for it." He gave a little chuckle. Lily wanted to wring his neck.

"It would be best if you just told us," Charles said. "We have already been dealing with this for a long time."

The doctor nodded. "Will is not developing normally."

"We know that," Lily snapped. "We've got twins and we're not blind."

The doctor nodded. "You're lucky there," he said. "Most children are diagnosed later than Will, which makes it harder."

"Harder to cure?" Charles asked. The doctor looked at him, his eyes compassionate and kind. Charles knew it was the way he himself looked at parishioners when they sat across from him, when there was nothing he could do to fix the problems of their lives.

"No," the doctor said, slowly and clearly. "I'm sorry. This will be hard to hear, but Will's symptoms are permanent impairments, and as he grows they will become more pronounced. He will be too heavy to carry, too big for you to bathe. He will not play with other children, go to school, learn to read. As an adult, he will not be able to work. He may become violent. What I'm trying to tell you is that the longer you have him with you, the harder it will become to send him away."

The room was suddenly silent. Charles was aware of the carpet, the desk lamp, the crisp whiteness of the doctor's coat. Lily was so still Charles wondered if she had died. Then she took a stiff, shrill breath and said, "What the hell are you talking about?"

"My recommendation is that you send Will to a home."

"He has a home," Lily said.

"To an institutional home." A heavy stillness fell over them. The doctor looked at Charles, who said nothing.

"We're not going to do that," Lily said. She looked as if every bone in her face had been sharpened by a whetstone.

"Perhaps you'd like to discuss it," the doctor said. "You need to think about each other and about your other son."

"I am thinking about him," Lily said. "We will not keep one son and send his brother away."

"Lily," Charles said, his voice thin as water.

"What?" she asked, turning toward him

like the crack of a whip. "You're not considering it, are you? You're not entertaining the idea, wondering if it is some sort of sacrifice God wants you to make?" Each word was a jab with the tip of a sword.

Charles did not answer. He needed a moment, just a moment, to think about things, to pray. He felt Lily grow as hard as cement.

He met the doctor's eyes and said, "It would help if we knew what to call it. Does Will's diagnosis have a name?"

"Not universally," the doctor said, "but we have started to call it autism."

Charles felt Lily relax, just a little, as he knew she would. A word was a hook to hang things on. A word was something to research, to dissect and analyze. A word was a definition; a word gave Will a place on the page.

"Thank you," Charles said, and led Lily out of the room.

"I want another doctor," Lily said as soon as the door had closed. "One who doesn't chuckle." She was clutching the neck of her coat.

So they went to see more doctors, any doctor anyone mentioned to them. The waiting rooms were all poorly lit, cold, manned by women in glasses who did not smile. The doctors sat behind huge desks and never came out from behind them, never shook their hands.

One sat behind his desk and said, gravely, "This could be schizophrenia."

Lily stood and walked out.

The one after that asked her to leave the room and said to Charles, "Unfortunately, we have found that the cause in many of these cases is unfeelingness in the mother — coldness, if you will. I see from her file that her parents are deceased. Have you noticed that she harbors any animosity toward the boy?"

Charles stood and walked out.

The third said, "Not schizophrenia. But I'm not a specialist. Let me give you a name." He wrote it out on a slip of paper, and it was the name of the chuckling doctor.

"We're back," Lily said, sitting down in a chair across from his desk. "And we're not sending him away."

Charles said, "What do we do?"

The doctor kept his face grave. "That," he said, "is the bad news. We don't really know."

"There's no treatment?" Lily asked.

He shook his head.

"What happens next?" Charles asked.

"It gets worse, I'm afraid."

And it did, though not as terribly as they had dreamed. Bip got bigger, more outgoing, sunnier. Will stopped following him with his eyes. Stopped following all of them, assumed a downcast gaze. Bip stopped banging on tables, and Will kept rocking back and forth. Bip learned how to dance, and Will seemed entirely caught up with the strange, silent music in his head.

Nan's calendar reminded her that the twins' second birthday was approaching, but there was no invitation to a party, no mention of a gathering, no news at all. In fact, it had been weeks since she had been to Lily's house.

Lily had said, "The boys have doctor's appointments this week. Can I call you when we're ready for you to come back?"

Nan had not heard from her since.

Something would have to be done. These people were her friends and they were in trouble. She would not abandon Lily, even if Lily wanted to be left alone. She went to the brownstone. She took, after much thought, a box of clementines, because they were bright enough to be cheerful and practical enough to not seem as if she were trying. She arrived in the late afternoon.

It was a cold day, but Nan had not worn

gloves; the doorknocker was freezing. She raised it gingerly and rapped it three times against the grey door. She heard footsteps and then the peephole cover swung up and down. There was a pause. Nan guessed Lily was sighing. The door opened. Lily stood with her hand on the edge of it, half in and half out of the entryway.

She stared at Nan and then said, "Why are you here?"

"We're worried about you," Nan said, her feet cold from the chill of the stoop.

Lily stared at her, as impassive as Nan had ever seen her, all of her armor back on, as if none of the past year had happened, as if Nan had never helped her, as if they had never learned how to be comfortable with one another.

"Did someone die?" Nan asked.

Lily closed her eyes for a long moment. "No," she said, finally. "Will has autism."

"What?" Nan said, too stunned to say anything more.

"It's a brain disorder." Lily's voice was factual. Nan covered her mouth with her hand.

"Oh, all right," Lily said. "You might as well come in. I know everybody's beside themselves, and it will be easier for you to tell them than for me." She stepped back and gestured Nan through the hallway into the kitchen. Nan put her gift on the plain wood table and sat down.

"Thank you for not bringing flowers," Lily said as she filled the kettle. "Will can't stand the smell."

"You're welcome," Nan said, looking around the room, out the door to the garden. She should get a group of people together to help Lily keep the house clean, help her plant and weed.

Lily took a tin of tea from the cupboard, started spooning it into a white teapot. She put the teapot on the table in front of Nan, placed the strainer beside it. She turned to take two mugs off their hooks above the sink. She sat down.

"I'm lonely as a tied-up dog," she said.

Nan opened her mouth.

"Don't say how awful," Lily said. She placed the strainer over Nan's mug, filled it with hot tea. "Say: 'Don't be ridiculous.' That's what my parents always used to say."

"Don't be ridiculous," Nan said.

"It's not quite as desperate as it sounds," Lily said. She took a sip of tea. "It could be so much worse — they tested him for things that were so, so much worse. But it's hard, and it will not get easier. He will not grow out of it. He will never dress without a fight, bathe without a struggle. I will always have to force him," she said, as if she were realizing it for the first time.

"Every day I will have to make him kick and bite and scream. No matter how clearly I know that it is best for him, it's just awful, and every night I know it's waiting, like a bludgeoning. The doctors say we should institutionalize him. But I won't do that. I won't make him an orphan."

Nan felt as if she had come out of herself, as if she had picked herself up out of her body and was standing in the corner. As Lily spoke, Nan knew with excruciating clarity that this was what she had once hoped for — to have her revenge, for Lily to be knocked from her pedestal. Even now, she could feel a small part of herself thrilling to the information like a hummingbird. She wanted to knock herself to the ground.

Lily took a long sip of tea and then said, "I used to think my parents died for no reason." She ran her finger along a groove in the table. "But now I think they died so I would know that Will isn't dead. I think they died so I would know that Will's life is *life* — no matter how awful it appears." She set her mug down. "It took a long, long time for their deaths to be useful," she said. "I had to persevere."

Upstairs, Bip called out, and Nan could hear both boys banging at their cribs.

"Now you're in for the whole show," Lily said, heading upstairs. She returned carrying Will, Bip running in front of her.

"Here we are!" she said, almost cheerful. She jogged Will up and down a bit and put her cheek to his hair.

"Would you take him?" she asked Nan. "Then I can get Bip a snack." She maneuvered Will onto Nan's lap. He was heavy and stiff, as angular as the room around her. He dug into her like a stick.

Lily found bread and took cheese out of the fridge.

Nan was stunned. The child on her lap was pitiful. His hair was so short Nan could see his scalp; his arms and fingers were cricked at strange angles. He seemed beyond repair.

Lily saw her looking at Will but looked away.

"Now, Bippo," Lily said. "Two slices of cheese or one?"

"Two!" Bip yelled, and Lily smiled.

Will made his strange howl that passed for crying.

"They think he can't hear well." Lily did not look at Nan. Her voice was clinical. "But they don't know. He wouldn't respond to noises even if he could hear them, so they can't tell."

Nan nodded. Will struggled to get off her lap, his movements stiff and clumsy. She held on to him; he struggled harder in her lap. She couldn't tell if his squirming was natural, or if he just didn't like her. It was overwhelming, this stark house, this lifeless boy, this vibrant toddler, this exhausted mother. One dream given; one dream taken away. What was the point of persevering? What was the reward?

The human body is a clear and honest thing, Nan thought as she sat there encountering this boy who was the clear and honest manifestation of all the things in the world she did not want to be true.

"Here, give him back," Lily said. She stood over Nan, stony with anger.

"No, it's all right," Nan answered.

"It is not. You can't stand him. Give him back."

Lily was correct. On that day, in that moment, that instant of Nan's life, Nan couldn't stand him. She depended on the world outside herself, where the sidewalks were sturdy, the walls upright, where she could tell herself, *Good things happen to people, so good things will happen to me.* Lily's house, that day, was underneath a rock, the place where bad things happened and could not be fixed. It frightened Nan: What if, after all she had been through, she had a child who did not look at her, who never smiled, who shut himself away?

"I'm sorry," Nan whispered.

Lily stared at her with a mixture of hate and resignation in her eyes. She could have said that Nan was a terrible friend, a hypocrite, a faithless Christian, and Nan would have agreed with her. Instead she said, "Please don't come back here anymore."

Eighteen

The boys turned two. When they went to the park, Bip found other children to play with, running after them up the slide, showing them his toys and looking at theirs. Will sat under a bench, unmoving. It was hard to think that he would never be like his brother.

"Is he okay?" other mothers asked her.

"Yes," Lily said plainly. "He's autistic."

"Oh," the other mothers said, then stepped away to confer with one another.

"Is it contagious?" Lily heard them whispering. "Do you think she has him under control?" Plenty of women called their children to them, shielded them from Will with the flats of their hands.

It didn't matter. Lily was determined that Bip have a normal childhood, that he go to the park and eat peanut butter sandwiches with the crusts cut off and swing on the swings. Since she no longer had Nan to help, Will would have to do those things as well, even though they were not the things he liked to do.

Will liked sidewalks. He liked to step over the cracks, could walk up and down their block for hours. Every Saturday morning, when Charles was home to watch Bip, Lily took Will outside alone. One of the marvels of New York City was that it was deserted on weekend mornings, quiet and still, so she and Will could stay on their street for hours and not see a single person or car.

As they walked down the steps of the brownstone, Lily could see Will set up his perimeter, deciding how far he would go, how many squares of pavement he would traverse today. Then, head lowered, he walked his proscribed section of sidewalk again and again, stepping over each crack and laughing. It was not a laugh that brought Lily joy. It was more like the "hah" sound that Bip made when he jumped on something deliberately. Still, she could sit on the stoop and enjoy the quiet, enjoy the sight of her son engaged in activity. Will would walk as long as she would let him, actually making sound.

Lily liked these mornings, these predictable hours when she had the time and space to give Will what he wanted, to leave him alone in his self-created world. She liked when his desires intersected with what she found acceptable. She was outside with her son. He was breathing fresh air. She could sit still. It was almost normal. Of course, he would scream and kick when it was time to go inside, and she would be swift and merciless in restraining him, sweeping him indoors so as not to wake the neighbors. It always ended badly. Everything did.

Nothing ended badly with Bip. He was delighted with everyone and everything, his eyes wide, fingers pointing. "What's that?" he asked, awestruck at a new animal, a new tree, a new car.

"That's yellow," Lily reminded him. "That's a taxi."

"Taxi," he said, as if it were the most marvelous word he had ever tasted.

He reminded her of her parents: how gay they had been, how lilting and full of life. She thought of how often her father would pinch her mother's cheek or kiss her on the back of the neck, and how often they would laugh and laugh. She thought of how comfortable they were in their skins, how they had moved in a buoyed, carefree way, like ships in a harbor.

Bip tried to share his joy with Will. When Will sat in a corner of the kitchen, Bip ran in and out of the backyard, bringing leaves and dirt to set on the floor — far enough away that Will would not be disturbed, but close enough so Will could see them. He spoke to Will. He dragged his canvas bag of blocks into Will's room and built towers while Will hid under a blanket. It was Lily's greatest solace that Will did not push Bip away.

Her greatest anguish was their difference. It was dreadfully clear to her that while Bip was like her parents, Will was like her: always serious, distracted, dissatisfied. If she had been different, if she had let her parents cajole her into going to parties, to have more fun, to try something new, would Will be normal? If she had joined in the fun, would Will not be alone? She missed them. She wanted to be more like them, but day by day she became more entwined with Will.

It wasn't fair. It wasn't fair that, after all her grief and loneliness, she could not just enjoy Bip, her lovely boy who played, sang songs, and held her hand. It wasn't fair that she gave him divided attention, would never look at him without a trace of impatience or despair. It wasn't his fault that Will had been born the very definition of a soul apart. It wasn't Will's fault that Bip had been given all the easiness, while he had been given all the hard. And it wasn't fair that she knew so intimately the ways in which Will suffered, the agony of living in a world that did not offer comfort, the particular desperation that drove a person to howl.

She wanted to believe that Will might be content in his own world, that he didn't need the same things everyone else did to be happy. That it was possible to be happy in a million ways. Charles had preached that a hundred times, that people did not have to be alike to be connected; being different need not be a tragedy. But she could not believe it, then or now.

She was angry. She railed at God. *I married a minister,* she yelled. *Against all my better judgment. And he loves you. He believes in you with every fiber of his being, and this is what you do?* She hated that her anger made Charles's God seem real to her. Acid burned through her bones. But she knew how to put it away. She knew how to cry, how to pound the bed and kick the wall. She knew how to arrange herself so that her grief sat quietly behind the closed closet door. It was torture.

Charles had given James permission to tell the congregation that Will was sick, as long as he didn't mention autism. All day long,

James took calls from people asking, "What can we do?" "How can we help?" He also spent every free minute calling experts he thought might know the answer to those questions. But he'd gotten all the answers there were on the first two days: the name of one doctor in Los Angeles, one in Baltimore, and two mental institutions. That was all. Everything there was to be known about autism could be learned in a week. The books and articles he'd found took up one lone corner of his desk. And it exhausted him. He was used to forging a path, to deciding on a course of action and chasing it as fast as he could. That was his call, and it invigorated him. Standing still drained him of everything.

"I don't mean to add more work to your pile," Marcus said, one day, "but there's a boy at my own church like Will."

James looked up. Marcus did not often talk about himself. James knew he lived in Harlem, took the subway to work, drank Coke instead of coffee. He arrived at work with a backpack, and James knew he studied at his desk on slow days, but he had never volunteered any specific information about his classes, or his family, or his friends. James put down his pen, closed his file; he did not want to miss anything.

"I used to be afraid of him," Marcus continued. "Not like he was going to beat me up or anything — he's just a kid. But I didn't know what to do. I didn't know if I should look at his mom, or not look at her; I didn't know if she wanted me to see him as different or if she wanted me to try to see him as the same. So I just avoided her. And the more I avoided her, the guiltier I felt, and the guiltier I felt, the more frightened I became. That's how I knew it was wrong — the avoiding. That's how I knew I had to do something different."

"What did you do?" James asked.

Marcus shrugged. "I tried to give him a cookie," he said. "Just like I would any other little kid at coffee hour. His mom came running up to me and grabbed my arm so hard I thought she was going to twist it off. He can't eat sugar. It makes him crazy. Lock him in the closet crazy."

Before he could stop himself, James laughed. "I'm sorry," he said. "It isn't funny."

"It *is* funny," Marcus said, smiling a wide smile. "I did something stupid. But now his mom talks to me sometimes, tells me a little bit about her life. It's hard. She feels totally alone. When I told her that Will was just like her son, I thought she was going to cry."

He looked at James sheepishly. "I said I'd tell her if Charles finds a doctor, or a medicine. Do you think it's all right to pass that kind of stuff along?"

"Of course," James said. "Charles would want you to. But they haven't found anything, yet." As the words came out of his mouth, James realized how tired he was of saying them.

Marcus cleared his throat. "She asked about sending him away." He looked down as he said this. "She doesn't want to, but he bites and kicks, and she has a younger kid."

James nodded. "I know a couple of places," he said. "I can give her some names."

"Have you seen them?" Marcus asked. "She can't pay, and she's afraid that the free ones . . ." He lifted his shoulders and trailed off.

"I haven't seen them," James said, straightening in his chair. "I *haven't.*" He couldn't believe this was true. He couldn't believe there was an option he hadn't explored.

"Let's go," James said to Marcus. It was something useful to do.

But first, James went to see Charles. The brownstone was as Nan had described it: solemn and tired. Lily's lean furniture gave no quarter for comfort, and James was relieved to walk into Charles's office, in which there were two leather club chairs and a brass-tufted ottoman on which to rest one's feet. Charles looked more alive than he had at church in the past weeks, but still frail.

"How are you?" James asked.

"Not well," Charles answered, clearly far away. "How are you?"

"Tired," James said. "Pretty much alone."

"I'm sorry," Charles said. His eyes were sunken and empty. He looked at James, his whole body an apology.

"Tell me," James said.

Charles took a deep breath. "I don't know what to do," he said. "The appointments are agony. Every time they examine Will, they put him in a hospital gown. It's torture for him to change clothes, but they make him. And they don't let us stay in the room. We have to sit in the waiting room and listen to him howl. Can you imagine what that does to Lily?"

James wanted to take Charles's hand, to enfold him in a hug, but the strain had starched them both into formality. "What does it do to you?"

Charles shook his head like a dog shaking off water. "I can't explain why we just sit there." He paused, now vibrant in his pain. "Except that we want them to see that we can handle this. They think we can't. They think we're endangering our family."

"Are you?" James was searching.

Charles let his head hang. "I don't think so. Not now, not while the boys are little. Bip loves him. But when Will gets bigger . . . the prognosis is so dire."

"Who makes the decision?" James asked, softly, gathering information, hoping to ground them in the present.

Charles laughed, the clang of a spoon on a tin can. "There's the rub. I do. Just me. Because I'm the husband, the father, the man. They only need one signature."

James could not imagine a world in which either of them would do that to their wives.

"I have an appointment to see one of the homes," James said. "I'm taking Marcus with me. Do you want to come?"

Charles put his fist up between them. "He isn't your son."

It was the first time James had ever seen Charles angry, and it was terrifying. "No, he isn't. But Marcus knows another boy like him. And you know me, Charles. I have to do *something*."

Charles stared at him. Of course he wanted to go with them. Of course he wanted to know what the future held; he needed to prepare, to research, to form a thesis, to prepare an argument. But he needed Lily more than he ever had or had ever thought he would. He could not betray her.

"Tell me how it is," he said.

Charles and Lily saw more doctors.

"Autism," one told them, following the words in the medical dictionary with his fingertip, "is absorption in fantasy to the exclusion of reality." He looked up and stared at them.

They stared back. Charles did not speak. He had stopped speaking, for the most part. He said *Good day* to people on the street and inquired whether Lily wanted coffee in the morning, though he knew she always did. But he did not ask for people's thoughts and did not share his own. He did not want to say the words that now defined him: sick, harrowed, apart. Apart from the church, which expected him to work, though he could barely hold his eyes open. Apart from his city, which had once seemed full of possibility and now seemed full of hopelessness and incompetence. Apart from his wife, who was persevering in spite of everything — who had picked herself up and was carrying on. Most of all, apart from his own sons, one of whom sat like a gargoyle in his room, and one of whom needed a gladness Charles did not possess.

Finally, Lily said, "I don't mind that definition, except that it's completely inadequate."

The doctor looked back down. "Mental introversion in which the attention or interest is fastened upon the victim's own ego."

Lily shook her head. "Victim," she said.

The doctor raised his eyebrows. He moved his finger down the page. "A self-centered mental state from which reality tends to be excluded."

Lily turned to Charles. "Do you think that's true?" she asked. "That he's just created his own world?"

Charles did not answer, though he thought it might be possible. Will did not seem vacant. He was focused on something, cared enough to demand sameness, monotony, day after day.

"Do you think he's happy in there?" Lily asked.

Charles did not answer.

The doctor said, "I don't see how anyone could be happy, not in this abnormal state."

Lily stood up, almost flung her chair across the room.

Finally, they went to see a young psychiatrist who had long hair and wore a brown tweed jacket. He ushered them into a brightly lit office, motioned them to a hard, shallow couch, and sat across from them with his elbows on his knees, ready to listen. Charles and Lily sat stiffly, hands on laps.

"What we want to know," Lily said, "is if Will's happy. Or if he *can* be happy like this. In his condition."

The doctor sat back in surprise. "Oh," he said, "I thought we were going to talk about you."

Charles and Lily looked at him questioningly.

He fumbled in his jacket pocket, found his datebook, opened it. "Yes, right here. The Reverend and Mrs. Barrett."

"Doctor," Charles said.

"Doctor and Mrs. Barrett."

"No," Charles corrected him. "The Reverend and Dr. Barrett."

The psychiatrist looked panicked and confused. "I'm not an expert in children," he said. "I treat parents coping with abnormal offspring. I thought we were going to talk about you."

"We want to talk about our son," Lily said.

The psychiatrist did not meet her eyes. "I imagine you are asking 'Why did this happen to me?' "

"No," Lily corrected him. "We are asking why this happened to Will, and what we can do."

"But you must not ignore your own needs."

"What I need," Lily said, "is for someone to tell me how to help my son. I need someone to tell me how much help is enough, to tell me what will make him happy. I don't care what happy looks like. I don't care how uncomfortable his happy will make other people feel. If he wants to swing from the lamppost every day at five o'clock — if doing that will make him laugh, will make him feel *something* — then he can swing from the lamppost every day at five o'clock. We are not concerned with what other people think of him. We are concerned only with how he feels within himself."

Charles forced himself to speak. "We want to know more about him. To understand how his mind works; how he might express his needs. Things we might not be able to guess on our own."

"I'm afraid that's impossible," the doctor said. "These children give us so little; it's almost futile to study them."

At the word *study,* a part of Charles collapsed. Study was his bulwark, his chart, his compass. If Will could not be studied, what kind of father could he be?

He felt Lily looking at him and knew she sensed this sharp splinter of pain. It was ironic that they understood each other so well, now; that intimacy had come to them through the suffering of their child.

"I think you should just tell us what you want to tell us," Lily said. "Tell us the worst thing you have to tell."

"All right," the psychiatrist sighed deeply, adjusted his glasses. "Children like Will can't interact with others. They can't look outside themselves. So, I think the worst I can tell you is that he will never love."

Charles felt his eyes jump, his heart slow.

"We love *him*," Lily said.

"But he cannot love you. He cannot even know you. He cannot understand abstract concepts. He will only ever connect to the concrete. He will not know friendship or passion or God." The doctor closed his book.

Lily put a hand on Charles's arm. It was a gesture so vulnerable he almost pulled away.

"God knows him," Charles said quietly.

The doctor shrugged.

In that moment, Lily vowed she would put her anger to good use. Since she could not be a gracious or patient mother, she would be a determined and tenacious one. She would prove these doctors wrong. She would find other doctors, commission studies, raise money, and find a cure.

James and Marcus decided to start at the home with the best reputation, so they had something to compare the others to. James made the appointment. The school, as it called itself, was housed in an old hospital far uptown, on the edge of the East River, where it had been built so that the current could carry infections swiftly away.

"Don't worry about the money," James told Marcus when they met on the subway platform. "If this is the right place for your friend's son, we'll get her the money. That I know I can do."

The director met them on the front steps of the building, which was smaller than James had expected, and shabbier. The columns holding up the porch were chipped and scuffed, there was moss growing on the foundation. In contrast, the director was a crisply starched woman with a white headband holding back her curly hair.

"Good morning," she said, shaking their hands. "We're so glad you're here."

"Really?" James was surprised. "May I ask why?"

The director opened the door and led them inside. "We don't get much recognition from the churches," she said. "Or from the government. There are so many other things to be outraged about today."

James and Marcus followed her down a marble hallway that smelled of disinfectant. She took a key ring from her belt and unlocked a metal door.

"This is the nursery," she said. James looked past her into a wide, square room full of light. There were cribs pressed next to one another along every inch of wall. In the middle were four rocking chairs, and two old blankets lay on the ground. A nurse was sitting in one of the rocking chairs, dangling a rattle in front of a baby who had crawled off the blankets and was sitting on the floor. "Mostly, we have mongoloid children here," the director said. "That's really the only condition we can diagnose at birth."

She turned and led them back into the hall, up a wide staircase with an ornate banister. The building, obviously, had once been very grand.

"It's a nice thing you're doing," the director said as they followed her up the stairs, "touring for your friends. Very thoughtful. Parents have a hard time making a decision.

So often they pick the first name on the list, wherever their doctor tells them to go. They don't know they have choices."

When she reached the landing she stopped, turned, and smiled. "We keep everything clean — you've seen that. The floors are mopped daily, beds are changed at least twice a week, more if necessary." James could tell she had begun her standard speech. She stood with one hand on the banister; her voice was practiced and a little loud for the space. "We've passed every health inspection," she continued. "Not that we do it because of the inspections. We'd do it without the inspections. But it's a feat. We spend most of our time handling our students."

James took note of the word *students* and the word *handling.* "Do parents visit?" he asked.

"Not often," the director said. "They're always welcome to make an appointment, but most don't. Most don't want to know."

She led them down another hallway, this one darker and narrower. James could feel Marcus starting to lag behind.

"These are the boys you asked about," the director said grandly, opening another door. Inside the room were ten boys. Half were sitting on their beds, staring into space. One boy was at the window, pushing his finger in and out of a sunbeam. One was sitting on the floor, a meticulous stack of blocks in front of him. There were no nurses.

"These are some of our easier ones, really," the director said, giving them time to take in the room. "Everyone here is prone to outbursts, but these boys respond to medication quite well."

James understood she was talking about sedatives, not medicines to make them speak or learn.

"Do you teach them anything?" Marcus asked, his voice smaller and tighter than James had ever heard it.

"Of course," the director said. She took a small notebook from the pocket of her skirt and read from a list she had written in pencil.

"And is that enough?" James asked when she was done.

"Enough for what?" the director asked. Her voice had changed, become hard, almost challenging. She pointed into the room. "Before he came here, this boy never had a bath. Most of them arrive with mats in their hair, severely malnourished. I'm not saying their parents don't love them. All the parents love them, Reverend MacNally. But they don't know how to care for them. We do."

As she spoke, James heard a banging — loud, insistent — and voices yelling over it.

The director's eyes flew to the ceiling. "Now, those are the boys who were kept in closets," she said. "Those were the ones who came here with concussions and broken arms." She put her notebook back in her pocket. "Tell your friends we keep them separate here — the quiet ones and the violent ones. Some places don't have enough space, have to keep them together. That results in injuries, as you can imagine. As long as he's calm, your friend's child would be kept here. You should tell her that. Tell her we hardly ever have to use the locks on the doors."

Afterward, James and Marcus stood on the greyed marble steps of the building, unable to say a word, trying to absorb what they had seen. The river in front of them was the color of steel, its currents the shape of hooks and cords. James felt that he would drown in what he had seen: the ignorance, the callousness, the cunning. He was short of breath, suffocated by the understanding that some things *should* break a man — that to remain whole would be inhuman.

"How can this be?" Marcus asked faintly.

James felt cruel for bringing him here, for making it an outing, for thinking Marcus was prepared. He wanted to apologize, but that wouldn't do either of them any good.

"It can't," he said.

As soon as he got home, he called Charles and shouted, "If you ever send Will to a place like that, I'm going to punch you in the throat."

NINETEEN

Another year passed. Lily spent every hour she could at the library. Marcus had agreed to watch the boys during his lunch break and for a few hours on Friday afternoons. He needed the money, and she needed someone who was not utterly shocked by Will's affect. She fed both boys before he arrived, put them down for their naps, and called every hour from the phone booth next to the ladies' room in the library lobby to see if she needed to come home.

"We're fine," Marcus said, even when she could hear Bip bouncing a ball in the background. "You know kids are always better for the babysitters."

So she stayed at the study tables as long as possible, reading every study about children's medicine, every footnote, just in case there was something to glean. At home, she set the alarm to wake up in the middle of the night to call doctors in Zurich or

London, had learned to take notes while cradling the phone on one shoulder and holding one of the twins in the other arm.

She lugged home bags full of books. This produced in Charles an aching wave of nostalgia. As she sat at the kitchen table turning pages, the smell of book dust and marble floor cleaner drifted across to him. Immediately, he was twenty-two again, secure in his place at the university and in the world. He was the boy who loved the girl with the furrowed brow and the hunch of concentration. He was the boy who loved her so much his throat constricted when she walked by and whose head went light when she spoke. Now, when she spoke, his heart was lead.

One night, late, when the living room was dark except for their two reading lamps, Lily looked up from her latest medical journal.

"Maybe we should go back to the psychiatrist," she said. "It says here that there are hidden benefits to psychiatry, surprise results."

Charles did not answer. He was lying on the couch reading a plumbing manual. He liked, now, to read manuals, to imagine assembling parts into systems. He was hoping to fix the pipe under the kitchen sink, which leaked when the weather was cold. He wanted to repair one thing in their house, the house that had been here long before them, and would be here long after them, its sturdy bricks and good windows sheltering families, children running up and down the stairs. He wanted to preserve it, because that was how he had once felt inside of it: protected and preserved.

It was the way he used to feel about God. He wished he still did. He tried to; he tried to pray in the bathroom at night, leaning on the sink, head bowed in front of the mirror. He wanted to bring prayer into this house, like heat from the radiators. But the words did not come. Or rather, the only words that came were the ones to the prayers of intercession, prayers he used to make every Sunday, prayers for the poor, the hungry, the sick, and the suffering, for prisoners and those who imprisoned them, for those who were dying and those who mourned.

But Will was not any of those things. He was not poor; he was not dying. He was not hungry or oppressed. He wasn't even sick, not really. Autism was not a disease, it was a condition. Charles supposed it could be said that Will was imprisoned in the state of being called autism and that he suffered there. But no one was sure. No one knew what Will thought, because Will did not tell them. All their worry about him could be unnecessary, or it could be wildly insufficient. They would never know.

Charles did not want to go back to the psychiatrist; their first visit had been the worst day of his life, the day he had discovered a chasm in the middle of his soul. On one side sat Will. Will who would never be normal, would never be the boy Charles had wished for, would never even know how much Charles loved him. Will, who would feel, despite all Charles's best efforts, exactly the way Charles had felt around his own father — overlooked and misunderstood.

On the other side sat God. In spite of everything, Charles had not lost his faith. He felt its solace shimmering across the divide, warm as a campfire. Oh, how Charles wanted to walk into the expanse of peace he had once known. It was still there, as beautiful and delicious as it had been on the first day he had experienced it, the first day he had stepped into it and felt all his doubt melt away. He knew he could give himself to God and God would make him at peace with Will's suffering.

He said nothing to Lily.

He understood, now, that he had failed her. He had never understood her grief. He had not fathomed how distinctly it defined her. He had thought he could heal her. Now he knew he had been a fool, useless to her and to so many others he had counseled, asking them to look beyond their suffering, believing that his empathy was any kind of balm. He did not want to count the times and ways in which he had been wrong.

And he had failed Bip. He had no energy for running or singing or jumping up and down the front steps. He did not want to tell stories at the dinner table or kneel at the side of the bathtub to play with the blue and yellow boats. The thought of teaching Bip to throw a baseball was grief incarnate. How could he take joy in one son's childhood, when his other's was so bleak? But also, how could he not?

Shame was the ground in which he now lived. Its dirt was dry and coarse and laced with an arsenic that paralyzed him, so Charles did not try to rise. He laid his head on a cushion and let the darkness hollow him out.

Lily threw a pencil; it hit him just above the ear. He dragged himself upright and forced himself to look at her. Her face was dark and jagged. She was no longer sturdy; she was gaunt and fragile. He realized he had not kissed her for months, or held her hand, or hugged her. These thoughts came from far away and took a long time to reach him. Long enough for him to realize that he was, once again, failing.

"You're just like Will," she said. "You've gone cold and stony and silent. I can't have two of you like that, Charles. I really can't."

Charles watched her lips move and knew she was the perfect mother for Will: ordered, precise, uncomplicated by God or any sense of calling except to arrange Will's life to make it bearable. She had not given up on him for one second since he had been diagnosed. And, despite her tireless efforts to find a treatment, she wasn't desperate to change Will; she just wanted to help him be happy.

Charles was not even a mediocre father. He was a man whose life had been propelled by love and God. Two ideas never seen, never proven to exist. He lived entirely in the abstract, and therefore, he was a man with a life his son could never share.

For the entirety of their marriage, he had wondered if Lily had as much to offer him as God. Now, it seemed, she was offering him more.

"Okay," he said to his wife. "Hand me a book."

And so he began to study with her, to

learn medical words and phrases, to read between the dry, clinical lines. They were both aware of how closely this paralleled their courtship: days researching, nights of discussion. And they were both aware of how much they'd changed. Then, there had been hundreds of books on the topics they had debated; now there were two. Then, books had been full of possibility, now they were cruel and dire. But it felt familiar, an echo of who they had been when they were young, even if, now, they were ancient.

Charles had not been in the church for weeks. There was nothing James could do to hide it, no excuse he could give the parishioners who called. They were tired of seeing James in the pulpit; they coughed as he spoke, turned the pages of their programs to find the number of the next hymn. Without Charles's deep insight, James's calls to service seemed chaotic, his explication of the scriptures ordinary.

James no longer begrudged Charles his absence. Having seen the reality of the options, he knew Charles had chosen the right one, and if it meant Charles had to stay at home, James would help him. He took Bible study back from Betsy Bailey, he lengthened his own office hours, he thought about offering to read one of Charles's sermons for him, so that the congregation could hear Charles's words without his having to come to church. He thought about writing a sermon for Charles, himself. He would do anything to keep the session from officially declaring that Charles was not doing his job.

It didn't work. Alan Oxman came to see James. He sat in the chair in the corner, crossed his legs, wiped his glasses on his tie. "Charles is not . . . around," Alan said.

"No," James answered. He closed his eyes. "He needs some time."

"We've given him time."

James opened his eyes, angry. "He's in the dark, Alan. His son is ill and he doesn't know what to do."

Alan nodded. "I understand," he said. "But this isn't what we signed up for."

James realized he meant that *he* wasn't what they'd signed up for, at least not without Charles's tempering hand. "I'm doing the best I can," he said.

"But you can't go it alone for much longer."

"What's the alternative?"

"Ask Charles to take leave, officially, and then we can bring in an interim."

James shook his head. He was afraid that

if Charles knew the church was in good hands, he would never come back.

"Just hang on," he said. "Let me talk to him some more."

Alan Oxman nodded again.

As soon as Alan had left the building, James strode straight to the manse, paced through the rooms looking for Nan. He found her sitting on their bed, annotating sheet music.

"They want to let Charles go," he said. He realized he was more afraid than he'd ever been of anything, except going to war. He sat down on the end of the bed. "I'm afraid they're going to let him slip away." He took a deep breath to crack the hard surface of his foreboding. "I can't let that happen. We have to find the doctors and the scientists, the teachers and the nurses and the politicians. We can't make him do all of that on his own."

James stopped, because Nan was frozen. She had put her music aside as he talked, moved to sit on the edge of the mattress as he had paced in the small space between the bed and the wall. Now she was staring straight ahead, back stiff, hands clasped tensely in her lap. He stepped forward to touch her shoulder, but she bent over until her head was almost touching her knees.

"I already let them go," she said, her voice muffled. "I went to Lily's house, and I held Will, and he was so awful. I couldn't bear it. I didn't help. I ran away."

James knelt in front of her, as quickly as he could, and put one hand on her hair.

"I've just been pretending," Nan said, woodenly. "My father took me to see all of those people, made me shake their hands. He cared about them, really cared. But I was afraid of them. I hated looking them in the eye."

It was not a small confession; James knew Nan had been carrying this gnarled pith of shame almost as long as she had been alive. For once, he took a moment to think before he spoke. She needed him to absolve her.

But he needed her more. He needed her diplomacy and tact, her clear-headed composure, her stubbornness and poise. He needed her faith to be unclouded and insistent. He needed her, just for today, to not need *him.*

"You have to tell me what to do," he said.

To his relief, Nan straightened up and looked him in the eye.

"You have to get Charles back," she said.

So James made another trip to the brownstone, sat across from Charles in one of the

418

low-armed chairs.

"Don't leave me," he said.

"What?" Charles said.

"I can tell you're thinking about leaving, and I don't want you to." James was gripping the leather with both hands.

Charles smiled wanly, looked James in the eye. "I've seen the limits of my faith," he said. "I see the end of the illusion — where the sea turns to cardboard, peters out, is left to sand. I see the desert. I see how close it is. One more disaster, one more sickness, one more death to grieve — one more piece of my faith given away and I will be lost. I no longer have enough to share. One more person asking me to confirm the love of God, and I will be empty."

All James could do was nod. "You've always said that doubt, the limit, was in us, not in God."

"It is," Charles said, "and that's the tragedy." He looked at the ceiling. "Can you do it alone?"

"I don't want to," James said.

Charles nodded, but James could tell from the length of his face and the hollows in his eyes that Charles did not have any reassurance to give him.

"You need to preach," James said.

"I don't have anything to say," Charles

419

told him.

"You have to think of something," James countered, his voice urgent. "You have to tell them what's going on. You don't have to be wise or inspirational, but you have to tell them something about Will."

Charles looked at him blankly. "I don't want to parade him about like a monkey at the zoo."

James sighed. "You can't keep pretending," he said. "They think he's going to be cured. They think you're going to stand up one day and say he's better. So they don't understand what you're going through. You have to tell them the truth. This is your *life*. Preach about it."

At a loss for what else to do, Charles took James's advice. He put on his black robe, sat through the hymns and the readings, prayed over the offering plates, and climbed the stairs to the pulpit.

"If you haven't seen my son Will lately," he began, "you might be startled. He keeps his head down, looks at the floor instead of meeting your eye. He moves awkwardly, jerks his hands and legs." Charles looked out at his congregation, saw those who had bowed their heads in hopes of evasion, and those who looked straight at him, bright-eyed with pity. He saw people who understood, the people who could not understand but wanted to, people who wanted him to just stop talking. He cleared his throat. "He has been diagnosed with autism." The church seemed twice as large to him. He was aware of the darkness of its pews, the dullness of its marble, the somber grey suits, the sparkling rings and bracelets. He was aware of the echo of his own voice.

"There is no treatment." He took a slow breath. "I have seen enough doctors to know that Will cannot be cured. That prayer will not be answered." He felt the church grow still, the faces of his congregation attentive, waiting.

"I expect that what you want to ask me is, have I lost my faith in God? Despite this evidence to the contrary, do I still believe God is with me?"

The congregation rustled, sat forward, looked at him with apologetic fervor in their eyes.

"Yes," Charles said. "I do. God *can* ease this suffering, as God has eased all of my other suffering. God can help me to believe that there is a reason and a plan. God can help me be happy. The lure of that is almost irresistible."

He put down his notes, put his hands on

421

either edge of the pulpit. "If I turn to God, God will allow me to look at my son, to watch him playing, solitary, in his room, and think: *This is all right.*"

Charles found that his throat was tight and the rest of him was electrified. This was why he had not spoken for so long: because this was the only truth he knew.

"How can I let that happen?" he asked, urgently. "How can I ever let Will's suffering be all right? How can I ever let my son struggle alone?"

The church was silent. Charles felt hollow and small. He wished Lily were there.

"I cannot," he said. "I do not want to find solace in Will's condition. That seems, to me, abandonment. I do not want to leave Will's future in God's hands. I want to take it in my own. And that is a failure.

"I want to be clear," he continued. "This is not a failure of God, but a failure of man. I have come here, today, to admit that I have turned away from God. That is why I have turned away from you. I am ashamed of it. God, I believe, could give me all the possibilities of thought, of interpretation I could ever need. It is just that I don't want to hear them. I want to close that door."

James stared at Charles as he descended from the pulpit. The two of them stood, as they did every Sunday, waiting for the opening chords of the hymn. When the organ sounded, James leaned over to Charles and whispered, "I didn't mean quit your job."

Nan and James got into bed that night. James was used to Nan turning away from him, curling up on her side. Instead, she sat up close to him.

"What happens," she asked, "if Charles is asked to leave?"

"They won't ask him to leave." Nan could tell by James's face that he was trying to convince himself.

"They might. Do you think he'll get another call?"

"He got *this* call. That's what a call is." James got out of bed and started pacing. "It means you find a church that's right for you, and a church that's right for you can handle a little uncertainty, a little crisis of faith."

"Can you get a bad call?"

James stopped pacing. "Yes," he said. And she knew from the drape of his pajamas and the harrowed set of his skin what he meant.

"I feel those things all the time, those things Charles said. And on top of it, I don't even have Charles's clear and certain faith that there is a God. I only believe there's a better way to live. What if they ask me to take over? What if they ask me to do it alone?" He sat on the side of the bed, suddenly small.

Nan felt as certain as a rock. If Charles went, James went. There was only one call. They were, the four of them, married to each other, in a strange way. They had turned in their quarters and the church had given them a silver dollar. She was not James's only wife, now; he was just as committed to the church, and through the church, to Charles and Lily. They were in it for the long haul, and something would have to be done.

The next day Nan knocked at Lily's door.

"All right," she said, when Lily opened it. "You're right, I can't stand Will. I don't know how to stand him." The words came out before she could stop them. Lily examined her face, hard.

"Okay," Lily said. "I don't know how to either some days."

Nan looked into Lily's eyes, really looked for the first time, and saw that she had changed. She was no longer closed off, no longer belligerent or challenging. In her eyes, Nan saw acceptance. It was not the acceptance she had known as a child: the acceptance she had earned by being perfect. It was an acceptance that acknowledged

Nan's flaws, an acceptance that saw them, simple, exposed. Lily knew the worst in her.

She pulled herself together, determined to give Lily the one thing she had to give her. "James found this," she said, pulling a slip of paper from her purse. She thrust it forward, forcing herself to look Lily in the eye again. "It's the name of a doctor he heard about yesterday. I know you have had a horrible time with doctors, but this one is supposed to be different."

Lily's eyes remained impassive. It would take more than a gesture to bridge the rift between them. But Lily did not send Nan away.

"I'll think about it," she said.

The session asked for a copy of Charles's sermon in writing and met to discuss their options. They solicited opinions from certain members of the congregation, wanting to discover if this admission of uncertainty was pardonable. Would their congregation be able to believe in their pastor, even when he did not believe in himself?

They met in the library, next to the fellowship room. They sat at the long, polished table. James and Charles watched from folding chairs in the corner of the room. Alan Oxman cleared his throat, preparing to read from a sheaf of notes typed onto white paper.

Marcus had typed the notes, lips pursed, shaking his head all the while. "These people need a good disaster," he said. "They need to know what it means for life to be hard. And I'm not talking about *death* hard. I'm talking about *suffering.* Don't they know there's a war on?" He whipped one piece of paper out of the typewriter and started a new one. "Everybody in the world is out there doubting God. And they're mad because their minister is doubting *himself?*"

"It says here," Alan Oxman began, leafing through the sheets, "*I am outraged. I am encouraged. He should be ashamed. I am amused.* There is no consensus," he said. "So I've invited our pastors to take a stand." He turned to them. "Charles?"

Charles shook his head.

"James?"

James stood and adjusted his coat sleeves. He began: "If you believe in a call, you believe we were brought here for a reason. Now, you can look at us today and think you made a mistake. You can look at us and see we've done something that makes you uncomfortable. What you have to decide is: Was making you uncomfortable a mistake? And, if so, how big a mistake?"

He took a breath. "You expect us to have seen God, I think. But I have not. I have never had a vision or seen a miracle. Honestly, I am one of those who must concede that the stories in the Bible are, in all probability, metaphorical — fables attempting to explain the way that faith made the writers feel. And so I read them *as if* there were forty loaves and forty fishes, *as if* the water had turned into wine. I am one of those for whom this interpretation does not diminish the beauty of the stories. I do not care if they are true — I care only that this feeling is available to us: that we can feel as if we have been reborn, as if we have been saved.

"Seminary does not offer the opportunity to see God. Seminary offers only the chance to study other seekers, other walks of faith, to learn from them what we can, to examine our beliefs in the light of theirs. It does not give us certainty; it gives us the tools to deal with uncertainty. That is the call.

"Charles believes he has lost this ability. So your decision comes down to whether you believe him. Do you believe Charles is irretrievably lost? Gone from the church, from the fold?"

He found himself calming down. He smoothed his tie and tugged the back of his jacket into place. He put his hands in his pockets. "Don't you want to know what happens?" he asked them. "Don't you want him to preach about his journey? Don't you think there will be a great reward at the end of that road? He could come back empty, but what if he comes back full? What if he struggles and is given a sign, is given a feeling, is given an utterly new way to believe? Don't you want to hear it? Isn't that your call?"

They were retained by a vote of six to four.

"Thank you," Charles said to James afterward.

TWENTY

The name on the piece of paper Nan had given Lily was Dr. Madeline Foster. Lily arranged to meet Dr. Foster without Will, this first time. She felt like she was going on a date. She stood in front of her closet, trying to get dressed. For the past six months, she had worn tan Capri pants with a blue or white button-down oxford shirt every day. These clothes could withstand toddler detritus and did not ride up or pull down as she grabbed and was grabbed by little hands. The butterflies in Lily's stomach felt exactly like those she had encountered when she'd met Charles. She took this as a good sign.

She was beginning to believe in signs. There were signs in Will all the time: signs of temper, signs of joy, signs that passed over him as quickly as the shadows of clouds on water. She had come to understand the importance of being attuned. When she was attuned, she could sense Will's moods, even when he was out of the room. She could sense when he had found a little space, when he was quiet, calm. She could sense when Bip was encroaching on that space — his exuberance too close, too loud, too *there* — and knew she had to separate them.

She could see now that when her parents died, she had become dis-attuned. She thought of it as static, the kind that creeps from the radio when you've spun the tuning knob instead of the volume and are left in a limbo of crackling, patchy grey. Her parents' deaths had bumped her radio, and she had not had the energy to move the dial back, had seen no purpose, had forgotten where the channels were, what they sounded like.

Charles had tuned her to his station, and she had listened. Bip had a station, too — a clear, bright station full of brass sections and music you could dance to. But Will had no single station. She had to sit, urgently patient, painstakingly shifting the dial millimeter by millimeter, listening for the finest modulation in static, the sign of a channel far away, one that she could get, if only she lived in Fiji or in Britain. Sometimes she came across clear ones, like tantrums, spasms, or sleep. But mostly she crept slowly up the dial, listening for the hiss and whine, inching as close as she could before she lost it, holding the transistor to her ear, listening, listening, as if it could one day become clear.

She expected Dr. Foster to understand this. The other doctors had not. They had been interested only in why Will didn't have more channels, what was wrong inside his little steel-and-wire box. Maybe someday they would know what caused autism, but not in time for Will. Scientific studies were marathons, and childhood was a sprint. She knew that saving her son's life depended on learning his language, meeting him under his own sun.

Lily finally chose black pants and a white shirt of a finer fabric. They were sober clothes; she did not want to appear too bright, too cheerful. She wanted to appear educated but desperate. And that was exactly how she looked.

Dr. Madeline Foster wore a white lab coat and tortoiseshell glasses. She came out from behind her desk to shake Lily's hand. She had trim legs underneath her skirt. She had no time for chitchat.

"I've been reading about Will," she said without looking at her notes. "I think I might be able to help him." She spoke matter-of-factly, like someone Lily might have met at college: serious, but open to a good time. She leaned across her desk.

"It's not easy," she said. "It's totally experimental. I have no idea how it works and no idea if it works for everyone. I'd be using your son as a guinea pig. Some people consider me a total quack."

"Some people consider me an unfit mother."

Dr. Foster smiled. "I know those people," she said. "They accept the status of the child. They accept the reality of symptoms, and so go looking for their roots. I say: Let's not accept symptoms. Let's break through stasis. Pathology takes years. These are children. Let's try behavior."

Lily looked at her and saw the woman she herself might have been if she had listened to all the stations as a child, if she had lived outside of books, experimented every once in a while. Her father had wanted her to be a doctor. He said she had a clinical mind.

"What is the one thing you most want to change?" Dr. Foster asked her.

"The howling," Lily said.

"Howling is the only way he has to express himself," Dr. Foster said. "We must give him another way." She took a notepad out of her desk drawer. "I'm going to give you the number of a girl."

432

■ ■ ■ ■

Annelise Winny was a student of Dr. Foster's. She had wanted to be a teacher when she took Dr. Foster's child psychology class in college.

"She wrote an essay on crying," Dr. Foster told Lily. "She said crying distresses us because we don't do it all the time. When we do cry, it seems abnormal, a rip in the fabric of daily life. Therefore, we interpret a baby's cry as an emergency. Perhaps, she wrote, if we cried all the time we would not view it as such. Perhaps, if every time we wanted something and could not get it for ourselves, we too would cry. Perhaps what mothers really need to do in order to understand their children is to be strapped to a bed and told to cry whenever they need something."

Lily laughed; Dr. Foster smiled. "Naive, yes, but there was something to it. An understanding that most students don't have — of a baby as an intelligent being — and a willingness to say things others would censor as inappropriate. She's brilliant. I wouldn't place her with just anyone, but you strike me as a family who can handle a mind being spoken."

433

Annelise had long blond hair that she wore in two ropelike braids fastened with office-issue rubber bands. She wore loose-fitting bell-bottoms and a wide leather belt with a plain white T-shirt. She had a phenomenal, long-legged, high-chested body. She looked like a cross between Heidi and Supergirl. She had incredibly clear skin and said everything that popped into her head.

When Charles and Lily first met her, Annelise said, "You're terribly good-looking." Then she said, "I don't really want to live in anyone's house, but I need to see autism in the home. Can you imagine what it's like for these kids to come to offices — all that carpet and antiseptic smell?"

They signed releases allowing her to use the knowledge she gained from Will in any papers she might write, providing she changed their names. "I'll think of something excellent," she said. "Like Thor and Vera." Lily liked her immediately. It was decided that she would live in the basement apartment Lily had fixed up with the intention to rent out.

Annelise arrived at the brownstone two weeks later, with a small, leather-piped suitcase. She said, "Good grief, your house is big."

She was wearing jeans with a white peasant blouse. "I know," she said when she caught Lily looking at her outfit. "It's plain. I wish I could wear tie-dye. I love tie-dye. But it drives kids like Will mad."

Lily felt like a cool autumn breeze had blown between her eyes. No one had ever said "kids like Will" before. No one had ever referred to him as part of a group. She could have wept with gratitude; instead, she took Annelise's suitcase and carried it downstairs.

Annelise looked at the little apartment with its tiled floors and white-curtained windows.

"What an amazing place," Annelise said. "You own this?"

"With the church," Lily said.

"Oh, hey, about that," Annelise said, "I hope it's okay that I'm not into it. I mean, Will should go to church, if he likes it. Some kids like the music and the repetition, but I just don't go in for that kind of thing."

"Neither do I," Lily said. "You and I can spend Sundays at home. I'll tell them we're trying some treatment with Will."

"If you don't go to church, how come you married a minister?"

"I didn't marry a minister. I married the man."

Charles wanted to like Annelise. She was eminently likeable. She laughed when she said hello, leaned forward when people talked to her. She sang when she walked down the street, picked leaves off trees and wore them in her hair. She cooked good food and listened to good music, so the smells and sounds that came up through the floor from her apartment were appealing. She always found a brightly colored windup toy for Bip to play with while she worked with Will.

She reminded Charles of Harold Evans. They were both extravagant and abundant. They both had a surfeit of energy and ease of being. As soon as either of them entered a room, it felt more relaxed, potent, and full of opportunity — the same way libraries had once felt to Charles, or prayer. Still, he shied away from her, kept himself out of her gaze. She was too *of God* — too curious, too sincere, too accepting, too forgiving, too encouraging, too involved. She could help Charles feel better. She could give him hope.

And so Charles managed to be out of the house during the hours she worked there.

When she stayed late for a glass of wine, he volunteered to put the boys to bed. He made eye contact with her as little as he could. He felt guilty for it; he knew she was insulted by his reserve. Worse than that, he knew she understood it. She saw exactly what he was going through, knew precisely how awkward he felt, how tortured, how confused. He knew it took every ounce of willpower for her to let him avoid her so completely.

"We want to train Will," Annelise said to Lily and Charles. She pointed. "Look at Bip. You have trained him to say *please* and *thank you,* to sit at a table, to ask for things nicely."

"We've *taught* him," Charles said.

"Before they have language, I call it training," Annelise said, "because there is no reasoning. You can have the same results with Will. But you have to let *yourself* be trained. You must let him teach *you* what will please him. You cannot train the boy's reaction to life. You must train your life to elicit the reaction from the boy."

"How do we do that?" Charles asked.

"That's what I'll find out," Annelise said. "I'm going to test him. We're going to see what happens. And then we'll build a life around him that we all can live with."

They started with food. Annelise said, "Kids like Will often eat anything, but not in combination." And she was right. They gave him peas, then potatoes, then carrots, and in that order he ate each one.

"Remember the order," Annelise said, "and do not change it. Give him the same thing until he seems disinterested, and then change only one."

Lily wondered if that was the way Bip might have liked to eat, too, if they had given him the chance. She wondered if Bip would have liked to sit quietly, but they had encouraged him to play. They *had* trained him, she saw, and it was just that Will had refused to be trained.

Annelise spent two hours a day with Will, behind closed doors, painstakingly trying out stimuli to see what he could handle and what he couldn't. When they emerged, she would say things like, "He likes classical, but not jazz. He likes pickles, but not gherkins. He likes cats, but not dogs."

One evening, after the boys were asleep, Annelise joined Charles and Lily for dessert and a cup of coffee. She was good company: She spoke only when something was on her mind. "I think Will likes trains," she said.

Lily finally had to ask, "How do you

438

know?" It pained her to admit she did not know what her son liked, or how to tell.

"I assume that stillness is happiness," Annelise said. "Things that don't bother him he doesn't react to. That's different from other children — most children will grab what they like. Things Will finds disturbing agitate him, and he protests. That's very much like other children, don't you think?"

Lily was constantly amazed at how normal Annelise considered her odd, difficult child.

"You're so matter-of-fact," she said, "so unembarrassed."

"I've never understood embarrassment," Annelise said. "Why are we bothered by what is difficult? Why are we unsettled by what is strange? I've always just been curious. I always just want to find out as much as I can."

"But you're not just learning." Charles said. "You're trying to change him."

Annelise cocked her head to one side and squinted. "I'm going to see if he wants to be changed. I want to give him the chance to live as full a life as possible. If he doesn't want to, if it seems impossible, then we'll leave him alone. But he deserves the chance, doesn't he? Doesn't everyone?"

Lily looked at Charles, hoping to see on

his face the same enthusiasm she felt. This woman was saying everything they had ever wanted to be true. Charles had been quiet for so long, but he had to at least *hear.* He was looking at Annelise with need and fear, as if she might take off her clothes at any moment, as if he were terrified he might find her beautiful.

"Will doesn't like to be touched," Annelise said. "But I don't think he minds being held."

"What's the difference?" Lily asked.

"Touch involves movement," Annelise said, taking Charles's hand and rubbing her fingers on the back of it. "Being held involves stillness." She came around the table, wrapped her arms around Charles and he let her stand there for a moment, embracing him. Lily had never seen another woman hold her husband. Jealousy flared inside her.

Annelise let go. "You can't squeeze him, of course. Kids like Will tend to hate that. But if you're very still, he might sit in your lap."

Lily had never thought of letting Will sit in her lap without holding on to him, but Annelise was right. When she tried it the next day he sat on her knees without complaint. Lily decided that if Annelise wanted to have an affair with Charles, it would be worth it.

"What else should I do?" she asked.

Annelise thought for a moment. "Try to live like him," she said. "Try to get behind his eyes."

So Lily made time to sit with him every day, to watch him, to not avert her eyes, to become fascinated. And she began to see a pattern to his moods. She began to see changes in his breathing, the way he changed position, the times he twirled his hair, the times he lined up the dominoes. She began to see a rhythm, and saw a personality in there, saw that he found comfort in these activities, and it helped her. She made time to sit in the garden and contemplate what his life might be like. She felt how hot the sun was, how bright. She sat in the kitchen while Bip ate and heard how loud he was, how unpredictable. She jumped each time he dropped a fork on the floor. She went into Will's room, where it was dark and cool, and she took out the dominoes, lined them up in front of her. She twirled her own hair. She twirled it hard, until she felt strands tearing themselves from her scalp, and she was calm. She felt it: All these things brought order, gave her a deep sense of control.

And so she let Will do them. If he wanted

to take toys apart and not put them back in the box, line the parts up in rows instead of putting them back together, what was wrong with that? If he wanted to sit for hours alone, in the quiet, in the dark, what was wrong with that? He needed the ocean around him to be glassy and motionless. He needed to sit in the middle of it. Why did the world find that so disturbing? It was not disturbing to her.

There were many things that Will liked, and many he did not, and slowly themes emerged. He began to have, by process of elimination, a personality. Their lives assumed more structure. They woke Will at the same time each day. They ate at the same time, exactly. They bought him seven sets of the same clothes. If they went to the park at the same time each day, Will would come out from under the bench.

"It's all about routine." Lily said to Charles. She did not let herself think about the future, about how hard it would be to keep a routine once Bip was bigger and went to school and had friends over. She did not let herself think about the fact that Will would not go to school.

Charles watched Lily come back to herself. He watched her stand straighter, breathe

442

deeper, reinhabit her skin. Will was improving. He no longer howled. He could sit at the dining room table for ten minutes at a time. He went to sleep at night without banging his head against the headboard. Sometimes, if he wanted something, he would take Lily's hand, or Annelise's, and point to it with their fingers. When he did this, Lily's astonishment lit up the room.

Will never took Charles's hand, though. Charles had not practiced, had not gone in the little workroom to make Will point to bits of cookie, to withhold them when Will would not use a gesture or move his eyes. Charles interacted with Will the way he always had: He took care of him. He fed him, buttoned his shirts, forced his mouth open to brush his teeth, held his head to brush his hair. When he found Will sitting in the front hall, he brought him a box of dominoes. He sat by Will's bed until he was asleep. He could not do more.

But Charles knew Annelise was helping. He read her exhaustive daily logs. He read that Will pointed eight times, then fifteen times, that Will followed orders, waited to pick up a domino until Annelise told him it was time. Charles read that Will let his hands be washed without crying, then his feet, then his hair. He knew that Lily felt she could leave Will in the house alone with Annelise, that Annelise could handle him, that Will accepted her. He knew Lily got to go out with Bip now, just the two of them, that they went to the park and ate ice cream cones. He knew this made her happy. She slept now without crying out, had stopped waking at four a.m. Their life was getting easier, and Charles did not know what to do.

It seemed a miracle. It seemed he had asked God for more than comfort and God had given it. It seemed he had asked God to cure his son, and God was trying. It seemed that, despite Charles's abandonment, God was present in his life, and Charles was unbearably ashamed.

Twenty-One

Nan walked slowly down Fifth Avenue, headed for Washington Square Park. As she made her way past the graceful apartment buildings on either side of her, the arch beckoned her, friendly, like a big white dog.

It was just about to be summer. The park was green. The huge sunken fountain sprayed the children splashing in its basin. Everywhere there were kids playing, old women and old men gossiping with each other on benches on which they had sat for forty years.

She was finally, securely pregnant.

She and James had both had small surgeries, outpatient, which had not resembled her miscarriages as much as she thought they would. Still, they had made her feel inorganic, like a tree felled, planed, reduced to a box. When the surgeries worked, when her doctor smiled at her and shook James's hand, she felt engulfed by dread. She did not know what to do with an accomplishment that had not been earned. It felt mechanical to her, absolutely mundane.

But today, Nan was afloat with hope. Today was the first day of her third trimester and she had not had one cramp, not one spot of blood. Now she was round and firm as a pumpkin, and the baby was due on Halloween, so James was calling it Spook.

"What if it's a girl?" she asked.

"Spookette," he said. Nan had an image of a girl in an orange dress, shaking her hips behind a microphone on a lit-up stage.

She was assiduously trying not to worry.

For months, she had been ashamed of her good fortune, ashamed that she had the resources to fix such a secret, transcendental problem. She was ashamed that she could not help Lily in the same way. That there was no small surgery for autism, no scalpel, no stitch, no specific tool. She was ashamed that only some problems could be fixed, and that those problems were hers. It was not fair. She had suffered little, and Lily had suffered much.

Nan received baby booties, silver rattles, and advice, but they were given surreptitiously, almost with a sense of shame. The women of the congregation were still troubled by Will; it felt wrong to celebrate with her. When they saw Nan, they said, "Would you tell Lily that my cousin knows a doctor in Ohio (or California, or Switzerland) who keeps up with all this autism, if she wants to call him."

Nan did not want to feel ashamed of her luck. She did not let herself think that her baby might be born with the same issues as Will, or worse. She did not let herself believe she might deserve that. She was determined to enjoy herself, to let her pregnancy unfold like a brand-new book. She went to the park. The sun was warm, the breeze soft, and as the baby did a backflip in her belly, Nan freed herself of all her anchors and just floated happily away.

She and James made a nursery in the small bedroom next to theirs, with a white wood crib, yellow walls, and an oversized rocking chair they'd found in the church basement. Her parents had sent some extra money, which they'd put in a separate bank account, with its own little red bankbook.

James's favorite baby accouterment was a Moses basket.

"They really call them that?" he asked incredulously as Nan unwrapped it and set it by her side of the bed.

"Of course."

"Can they do that? I mean, what about all the mothers who don't believe in Moses?"

"Who doesn't believe in Moses? It's a story — like *Br'er Rabbit* or *The Three Little Pigs.*"

In fact, James had always thought the story of Moses's birth the most miraculous of all. It was a mother's desperate, selfless act of protection, another woman's softening heart.

And it seemed even more of a miracle to him now, as he contemplated his wife's pregnancy. He thought of his own soon-to-be child, tucked in a woven basket on the river of their life. He wondered if this feeling was what some people called being reborn. He thought of Charles and Lily and knew their life was what most people would call hell.

He redoubled his campaign of usefulness, adding childcare, health care, education. Parenthood, his and Charles's, drove him toward these labors, exposed him to new nightmares that woke him in the middle of the night: his baby left in a home, or Nan forced to give up music in order to care for him, compelled to renounce everything that made her smile. He thought of Marcus's friend, a woman on her own with a son to care for. When the feminist group approached him about starting a day care in the church building, he immediately agreed.

"That was a mistake," Marcus told him.

"You're against childcare?" he asked.

"No, but this feels like just one more of your impulsive, arbitrary projects."

James narrowed his eyes.

"Sorry," Marcus said. "But I've watched you for a while now, and you don't always put two and two together." James shifted on his feet, wanting Marcus to get to the point. For all of his new empathy, he was still horribly impatient.

"The boy at my church can't go to school," Marcus said abruptly. "His mother tried to start him in kindergarten, but he bit the teacher, so they asked her to keep him home."

"They can't do that," James said fiercely. "It's against the law. They have to find him a place somewhere."

Marcus raised his eyebrows. "And you want to start a *day care*?"

After a long moment James said, "Oh. I need to think bigger." One part of him was embarrassed, one part was rising like a lion from a nap. "I need to start a school for boys like Will."

Marcus shrugged. "It seems like the kind of thing you like to do."

449

"In fact," James said, clapping his hands together, "I think we can do both. I think we can start two schools."

Nan had not seen Lily since the day she had passed on Dr. Foster's number. Lily had not thanked her or asked Charles to thank her. But one morning, Nan walked out of the church and Lily was there, leaning against the brown bricks of the outside wall.

"Oh," Lily said, running her eyes over Nan's huge belly.

Nan was coming from rehearsal and was full of song, which made her obviously serene.

"You look wonderful," she said to Lily. It was almost true. Lily looked better. She had showered and brushed her hair, and she was out of the house alone. Nan hadn't seen Lily without Will since the boys were born.

"Thank you," Lily said, stepping back. She did not know how to respond to a Nan this cheerful. She realized she had never seen Nan truly happy, blond and rosy and smiling without regret.

"How are you?" Nan forged ahead, determined not to be embarrassed. "I've just been preparing for rehearsal on Sunday. Dr. Rose lets me use the organ from ten to noon. He's playing now, if you want to listen. He won't mind. It's so wonderful to sit in the church and listen to him, to be the only one there."

"No, thank you," Lily said. "I'm just waiting for Charles." She and Charles were going to eat lunch together for the first time in as long as she could remember. They were going to sit in a restaurant and not think about doctors or diagnoses. They were going to talk about books or the weather, or nothing at all.

"I don't think they'll be out for a little while yet," Nan said. "They're passing the budget."

"Oh," Lily said for the second time. She did not like Nan's smugness. She did not like that Nan knew Charles's schedule better than she did. She did not like that Nan was part of Charles's life at all.

"Everyone is so pleased Charles is back," Nan continued. Lily thought about what that meant. For the church, it meant a return to stability and, of course, that made Nan happy. But at home, Charles still retreated to his study — not as much as he once had, but enough that Bip noticed when he was gone. So the church had its minister, but Lily did not quite have her husband. Something in Charles was still missing, some weight he needed to be secure.

Nan smiled at her again, brightly, and Lily realized what it was. Charles was still missing God.

Annelise looked at Lily inquisitively when she returned home. Lily had dropped her bag on a chair, was pacing up and down the front hall.

"What's up?" Annelise asked. "I thought you were going to lunch."

"I'm understanding," Lily said, without stopping her steps. "It isn't fun."

"Is this about Will?" Annelise asked, standing in the doorway between the kitchen and the hall.

"No," Lily said. "It's about everyone else. I'm suddenly seeing that everyone else cares about Will, too."

"Is this about Nan?" Annelise asked curiously, casually. As if Lily paced in the front hall, wild-eyed, every day. "Because she seems perfectly nice. Why don't you like her?"

Lily forced herself to focus on Annelise's normalcy, to let it steady her, set her to rights. She shook her head. "It's about Charles . . . I don't know where to begin." She sat down on the black-and-white-tile floor, leaned her back against the wall, imagined Nan in her mind. "I hate that Nan is a part of his life. She's too cheerful. She likes chintz. She doesn't stand up for herself, she waits for others to speak, she always seems frightened. She wants everything to be pretty and soft."

Annelise smiled a rueful smile. "And that's just the opposite of you."

"What?" Lily gaped at Annelise.

"It's not an insult," Annelise corrected herself. "It's just a fact. She's a woman in your husband's life. You're jealous. She's jealous too."

"I'm not jealous," Lily protested. "I just remembered that Charles has a whole life he lives without me. And I haven't tried to understand it at all."

"And Nan does," Annelise said. "What's the point in hating her for that? She doesn't hate you. She wants to be your friend. She's lonely."

"You can't fix loneliness by finding friends."

"You can't?"

Lily stretched her legs out. "No. That's ridiculous. Loneliness never goes away."

Annelise sat on the floor across from Lily. "I don't think Nan believes that," she said. "I think she would feel almost completely better if you and she could be friends.

Wouldn't that be nice for you, too? Your husbands are friends — the four of you could have a cozy life together." She looked directly at Lily, waited for her to meet her gaze. "You can't forgive her?"

Lily paused before answering, assessing Annelise. "I can't lie to you, can I?"

Annelise shook her head. "Well, you can, but I spend all day looking at a child who can't communicate with words, trying to figure out what he's really thinking."

Lily looked past Annelise, through the kitchen doors to the garden. The tulips were up, and she saw tiny green tips in the far planter box that meant the irises would be blooming soon.

"I used to believe everything was random," Lily said. "I used to think that what you did with your life didn't matter — look at me: I believed I could marry a minister and not ever come into contact with God. I thought that, at the root of it all, things were unconnected. And now I know I won't ever be alone. If I'd had two regular children, I don't know if I could say that to you so clearly. I think, maybe, I would have raised them to be independent, to not need me, to be able to walk away. But Will will always need me, so I know, now, what it means to be connected. I'm connected to Charles and to you and to the boys. And I suppose I'm going to have to admit that I'm connected to James and Nan, too, whether I want to be or not. I suppose I'm going to have to allow that being connected is better than being alone."

"I've always believed that," Annelise said. "Have you not? Oh my goodness! How can you live without believing in people *or* God? Haven't you been terribly sad?"

Lily smiled. "Yes," she said, "I have been terribly, terribly sad."

Annelise crawled across the floor and hugged her.

Lily called Charles and told him to meet her at home. She sent the boys to the park with Annelise, made beef bourguignon, and poured herself a glass of wine. When Charles arrived, the kitchen was full of olive oil and rosemary.

"Where are you, Charles?" she asked, as he walked through the kitchen door.

"I'm here," Charles said, stopping short.

"No, I mean, where are you with God?"

Charles stared at her with the same astonishment he had that night on Nantucket when she had told him she was losing her mind. He pulled out a chair and sat down across from her. His face was heavy; his hair was dull and dark. His eyes, which had once been so encouraging, were desperate.

"I don't know," he said.

"I know," Lily told him. She put down her wineglass and folded her hands in front of her, a schoolteacher in front of a class. "You're going a little bit crazy," she said. "You've decided God is dead to you, and I have to tell you — I think that's ridiculous. It is ridiculous to decide someone's dead when they are not. To act like they're dead when they are not. Why would you want to live that way? Why would you want to deny yourself their life? The joy of their existence?"

"Are you talking about Will?" Charles asked.

"No," Lily said forcefully. "I'm talking about God. I'm talking about the way you're punishing yourself." She stood up and walked to the garden door, turned around to look at him. "You spoke badly of God. You abandoned God and now you're sequestering yourself out of some noble sense of shame." She came back to the table and sat down, leaning forward. "God isn't your father, Charles," she said. "It doesn't matter to God if you always get it right."

"How would you know?" Charles asked. His voice was almost mean. Lily sat back.

456

"I know that Will's not my parents," she said. "I thought he was, for a little while. I thought he had abandoned me. I treated him like he had. I missed him; I grieved for him. I missed him and grieved for him just as badly as I did for them. I missed him and grieved for him because I missed *them.*

"And now you're grieving because Will made you question God. You're avoiding him because every time he won't look at you, you feel the loss of God. You won't work with him because every bit of progress makes you feel like abandoning God was the wrong thing to do."

She could tell by the twist of his face that she was right. She could tell by the tears in his eyes, so she stopped talking and sat still in the moment of knowing him completely. It was still, and silent, and beautiful. She wanted to give him the same feeling.

"I accept your faith, Charles. I understand it now, because I have faith in Will. Because I will choose to believe, for my entire life, that we can help him, and that he loves us, in his own way. If I do not, I will go crazy. I understand, now, what your faith in God gives you — what it gives everyone who believes. It's worthwhile, Charles."

Charles did not answer. This was a miracle. Even without God, he could see that.

He put his face in his hands.

"You have me, and your sons, and there is progress — real progress — and you are not happy. You are missing something. I want to give you something as substantial as this house you gave me. And the only thing I can think of is God."

Charles took his face out from behind his hands. He knew it was the hardest thing she'd ever said to him, and she deserved for him to look her in the eye.

"I wish I could believe," Lily said quietly. She laid her hand on the table and he took it. "I wish I could believe with you. I wish I could share it with you. I wish you didn't have this whole part of your life in which you feel alone."

Her face was earnest and open. He wanted to turn toward it, to let it lead him back to her, to his sons, even back — however improbably — to God. "You still don't believe?" he asked. It was the question he had not asked since they had been dating, since they had first been married. The one that had been like a tiny pebble in his shoe. She shook her head. There would be no easy path to grace.

"Still, I needed a miracle," Lily said. "And Annelise came. It's not exactly a co-incidence. But I think we die, Charles. I think we die and are buried and become fertilizer for grass and home for worms. I think we go to sleep forever." She paused. "And it doesn't scare me. It happens to every one of us, and that's comforting to me. Isn't that what it's all about?" she asked, sounding tired. "Don't we just have to find the thing that lets us not be scared to die? The thing that lets us not be scared, so we can live?"

No, he thought, that wasn't all faith was. But he wasn't sure he knew anything about the rest of it anymore. He squeezed Lily's hand to let her know he was still listening, that he wanted to hear the rest of what she had to say.

"I'll pray with you," she said. In his astonishment, he almost pulled his hand away.

"Well, I'll let you pray with me," she continued. "If you want to. I've barricaded myself against it forever, as if it would attack me. But it won't; it's just you."

So they sat across from each other at the kitchen table, holding hands, and he said, with trepidation in his chest like sandpaper, "Lord, help us. Make us useful even when we do not know what to do. Make us perceptive when we are dull, make us compassionate even as we try to turn away.

Make us intelligent. Our ideas are so small. Yours are limitless. Please help us learn the things we need to know."

TWENTY-TWO

In the second week of October, Nan went into labor and, sooner than they had expected, they were parents. It was a girl. She lay in a tightly wrapped pink blanket in Nan's arms, wearing a tiny pink hat.

"Let's name her Louise," Nan said.

"And call her Lola," said James.

"That sounds like a woman of the night," Nan objected. But the name stuck.

Lola came to the yellow nursery in her Moses basket and slept and ate and cried her tiny newborn cries. Nan sat in her window seat, Lola in the basket on the floor beside her, musing about babies. She had thought, after all they'd been through and witnessed, that Lola would be a bit less magical — less like an elf or a fairy and more like a human being. She thought they would see, simply, a small person — someone to hold and nurture and raise.

But this was not so. After so many years

of bracing herself for bad news, of tempering expectations, Nan found that her fondest dreams had come true. The part of her that had been cold was now warm. She could not imagine a more wonderful sensation than holding her daughter, bouncing her gently around the room. Lola had, in the space of one tiny day, completely restored Nan's hope. Nan, who had stopped wishing, stopped dreaming, now imagined Lola in a school pinafore, in ballet class, running in the park, swinging on swings. She imagined her curled up in the corner with a book. She imagined her in her first high heels, on her wedding day. She imagined her happy, happy, happy.

And as she imagined Lola happy, she herself became happy. In the little child were boundless opportunities, and so there were for her, too. For every time Lola was happy, she would be happy. Every time Lola was unhappy, she would be unhappy. Her life was doubled, instantly, and she felt the new length of it, the breadth of it, like opening a door one day and discovering her kitchen had turned into the Hall of Mirrors at Versailles. She wanted to wander the halls endlessly. She wanted to know everything, everything there was to know about her child. She felt as perfect as Lola's silver spoon.

James sat cross-legged by the basket, Lola's finger in his hand.

Before she was born, James had been working on yet another sermon about action — about medicine, medicine as God working through man. He was thinking about Nan as he wrote it, and about Will. It was not difficult. His faith was rooted in the idea that God worked through man. God did not act upon people; God inspired them, existing only as an animating force. Therefore, medicine *was* a miracle. But what, then, was the failure of medicine? He thought of Charles, whose soul was crying out for progress, who wanted to lock doctors in their offices and make them study harder, faster, who wanted people to give money, to call congressmen. Charles, who had given up on ideas and wanted, now, for action to lead to success. When it didn't, whom would Charles blame?

Now, James would have to rewrite it. Children, he understood, didn't engender action. They engendered awe. They engendered reverence. He felt, looking at his daughter, that he could let the whole of world history pass him by, if he could just sit and look at her like this forever.

"You can't be serious," Nan said. "She makes me want to go out there and fix everything. I understand now," she told him. "I understand why you want the world to change. How can you look at her and not want to erase every terrible thing that's ever been?"

"She erases them for me," he said.

Nan was willing to forgive this insanity because James hadn't been carrying a baby for nine months, hadn't felt it roll and twist in his stomach, hadn't felt it grow, day after day. He was just now experiencing the magic of it. She would give him a couple of weeks. But as soon as she was back on her feet, they were going to get cracking.

The first thing Nan and James did was take Lola to meet Will and Bip. Together.

"Is a baby going to freak Will out?" Lily asked Annelise.

"I have no idea," Annelise said. "Why do you keep thinking I know things?"

"Because you're brilliant," Lily said. She accepted this now, as complete fact. Annelise had transformed Will from a gargoyle into a child.

Nan dressed Lola in a white dress and brushed down her fuzzy newborn hair.

"This way Lily won't think I'm afraid of

Will spilling on her," she told James.

Charles met them at the door. "A girl," he said stoically. "I always wanted one of those."

Lily, Bip, Annelise, and Will were in the kitchen. Lily and Bip were stirring a bowl of chocolate chip cookie dough. The batch in the oven perfumed the air. Annelise had Will on her lap and was showing him cards. They did not stop when James and Nan came in the room.

"We're not supposed to react suddenly," Charles explained, offering them a seat at the table. "Will knows you're here, but if we skid out of our routines, he'll think you're dangerous."

"Not dangerous, Charles," Annelise corrected him, "just different. Kids like Will hate different."

Bip finished stirring and noticed Lola. "Baby!" he cried.

"Yes," Nan said. "Do you want to see her?"

Bip came to her side and peered at Lola with wide eyes. He put a hand out to touch her face. "She's like Will," he said.

Lily looked at him. "What do you mean, Bippo?"

"She can't talk," he said, "and she gets carried."

All five adults suddenly realized he was the only child in the room not being held. Lily came and knelt beside him. "Do you want to sit on my lap?" she asked, her face stricken. "No, I'm a big boy," he said and toddled out of the room.

Lily stayed on the floor and looked at Lola. "She's beautiful," she said to Nan. She had not known how she would react to a perfect, shining new baby, all wrapped up, warm. But she found herself instantly drawn to her.

"Will hasn't moved," Annelise said. "I think that means he likes her."

Lily looked up at Nan. Nan met her eyes and finally, awfully, understood her. She understood the drawn face and the grey clothes, the terse words and the sharp turnings away. Nan did not need to fear her, pity her, or look away in shame. She understood. She, Nan, would know everything about her child. She knew every minute of her life already, short and contained as it had been. But Lily had a son whose life could never be known, nor even imagined. In Lily's house, it must feel as if every door had been flung closed.

Lily watched Nan's face rearrange itself from round bliss into the sturdier architecture of empathy.

"It is not subtraction for one of us to be completely happy," Lily said. "It's almost — not quite, but almost — more."

After James and Nan had gone home, after the coffee cups and napkins and Bip's tricycle and Will's dominoes had been put away, Charles and Lily found themselves alone in their bedroom. It was an awkward place to be. For so long they had lived separate lives — under the same roof, their minds distracted by different things. For months, when they looked at each other they did not see anything beyond the basic arrangement of features, the color of shirts, the length of hair. Now they looked at each other and saw two landscapes of emotion.

They looked away from each other. Charles went into the bathroom; Lily opened her dresser drawer. They dressed for bed silently. When Charles came out of the bathroom, he sat on her side of the bed and asked, "Have you forgiven Nan?"

Lily sat down beside him. "Yes," she said. "I can't stand myself for it, but I have." She stood up, went into the bathroom, washed her face.

When she came back, Charles said, "She knows she was wrong."

"I know," Lily answered, pulling back the

covers on her side of the bed. "She looked so sheepish and well-meaning. I can't help but forgive her. Even though I still think I should hold a grudge. I'm supposed to stand up for my children."

Charles pulled down the covers on his side of the bed and got under them. Lily slid in next to him. "Are you going to have an affair with Annelise?" she asked.

Charles stared at her. "Are you kidding? Annelise is a Swiss Amazon who could smite me with one look of her eyes."

"But she's beautiful."

"Not as beautiful as you."

"I'm mean."

"Sometimes."

"She's kind."

"I don't care. I love you. I've loved you since that day in the library."

Lily knew it was true. She knew that every doubt she had allowed herself, every moment of desperation, had been her own. Charles worried and puzzled, but he had never wanted to leave her, never needed to be untangled, never thought it would be easier on his own. She rested her head on his shoulder.

As soon as Lola started sleeping through the night, Nan joined James and Marcus on the school project. It wasn't easy. The Department of Education was, of course, eager to approve a new day care. The feminist cause was mainstream now, and powerful. They were mobilizing voters. A fully enrolled day care would cost the department little, and yet would provide them with newspaper coverage of happy, smiling mothers heading back to work. But a school for those with mental disorders would mean pictures of unsightly children. It would mean special equipment, special teachers, special training. They would have to open it to children in the five boroughs; they would have to pay to bus them in.

Nan countered these arguments with relentless patience and her sweetest southern accent. She made it clear that she was both a minister's daughter and a minister's wife, and implied that ignoring her might be seen by some as ignoring God. This got her all the way to the city's chancellor of education.

"We have schools for these children already," he told her. "We have spots for everyone who wants them."

"Do you mean the accredited homes?" Nan asked.

"Yes," he said.

"Have you seen those homes?"

"Not personally."

"Well, I think you should," she told him. "I'll have my husband arrange a tour."

"Mrs. MacNally," the chancellor said, "I really haven't got the time."

"I do," Nan answered. "I'm housebound with a new baby. I have all the time in the world to keep making calls."

The chancellor sighed. "I'll send my vice chancellor," he told her.

So James arranged a visit, and the vice chancellor met James in the lobby of Third Presbyterian. He wore a brown suit, tan trench coat, and aviator glasses that obscured half his face. He brought with him two Special Ed teachers in earnest cardigans with simple hair.

They took the subway up on a cold and sleeting afternoon. This time, the director was not so glad to see him.

"Reverend MacNally," she said, her headband crisp and forbidding. She guided them through the marble hallway without stopping at the nursery, led them once again up the marble stairs.

"You asked about the classrooms," she said to the vice chancellor.

"Yes, please," he said pleasantly.

"We conduct our instruction in here," she said, opening the door to the bedroom

James had seen before. It was much the same, clean and impersonal. The beds were still lined up along the walls, but now there were two long tables in the middle of the room, and a nurse sat at one of them with three boys. She had laid paper out in front of them and put pencils in their hands. "Write A," she said, as the door opened, and then she got up, stood behind each boy, and wrote the letter on their pieces of paper with her hand over their own.

"We're investigating the Lovaas method," the director said, searching the vice chancellor's face to see if he knew what that was.

"Very interesting," he said, nodding. "But do they learn?" James saw that, behind his sunglasses, the vice chancellor was noticing every harsh detail about the entire place.

On the way out, the vice chancellor stopped James on the stairs. "You have the space?" he asked James.

"Absolutely."

"And you think there is public support?"

James forced himself to breathe twice before he spoke. "I am certain there are parents who do not want their children to live in places like this," he said.

The vice chancellor nodded. "I can't promise anything," he said. "I would bet all my money that getting the state to pay for schools instead of homes like this will take a long legal battle. But if you want to open your own school, with private funding, I will do my best to get it approved. You'll have to get certified Special Ed teachers. And you'll be monitored, I can tell you that. But if you see results, good results, you'll have a leg to stand on. Though you should be realistic. This kind of thing can take years."

James heard nothing but the absence of *No*.

Marcus was waiting for him at the church. "We've got to tell people," James told him as he folded up his umbrella.

"What people?" Marcus asked incredulously.

"Everyone," James said, pulling a piece of paper from the stationery shelf. "Everyone we know." He started to draft a letter in his huge, impatient scrawl.

"What are we telling them?" Marcus asked.

"That we need money. That the state says if we fix up the space and pay the teachers, we can open."

Marcus pulled down a piece of paper for himself.

They wrote their appeals, photocopied them, stuffed the envelopes, and put stamps on them. Then they waited.

TWENTY-THREE

While they waited, Marcus and Annelise fell in love. It happened one Wednesday afternoon, in the Barretts' garden. Lily was there, and Nan, and the ministers were expected shortly. It was not a birthday or any other special occasion. It was simply a glorious day, and they had all decided it would be wasted if they went home alone. So Charles had called Lily and said, "Do we have any wine?"

"Miraculously, yes," she said, "and steaks, too."

And so a barbecue was decided upon, with Marcus sent for tomatoes, lettuce, olives, and cornichons for the salad. Nan and Lola brought a loaf of Italian bread from the bakery next to the park, the one with the blue awning.

It had been a good day. Annelise had spent two hours with Will, and when they emerged, Will was calm and looked at his mother when she said hello.

Lily stopped. "Did he look at me?" she asked Annelise.

Annelise, beaming, smiled. "Yes. And he looked at me three times."

If Lily hadn't known it would undo every bit of progress they had made, she would have hugged him.

Later, she greeted Marcus at the door, the Beach Boys on the radio behind her. Will had already gone to bed, but Bip was dancing in the living room.

Annelise was in the garden, setting the table. She was wearing a peasant blouse and a flowered skirt. She had sat a little too long in the sun, so her nose and shoulders were sunburned. When Marcus looked at her, all he saw was white and pink: the absolute opposite of the woman he thought he would love. But there it was.

Bip came out and pulled at Annelise's skirt, kept her from noticing that Marcus could hardly breathe. Marcus managed to keep himself upright until she took Bip's hand and said, "Let's go get the silver."

Then he said, to no one in particular, "I think I'd better sit down."

"Marcus!" Nan cried. "You look awful. Are you sick?" He shook his head. Lily got him a glass of wine, half of which he drank in one gulp. He had just set his glass down when Annelise came back outside.

"Hello," she said, extending her hand. "I'm Annelise."

"I'm Marcus." Annelise's eyes were very blue and her face was very open.

"You're very handsome," she said. The blood came back to him in a rush, and he was suddenly overheated. He said nothing. He was trying very hard just to stay alive. He felt like a salmon flapping its way upstream.

James and Charles arrived and kissed their wives. James took Lola in his arms and started dancing with her. Charles turned Bip upside down, unleashing peals of laughter.

Annelise watched them. Marcus recognized that he should say something. "I hear Will is making progress," he said.

"Enough that his mother can have a party." Annelise smiled.

They sat at different ends of the table through dinner. Marcus tried to pull himself together. He tried looking at Annelise, thinking that if he saw enough of her he would not feel so desperate to see more. Then he tried not looking at her, thinking that if he could break the spell her face had over him, he could forget her. But looking

475

at her made her seem more beautiful, and not looking at her just made him more aware of her voice and the sheen of her hair. At the end of the evening, he took a deep breath, held it for a moment, and offered to walk her home.

"But I live here," Annelise said, "downstairs."

"Then can I walk you somewhere else so I can walk you home?"

They walked through the Village, past the old Italian coffee shops, past the street musicians, past the chess stores' windows stacked with hand-carved pieces. They talked about their families, their friends, their favorite music, their schools, the war. They talked about Will and boys like Will.

"Well, that's that," Annelise said when he dropped her off at home.

It was obvious to everyone what was going on.

"I'm in love with a white woman," Marcus said to the ministers the next day. "I'm going to be disowned."

"Does it matter?" Charles asked.

Marcus thought for a moment. "No."

Annelise asked Lily, "Do you think it will really be so much trouble? Do you think we will really find it very hard?"

Lily said, "Yes. Yes, I do."

"But that's awful," Annelise said. "And I don't care."

Lily took her hand. "That's exactly how I feel, Annelise, about Will. It's just awful, and I don't care."

"Is it worth it?" Annelise asked.

"I don't know," Lily said. "But what else are you going to do?"

James asked Annelise to come to his office. She arrived in a white crocheted shirt and jeans with multicolored patches on the knees.

"I'm starting a school," he said, pulling out a chair for her. "For kids like Will." He sat behind his desk, opened a green file folder, and passed it to her. "This is what I think we'll need."

Annelise opened the folder on her lap, bent her head to read. Her hair fell down around her face, and she followed the words with a finger.

"This isn't enough," she said, looking up and pulling her hair back with one hand. Her cheeks were flushed. "You'll need one teacher per child, I think — at least for the really young kids. Maybe one teacher for two when they're older. And you'll need enough toys so they don't have to share, and you'll need more equipment."

For one moment, James faltered. One teacher for each child; he had not asked for enough money. One teacher for each child; they did not have enough space.

Annelise looked at him, her eyes as blue as a lake. "You're overwhelmed," she said.

"Indeed, I am."

"That's all right," Annelise told him. "It's only because you're trying to do it so fast, and all on your own."

"I need more money," he said simply. "I don't know who else to ask."

She nodded. "I do," she said. "You can apply for grants, if you're willing to have scientists in the classroom. And of course, some of the parents who will want their children to come can pay their own way."

She said it so plainly that James was too embarrassed to admit he had forgotten that not everyone who needed help needed it to be free.

Annelise was looking at him steadily, so he looked back at her. "You have to realize that it takes time," she said. "Everything with these children takes time. Everything that happens in the whole world takes time, even if it seems to happen in an instant."

He was silent for a moment. Then he said, "If I can make this happen, I want you to be the principal."

Annelise stared at him. He had a feeling it was as unusual for her to be struck silent as it was for him. "You'll have to get certified," he told her. "In Special Ed."

Annelise clutched the folder to her chest. "I'll do whatever I have to do."

"You have to keep it a surprise," James said. "At least from Charles. I don't want to tell him until I absolutely know it's going to go through."

Annelise walked around the block six times before she went back to the brownstone, trying to stifle her good mood. When she went in, Lily was at the kitchen table folding laundry. She narrowed her eyes at Annelise.

"Why are you so bubbly?" Lily asked, picking up a pair of jeans and snapping them to force out the wrinkles.

"I think you should have another baby," Annelise said.

"Are you crazy?" Lily answered. She pushed the stacks of laundry to the side of the table and pulled another chaotic mound toward her.

"Maybe," Annelise said, taking up a spot at the table across from Lily, picking socks from the pile and folding them together. "But I've been thinking. The thing that so upsets you about Will is that you think he's the last. You think it will be Bip and Will, and that your lives will be divided: one normal, one different, that you will have to turn yourself around and around to speak to both of them. What if you had another? What if you had a triangle instead of a straight line? A pentagon instead of a square?"

"What if the new one's just like Will?"

"Then he wouldn't be so different. He wouldn't be alone. Then we'd know twice as much about him."

Lily thought of two transistor radios, and not enough hands to hold and tune them at the same time.

"Just think about it," Annelise said. "What if you had a girl?"

What if they had a girl, Lily thought, and then stopped herself. It would be like trying to make up for Will. It would be like trying to prove they could do better. She would not consider it. A baby would be agony for Will, the cries would hurt his ears, the smells would offend his nose. And she would never trust him to hold the baby, never want to leave the two of them alone.

"What's the matter with you?" Lily asked.

Annelise took a deep breath and smiled.

"Don't tell Charles, but James wants to

start a school."

"What?"

"James wants to start a school for kids like Will. In the church, except it will be a public school, eventually."

"Who's going to pay for it?"

"You," Annelise said. "You're going to spend every last cent you have on it because it's a school. The school to which you are going to send Will."

Will might go to school. He might go to school and he might have friends. Well, maybe not friends. But he would have peers. And Lily would have people who understood her. She felt herself start to cry. She felt the tears pool wet against her eyelashes. She looked at Annelise.

"What about you?" she asked, feeling the tears start to roll down her cheeks like marbles.

"Oh! Yes!" Annelise clapped her hands. "I forgot. You won't have to pay for me anymore, because I'm going to teach there," she said. "I'm going to run it."

"You're going to leave?"

"No!" Annelise said, rushing around the table to stand beside her. "I'm still going to live here, in your basement. If you'll let me, I mean. You'll let me, right?"

Lily nodded.

■ ■ ■ ■

It had been hard for James not to ruin the surprise. Sometimes he felt he should; it might jar Charles out of his limbo. Though Charles had returned to office hours and some services, he had not preached since the day he had spoken about Will. James missed him. They no longer puzzled over sermons together or sighed about disgruntled parishioners or discussed their lives in any meaningful way. This made James hollow with sadness, which he wanted to counter with good news. But it was easier for him to build while Charles was distracted. It hadn't been a lot of work — they hadn't had to knock down walls or replace windows, but there had been cleaners and painters and deliverymen in the church for weeks. It had been easy to encourage Charles to spend more time at home.

Then, finally, it was done. James waited outside for Charles to arrive.

"I have something to show you," James said. Charles looked at him warily.

"All right," he said.

James led the way to the elevator. They rode in it without speaking, looking straight ahead at the quilted metal door. James hoped Charles would not feel grateful, would not turn to him with abject thankfulness in his eyes. And he hoped Charles would not be offended, would not feel like James was interfering in his personal life.

"I hope this is okay," James said when the elevator door opened. They stepped out onto the fourth-floor landing. The old tiles had been covered with blue speckled linoleum. The new doors had windows in them and round metal handles.

"What's this?" Charles asked, walking forward, then turning to James.

"It's a school," James said. Taking a set of keys out of his pocket, he went to the farthest door from them and unlocked it. He pushed the door open, leaned against it, gestured Charles inside. "This is the physical therapy room," he said.

It was the sunniest room on the floor. Even as dusk fell outside, the space felt open; from every window Charles could see the sky. The floor he stood on was covered in blue felt carpet. To his left was a pile of blue padded gym mats, folded to the ceiling. In the corner was a bucket of red balls. To his right was what he could only call a contraption: an indoor hammock, it looked like, a metal stand suspending a full-body-sized sling. There were pictures on all the walls, simple figure drawings of children doing things. One picture read: *pull down a mat.* Two: *unfold it.* Three: *sit down.*

"These look like the pictures Annelise draws for Will," Charles said, turning to James once again.

"Annelise drew them," James said, still leaning against the door. "For this school." Charles looked at him, puzzled.

"It's a school for Will, Charles. It's a school for autistic children. We have a boy from Brooklyn enrolled, and a boy from Marcus's church. Will would make three, if you want him to come."

Charles did not answer, just looked around the room, his arms by his sides.

"It will be a public school," James said. "It will be open to anyone who wants to attend. Open to any parent who is trying to raise their child at home, who doesn't want to send him away." James's throat tightened as he said this. He understood, now, what it would mean to send a child away.

"How did you get it done?" Charles asked without looking at him, his voice heavy and high.

"The congregation," James told him. "Marcus and I sent a letter, and I think everyone replied. I think everyone sent money. I think we finally found the cause behind which they can all unite."

Charles still did not look at him. James understood. He understood that, in this moment, the gesture felt like charity. He understood that Charles felt he was receiving special favors, that people had taken pity on him, had seen his life and felt sorry for it. He understood that, in light of all that had happened, it might be too much for Charles to bear.

But he also knew that Charles would come around.

James and Nan asked Charles to officiate Lola's christening. They were not sure he would agree. He was not yet fully himself. The gift of the school had overwhelmed him. He had tried to write a sermon about it; he felt his congregation deserved a full expression of his gratitude. He knew an offering of such devotion should be enough to inspire him back into the pulpit, but he could not climb the stairs. He was not yet sure if it was because he felt like a fraud or a failure or both. He thanked them in the prayers, with affection and respect, but his voice was not as strong as it could have been and did not fill the church with certainty. He was afraid he would sound the same way at the christening. He knew Nan and James wanted him to say a few words, and he had no idea what those might be. For most baptisms, he relied on the Book of Common Worship, which had quite enough pomp and circumstance for most parents. But this was not a common baptism. Nan and James had decided not to hold it in front of the entire congregation, because they wanted Will to be able to attend. Charles wanted to bless their child in the usual, wholehearted way. So, despite his hesitation, he agreed.

Nan's father harrumphed, but her mother said, "You're already her grandfather. That's enough responsibility for one day."

Charles was nervous that Will would protest, that on the day he would not get dressed, not leave his room, but Annelise practiced with Will in the church for a month, so he could get used to the space. He would have his own pew, where he could rock back and forth through the ceremony, if he needed to, and for his sake there would be no music.

The day came. Outside, it was bright and sunny. Charles, Lily, Bip, and Will walked to the church together. This, in itself, was a miracle. He had been afraid he would have to scoop Will up, carry him under his arm, listen to him cry the whole way. Instead,

Will walked straight up the block, stepping over the cracks, calm as Charles had ever seen him.

He left Lily and the boys at the church door and went into his dressing room to robe. He had told James not to check on him, to just enjoy the morning with his family and arrive like any other member of the congregation — a little bit late and in an ordinary suit and tie.

When Charles walked into the sanctuary, the little group was already circled around the baptismal font. It was the most ornate decoration in the church, carved from one piece of Carrara marble, cherubs and lambs on every side. It was positioned in front of the first pew on the right, in which Will sat pressed in the corner, knees to his chest, staring at his shoe. Bip was in the pew behind, running a toy car across its wooden ledge as quietly as he had been told to. The adults stood behind James and Nan, all in festive dresses and ties. Lola wore a knitted gown.

Charles was used to this moment at the beginning of each service, when the church was electric. He was used to waiting, to prolonging the moment until the church settled, the air descended, and everyone became completely still. But it had been a long time since he had stood alone at the altar.

At one point in his life, Charles would have considered this a moment of possibility, the beginning of a child's life inviting others to renew themselves as well. But he was not sure, now, that he believed in infinite possibility. It was not possible his son would become normal, or that his wife would be the same woman she once was, or that this tiny child in front of him would definitely come to believe in God. He had once tried to inspire people to believe. Now he knew that people believed or did not believe. It was not he who did the convincing.

"Dearly beloved," he began. They were the words that started weddings, not baptisms, but the people in the church were his beloved, so dear that as he spoke his heart and throat grew tight. He loved every person in this church more than he would have ever thought possible, loved them not with the automatic love of childhood or the easy love of coincidence, but with the tautly stitched love of people who have faced uncertainty together, who have stuck it out, the strong love of people who looked to their side while suffering and saw the other there. Together, they would send all of these young people out into a world they knew was full of injury and hard to bear. Somehow, they would wave and wish them well and have faith that they would avoid the worst of the darkness, live mostly in the light.

At Marcus and Annelise's wedding he and James would say, *We have gathered here today to join two people.* But they were already gathered and joined, he thought, all of them made useful together, like the mechanisms of a clock. These few people, here in this church, were the gears and switches in his life, the tiny metal pegs that made it turn. If he opened any hinged door in a shadowed room, one of these people would be there.

He performed the service. He asked Nan and James if they wanted their child to be raised in the church; he asked the small congregation if they would support Lola in her faith. They said yes. He scooped water from the font and tipped it onto Lola's head; her blue eyes opened in surprise. He felt, suddenly, the overwhelming need to speak, not as a figurehead or a channel for the word of God, not as a minister — only as a man.

"James and Nan," he said. They smiled. "You have given me the gift of speaking at this very special occasion, and I will try to make it worth your while. I have been thinking of what I might tell Lola about life, but since she won't understand any of it, I will tell the rest of you what I have come to understand."

Charles paused for a moment, and cleared his throat, as he put his thoughts in order. He was not sure they were entirely true, but they felt true to him in that moment, and he was tired of thinking too hard, tired of talking himself out of things he believed.

"There are three kinds of trials in life," he said, relishing the simplicity of the idea. He heard his voice grow stronger, stood straight to accommodate it. "There are the trials God gives you," he continued, "which almost always lead to wisdom, and so are worth the trouble. There are the trials you force upon yourself, which should be abandoned at their onset." He nodded to show them that he realized he was speaking about himself. "And there are the trials we create for one another," he continued, "which are more complicated because it is impossible to know whose hand is guiding them.

"The only advice I can give anyone is this," he said. "Don't ever shrink from those last trials. Run to them. Because only in the quality of your struggle with one another will you learn anything about yourself. Sometimes that struggle is nearly impossible to survive, but it is those trials which make a life."

When he was finished, Nan and James hugged him, and Nan's father shook his hand. Lily looped her arm through his, and they followed Annelise as she guided Will and Bip out to the church steps, where the little party had decided to take a picture. Annelise ran to the gate and flagged down a woman passing by. As the woman held up the camera, and they stepped closer together, Charles knew all was not well. All was not well, all would never be well; but all was not lost. Charles put a hand lightly on Will's shoulder and Will did not pull away. The day was warm, his wife was cheerful, his friends finally had their child. The shutter clicked. The dogwood and apple trees had suddenly thrown down the confetti of their new year.

EPILOGUE

On the day Charles died, Lily pulled one of her white kitchen chairs up to the window that faced the garden. It was barely dawn. She had found Charles slumped over his desk, still dressed in a blue oxford cloth shirt, his head on the green felt blotter at such an angle that she could not question what had happened. Still, she said "Charles?" into the silent room. She stood next to him, in her nightgown, for a long time. It would be the last moment she would have with him, so she took in everything: the plaid curtains, the leather chairs, the books on the shelves behind him, the fireplace, the nape of his neck. What a relief, she thought, for him to die in the privacy of their own home, on a night they had spent together, so she did not have to stand again, cold and astonished, in the green-lit hall of a hospital. She put her hand lightly on Charles's back. Then she walked into the kitchen and telephoned James.

"Don't bring Nan," she said.

James arrived as the ambulance pulled up, bounded up the steps before the men with the stretcher could pass him, cheeks red, hair disheveled.

"Are you all right?" he asked. Lily nodded. Death was not a mystery to her, this time. Soon, there would be grief. She recognized the dull, electric imminence of its hurricane off the shore. Her nights would be full of wind and darkness. But she was well rehearsed, and her boat was stronger now; her sail and rudder would hold.

And Charles's death was not a tragedy. They'd had fifty years together, decades of parks and bicycles, soccer fields and swimming pools, school meetings and city petitions, a house cobwebbed with worry and swept clean by relief. He had seen his children grow up. He had preached and preached again, grown both more impatient with the world and more compassionate. He had stooped and shuffled; she had grown even more thin and angled. For their fiftieth anniversary, she had given him a hat with flaps to keep his ears warm, a luxury he would never allow himself. But, despite his bowed shoulders, he had remained taller than everyone, at the mercy of buffeting wind, and she had not wanted him to suffer. He had given her fifty boxes of tea. Now, they would be the tally of days she would live without him, the last one a marker at the end of the paved road from which she would have to step alone onto an untamped path.

The stretcher creaked and clicked. There was a sound like snow falling from a roof as they laid Charles's weight on it. James came out of the study and held her hand.

"They'll take him out now," he said. "Do you want to see him?" Lily shook her head. She wanted to remember Charles's face as it had been in life. She went back into the kitchen and sat down on the white chair. The sun was up, dew beading on the garden's small batch of grass.

Charles had been dead five hours. Any minute now Nan would arrive. She would bring cinnamon rolls, and grapes, and coffee in a blue deli cup. She would bring a casserole and fruit salad, crackers and cheese, bottles of juice and milk. It would feel like too much, a bounty when Lily felt most bare, but it would be just enough to feed Bip and Will, when they arrived, and Bip's wife, Laura, and Marcus and Annelise. Nan would pack it all in separate containers, because Will did not like different foods to touch, and she would bring fresh white bread and soft butter, because they were all Will would eat when he was sad. Who else but Nan would think of all that?

Nan would organize everything. She would choose the hymns and the flowers; she would stand next to Lily on the church steps as they greeted guests before the service. There would be hundreds; the church would be full. Will would pace the long, cracked aisle, as tall as Charles had been, and bearded, but still making figure eights with his hands and pulling at his hair. Nan would make certain that no one asked him to sit down. She would hold Lily's hand while James gave his eulogy, and Lily would let her. Lily would be her best self for as long as it took everyone around her to let Charles go.

And then she would move to the Vineyard. After Charles's parents had died, she and Charles had bought a house there, close to his cousins. She could have dinner with them, sometimes, and walk on the beach every day. Bip and Will lived together in Boston; she could visit them on weekends, drive Will to his job at the small company that made Shaker boxes: delicate oval catchalls for rings and extra buttons. Charles had put a pair of them on each of his desks;

Lily thought them a perfect reflection of the love he had found for his son, practical and fragile, sentimental and searching, willing to be empty or filled. It made her light-headed to think about it.

The Vineyard house was too big for her; she would be lonely, but she wanted to look out at the water and know Charles had seen the same view, so she would live there, adding on to a life he had known. Nan and James would visit her for long summer stays. There would be lobsters and bonfires and wool blankets wrapped around their knees on cool nights. It would not be the same, but it would be familiar.

Nan's loud knock on the door broke the silence. Lily took a sharp breath. Charles had not left her alone, she realized. The thought was a surprise. She and Nan and James had lost him, but not one another. He had worked on them all carefully, every day, bending and shaping, folding and binding, so that if he went first, they would not be adrift; they would be inextricably linked, these people who had known him longest and best. How she loved him, she thought — how improbably — for ensuring these friends would forever be her stitches, her scaffold, her ballast, her home.

ACKNOWLEDGMENTS

One of the true joys of finishing this book is that I finally get to publicly acknowledge all the people who advised, encouraged, and sustained me for the many years it took to write it. Everyone on this page believed I could publish this book even when I was ready to give up. I am humbled to thank:

Wendy Levinson, my astounding agent, for championing this book with her rare combination of tenacity and grace. Marysue Rucci, my gifted editor, who polished this story until it shone. The rest of the Simon and Schuster team, for their overwhelming warmth, support, and advocacy: Jonathan Karp, Richard Rhorer, Cary Goldstein, Elizabeth Breeden, Samantha O'Hara, Jackie Seow, David Litman, Ruth Lee-Mui, Jonathan Evans, Dominick Montalto, Allison Har-Zvi, Lana Roff, and especially Zachary Knoll, for answering my many questions. My earliest readers: Laura Murawczyk, Jack

Livings, Kristina Loverro, Mariko Tada, Lydia Snape, and Alix Ford, for critiquing with kindness. My later readers: Lewis Buzbee and Jan Geniesse, for helping me understand my characters in a deeper way. The Reverends Will Critzman and Gina Gore, for sharing their experiences of ministry. The BBBW: Catherine Anderson, Jan Brown, Alix Ford, Leah Guggenheimer, Lara Rosenthal, Lydia Snape, Darnley Stewart, Mariko Tada, and Sandra Weathers Smith, for almost twenty years of book club and never doubting I would get this done. Anne Wall, Jan Geniesse, and Julianne Mulvey, for parenting my child as if she were your own — and me, too, when I needed it. For Deborah Claymon, Christina Hall, Jennifer Huber, Kristina Loverro, and Lydia Snape — the gratitude I have for you could fill another book. My partner, Alfred Culliford, who puts up with my mess, tells excellent jokes, and challenges me to be my best self. Grayson Culliford, who adds her special laugh and lightness to my life. And finally, Eleanor Livings: I wrote the first draft of this book while I was waiting for you to be born, and I finished it so you would be proud of me. You are my truest inspiration.

ABOUT THE AUTHOR

Cara Wall grew up in Greenwich Village. She attended Stanford University and The Iowa Writers' Workshop, where she helped establish and then directed the Iowa Young Writers' Studio. Her work has been published in *SF Gate, Glamour,* and *Salon.* After wandering the world, she once again lives in New York City with her family.